W9-CQS-616

By Deborah Harkness

A Discovery of Witches
Shadow of Night
The Book of Life
The World of All Souls
Time's Convert
The Black Bird Oracle

THE BLACK BIRD ORACLE

THE
BLACK BIRD
ORACLE

A Novel

Deborah Harkness

Ballantine Books
New York

The Black Bird Oracle is a work of fiction. All incidents and dialogue, and all characters with the exception of some well-known historical figures, are products of the author's imagination and are not to be construed as real. Where real-life historical persons appear, the situations, incidents, and dialogues concerning those persons are entirely fictional and are not intended to depict actual events or to change the entirely fictional nature of the work. In all other respects, any resemblance to persons living or dead is entirely coincidental.

Copyright © 2024 by Deborah Harkness

All rights reserved.

Published in the United States by Ballantine Books, an imprint of Random House, a division of Penguin Random House LLC, New York.

BALLANTINE BOOKS & colophon are registered trademarks of Penguin Random House LLC.

LIBRARY OF CONGRESS CATALOGING-IN-PUBLICATION DATA

Names: Harkness, Deborah, 1965– author.
Title: The black bird oracle: a novel / Deborah Harkness.
Description: First edition. | New York: Ballantine Books, 2024. |
Series: All Souls series; #5
Identifiers: LCCN 2024006112 (print) | LCCN 2024006113 (ebook) |
ISBN 9780593724774 (Hardback) | ISBN 9780593871461 (International edition) |
ISBN 9780593724781 (ebook)
Subjects: LCSH: Bishop, Diana (Fictitious character)—Fiction. | Witches—Fiction.
| LCGFT: Paranormal fiction. | Fantasy fiction. | Novels.
Classification: LCC PS3608.A7436 B56 2024 (print) | LCC PS3608.A7436 (ebook)
| DDC 813/.6—dc23/eng/20240214
LC record available at https://lccn.loc.gov/2024006112
LC ebook record available at https://lccn.loc.gov/2024006113

Printed in the United States of America on acid-free paper

randomhousebooks.com

2 4 6 8 9 7 5 3 1

First Edition

Book design by Virginia Norey
Title page art: elegant tree by Matorini_atelier/stock.adobe.com,
black bird by Weasly99/stock.adobe.com, oracle ornament by Cocorrina
Family tree branch: dariachekman/stock.adobe.com
Part title art: owl/Dover, raven by Norhayati/stock.adobe.com,
glass bottles by BOOCYS/stock.adobe.com
Spot art: feather 1 by Norhayati/stock.adobe.com, feather 2 by Shy Radar/stock.adobe.com,
wolf/Dover, wolf tracks by AnNiStok/stock.adobe.com, bottle by lynea/stock.adobe.com,
raven by Morzan/stock.adobe.com, bird on branch by Andrei Kukla/stock.adobe.com,
mystical card background: Murhena/stock.adobe.com, card ravens/Dover

For Tonya and Tracy,
who understand the magic of twins

CLERMONTS & BISHOPS FAMILY TREE

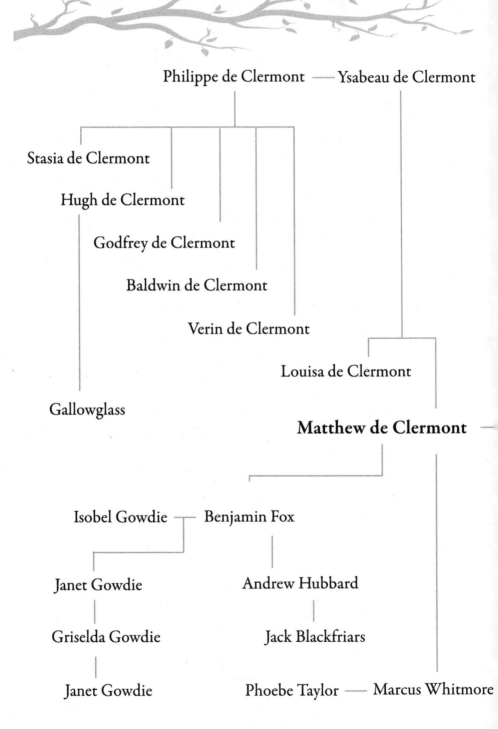

Philippe de Clermont — Ysabeau de Clermont

Stasia de Clermont

Hugh de Clermont

Godfrey de Clermont

Baldwin de Clermont

Verin de Clermont

Louisa de Clermont

Gallowglass

Matthew de Clermont —

Isobel Gowdie — Benjamin Fox

Janet Gowdie

Andrew Hubbard

Griselda Gowdie

Jack Blackfriars

Janet Gowdie

Phoebe Taylor — Marcus Whitmore

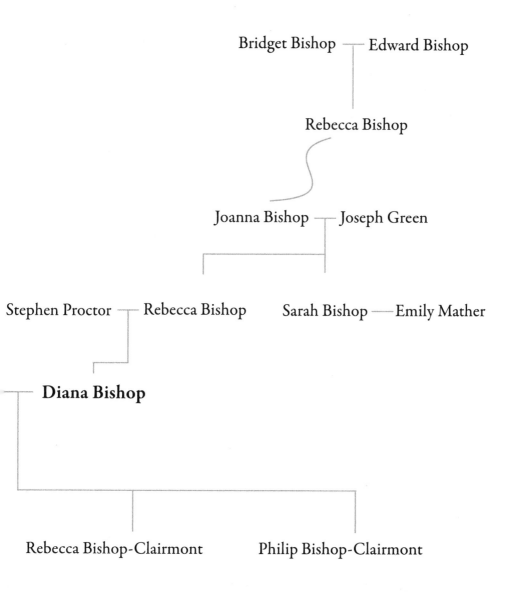

THE BLACK BIRD ORACLE

With heron's bone and owl's wing,
Through vulture's silence, the ravens sing.
Through absence and desire, blood and fear,
A discovery of witches will carry them here.
Four drops of blood on an altar stone,
Foretold this moment before you were born.
Three families joined in joy and in struggle,
Will each bear witness to the black bird oracle.
Two children, bright as Moon and Sun,
Will Darkness, Light, and Shadow make one.

PART ONE

Chapter 1

In every soul, there is a place reserved for Shadow.

Mine was safely hidden, tucked in a blind spot at the corners of my memory, under a hollow bruise that I thought had healed long ago.

Then the ravens came to New Haven, carrying an invitation that neither Shadow nor I could refuse.

It was a Friday in late May when the invitation arrived.

"Hey, Professor Bishop! I just put your last mail delivery through the slot!"

I'd been woolgathering on the familiar route home from my office at Yale, listening with half of my attention to Becca's excited chatter while the rest of my mind drifted. I hadn't noticed that we'd arrived at the ornate iron gate that guarded our house on Orange Street, or that our regular mail carrier, Brenda, was just leaving the property.

"Thanks, Brenda," I said, giving her a limp smile. The heat was withering. It was always like this in New Haven around graduation time, which led to frazzled tempers, damp academic regalia, and long lines for iced lattes at the city's many coffee shops.

"You must be excited about getting back to England, Becca," Brenda said. She was already wearing her USPS bucket hat and shorts, prepared for New Haven's warmer temperatures and sky-high humidity.

"I am." Becca hopped from one foot to the next to prove it. "It's Tamsy's first trip and I get to show her *everything.*"

Tamsy was a recent addition to the family: one of the historical dolls that were all the rage among the thirteen-and-under set. Marcus and his mate, Phoebe, had chosen the colonial era doll for Becca because of her fondness for Marcus's house in Hadley, and her delight in the stories he told about growing up there in the 1760s and 1770s. Though she had been given a different name by the manufacturer, Becca had rebaptized her the moment she had seen the doll's green eyes and red hair peeking out from the box's clear, round window.

Since receiving the doll, Becca's active imagination had been fully engaged with Tamsy and her world. She came with a variety of outfits and accessories that helped Becca bring her to life, including a horse named Penny. Tamsy was well supplied with home furnishings, too. Matthew added to them with a small replica of the Windsor chair at Marcus's house that had once belonged to Grand-père Philippe and a Tamsy-sized version of a painted Hadley chest like the one Phoebe used to store household linens. It was fitted with a tiny lock, and Becca had already packed Tamsy's clothes, her schoolbooks, her quill pen and ink pot, and her collection of hats for the journey to England.

Brenda gave Tamsy, who was hanging from Becca's hand, a wave. She turned to me. "You must be excited to get back to your research, too."

At the end of every school year, Matthew and I would take the children to England, where we spent the summer months at our house in Woodstock. It was only a few miles outside Oxford, which put me within easy reach of the Bodleian Library and made it possible for Matthew to work in his quiet Oxford University laboratory, with no colleagues or graduate students to interrupt him. Becca and her brother, Pip, had acres of land to roam, hundreds of trees to climb, and a house filled with curious treasures and books to occupy them during the inevitable summer downpours. There were trips to France to see Matthew's mother, Ysabeau, over long, lazy weekends, and a chance to see more of Marcus and Phoebe, who would spend part of their summer in London.

I couldn't wait to get on the plane and put Yale, New Haven, and the spring semester behind me. The prospect of a new research project focused on the wives and sisters of early Royal Society members beckoned, and I was eager to get my hands on rare books and manuscripts.

"I expect you have lots to do before tomorrow," Brenda said.

She had no idea how much. We weren't packed, the houseplants were still inside and not neatly arrayed on the back porch so the neighbors could water them, and I had at least three loads of laundry that needed doing before we could leave for the summer.

"I double-checked your mail hold. You're ready for takeoff as far as the New Haven post office is concerned," Brenda said, drawing our conversation to a close.

"Thank you," I said, removing Tamsy from Becca's grip and sticking her, legs first, in the top of my tote along with the campus mail.

"You and Pip have fun, Becca, and I'll see you in August," Brenda said, adjusting the thick strap of her mailbag.

"Bye!" Becca said, waving at Brenda's retreating form.

I stroked her shiny hair, blue-black and iridescent as a crow's wing. Becca resembled Matthew so closely—all long lines and contrasts, with pale skin and heavy brows. They were alike in temperament, too, with their confident reserve that could erupt into strong emotions in a heartbeat. It was Pip who resembled me. Comfortable with expressing his feelings, and quick to cry, he had my sturdy build, fair hair glinting with strands of copper, and smattering of freckles across his nose.

"We *do* have lots to do, peanut," I said. "Starting with taking care of Ardwinna and Apollo and sorting all this mail."

After that, the house would need to be put in apple-pie order—a daunting task. My little house on Court Street had been far too small to contain a vampire, a witch, two Bright Born children, a griffin, and a deerhound. Matthew's son Marcus had offered us his palatial home on Orange Street instead. He'd bought it just before the Civil War, when he was first studying medicine at Yale and mahogany and formal entertaining were very much in fashion. Every surface in the house was polished, carved, or both. It was a nightmare to keep clean and the spacious rooms filled all too quickly with the clutter of modern living.

Despite its vast size and formal appearance, the house had proved to be surprisingly well suited to family living, with expansive covered porches that provided a place for the children to play in rainy weather; a private backyard where Philip's griffin familiar, Apollo, and my Scottish deerhound, Ardwinna, could join in the twins' games; and numerous downstairs rooms that had once been allocated to residents according to gender and function. At first, Marcus's house seemed too grand for our small clutch of vampires and witches, but families have a way of expanding to fit the space allotted to them. What we thought would be a temporary stay had turned into years of permanent residence.

Becca, who was attuned to my changing moods, felt my anxiety rise.

"Don't worry, Mom. I'll help you." Out of her hip pocket, Becca pulled a Yale-blue kazoo that she'd found in the office, hoping to rally my flagging spirits by piping us the last few feet home. The kazoo's strange, bleating squawk disturbed the birds settled in the nearby trees. They took flight with an irritated flutter of wings, the murmuration of dark shapes and raucous cries protesting this interruption in their sleepy afternoon routine.

I shielded my eyes, mesmerized by the swirling, attenuated black cloud of birds that rose and fell on the damp currents of air. Becca was also rapt at the sight, her eyes wide and filled with wonder.

A single bird broke from the formation, its shadow falling over our clasped hands. The outline of the bird's head and curved beak extended onto the walkway, pointing the way to the front door.

A sudden chill fell, and I shivered. Curious as to what had caused the drop in temperature, I looked up, expecting to see clouds blotting out the bright sun.

Instead, all the color had leached out of the world. The mellow stucco of the house, the green canopy of the trees, the splashes of blue from tall stalks of delphinium and bearded iris in the perennial borders—everything was reduced to gray scale like a washed-out photograph of foggy London taken in the 1940s. My perspective was altered, too, the house looking too tall and wide, and the trees too short. The clear tang of petrichor replaced the usual green scents of summer, along with a sulfurous note of brimstone. The usual sounds of the neighborhood—traffic, the call of the birds, the hum of lawn mowers—were all too loud, as was the drumming of my heart when a wave of the uncanny crashed over me.

Power, prickling and ominous, flooded my veins in response to the surge of magical energy that held us in its colorless shroud. I drew Becca toward me, sheltering her with my body.

The solitary bird that had been gliding overhead plummeted to the ground in front of us, wings outstretched and its head bent to the side at an angle that told me its neck had snapped on impact. Its curved, ebony beak and the ruffle of feathers at the neck told me this was a raven.

A rustle of birds' wings filled my ears as the raven's companions settled on the branches of the nearby tree, dark spots in the ghostly world that stood out in sharp relief like a string of silhouettes cut from black paper. There were not just a few ravens, but dozens.

Everything I knew about the significance of ravens—magical, mythical, and alchemical—raced through my mind. Messengers between the dead and the living, ravens often symbolized the first step in the alchemical transformation that led to the philosopher's stone.

Some traditions linked ravens to the power of prophecy. What it meant to have one fall dead before you, I couldn't imagine—but it couldn't be a sign of good fortune.

A pool of blood, crimson and thick, spread out on the pavement underneath the raven's body. With the release of the bird's life force, the color bled slowly back into our surroundings. Becca's denim shorts were blue once more. The floral sprigs on my blouse turned a rosy pink and bright yellow. The irises returned to their usual indigo.

"That bird is dead, isn't it?" Becca peered out from my arms at the raven lying motionless before us, its eyes open and staring. Her nostrils flared at the scent of the raven's blood and an expression of hunger passed over Becca's face, making her look every inch a vampire. Becca had demanded blood as an infant, and though her avidity had waned over time, its coppery smell still roused her need for it.

"Yes." The outpouring of blood confirmed it, and there was no point in avoiding the truth.

"When the bird died, why did the colors die, too?" Becca's eyes were as wide as those of the dead bird. In their depths was a dark spark I had not seen before.

"What do you mean?" I asked carefully, not wanting to dilute her response with my own reactions to this afternoon's events.

"Everything went gray, like the ashes in the fireplace," Becca explained. "Didn't you see it?"

I nodded, surprised that my daughter had noticed it, too. Becca's powers of observation were second only to Matthew's but, unlike Pip, she was not usually attuned to the magical forces that swirled around her.

"Was it magic?" Becca wondered. "It didn't feel like your magic, Mommy."

"Yes, sweetie, I think it was," I replied.

Whatever magic had visited our New Haven neighborhood, it had retreated now. Even so, I wanted to be safely in the house, away from the dead bird and the dark shadow it had cast over me and my daughter.

Before I could move Becca in that direction, the unkindness of ravens perched in the trees started a mournful chorus. Their song was made up of screams of pain, gurgling croaks, throaty chuckles, and raspy cries. One particularly large raven took flight. The slow, heavy motion of its wings quieted the other birds. The raven opened its beak and out poured the sound of bells, high and chiming, to replace the previous cries of grief and despair.

The sizable raven landed safely on the pavement before us, light and sure-footed. The bird's feathers shone deeply black with a hint of darkest blue that reminded me of Becca's hair, and its neck swelled so that it looked as though the raven had donned a black ruff. With a snap of its formidable beak, the raven cocked its head.

Becca returned the gesture. Cautiously, she approached the bird.

"Careful," I murmured, unsure of its intentions.

The ravens in the trees cried out with loud *kra kras,* indignant that anyone would think they would harm a child.

Becca crouched by the dead bird. Its lively companion took a few two-footed hops to narrow the distance between them, and strutted back and forth, emitting a bubbling stream of chatter. It picked something out of the dead raven's beak and dropped it before her.

It didn't clatter like metal, but the round hoop suggested it was a ring—albeit one that would have fit only a very slender finger.

"Don't touch it!" I cried. My aunt Sarah Bishop had taught me never to touch an unidentified magical object, and for the most part I obeyed her rules.

Our daughter was made of more independent stuff.

"Thank you," Becca told the raven, slipping the ring over her knuckles. It left streaks of the bird's blood as it traveled down her finger.

The raven chirruped a reply and Becca listened attentively, nodding as though she understood what it was saying. Tamsy stared at the raven from my tote bag, blinking slowly every now and again like she was clearing the sleep from her eyes.

As Becca and the raven conversed, a prickling sensation in my left thumb and the pucker between my eyebrows told me that the strange magic had not retreated after all. It had simply shifted to something else that was equally unfamiliar. I tried to probe the nature of the magic, sending out inquisitive feelers in the hope of identifying it, but it was smoky and murky, without clear intentions or any discernible knotted structure. It had a strange scent, too: sea salt, pine, barberries, and brimstone all garbled together.

"I'm sorry your friend died," Becca said, when the raven at last fell silent. "You must be sad."

The raven's head rose and fell in time with guttural chirps that sent its throat feathers sticking out even farther, like a porcupine's quills.

"We'll bury her in the backyard." Becca crossed her heart just as Matthew had taught her to do. "I promise."

Becca's solemn oath was a large commitment for such a young person. Given the enchantment unfolding around us, the ravens had not come to Orange Street by accident.

Someone had sent them, and they had come bearing a gift for my daughter. I had learned the hard way that magical gifts always came with strings attached.

"Let's go inside, and give the birds a moment with their friend," I suggested gently, still wanting to be behind closed doors rather than outside and vulnerable to whatever complicated spell was unraveling. I held out my hand and Becca took it.

"We can't! We have to stay until her friends sing her on her last flight, Mommy," Becca explained, rising.

On cue, the ravens sitting on the branches began another haunting dirge, this one rattling like bones against wood and full of grief and longing. It was a privilege to listen to the inner life of these magnificent birds. Emotion filled my throat as I, too, felt their loss.

Becca gripped my hand tighter as the birds sang. Heavy tears fell from her eyes, and though she tried to sniff them away, they mingled with the dead raven's blood, forming clear, saline puddles in the darkening stain around the bird.

The ravens took flight, their song of grief turning to one of hope as the sound of bells once more filled the air. The birds soared and tumbled over their fallen sister, their feathers shimmering with otherworldly brilliance.

"Thanks for delivering her message," Becca told the lone raven who remained. "I won't forget."

With a few powerful strokes of its wings, the raven joined the rest of his unkindness—though that seemed like a collective misnomer based on what I'd just witnessed. Together, the birds rose higher and higher until they were nothing more than black specks against the sky.

"What was the bird's message, Becca?" I asked, eyeing the dead raven with concern.

"He told me it was time to come home and gave me this." Becca held out her left index finger.

I examined the ring as closely as I could, given it was smeared with gore and had clumps of earth attached to it. The ring was blackened with age in places, but white as bone in others. Its surface was pierced, and coarse, dark fiber was woven through the holes.

"But we're already home. It's awfully sad that his friend died delivering a message that we didn't need." Becca's tears resumed as she looked up at me. "Is it my fault she died?"

"Of course not." I drew her close. "The raven just misjudged the distance to the ground."

Becca sniffed.

"Come on," I said firmly. "Inside."

"But the bird—" Becca protested, putting all her weight into resisting me.

"Your father will take care of the raven," I said.

The colors may have returned to the world, and the sounds and smells of a New Haven summer filled my nose instead of the strange resinous mix that had accompanied the ravens, but there was no mistaking that something had happened on Orange Street today. Something magical that was both uncanny and unfamiliar.

Once we'd gone inside the house's cool entrance with its marble floors and high ceilings, I let out a quiet sigh and leaned against the closed door. My overflowing tote bag slipped from my shoulder, joining the mail at my feet that had been delivered through the brass-plated slot. Tamsy tumbled out of the bag, and Becca rushed to retrieve her.

Becca's eyes bored into me. She was a watchful child, and little escaped her notice, whether it was a mouse out in the garden scrounging for food or the shifting emotions of the people around her.

"Do you need a cup of tea?" Becca asked.

Everyone in the family knew that the quickest way to soothe my ruffled feathers was to put a book in one of my hands and a cup of tea in the other.

"I most certainly do!" I laughed. "And you look like you could use a snack. Peanut butter and apple slices?"

It was Becca's favorite treat, the crisp half-moons of apple providing the perfect dipper for the creamy, salty spread.

"Yes, please," Becca said solemnly, her mood still affected by the raven's death.

I scooped up the mail and tote bag and we made a beeline for the kitchen. This sunny room in the back of the house was my favorite space in Marcus's otherwise wallpapered and well-upholstered home. Because the purpose of a vampire kitchen was comfort, rather than food preparation and consumption, it was often designed around aesthetic considerations instead of the practical needs of a cook. The kitchen felt more like a living space as a result, with ample seating and warm, inviting lighting. The cabinets were painted a cheerful duck-egg blue and retained the original glass-fronted upper doors to display crockery and a large selection of wineglasses that sparkled in the light.

Ardwinna and Apollo were fenced in the former sewing room just off the kitchen. Apollo was sporting the disguising spell I'd designed for him that made him look like a large yellow Labrador retriever.

They greeted us with their own chorus of barks and chortles.

"Why don't you take the animals outside?" I suggested to Becca, who was still watching me like a hawk. My hands shook as I dropped the mail and my bag on the kitchen table. Now that the eerie moment with the birds had passed and the adrenaline was leaving my body, I was aware of the tension I'd been holding.

"Okay, Mommy." Becca opened the door and led Ardwinna and Apollo into the backyard to stretch their legs and pick up any messages left by the neighborhood's other beasts.

Musing over the raven's gift and its strange message about going home, I took the kettle to the sink. I was so consumed trying to recall every detail of the mysterious magic that had settled around us that I forgot to remove its lid, and the water hit it with such force that it splattered all over me, the counters, and the window. I mopped up the mess, filled the kettle properly, and set it on the stove. Then I took down a small bowl for Becca's snack and gathered a knife from the drawer. Still distracted, I narrowly avoided slicing the tip of my finger rather than the apple.

By the time the dog and the griffin had sniffed every plant and tree in the garden, I'd managed to safely slice the fruit, put some dollops of peanut butter into the bowl, and make myself a bracing cup of tea.

"Wash your hands before you sit down," I reminded Becca as she came inside, not wanting the blood and grime of this afternoon to get into my daughter's reactive bloodstream.

The five of us settled around the scarred but substantial piece of furniture that had been used as a chopping block when the house was built. Now, it was where we gathered for family meals rather than in the stuffy dining room. Tamsy was in her high chair, listing to one side with a bemused expression and a buckled shoe dangling from her foot. Ardwinna curled as close to Becca as possible in case a peanut butter–smeared finger or half-bitten piece of apple came her way, while Apollo positioned himself so that he could keep one tawny eye on the hallway, alert for Pip's return.

My son and his griffin were tightly connected by the mysterious bond that developed between weavers—witches like Pip and me, capable of making new spells—and the magical companions who supported them on their magical journey. My familiar had been a firedrake, and I still felt pangs of loss whenever I thought of Corra, whom I'd freed from service after she helped me save Matthew's life.

Becca did not have such a creature at her side. We weren't sure when—or if—one would appear. Our daughter's magic was not progressing by leaps and bounds like Pip's was, and Matthew and I were fine with that. Becca's vampire instincts were sharp, and her hunting skills excellent. Still, I needed to pay more attention to Becca's development as a witch this summer. I'd been so preoccupied in the last few years with my responsibilities at Yale that I hadn't been doing much magic at all.

As she sat, Becca took my emotional temperature and seemed to find it improved, since she tucked into her snack without mentioning Yale, Brenda, or the raven on the front pavement. I flipped through the mail delivered to Orange Street. It was mostly bills that needed to be paid before we left.

In between sorting items, I cast long looks at the ring on Becca's finger. Now that it was free from dirt and blood, I could see its intricate carvings. It was made of bone, though what kind of bone I couldn't tell. The black thread woven through the piercings gave both texture and color to the ring and reinforced the delicate tracery. Magic was woven through it, too, and I wanted a chance to explore it further.

"Can I see your ring?" I asked.

"Sure." Becca tugged at it, but the ring didn't budge. She put her finger in her mouth and sucked on it before I could stop her, then pulled on it again. "It's stuck."

"Let me try," I said, beckoning her over. She extended her finger toward me. The tip sparkled and shone.

"Look, Mommy!" Becca hopped up and down with excitement. "My finger is on fire, just like yours is when you do magic!"

"So I see," I replied calmly, though my heart had dropped into an ominous drumbeat. I touched the ring, hoping to learn its secrets, and the light at the tip of Becca's finger dimmed. The magic was stuck inside the ring just as the ring was stuck on Becca's finger.

"Can I wait for Daddy and Pip in the library?" Becca asked, impatient with my fussing. The colored paper, tubs of markers, pencils, and all the bits and bobs she used in her craft projects were stored there, and she would much rather play with them than stay in the kitchen with me.

"Of course you can," I said, letting go of her finger. "Are you going to draw a picture of what you saw at Yale to show Daddy and Pip when they come home?"

Becca picked up Tamsy and shook her head. "I'm going to draw a picture of the raven—so I won't forget her, or her message." Becca was an exceptionally resilient child, but the raven's death had made a deep impression on her.

"Okay, sweetie." I kept my voice light. "I'll join you soon."

Becca skipped off to the library and I sipped my tea, staring into its depths as though it might tell me what to make of the unkindness of ravens, their strange behavior, Becca's even odder reaction to it, and the unbudgeable ring.

Was Becca's magic waking up at long last? Would I have two teenage weavers on my hands in a few years and not just one? Matthew was bound to have similar questions when he discovered the dead bird outside. For now, I had no answers for him—or myself.

I returned to the mail with a sigh. Bills. Sale flyers. More bills. I quickly pitched them onto an empty chair to be recycled. My hands stilled when they touched a thick, creamy envelope with Italian stamps.

This was not junk mail. It was a letter from the Congregation, the ruling council that oversaw creature affairs in an often-hostile human world.

Holding the thick envelope in my fingers, I was reminded of my office in Venice and the work I'd done to integrate daemons, witches, and vampires into the Congregation, disrupting the status quo and breaking the tradition that a member of Matthew's extended family should preside over its proceedings. Today my friend Agatha Wilson led the nine-member council—a daemon who had brought many creative solutions to perennial Congregation problems. The occupant of the de Clermont chair after me had also broken with precedent. The vampire Fernando Gonçalves—the mate of the revered and long-dead Hugh de Clermont—represented the family, not Matthew or his older brother Baldwin.

I flipped the envelope over, expecting to see a swirl of black, silver, and orange wax impressed with the official Congregation seal of a flaming triangle with a sun, star, and moon held within it. This seal was all silver, however, with an unblinking eye in the center.

The all-seeing eye was the personal emblem of Sidonie Von Borcke, one of the Congregation's three witches. She had been the bane of my existence even before Baldwin had appointed me the de Clermont representative to the Congregation. While I was on the ruling council, Sidonie had made it her personal mission to thwart me at every turn.

Braced for bad news, I cracked the wax and opened the envelope. A whisper of rose and cedar escaped from the broken seal. I drew out the distinctive marble-edged paper, made by a *maestro marmorizzatore* at a shop where the Congregation had been purchasing their stationery since the 1860s. The letter began:

> *Dear Professor Bishop and Professor Clairmont,*
>
> *As you know, we assess the talents and skills of all children who have a legacy of higher magic in their family. Because both of Professor Bishop's parents came from such a lineage, we feel there is some urgency to proceed with your children's evaluation as soon as possible.*

Sidonie was wrong. My mother, Rebecca, had dabbled in higher, darker magic for a time in her teens and twenties. She'd first encountered my nemesis and her rival, Peter Knox, at some Congregation event for higher magic hopefuls. But my father, Stephen Proctor, had been notable for his lackluster magical talents. My father was a weaver, like me, unable to work other witches' spells. Aunt Sarah had told me that Dad wasn't interested in the craft, never mind its advanced practices. As for his lineage, the head of the Madison coven, Vivian Harrison, didn't believe the Proctors had produced any witch of real talent for generations.

We will be in touch with you in August to arrange for an examination in the early autumn, before Rebecca Bishop-Clairmont and Philip Bishop-Clairmont turn seven in November.

Kind regards, Sidonie Von Borcke

I shivered despite the heat. The fractured memory of Peter Knox's examination still had the power to unsettle me. He had come to Cambridge when I was seven and my parents—who had no doubt received a letter like the one I held—had spellbound me before he arrived, tying my power in knots and removing my memories of childish magic to guard me from the Congregation's interest. It wasn't until I found the Book of Life and met Matthew that my parents' spellbinding loosened, and my memories of those dark days slowly started to return, along with my magic.

But Knox's curiosity must have been roused despite my parents' desperate measures and the Congregation alerted to something strange in our household, for a few weeks later my mom and dad went to Nigeria to conduct research on ritual magic, drawing their focus away from me. They both died there, under mysterious circumstances I still didn't completely understand, although the role Peter Knox and his allies had played was evident. After their deaths, I'd had to figure out the contours of my own power without their support or guidance.

"No," I said fiercely. "Absolutely not."

The Congregation was not going to probe the twins' magical abilities so they could make use of them, as Peter Knox had tried and failed to do with me. The witches in Venice would not be given access to knowledge of my children's potential. I would go to the Congregation myself, and take this up with Sidonie and the other witches.

I turned my tote bag over, dumping my wallet and everything else I'd gathered from the office all over the kitchen table, scattering the freshly sorted house mail and undoing my earlier work. As usual, my phone had sifted to the bottom. It was now on top of the small mountain of campus mail that I had yet to go through.

Matthew was the first number on my speed dial. With more force than was necessary I pushed the button on the screen to connect us.

"Hello!" Matthew's voice was warm, and I immediately felt supported in my determination to protect Becca and Pip from Sidonie and her Congregation cronies. "Are you home?"

"Yes. And I need you to come home, too," I said. "They're after the children."

"Who is?" Matthew asked, his tone now blade-sharp.

"The Congregation. We got a letter," I said. "They want to test the children's magical talents. You'll have to take Becca and Pip to the Old Lodge while I go to Venice and sort this out."

"Slow down, Diana." Matthew was trying to calm me, but the urgency of the situation had me in its grip and his words carried little weight.

"If we let Sidonie test the children, the Congregation's witches are bound to discover that Pip's a weaver," I cried. "And they might be able to sense if the twins have blood rage, too."

Blood rage was the scourge of vampires, an inherited genetic condition that resulted when daemon, human, and vampire blood mingled. It manifested in uncontrollable anger, violence, and bloodlust. Matthew was afflicted with it, as was his great-grandson, Jack. Matthew had refused to perform tests on the children to see if they, too, had inherited his genetic mutation.

"I can't spellbind Becca and Pip," I said, my heart breaking and my voice following suit. "I can't, Matthew. I thought I could, if necessary, but now—"

"I'm on my way," Matthew said, his keys jangling as he gathered his things at the lab.

The line went dead.

In the silence that followed the call, I was aware of the distance between Becca and me in the house. Needing to close it, I swept the contents of my tote into my arms. I could sort through my campus mail in the library just as easily as in the kitchen.

Marcus's impressive, paneled library served as our family room, a quiet place tucked away from the street at the back of the house. It had windows that opened onto the garden, walls lined with books, a cozy fireplace, and a long table like those at Sterling Library.

Becca glanced up from her drawing and splayed protective hands over her work. "Don't look, Mom. It's not finished."

"I won't," I said, dumping my possessions on the far end of the table. "Cross my heart."

Though I was tempted to peek at Becca's creation, I dove into the drifts of paper instead, looking for my planner so that I could begin to make the arrangements for Venice. Matthew had told me to wait, but there was no harm in looking at dates and imagining how we could adjust our summer calendar.

I located the slim diary and drew it from the pile. Sticking out from underneath it was a letter addressed to me at the Yale history department. The sender's identity was embossed in navy on the upper left corner: *Professor G. E. Proctor, Ravenswood, Ipswich, Massachusetts.*

I stared at the return address, unable to believe what I was seeing. Professor? Proctor? Ravenswood? Ipswich? Sarah had assured me that all my nearest Proctor relatives were dead. But the postmark indicated that the note had been sent three days ago.

As far as I knew, ghosts did not have access to the U.S. Postal Service.

I took hold of the letter and slid my finger under the flap, ripping a clean tear across the top, releasing the scent of petrichor and brimstone I'd noticed outside with the ravens. The thick card inside bore a formal inscription: *From the desk of G. E. Proctor.* Below were three lines written in a sloping script no longer taught in American schools.

It's time you came home, Diana.

Your great-aunt,

Gwyneth Proctor

It was the same message the raven had delivered to Becca.

It couldn't be a coincidence that both messages had arrived from two different sources on the same day I'd received the ominous letter from the Congregation. Had this mysterious great-aunt of mine sent the ravens in case her invitation was lost in the mail? Could the invitation to Ipswich have something to do with the Congregation?

"Professor Gwyneth Proctor." I traced her name with my finger. I knew almost nothing about my father's family, and I was surprised to discover that there were academic women among them.

I looked to see if there was anything else in the envelope. I tipped it over and out slid a playing card. Someone had drawn a hexafoil on it, the most popular apotropaic mark used to protect humans from witches and magic. It resembled a simple six-petaled flower. You could still see the tiny hole where the point of a compass had rested.

I took up the card, and the weaver's cords on my left hand flared in response. Usually, weavers had a clutch of colored cords that helped them make new spells tied to the corresponding powers woven into the universe. Mine had been absorbed into me like the mysterious Book of Life, becoming part of my body as well as my magic. They had been quiet for years, but today's events had awoken them.

When I flipped the card over, I saw a woodcut of a man in dark clothing and stout buckled shoes walking along a dark path bordered by low grasses. Clouds gathered above his head, and one hand was outstretched as if pointing the way. The image had been cut from some broadside or book, and glued to the card.

Home, my witch's sixth sense whispered, as I stared at the man's outstretched hand.

Another piece of paper slid from the envelope and fluttered down into my lap. It was small and tissue thin, folded neatly in half. The crease in the paper was soft and worn, as though it had been opened and closed many times.

On it was a pencil drawing of two clasped hands with a raven's shadow falling across them. One hand belonged to a child. The other was adult and wore an intricate ring.

My ring. It had been a gift from Philippe de Clermont to Matthew's mother, Ysabeau. She, in turn, had given it to me and I'd worn it ever since. I looked down at my left hand and compared the rare jewel to the pencil drawing. The similarities between them were unmistakable, with the tiny hands holding a heart with a diamond embedded in the center of the ring. I searched the paper, looking for further clues about who had drawn it, and when. *Rebecca and Diana* was written on the back, along with a set of initials—MFP—and the date 1972.

It was impossible that a drawing made decades ago, before I was born, could depict something that had happened just this afternoon in such detail.

The weaver's cords on my left hand stood out, trailing from my fingertips, over my palm, and down to my wrist in strands of white, gold, silver, and black. A round figure appeared around my pulse point, woven from the cords: an ouroboros, the snake with its tail in its mouth. It was the de Clermont family symbol, as well as a representation of the tenth knot of creation and destruction that so few weavers had the power to tie. These were the colors of darker, higher magic. I looked to my right hand, where the colors of the craft—brown, yellow, blue, red, and green— normally appeared when my power was stirred.

There was no trace of them. The card and the drawing that Gwyneth Proctor had sent had only captured the attention of the cords of higher magic, which I had rarely used.

I drew Sidonie's crumpled letter from my pocket and held it next to my great-aunt's simple missive. In one hand I held the prospect of danger and a threat to my family. In the other, I sensed a thin lifeline of hope and possibility.

I glanced at the picture made in 1972 of my daughter's hand inside my own, the shadow of a raven's wings falling like a benediction where our bodies met. I felt a pang of intense desire for something I could not name, and a place I'd never heard of before, where a great-aunt named Gwyneth Proctor waited for me.

I flexed my fingers, and the ouroboros at my wrist appeared to move, shifting slightly underneath my skin while shimmering colors of higher magic brightened in the air around me.

I was not going to England or Venice. Not yet. First, I was going home. To Ravenswood.

Chapter 2

I moved to one of the deep chairs by the fireplace, my feet on the brass fender that surrounded the hearth, as I reexamined the pencil drawing—accurate to the last detail—depicting the events of this afternoon. The aged card, the note from Gwyneth, and the official missive from the Congregation rested in a pile on my lap.

"Who drew that?" Becca had come to look over my shoulder, silent as a panther and curious as a cat.

"I don't know," I replied, making room for her in my lap. Becca climbed up and rested in the hollow of my arms. "I think it might have been one of Grandpa Stephen's relatives."

Becca's fingers reached out for the drawing, and I gave it to her so she could take a closer look. She held the edges carefully. Phoebe had been teaching the twins to treat priceless objects with respect, and while Pip could still be dangerously exuberant with a piece of porcelain, Becca was an excellent pupil.

"That's your ring," Becca said, "the one that Gammer Ysabeau gave you."

I nodded, my cheek sliding along Becca's smooth hair.

"I'm going to draw the next thing that happened," Becca said, hopping down and returning to the table and her coloring supplies.

I returned to the playing card. It was old, based on the thick, rough card stock that had once been white but was now a mellow ivory tinged with amber. The walker's clothing was from the seventeenth century, and the high-flying feather in his cap indicated the image dated from the reign of Charles I or Charles II, as did the lace-trimmed cuffs and collar. The glue that held the image to the card was brittle and yellowed. The item gave off a homemade air, as though someone had been doing a craft project between 1629 and 1685 with scissors, a glue pot, and a pile of old playing cards and pamphlets.

As for the significance of the card itself, I wasn't sure. Was this a one-off image, something intended to be kept in a document box or between the pages of a book and mounted to card stock for durability? Did the hexafoil signify the curious card was a magical talisman of some kind? Or did it belong to a larger deck?

I found myself wanting to follow the solitary walker to his unknown destination as though the answers might be found at the end of the road. Though his route was not signposted, my feet itched to step into the prints made by his heavy soles and match his progress stride for stride.

Go home, the walker seemed to say, urging me to accept Gwyneth's invitation. *There are answers there.*

I studied the card as if it were one of my alchemical manuscripts, hunting for anything I might have overlooked. I spotted a faded letter, and another. There was a faded number, too, along the top margin. I picked up my cellphone and took a photograph, then fiddled with the settings until a negative version of the card appeared on the small screen. This was a trick I'd learned in the archives, and it often saved me from having to reserve time with the ultraviolet light that revealed faded or obliterated writing.

Happily, the trick worked. With the help of magnification and a few more tweaks I was able to read the old inscriptions. Written in a copperplate from around 1700 were the words *The Dark Path* and the number *47.*

Puzzled, I sat back against the chair's plump cushions. Playing card decks had fifty-two cards, but not a card titled The Dark Path—nor were they usually numbered above ten. Tarot decks had seventy-eight cards, but only the first twenty-two cards of the major arcana were numbered sequentially. As this was numbered *47,* the card couldn't be from a tarot deck, either.

Before I could take my thinking any further, the doorbell clanged. Then the door banged open.

Pip was home. Whether the house was empty or full, whether he was with a creature holding a key or not, Pip couldn't resist turning the crank of Marcus's doorbell, which released a blare of tinny sound capable of raising the dead. A low murmur of voices followed, then Ardwinna's sharp bark and Apollo's answering chortle as the animals raced to meet the new arrivals.

"Hi, Mom!" Pip bellowed. "We're home!"

"Daddy!" Becca's voice was loud and piercing as she left the table to follow the dog and griffin. "Did you see the dead raven?"

"Yes, moonbeam. Where's your mother?" Matthew replied from somewhere in the middle of the house.

"She's in the library." It was Becca's turn to shout. "Mom! Daddy's home. Pip, too. And Uncle Chris and Aunt Miriam!"

"Hey, Diana!" Chris called. "I'd like to give those witches on the Congregation something *really* scary to worry about—a pissed-off god-father!"

"Where is it?" Matthew asked from the library threshold. His hair, dark as a raven's wing like Becca's, stood up in agitated patches and his brows were dangerously low over his gray-green eyes.

I picked up the Congregation's letter from the nearby table and extended it to him.

Matthew knelt by my chair, searching my face for signs of distress.

"We will figure this out, *mon coeur*," he said, bringing my hand to his lips and pressing it into his cool flesh. "You will not have to spellbind the children. We can go to Sept-Tours, rather than the Old Lodge. No one will disturb us there, and Baldwin and Fernando will have something to say to the Congregation about the fate of our children. We'll be safe."

My parents had thought I'd be safe in Madison with Sarah, and I had been—for a time.

I wanted more than temporary security for Becca and Pip.

"What happened to that raven?" Chris asked, arriving a few steps behind Matthew.

Pip shot past him to give me a kiss. Becca was right on her brother's heels, headed toward the library table.

"It was bringing me a message, Uncle Chris, and then it hit the pavement. See!" Becca waved the pencil drawing from Gwyneth Proctor and her own drawing of a flat raven outlined in vivid red. "Mommy said it was an accident. I'm not sure, though. I should have asked her friend."

"Wait." Chris performed an Oscar-worthy double take. "You got a message from a bird? Are you enrolled in a school of witchcraft and wizardry now?"

"That was an owl, Uncle Chris," Becca replied. "This message came from a raven."

But the message was not the only thing the ravens had brought to New Haven. They'd brought Becca a ring, too. I was surprised to see it was no longer on her finger, given how tightly it had clung to her skin earlier. Where had it gone?

"Were you expecting a message from the dead, Diana?" Miriam asked, slipping into the room at her usual, unhurried pace. She was an ancient vampire, and capable of great speed, but she was temperamentally averse to haste. "That's what ravens usually carry."

"No," I muttered under my breath, "but I got one anyway."

My quiet words captured the full attention of the adults.

"We got several messages today," I explained. "One from Venice, one from the raven, and one from the Proctors."

"The Proctors?" Matthew's face went blank as he processed this revelation. "I thought all of your nearest relations were dead?"

"So did I." Sarah had told me so, repeatedly.

"Three messages," Miriam said thoughtfully. "All of them magical. That can't be a coincidence."

"My aunt Hortense swore that bad things come in threes," Chris said, his voice ominous.

"So do Newton's laws of motion," I said, wanting to squash this superstitious talk as quickly as possible.

"Pigs, too," Pip chimed in, presenting evidence from his own area of expertise. "And bears. And French hens."

"And musketeers," Becca added, a piece of paper in each hand. She charged at her father.

"Careful, Becca!" I cried, afraid she might damage the delicate drawing. I rose to my feet, and the old playing card tumbled to the floor along with Gwyneth's note.

Matthew's eyes fixed on the fallen items. "What are they?"

"A message from my great-aunt Gwyneth Proctor. She'd like me to come home." My voice was even as I made the startling announcement.

Matthew's eyes met mine, storm-dark and gleaming. I picked up the cards and handed them to my husband.

"Home?" Chris said. "You are home."

"Gwyneth's home. In Ipswich," I said, my gaze not wavering from Matthew as he studied my great-aunt's message, though my voice broke on the word *home*. "A place called Ravenswood."

"What about the Congregation?" Chris asked with a frown. "Shouldn't you be going to Venice?"

"What about England?" Pip cried, horrified at the prospect of a change to his careful summer plans.

"What about me?" Becca demanded. "The ravens said I needed to go home, too."

"Nothing's decided," I said lightly, even though I was fully committed to going to Massachusetts. "Let's talk about it after dinner. I don't know about anyone else, but I'm hungry. Who needs a glass of wine?"

The twins, distracted by the prospect of a warm meal, took charge of Tamsy and the animals and led the way to the kitchen. Chris and Miriam lingered behind in the library, as did Matthew.

"Ipswich?" Matthew's eyebrows rose. "You're going to Boston's North Shore on the basis of a six-word note from a great-aunt you've never met?"

But it was more than that, and he knew it.

"After dinner," I promised. "We can talk about it *after* dinner."

Once we were all gathered in the kitchen, everybody took up their usual Friday-night dinner responsibilities. It was a tradition for us to come together at the end of the week and have a family meal. While Matthew prepared the food, the rest of us fed the animals, cleared off the table, turned on the speaker to listen to one of Chris's playlists, and set six places with all the plates, cutlery, napkins, and glassware necessary to cater to a hungry mob. Becca plopped Tamsy in her high chair, and the doll surveyed the whirl of activity around her with the superior attitude of an aristocrat watching servants at work.

Around the doll's neck, suspended from the coral beads that she had come to us with, was the missing bone ring. Praying that no one would ask questions about this fresh addition to Tamsy's wardrobe, I poured a healthy slug of wine for each of the adults and took a gulp of my own to steady my nerves.

Soon, the comforting scent of cassoulet filled the kitchen. Matthew had been making pots of hearty French food once or twice a week all semester and feeding me and the children out of them one ladleful at a time. Ratatouille, *potée auvergnate,* beef and chicken stewed in wine—each one was delicious and different. Chris had started calling Matthew *Julia* and had arrived for one of our Friday-night suppers with a ruffled apron and a block of butter instead of his usual offering of wine and flowers.

We got through Matthew's delicious concoction—which Pip accurately called *fart stew*—and two bottles of red wine without incident, except for a few petty squabbles about portion size, the amount of French mustard Pip wanted spooned into his dish, Becca's desire for a slug of the blood she still liked to drink on special occasions, and one very loud expression of gas from the direction of the twins. Becca and Pip kept up an endless stream of lighthearted chatter and shared important neighborhood news, such as the arrival of kittens at the house on the corner, and all we adults had to do was follow their lead. Matthew drank a whole bottle of Burgundy himself.

By the time I served ice cream and espressos for dessert, my husband was casting hard, speculative glances in my direction, his patience now exhausted. Once the bowls and tiny cups were empty, I tried to hustle the children upstairs to bed so that we didn't argue in front of them. Something told me Matthew wasn't going to be amenable to the plan I'd cobbled together over dinner.

"I can't go to bed yet, Mommy," Becca protested, carrying her empty bowl to the dishwasher. "I have to take care of the raven first."

"Your father will do it," I said, making sure that Ardwinna had fresh water and one of the deep sinks was partially filled so that Apollo could give himself his nightly bath.

"No!" Becca's sharp cry was fueled by a surfeit of sugar. "I have to do it, Mom. I promised the raven's friend that I would bury her."

I put my hands on my hips, trying to judge my daughter's level of commitment to this lunacy.

"And your *maman* knows that our word is a solemn oath," Matthew said, rising from his chair and swinging his long-legged daughter into the air before setting her down, light as a feather. "Let's do it properly, *oui*?"

"*Oui*," Becca said gravely.

"Can I come?" Pip asked his sister. "Cuthbert, too?" The battered blue rabbit with the long ears was already tucked into his elbow.

Becca considered her brother's request. "I think that would be okay."

"Mind if I tag along? I've never been to a raven funeral before," Chris said.

"The funeral already happened, Uncle Chris. The other ravens took care of that. This is just the burial," Becca explained. "Ravens don't have hands. They needed my help with the shovel."

"Oh." Chris looked at Matthew and me, his eyebrows lifted. "Point noted."

"And me?" Miriam asked, though she knew the answer already, for Becca never refused the ancient vampire anything. Like Phoebe, Miriam was one of Becca's role models and close confidantes.

"Are you coming, Mommy?" Becca stopped by the door to the backyard. "You were there for the funeral, so it's okay if it's too hard for you to say goodbye again."

"I think I'll just stay behind and clear up the kitchen," I said, mindful of all that would need to be done if I went to Ravenswood tomorrow. "You go ahead. But it's straight up to bed after that."

"Yes, Mom," the twins intoned in unison.

While washing the dishes, I kept my eye on the proceedings outside. In the garden shed, Matthew and Becca found a suitable shovel to scrape the raven's remains off the pavement.

Miriam conferred with Becca about where the bird should be buried, and after much deliberation they decided on a spot under the canopy of the majestic tree outside the library window. It was one of the few specimens to have made it through the blight of Dutch elm disease, and my neighbors told me that in case of fire I should let the house burn and save the tree instead.

Miriam and Chris dug a hole for the bird while Matthew, Becca, and Pip went off to the front yard to retrieve the corpse. When the three of them returned, Becca led the burial cortege, carefully holding the shovel with the raven before her. Pip, in charge of Cuthbert and Tamsy, followed in the role of chief mourner. Matthew brought up the rear of the procession, his hands folded before his heart in a gesture of prayer.

Apollo, sensing that a ritual was afoot involving another winged creature, pecked at the doorknob. I let him and Ardwinna out and stood by the open door, watching as Becca came to a halt under the elm's spreading limbs.

"Bye-bye, black bird," Rebecca said sorrowfully, standing next to the shallow grave. She tipped the shovel and the bird tumbled into the hole, its body stiff and its feathers gleaming. "I'll visit you when we get back. Sweet dreams."

Our daughter had managed to organize a touching memorial in a matter of minutes using a combination of one of her favorite songs, a promise, and a few words from our family's nighttime ritual. My eyes filled at Becca's empathy for the dead bird, and her determination to give the creature a proper send-off.

"*Pack up all my cares and woe,*" Chris sang in his rich bass, picking up on the mood of the ceremony as well as a snatch of the same song Becca had woven into her goodbye. "*Here I go, wingin' low. Bye, bye, blackbird.*"

"*Where somebody waits for me, Sugar's sweet, so is she.*" Miriam joined in, her pure soprano soaring above Chris's resonant tones. "*Bye, bye, blackbird.*"

"*Make my bed and light the light, I'll arrive late tonight.*" Matthew added his voice to the choir on the next lines, providing a baritone note. He rested his hand lightly on Becca's bowed head. "*Blackbird, bye, bye.*"

I dashed a tear from my cheek. In the silence that followed, a few early fireflies flickered in the garden as if they, too, wanted to contribute to the occasion.

"Here, Becca." Pip handed Tamsy to his sister for emotional support.

Becca buried her face in the doll's streaming red hair, her sniffs audible in the quiet.

Chris and Miriam shoveled earth over the raven as the others watched. Once the bird was encased in its tomb, everyone waited for Becca to signal that she was ready to go.

"It's okay now." Becca took a deep breath and waved at the small mound of freshly turned earth. "Bye-bye, black bird. See you soon."

I stood aside as the burial party reentered the house, unexpectedly moved by the poignant sight of a raven being put to rest.

"**M**y plan makes perfect sense," I told Matthew, once we'd tucked the children in, read the obligatory bedtime stories, and returned to the library to join Miriam and Chris. "You'll take the children to England—or Sept-Tours if you'd rather. I'll go to Ravenswood to meet Gwyneth Proctor. She must know something about why the ravens came. Then I'll go straight to Venice to tell the Congregation to leave our children alone. I'll join you at the Old Lodge as soon as I can."

Chris put down his glass of bourbon and looked at me in disbelief. Miriam paused in her efforts to remove the cork from a bottle of Vouvray. The pair exchanged glances, then voiced their opposition to this cocka-mamie plan. Matthew crossed his arms, leaned against the library fire-place, and gave me the latest in a series of uncomfortable stares.

"Exactly what happened here today that's made you rethink our summer plans?" Matthew asked. "Not to mention abandoning your research proposal, and the countdown to departure that you started back in April?"

"Let's see." I put down my wineglass, the impact making a dull thud on the table. "A swarm of ravens descended on the house, one of them died, Becca talked to another, we got a letter from the Congregation, and I received a picture and a playing card from a branch of my family tree I thought had died out! Call me crazy, but I think a change of vacation plans may be in order!"

"You mean a conspiracy of ravens," Miriam said. "It's an omen, clearly. Where's the picture?"

Matthew held it up and Miriam took it from his fingers.

"What kind of omen?" I asked, worried. Miriam had been born back in the days when consulting auguries was part of daily life. Dead birds couldn't signify anything good, but an omen was on an entirely different level.

"The kind that comes wrapped in a prophecy." Miriam pointed to the date the picture had been drawn. "This says 1972—almost half a century ago. But the ravens didn't come until today."

"It says *Rebecca and Diana* on the back," I said. "I would have thought it was a picture of Mom and me, except for Ysabeau's ring."

"So it's a double prophecy," Miriam commented. "You weren't born until 1976. Someone with the initials MFP foresaw it all: your birth, and Becca's, Matthew, and the ravens, too."

"Whoever it was, I'm guessing that P stands for Proctor," I said. "A close relative of Gwyneth's perhaps?"

"How is it possible you know so little about your father's family?" Miriam asked me in disbelief. "Weren't you ever curious?"

This question troubled me, too, and my voice took on a defensive edge.

"The Proctors were never part of my life. We never spent any holidays with them before my parents died—or afterward, either. I don't remember there being any Proctors at the memorial service we had for Mom and Dad," I replied. "Dad never mentioned his family, so I suppose

I never questioned their absence. Sarah said the only Proctors left were far-distant cousins."

"Families aren't always reliable when it comes to their own history," Matthew said. "Perhaps this isn't the first time one of your father's kin reached out to you. Previous attempts might have been met with silence."

"I'm sure neither Gwyneth nor any other Proctor ever tried to contact me." To believe otherwise would mean that Sarah and Emily had been keeping another huge secret from me while I was growing up.

Though I sounded certain, a memory niggled at the edge of an oubliette left by my parents' spellbinding. Had Em mentioned the Proctors, once upon a time? Before I could chase down the elusive thought, Matthew spoke.

"When, exactly, did Rebecca talk to the raven?" The look Matthew gave me was not gentle like snowflakes but as penetrating as a falling icicle.

"After the world turned gray and the other raven plummeted to the pavement," I replied, supplying additional details of the encounter. "When the bird bled out, the color returned to the world. All the ravens settled in the trees—except the one who delivered the message to Becca. I think he was their leader."

I'd never witnessed our daughter talk to birds before, but she had so many imaginary friends I might have missed it. The sight of that single raven, hopping along the path toward her, kindled another spark of curiosity. Why had Becca been able to communicate with the bird, when I could not?

"So magic was already at work when Rebecca made her oath." Matthew swore and sat beside me.

"What kind of magic?" Miriam asked.

"I'm not sure." My left hand tingled and I shoved it under my thigh. "But the ravens were caught up in it. They sang the most mournful song after Becca spoke with their leader. It was like nothing I've heard before. The whole swarm—"

"Conspiracy," Miriam corrected me. "Or an unkindness, if you prefer."

"—unkindness behaved as though a family member had died," I finished. "Becca said that the raven who spoke with her was the dead bird's friend."

"Did you ever observe this kind of behavior in your research, Matthew?" Miriam asked.

My husband had done research on wolves, not birds. Confused, I waited for his response.

"Ravens form mating pairs, just like vampires and wolves," Matthew replied. "They grieve when their mate is gone, and their social group often participates in the mourning. In Norway, I witnessed wolves howling along to the ravens' lament when a member of their group passed."

I frowned. "You make it sound like ravens and wolves have some kind of relationship."

"They work together in the wild," Matthew said, nodding. "They play together, help each other locate prey, and even share kills. It's an unusual example of cross-species cooperation."

"Speaking of which," Chris said, "we'll need that spirit of teamwork to take on the Congregation. They're coming to test Becca and Pip— dead raven or not. Maybe we should focus on that and not some spooky omen!"

"What if they're connected?" I asked. Even a human like Chris had to see that the whole of the afternoon's events was far greater than the sum of its parts.

"Maybe they are," Chris conceded, "but right now I think we should work on a greater level of trust between the vampires, witches, and humans in this room. And I'd like some credit as a prophet myself. I knew something like this was going to happen—not that any of you listened to me."

Miriam shook her head in warning, but Chris plowed on.

"We can't let anyone, and especially not the Congregation, learn something about Becca and Pip that we haven't already discovered and come to terms with," he continued, becoming more forceful with every word. "It's long past time to run genetic tests on them, and get a sense of what powers and abilities the twins might have inherited before somebody else beats us to it."

"We've been over this, Chris." Matthew's voice was quiet, but the dark vein in his temple was ticking dangerously. "Diana and I want Rebecca and Philip to develop their talents and skills naturally—without laboratory findings shaping our ideas about what they might become."

Chris flung his hands up in exasperation. "You may not have noticed, Matthew, but there are a lot of smart, observant humans in New Haven. They know you and Diana are different, even if they can't articulate how. Pip grew an inch in the past month, and Becca is well on her way to mastering trigonometry. You can't keep the twins inside the Addams family mansion until they're eighteen, hoping nobody picks up on their advanced development."

Not only did Chris watch a lot of television, he wasn't fond of Marcus's house.

"Pip and Rebecca go to school," I pointed out, defensive at the notion that the twins were housebound.

"You think Maria Montessori is going to make them appear like average folk?" Chris snorted.

"It's a Waldorf school, actually," I said, gritting my teeth. "We felt that the focus on developing curiosity and channeling the imagination was a better fit for Becca and Pip."

"Pip has a pet *griffin,* D," Chris said. "And Becca is turning into some combination of Alan Turing and Dr. Doolittle. I don't think you have to worry about their imaginations."

"With respect, Christopher," Matthew said, "this is really none of your business."

"With respect, Matthew, that is utter bullshit," Chris replied, his voice rising. "Miriam and I are their godparents."

Along with half of the family. Still, Chris and Miriam had sworn to protect and defend the children. They had a right to speak their minds when it came to ensuring the best possible futures for them.

"We are not testing the children now." Matthew's tone said *do not press your luck.* "When they are eighteen, they can decide for themselves if— and when—they want to be research subjects."

"And the Congregation has agreed to your schedule?" Miriam asked pointedly. "Because I'm with Chris on this. It's time we knew the truth."

Matthew sipped his wine rather than responding.

My glance fell on the old bar cabinet where we'd arranged a group of family photos. A picture of Ysabeau and Philippe during happy times at the 1924 Paris Olympics shared the space with a snapshot of my parents' wedding. My maternal grandparents hovered in the background, beaming with joy. There was a marvelous picture of Phoebe throwing her wedding bouquet into a crowd of well-wishers gathered in Freyja's garden, a laughing Marcus by her side. Several photos of Sarah and Em were there, too, along with a photo of Jack and Fernando, wreathed in smiles, on a beach in Portugal. And there were pictures of the twins as well, captured in the active, happy moments of early childhood: Pip's first tricycle ride, a trip to a farm to meet the animals, Becca and I playing patty-cake, Matthew reading them a bedtime story.

My father was the only representative of the Proctor family among the photos. He'd never explained why his parents weren't in any of their wedding pictures, and I'd later assumed they must have been dead by the time he and Mom got married. When I was old enough to ask questions, my father, too, was dead. My great-aunt Gwyneth must have known where to find me for some time, but she hadn't reached out until now. Some intricate plan was unfolding, and though Gwyneth might not have been the architect of it, she was somehow instrumental to its workings.

"Gwyneth Proctor is the key to all of this," I said, half to myself. "It's her message that matters. She knew that the ravens were headed this way. She must have known about the Congregation, too. My great-aunt has more to divulge, or she wouldn't have invited me to Ravenswood."

"A Proctor relative would be a godsend, genetically," Chris said, pitched forward in excitement. "Her blood could answer so many questions about the kids' DNA."

"Not now, Chris," Miriam warned, putting a restraining hand on his knee. Nevertheless, he persisted.

"And it would shed light on the gray areas in Diana's genome that we still don't understand." Chris's excitement mounted at the prospect of even more DNA findings. "Gwyneth can't be the only Proctor in Ipswich. There must be more. Can I come with you?"

The thought of arriving at Ravenswood with a bucket of cheek swabs and Chris Roberts in tow was too much.

"No one is going with me," I said firmly. "Gwyneth invited *me* to Ravenswood. Whatever she has to say, it's a family matter. She isn't likely to share it with others listening in on the conversation."

"*We* are going to Ipswich with you," Matthew said grimly.

Chris gave Matthew a high five.

"Not you," Matthew said sternly, dashing Chris's hopes. "Rebecca, Philip, and I will go. This supposed relative could be luring you into a trap."

Supposed relative? Trap?

"There's no vast conspiracy of creatures impersonating members of my family," I said, taking on the first of Matthew's absurd comments. "Gwyneth Proctor must be in her nineties. I doubt she's sprinkling a bag of breadcrumbs between Connecticut and Massachusetts to lure me into some malicious web."

Matthew's expression told me that he wouldn't put anything past Gwyneth Proctor. I smothered a frustrated reply.

"You have to put the twins first, Matthew," I said, conviction making my voice rise. "And if you won't go to England without me, that means staying here, in New Haven. The twins shouldn't be anywhere near Ravenswood until we know more."

"She's right, Matthew." Miriam was an unexpected, but welcome, ally.

"I won't be long," I said more gently. "A few days at most."

"Very well," Matthew said reluctantly. "I'll stay here with the children while you interrogate Gwyneth Proctor."

Matthew was making it sound like a military operation, not a family reunion.

"But you must promise me you'll leave immediately if you sense something is wrong, and stay in touch while you're there. We'll decide what to do about the Congregation and our summer plans when you get back," he continued.

It's time you came home. Gwyneth's strange invitation whispered through my mind.

I didn't know where the road to Ipswich would take me, or what I would find once I arrived. But I was eager to follow the mysterious walker in his plumed hat and buckled shoes.

"I won't be gone long," I repeated to reassure him. "Just until Monday or Tuesday, at the latest. I pro—"

Matthew silenced me with a glance. "Don't make promises you might not be able to keep, *ma lionne.*"

That night, under the dark of the moon, I made promises with my body that Matthew was not willing—or able—to silence. With every gentle touch and press of my lips to his flesh, I promised more.

More intimacy, free from secrets kept too long.

More trust, free from the fear that made life feel impossible.

More love, unimaginably more love, to fill the remaining days we would share.

Matthew responded to my promises with his own.

That not even deeply hidden secrets would threaten our love.

That nothing was impossible, so long as we faced the challenge together.

That nothing would keep us from living every moment to the fullest.

The moonless night wrapped us in velvet when we were at last sated and at peace. I stole into Matthew's arms, stretched along the length of him. My husband's familiar contours were comforting in their coolness, accustomed as I was to the temperature of a vampire's body.

"I won't be gone long," I murmured once more, pressing another kiss into the muscles over his heart.

Matthew didn't say a word but gathered me closer as I fell into a dream-filled sleep.

Chapter 3

The sign on Route 1 that flashed past my window indicated that I was seven miles from Ipswich—and only eight miles from Salem. The shadows cast by the nooses that once swung on Gallows Hill were long, and I felt their chill.

It wasn't the first time I'd been to Ipswich. My mother had insisted we stop there *en route* to summer vacation in Maine and have fried clams in the town's legendary Clam Box. Dad had been uncharacteristically quick to anger and sharp of tongue during the ride from Cambridge, as he preferred to get to the small cabin in East Boothbay as quickly as possible, with a minimum of stops for ice cream and antiques. I sat outside at a picnic table, slurping down a frozen root beer slushie, while they fetched the food at the pickup window. My parents' raised voices floated toward the parking lot, setting my face afire with mortification at the thought that everyone could hear them argue.

I couldn't recall what they had been fighting about—though I now suspected it might have had something to do with our proximity to Dad's family.

I turned off Route 1 and onto the old road from Topsfield to Ipswich, leaving behind the land of strip malls, pizza parlors, and national donut chains. A quiet stillness descended as the traffic was reduced to a trickle and sprawling old houses with green lawns replaced the neon signs of commerce that lit up Boston's northern suburbs. It was like driving back in time to pass by the eighteenth-century houses, with their pristine paint and picket fences.

I drove into the center of Ipswich along Market Street, one of the town's main thoroughfares, and pulled the Range Rover into a parking spot outside a thriving café called The Thirsty Goat.

Outside, under a swinging sign with an image of a goat in seventeenth-century clothing tipping his head back to drain a goblet, the tables were filled with a wide range of locals: young mothers sipping lattes, their children parked next to them in strollers; old salts in overalls and worn baseball caps clutching paper cups full of steaming brew; and people with laptops clicking away at their email while downing mochas. The Thirsty Goat was clearly the hub of the local community.

It was also the perfect place to ask for directions to Ravenswood. Though I'd plugged Gwyneth's zip code and the word *Ravenswood* into the navigation system when I left New Haven, the directions had only landed me here in the center of town. Without a street name and number, I was going to have to rely on local knowledge to find my great-aunt.

I turned off the ignition and grabbed my tote bag from the passenger seat. I was in desperate need of hot tea to revive my courage before meeting Gwyneth Proctor for the first time.

When my feet touched the pavement, a nudging tingle filled the air as though a thousand witches were blowing kisses. My eyes swept the crowd, looking in vain for a witch among the prams and baseball caps, but I couldn't locate the source of the warning that witches were nearby.

My senses on high alert, I entered the café. It was a cheerful space with a lofty beamed ceiling. The crisp white on the rafters extended down until it met chair-height red paneling, and the work of local artists covered the walls.

The cozy atmosphere turned chilly as I felt the strong probe of a witch's gaze. Then another.

Behind the café's counter stood two witches. One had wild black hair piled into a topknot and a nose ring. Her arms were covered with tattoos: a new moon, an owl feather, a moth, a tarot card, and more that were hidden in the sleeve of her black T-shirt. Embroidered on her apron was a name—*Ann*—along with a vivid rendering of the High Priestess card from the Rider-Waite tarot deck. The other witch had a colder, more forbidding air. Her apron was embroidered with the name *Meg,* and the Queen of Pentacles was displayed across the bib. Meg wore a pin that read COVEN MEMBERSHIP COMMITTEE.

Not even the most obtuse human could overlook that these were witches. As if to prove it, I spied one of the industrial Italian coffee machines that Matthew adored. Though not a cauldron, it was black and set in a prominent place. Occasionally, it discharged a puff of steam. A sign taped to it read NO CAPPUCCINOS UNDER THE BALSAMIC MOON DUE TO POWER SURGES. TAKE YOUR COMPLAINTS TO THE TOPSFIELD COVEN.

"Can we help you?" Ann's tone was brisk, her power carefully banked and managed. It was not wild like the power of the elemental witches in London's Rede, or delicate and precise like a weaver who made new spells. The image that came to mind was that of a highly trained, magical figure skater willing to patiently inscribe modest school figures in the ice so that she could explode later into effortless quadruple spins.

I smiled brightly. "A hot tea with milk, no sugar. To go." I was grateful that my order wasn't restricted by the lunar cycle since I had no idea what phase the moon was in at present.

"Our specialty tea is Witches' Brew. It's not on the menu, but it's a town favorite." Meg's lips rose in a sardonic smile, the force of her stare intensifying. She had strange, mottled eyes that contained different hues: sea-glass green and bark brown, a mixture of water and earth.

"No eye of newt?" I asked sweetly, fishing for the wallet inside my Bodleian tote bag.

"Only in sorbet," came Ann's quick reply.

"English Breakast would be fine," I said, refusing to take the bait. These two may enjoy going full witch on the tourists who had straggled in from nearby Salem, but I wasn't going to encourage them.

"Anything else?" Meg demanded, her eyes narrow with suspicion.

"Everything all right, Meg?" A slight woman with jet hair iced with white and holding a parasol to shield her skin from the sun entered the café, power and magic following her like Cinderella's train at the ball. The witch studied us from behind round, rose-colored glasses.

"Just an unexpected visitor," Ann said, placing a slight emphasis on the last word. What she meant was *witch*. Did Ipswich's coven require magical passports for creatures like me?

"It's under control, Goody Wu." Meg bristled at the unwanted interference.

Goody was an old-fashioned form of address, and one that I'd not heard uttered in a community of witches since I timewalked to Elizabethan London.

"Oh, I think not," Goody Wu said softly, breathing out a stream of sea glass–tinged air that sparkled and chimed in the light. It reached me in curious wisps that tickled my ears and slid up my nostrils. "Quite the opposite."

How many witches were in this town? I'd been here less than ten minutes, and I'd already met three.

"Hellooo!" A tall, slender willow of a witch breezed through the door, adding another creature to my tally. She was wearing a pink canvas bucket hat emblazoned with a griffin and the kind of plaid madras shorts my mother had worn in the early 1980s, when preppy was high fashion. A messy ponytail attempted to capture her blond-and-gray hair, the length of it bundled up under the brim of her hat. An enameled pin proclaimed her to be MISTRESS OF COVEN CEREMONIES. As she drew closer, I could see that her energy and agility, along with her delicate features, had made me think that she was far younger than the fine lines around her eyes indicated.

"Welcome home, coz!"

I looked around to see whom the witch was greeting. After an uncomfortable pause, I realized she was referring to me.

"Hi." I waved weakly.

The witch flung her arms around me, knocking her own hat off in her enthusiasm. She whispered into my ear, "I'm Julie Eastey. Just play along and I'll get you out of here."

Eastey was a name to conjure with in this part of Massachusetts, just like Bishop and Proctor. Four victims of the Salem panic had been members of this old Essex County family. If Julie was indeed my cousin, then the list of my relatives caught up in the dark events of the hanging times would expand exponentially.

"Fancy meeting you here." Julie pulled me away so she could get a better look at me. She beamed with pride, but a warning sparked in her pale aquamarine eyes. "Aunt Gwynie is waiting for you out on the neck. She sent me to town so you wouldn't get lost."

"Gwyneth didn't mention she was expecting guests at the last meeting." There was a thoughtful note in Goody Wu's voice.

I was sure Goody Wu didn't mean the PTA or the local garden club.

"It's summer, Katrina. You know how it is," Julie said with a dismissive flap of her hand. "Ipswich is crawling with tourists. Not today, though! It must be pagan discount day. I see you've met Meg and Ann."

Two fresh sets of witchy eyes pinned their attention on my back. I turned to see that the exit was blocked by a woman in her forties wearing a navy suit and a crisp white blouse. She was carrying the same distinctive Coach messenger bag with the flap and the brass closure that my mom had taken to Harvard every day, and in the same tan leather, too. At her side was an elderly dumpling of a witch with tight white curls that were tinged pink to match her cardigan.

"Oh, look, Hitty Braybrooke and Betty Prince have arrived," Julie said cheerfully, though her eyes narrowed a fraction. "Busy day here at The Thirsty Goat."

"You called?" Hitty asked Ann.

Someone had hit an invisible alarm button to notify the community that there was a strange witch in town.

Betty stared at me with open curiosity. "Is that—a *Bishop*?"

"My cousin, Diana Bishop, yes." Julie gathered me into her arm. The firm squeeze she gave me was tight enough to make me wince. "She's here to visit with Gwynie."

"That's a disturbing procedural irregularity," Hitty observed. "Gwyneth should have notified us so that we could take proper precautions. I'll be taking this up at our next meeting." Though she wore no identifying pin like Meg and Julie, I suspected Hitty was the coven parliamentarian, the unlucky witch who had to master the rules and regulations.

"Precautions?" Julie snorted. "Goddess above, it's not 1692, Hitty. Give Diana a break."

The town's bells sounded one o'clock.

"Is that the time?" Julie exclaimed. "We need to get to Ravenswood. Gwynie takes a nap at three, and she'll want to catch up with you first."

I turned toward the door.

"Don't forget your tea." Meg held out a paper cup with the distinctive goat logo.

I hesitated, tempted to walk away without it. Meg smiled, slow and satisfied as a cat.

"Thanks." I marched over, plucked the tea from her grip, and headed straight for the door. "Ready when you are, Julie."

"Ready as I'll ever be!" Julie said. "Gwynie's been dying to have a good gossip."

Ann blinked at this announcement.

"I predict it's going to be an interesting summer," Goody Wu said, addressing the café's customers, all of whom—human and witch—were watching our drama unfold.

"And you're never wrong!" Julie said over her shoulder as she took me by the elbow and rushed me past Hitty and Betty. "Katrina is our chair of divination and prophecy, Diana. She always knows what the future will bring."

"I'm sure we'll meet again." Goody Wu's eyes fogged with possibilities. "Goodbye for now, Diana Bishop."

We reached the sidewalk and I took in a lungful of magic-free air. The power in the café had been stifling and the clean, salty tang was welcome.

"Keep moving." Julie's pleasant demeanor changed as soon as she was out of the café. "We need to escape before Meg starts working the coven phone tree, otherwise someone will flag us down at every intersection. Which is your car?"

I pointed to the large black Range Rover.

"Of course it is." Julie shook her head. "Vampires. Conspicuously consumptive with no regard for the environment."

I opened my mouth to defend Matthew's choice of vehicle.

"Follow me. I'm in the blue truck." Julie pointed across the street to where a pastel blue vintage Ford was parked at a sharp angle in a spot designed for motorcycles.

Julie waited until I closed the car door before she dodged through the thickening traffic. Once in her truck, Julie performed an astonishingly speedy U-turn without crashing into oncoming traffic and pulled alongside.

"Stay close," Julie said through the open window. "We don't want to get separated."

I'd fallen out of a fantasy novel and into a spy thriller, complete with a car chase. Julie's U-turn had been a sample of her driving style, which was erratic and confident in equal measure. After a near miss with a cyclist, and a brief conversation with a uniformed officer of the Ipswich police department, Julie slowed down and remained in her own lane.

This gave me a chance to observe the changes as we left Ipswich's dense center and turned onto East Street toward the old harbor. This had once been a bustling economic hub for the area. Now it was the site of a quiet marina for leisure craft. Crouched seventeenth-century houses popped up regularly among the statelier eighteenth-century buildings. Ipswich was clearly proud of its history, and white wooden plaques with black lettering identified each house, the person who first lived in it, and the date it had been built. I followed the signs back in time. 1671. 1701. 1687. How had these houses survived the pressure of development?

Julie's truck bounced along as the road swept to the northeast. We had arrived on a long spit of land that stretched out toward the water. I felt another prickle from the past, heard a window open and my mother laugh as she drank in the sea air. There was a song playing on the radio, and Mom was teaching me the words.

I nearly went off the road at the sudden flash of memory. And yet I had been sure I'd never been anywhere in Ipswich except for the Clam Box.

Julie's hand waved out the window to alert me that we were close to our destination. I spotted a battered sign for Ravenswood and slowed the car. We peeled off the paved two-lane highway and onto a worn carriage road. Someone had dumped gravel on it to fill the deep ruts left after winter's hard freezes and a wet spring. The ancient, overhanging trees created a luminous green tunnel that cast everything in an otherworldly glow.

I lowered the window, drinking in the scent of grass and marsh and muck, the earthy aroma sharpened with a faint tang of salt. There was no loud music playing from nearby houses as there was in New Haven, or the banging of doors and shouts of students. There was only the hum of insects and the raucous caws of the birds as they flew over us.

A man walked in the ditch at the side of the road. He was dressed in short, baggy trousers tied below the knee and held a pair of sturdy shoes in his hand. His long white shirt, the sleeves rolled up, grazed the top of his thighs. It was made of a coarse cloth, as were his breeches. A worn hat with a floppy brim and a wilted turkey feather stuck in the band shielded his face so that I could not make out his features. Still, he seemed familiar.

The walker from the card.

I had already passed by him, and I peered into the rearview mirror to take another look.

He was gone.

I slowed down, searching the trees to track him, but there was nothing to see but rough trunks and thick underbrush. Julie honked her horn impatiently and I pressed my foot on the gas pedal.

After sailing slowly over the dips and swells like overloaded galleons, we reached the first fork in the road. A sign pointing to the right read ORCHARD FARM. The only features of the house that were visible were the two chimneys that anchored its sloping roof.

Julie drove past the turnoff for the farm and proceeded up a barely visible dirt track. Another crude sign nailed to a post indicated we had arrived at the Old Place.

I tried to spot a house through the thick hedges speckled with white polka dots, but an aged chestnut tree blocked my view. It stood like a sentinel, ramrod straight on the rise, with limbs spread wide and distinctive ovate leaves. Its rough, gray bark looked like feathers, the ends tipped up and away from the trunk in delicate furls. Golden catkins dropped from the branches, their heavy scent filling the car.

But the fuzzy panicles were not the only ornaments on this tree. The chestnut was festooned with objects and pieces of paper, too. They were tied to the trunk with faded ribbons and frayed string and drooped from the branches on wire coat hangers and bits of old rope. Doll legs and heads swayed eerily in the breeze. A worn shoe beat against the trunk, a muffled toll to announce someone had arrived.

A witch's tree. My mother had written an article about such trees, once upon a time. People left messages and offerings on the branches hoping that the witch who lived nearby would pass them on to ancestors and other intercessors.

Even through the car's robust frame, I could feel a magic shimmering around the bedecked tree that was both protective and inviting. Visitors were welcome to leave their tokens and prayers here, but the tree would keep anyone from venturing farther—unless they were welcome at Ravenswood.

Ahead, Julie had stopped her truck. She honked again to capture my attention and waved her hat out of the window to make sure that I knew our goal was still unrealized. Out popped her blond head.

"You can visit the tree later!" Julie called. "Get a move on!"

As my heavy vehicle crested the rise, a primrose-colored clapboard house appeared below, hunkered on the edge of the salt marsh with a wide horizon of blue sea beyond it. It looked like it had been built in the late seventeenth century, with its simple saltbox shape and single central chimney. And unlike houses of the same period I'd passed in Ipswich, there was no busy road inches away from the front door or a gas station perched nearby. This house was a rare survivor, perfectly preserved in its original setting of deeply forested woodland and waterside meadows.

I took a closer look at the house after I switched off the ignition and set the parking brake. The clapboards were narrow, confirming its age, and layers of paint and lashings of wind and rain had made them bow and bubble, giving the house the wrinkled appearance of an old dowager. From the side, the Old Place seemed to have three floors. A single attic window was set in the peak of the gable, while two windows set at slightly different heights marked the second floor as though the house were squinting. The ground floor had two more windows and a door with an overhang to protect anyone entering or leaving from being drowned in a sheet of falling rain or impaled by an icicle.

Julie parked her car where the sharply sloped roof nearly met the ground, leaving only a scant three feet of wall between the tufts of green grass and the eaves. While this might have been the place where the road from town ended, it was decidedly not the front of the house, with its odd angles and tiny door. The two windows tucked under the low eaves were wider than they were tall, and reminded me of the narrowed looks I'd received from the witches at the café. The old house was peering out at me from under its lowered brow—and with just as much suspicion as Meg and Ann had showed, too.

Home, the susurration of chestnut leaves said.

Home, the bees buzzed.

Home, a raven called from its perch on the ridge of the roof.

Home, my heart echoed.

I belonged to this place where I'd never been, and a sense of rightness settled over me as Ravenswood exerted its pull, like the moon on the tides. I savored the feeling, drinking in a little more of its magic with each passing breath.

A slender, elderly woman with neatly bobbed gray hair held back with a velvet headband stepped out from the side door, her blue-and-white-striped shirt and trim gray cotton trousers straight out of a Talbots catalogue. An old pair of slip-on SeaVees, stained with salt, were on her feet.

She bore a subtle but unmistakable resemblance to my father, especially around the eyes and in the widow's peak that framed her forehead.

I released my seat belt and opened the door, sending one tentative foot toward the ground.

"Come down from there, Diana." Gwyneth took a few steps then stopped, her tone vinegar. "I'm eighty-seven, and too old to be scampering up hills."

I hopped down from my seat. When my feet touched the ground, the soles sent roots deep into the soil. I swayed in place, startled by the change to my center of gravity.

"Steady on." Julie put a supportive hand under my elbow. "You'll be fine. You just need to get your witchlegs under you. Who wants tea?"

I'd been so absorbed following Julie and looking at the local landmarks that I hadn't taken a single sip from The Thirsty Goat's cup. My stomach let out a gurgle.

"The kettle is on the hearth." Gwyneth shielded her eyes from the sun. "Come closer, my dear. I don't bite."

Silvered laughter sounded at Gwyneth's joke.

Canst thou remember a time before? My mother whispered the line from Shakespeare's *Tempest.*

"Mom?"

I had seen the ghostly form of my father, and my grandmother Joanna Bishop. I'd even caught glimpses of Bridget Bishop, my ancestor who had been hanged at Salem. But the one time I'd seen my mother was after the witch Satu Järvinen had dropped me into an oubliette. I had never been sure it was her ghost who visited me, or just a trick of my panicked mind that made me think Mom was there.

I looked for her in the trees, the meadow, and the marsh. At last I spotted her at the edge of the thick wood. Like the man on the carriage road, her outlines were clear, as was her familiar red Plimoth Plantation T-shirt, banded at the neck and sleeves in navy, with the passenger list of the Mayflower printed on the front. This was no ethereal ghost. Here was my mother, right down to her old boat shoes.

"Mom!" My feet sped down the hill, and another sharp memory surfaced, cutting through my heart. I'd run down this hill before, hand in hand with my mother. We were laughing as we ran toward—

I crashed into Gwyneth, who despite her frailty was able to catch me before I could reach the thicket of trees. She held me tight as my mother vanished into the shadows. Like the witches in town, my aunt's power was substantial and carefully managed, but it was not hidden. Nor was it dressed up in love spells and embroidered into lavender-filled pillows to help you sleep. Darkness frilled the edges of it.

"Not yet, Diana." Gwyneth's eyes were a shade greener than Julie's brilliant aquamarine, but had the same translucent paleness. "That's the Ravens' Wood, and the source of a Proctor's power. You need to get accustomed to the place—and it to you—before you barge around in the trees."

"My mother—" I struggled to break free, but my great-aunt's grip was surprisingly strong.

"Has been waiting here for you for some time, just as I have," Gwyneth replied, her voice low and compelling. "She's not going anywhere. But you're not ready to meet with her just now. Be patient."

I took a deep breath, inhaling Gwyneth's scent of cinnamon and buckthorn and crushed stone. It blended into the salt tang of the marsh air and conjured images of crackling fires and rocky, windswept beaches. The scent was both grounding and comforting.

"That's better," Gwyneth said, releasing me. "As for your witchlegs, you'll have to forgive Ravenswood for greeting you so enthusiastically. Like your mother and me, it's been expecting you."

"Are you two coming?" Julie had reached the low door into the Old Place and was squinting back at us.

"Wait," I said, planting my feet. There was a question that my aunt needed to answer before I went any farther. "Why didn't you reach out to me before? Why now?"

"The oracles told me it was time to make contact,"

Gwyneth replied. "It's a good thing they did, too, for the ravens took flight two days later. I hoped the U.S. mail would deliver my message before a flock of birds arrived."

"It did," I said. "But I didn't open your message until afterward."

"That's a pity," Gwyneth said sadly. "Was your daughter with you when they appeared, like my sister Morgana foresaw?"

MFP stood for Morgana Proctor—another unknown great-aunt.

"She was." My words were abrupt. I wasn't ready to talk about Becca and Pip and what my trip to Ravenswood might mean for them. And with every passing moment, I was more convinced that my current situation had as much to do with my father's past as it did my present, or the children's future.

Gwyneth took note of my tone, and her response was equally brisk and to the point. "There are things you need to know, Diana. About the Proctors. About yourself."

A sense of anticipation hung in the air of Ravenswood.

"Come inside. Have some tea. We'll take this one step at a time." Gwyneth's eyes were warm and filled with compassion. "After forty years of silence, our Proctor noise must be deafening."

I took a step, then another, down the dark path unspooling before me.

Chapter 4

The spring mechanism on the Old Place's ancient screen door screeched shut behind me. Coming from the strong sunlight into the cool interior blinded me temporarily, although neither Julie nor Gwyneth seemed affected by it. They both moved surely and swiftly, and I heard the clatter of crockery and the ring of silverware.

Once my eyes adjusted to the dimness, I saw that we were in a long, narrow room. There was a door at the far end, with another wooden-framed screen that created a cross draft and let in the scent of the wisteria that clambered outside. The uneven floor underneath my feet had been made from huge slabs of granite. Some effort had been made to keep the floor level, but time and damp had rearranged the stones. A few cupboards were nailed to the wall, and a run of open shelving surrounded the room on three sides. The hum of an old icebox (it was too aged to qualify as a refrigerator) and a scarred butcher block suggested this minuscule area of the larger room served as Gwyneth's kitchen. But where did my aunt cook?

That mystery was solved by the vast fireplace where the granite gave way to eighteen-inch-wide planks of pumpkin pine. Gwyneth was living in the house as her ancestors had, cooking over an open fire. The wooden flooring was nearly as dipped and bowed as the stone floor in the kitchen, and the wear of hundreds of feet and furniture legs had carved small hollows in the stout boards.

Julie looked up from her phone, which was resting on a stack of plates.

Her fingers had been racing over the screen since we entered the cooler confines of the house.

"Junior's standing by. Grace and Tracy are out of range," Julie reported. "They must be on the boat. DeMarco heard the news. They're already saying a Bishop's come back to town down at The Seagull." She sounded frazzled.

"Ipswich doesn't approve of secrets any more than Ravenswood," Gwyneth said calmly. "Every witch in Beverly, Danvers, Salem, and Topsfield will know the news of Diana's arrival by tomorrow morning. There's nothing for it, Julie."

"I knew we should have posted a lookout at the Route 1 turnoff," Julie grumbled.

"You were overruled. Let it go." Gwyneth pointed down the room with the knives she clutched in one hand. "After you."

I passed by the wide fireplace with its cooking cranes and iron cauldrons and the oven built into the back wall for baking bread. The heady aroma of yeast and flour filled the air, and a seaweedy steam escaped from the covered pot that made my mouth water.

Two more doors opened at the far end of the room. One led to the extension I'd seen jutting off the house and the other offered a glimpse into a sparely furnished parlor with nineteenth-century portraits of a dour man and woman dressed entirely in black and a few brightly colored pieces of pottery that stood out against the creamy milk paint that covered the walls.

Someone had scratched symbols into the doorframe—hexafoils and daisies and crude crosses, some of them overlapping in complicated patterns. Though the marks had been painted over again and again, the gouges in the wood were still visible.

"Apotropaic marks," I said. They were common in old houses and put on the sides of Amish barns to ward off evil.

"Keen eyes." Aunt Gwyneth nodded approvingly.

I ran my fingers over the scarred wood. Symbols and sigils sprang to life under my touch, each one illuminated for a moment as the faded hexes uttered when they were carved flared into life. I traced one intricate hexafoil with my finger and it emitted dark sparks, crackling with power as though the spell had been cast yesterday. Neither Aunt Gwyneth nor Julie blinked at this manifestation of magic that would have sent Aunt Sarah scuttling for the Bishop grimoire and the restorative powers she found in a bottle of Gentleman Jack.

"These wards aren't like any others I've seen." My fingers drew away from the scarred surface, and the old magic quieted.

"Most witches' marks are inscribed by humans to keep magic out," Aunt Gwyneth said. "These were made by Proctor witches to keep the magic in."

"If I don't get some tea and a blueberry muffin in the next two minutes, I won't be held accountable for the consequences." Julie wedged her body between us and wiggled into the room.

"Julie's known for her impatience," Gwyneth said dryly. "It's a Proctor family trait."

I wasn't sure the dad I'd known had inherited it, but I had more than a touch of it myself, and hunger only sharpened it. I followed Julie into the room, observed all the while by the couple on the wall.

"Your grandparents, from six generations ago," Gwyneth said, following my glance.

The historian in me wanted to know their names, when they were born, who their children were, and how they had died. Julie sensed in which direction the conversation might turn and put an immediate halt to it.

"If we start going over the family tree, Aunt Gwynie, it will be Yule before I get my muffin." Julie was bent over a round, brown teapot set on a spider over the coals of the hearth. She lifted the lid and gave the contents a stir. The malted scent of tea filled the room. Julie took a mug down from one of the hooks pounded into the mantel. "Here, Diana. I hope you like it strong."

"It's from Ceylon, and very good," Aunt Gwyneth said. "I get it from a witch in Chicago who makes custom blends."

Lured away from the portraits by the prospect of caffeine, I took the mug from Julie.

"How do you like your tea?" Gwyneth inquired.

"Like we do, I expect." Julie handed over a mug. "Strong, milk, no sugar."

That was indeed my preferred recipe.

"Milk jug's on the table," Julie said, pouring herself a cup of the bracing brew. She plopped down in one of the straight-backed chairs gathered around a venerable oak table. Without ceremony, she grabbed a blueberry muffin and put half of it in her mouth. Julie let out a moan of satisfaction. "Ewe still may da best mfns, Gny," she said in between chews.

My stomach gurgled again. I'd eaten a bagel somewhere between Hartford and Worcester but was already famished. Not only were there muffins on the table, Gwyneth had made sandwiches, too, delicate little triangles of white bread filled with eggs, mayonnaise, and herbs.

"Sit down, Diana. Help yourself." Gwyneth took up occupancy in the grandest, and most uncomfortable-looking, chair.

I sat and forced myself to count to five before I dove into the platter of sandwiches. I was chewing on one and pouring milk into my tea when Gwyneth slid a knife toward me. Confused, I wondered if it was a Proctor custom to stir their tea with knives rather than spoons.

"For the muffins." Gwyneth gestured toward my mug. The tea inside was whirling and swirling without any implement or aid. "We use tea-stirring spells in this house. It saves on the washing up."

While Julie and I devoured the food, Gwyneth studied me over the edge of her mug. It was white with a blue lion on it and emblazoned with *Class of '52*. Julie's mug was decorated with a red winged horse and *Class of '78*. I looked down at my own mug. It bore a seal in sky blue, along with *Mount Holyoke College* in Gothic script.

"Are you an alum?"

"Of course. So is Julie. Most of the Proctor women went to Miss Lyon's seminary—or Mount Holyoke if you prefer," Aunt Gwyneth replied. "They say Mary Lyon got her idea for a women's college when she was here, serving as the assistant principal of the Ipswich Female Seminary."

"The family was terribly disappointed when Stephen took that job at Wellesley," Julie said sadly.

"What was your major?" I asked my great-aunt.

"Geology," Gwyneth replied. "Tally and Morgana loved to collect shells on the beach, but it was always the rocks that captured my attention."

"Tally," I said, tasting his name on my tongue. It was exotic and familiar at the same time.

"Your grandfather and my older brother: Taliesin Proctor. Mother was going through a Druid phase." Aunt Gwyneth sighed. "Wore robes, played a harp, the whole nine yards. She believed she was a reincarnated Celtic priestess. We all got names from the Arthurian legends. I got two—Gwyneth and Elaine."

My respect for Gwyneth rose. Female scientists were few and far between, even now. I knew she was a professor, but if my aunt was a PhD student in the sciences in the 1950s, she was filled with grit and determination.

"Did you go on to get a doctorate in the subject?" I wondered.

"Yes, from Johns Hopkins," Gwyneth said. "They were one of the first programs to admit women for advanced study. After I received my degree, I returned to Mount Holyoke to train the next generation. I spent my whole career there. By the time I retired, my students claimed I'd spent as much time at the college as the dinosaurs in Clapp Hall."

Julie snorted into her tea. "Maybe more."

"You must miss it," I said, comparing the constant energy of a liberal arts campus with life on the quiet banks of the Ipswich River.

"At times. Especially in October, when the skies are Mary Lyon blue, and the leaves are at their most spectacular. I still get a call from the department secretary to tell me it's Mountain Day," Gwyneth admitted, her voice wistful. "Once upon a time, I used to lead the students on hikes up Mount Tom and Mount Holyoke."

A wave of grief at all that I'd missed by not knowing Gwyneth— including not having another academic role model in the family to rely on for advice and perspective—threatened to pull me under.

"Why didn't you contact me sooner, Gwyneth?" I cried. "Didn't you want me—before?"

"We all wanted you," Gwyneth said sharply. "But Stephen was determined that you not know us, and your grandparents died before you were born. Sarah had sole custody of you after he and Rebecca were murdered. As far as she was concerned, you were a Bishop—first, last, always. The lawyers told us we had few legal rights to challenge that, even though you were our flesh and blood, too."

"If Dad didn't want me to know you, then why is my mother here?" My questions were tripping over Gwyneth's answers, eager to be heard.

"Rebecca felt at home at Ravenswood," Gwyneth explained. "She always wanted to return, but Stephen wouldn't allow it. Your mother was creative, though—and persistent."

"So I have been here before," I said, remembering the feeling of running down the warm grass toward the house. "Not with Dad—but with Mom."

"Only once." Gwyneth's regret was etched into her face in painful lines. "We hoped that it would be enough to make an impression, but when we didn't hear from you—"

"I was seven years old!" Now that I'd vented some of my questions, my anger erupted. "What did you expect me to do? Hijack a Greyhound bus and follow my nose?"

"Exactly what you did do: live your life, grow into a woman, and make your own decisions," Gwyneth replied. "Time was on our side. Stephen and Sarah knew that they were fighting a losing battle. So did Rebecca. She understood that higher magic could only be denied and suppressed for so long. Shadow always finds us, in the end."

"You make it sound as though my parents were at war over magic." My stomach tightened at the implications.

"Not at war, but in an uneasy state of détente," Aunt Gwyneth said. "Stephen refused to let your mother practice the higher, darker branch of the craft, or to teach you its basic principles. It was a condition of their marriage."

My father's love for my mother couldn't have been conditional. It wasn't possible. What Gwyneth was saying went against everything I believed about my parents.

"Their relationship was built on a foundation of rules established by Stephen," Gwyneth continued, her voice disapproving. She ticked them off, one by one. "No higher magic, only the simplest workings of the craft. No contact with the Proctors. No further involvement with the Congregation. No local coven membership. No further intimacy unless Rebecca promised she would spellbind any child who showed an inclination to follow the Dark Path. It was quite a prenup."

I'd made a similar promise to Matthew's brother Baldwin—only my oath involved spellbinding any of our children with blood rage, not higher magic.

"Dad would never do such a thing." I was numb in the face of these latest revelations.

But something Sarah once told me made me pause and reconsider: *Rebecca seemed to lose interest in higher magic once she met your father.* Maybe Mom hadn't lost interest, but had been forced to give up these aspects of the craft?

"Your father didn't believe in negotiation. It was his way or the highway," Gwyneth said. "Rebecca loved Stephen so much she agreed to his demands. She would have been a formidable witch—a legendary one, perhaps—if only he'd let her hone her talents. Rebecca was relying on time and love to soften his stance. The clock ran out. Her love for him never did."

The silence in the house was absolute. Not a floorboard creaked. The logs in the fireplace stopped crackling. There was not even the soft tick of a clock to break the stillness.

"You still haven't answered my question," I said. "Why did you decide to go against Dad's wishes now, Gwyneth?"

"Because when you turned seven and the Congregation sent someone to examine you, two people I loved died." Gwyneth's tone was flat and tinged with weariness. "The oracles told me that your children were about to reach that milestone in a witch's life. I won't sit back and let tragedy befall the Proctors again. Not while there is breath and blood in my body."

"How long have these childhood examinations been going on?" I had always thought that Peter Knox's arrival at our house had been primarily because of his obsession with my mother, and by extension me—not because of an established schedule of magical assessments.

"The standardized Congregation tests are relatively new," Gwyneth replied. "Before the 1880s or so, it was left to families and local covens to send word if a young person showed a talent for higher magic. The old tests were straightforward, and required only filling out a form that the Congregation sent to witches who had been earmarked as having noticeable magical potential."

I'd never understood what, precisely, Knox had been looking for when he probed my mind on that long ago Cambridge afternoon. Matthew and I thought it might have been my ability to weave new spells. Might he have been searching for evidence of a propensity for higher magic instead?

"The world wars made it difficult for the Congregation to enforce any kind of global initiative, however," Gwyneth continued. "It wasn't until the 1960s that the tests started up again, with a new format and in-person examinations by a Congregation member or their representative."

A shadow crossed Gwyneth's face. It was fleeting, but a sense of darkness remained. There was more to the story than she was telling me.

"I suspect you're unfinished business, as far as the Congregation is concerned," Gwyneth said.

"The Congregation knows I'm different, if that's what you mean," I replied. "They know I'm a maker of new spells, like Dad—a weaver. Surely one of the witches would have noticed if I had other talents as well."

"A weaver, eh?" Julie's blue eyes sparkled. "We call them knotters around here, but I suppose it's the same thing."

"Maybe one of the Congregation representatives did notice." Gwyneth blinked at me like an owl.

Peter Knox. I closed my eyes at the sudden vision of him, fatally caught in my snare of magic. I had taken his life to save Matthew.

"Peter Knox was the witch the Congregation sent to examine me," I said. "He knew that my parents were hiding something. I always thought it was the fact that I was a weaver, but maybe Knox's interest was also connected to Mom's study of higher magic."

"Perhaps," Gwyneth said. "But Knox would have recognized that you'd inherited your mother's talent for higher magic, too."

"But it wasn't just the prospect of the Congregation examining your children that led me to write to you," Gwyneth confessed. "The oracles told me that you had also reached a point in your life's journey where difficult choices must be made."

She conjured up a bright green ribbon.

"Your father's Proctor heritage and your ability to make new spells."

Another ribbon, this one blue, blossomed out of the air.

"The Bishops, and their talent for higher magic." Gwyneth pulled out yet another magic ribbon, this one black as night. "Your marriage to Matthew de Clermont, and the children born to your union. These are the three paths that led you here, to Ravenswood," Gwyneth said, her voice ringing with power and prophecy.

The ribbons fluttered in the breeze from the open window. The currents of air carried a raven-black feather into the house. The feather sailed through the ends of the ribbons, the sharp point on the feather's hollow shaft piercing the soft fabric. Its weight dragged the ribbons down to the table, pinning them so that they were spread out in three directions with the feather at the center of a brilliant crossroads.

A crossroads usually had four paths, however, not three. One of the paths was missing.

"If Ravenswood is here," I said, lightly touching the feather with the tip of my finger, "and these are the three paths that have brought me here, where do I go next?"

"You must choose your own path forward," Gwyneth replied. "Not the road that Sarah chose for you, or Stephen, or even the one you embarked upon with your husband. This is a path you must walk alone."

I didn't like the sound of that, and Matthew wouldn't like it, either. I had come to Ravenswood to find out how to protect my children from the Congregation, not to go on a magical adventure. I drew the old card that Gwyneth sent me from the side pocket of my cargo pants and laid it on the table where the missing ribbon should have been.

"I saw this man, walking along the carriage road."

"I doubt it was this man," Gwyneth said.

"Wait." Julie stared at the card, her face drained of color. "That looks like descriptions of John Proctor. Diana saw John Proctor, Gwyneth. Out on the carriage road. In the middle of the day."

"*The* John Proctor?" If asked to name one of the poor souls executed at Salem in 1692, most Americans would rely on their high school reading of *The Crucible* and dredge up his memory. I knew my father was descended from him, but I had not been able to figure out how.

"Our many-times great-grandfather," Julie said. "Why didn't I see him? I look for him every Halloween when the veil between the worlds is thin. He never appears!"

"If it was our ancestor, I don't suppose John was here for a family visit," Gwyneth said, "or to answer your questions about his sundial spell."

"If only I could figure out the last part of it, I know it would work," Julie said, frustrated.

Gwyneth took a considered pause. "My oracle cards are in the cupboard. Could you fetch them for me, Julie?"

Something told me that Gwyneth's oracle deck was not available next to the register at Be Blessed, Sarah's shop in Madison, where impulse items tempted visitors as they checked out with their herbs, tisanes, and organic vegetables.

Julie scrambled to her feet. She returned with a black velvet pouch. I eyed it with curiosity.

The bag was threadbare in places, and someone had embroidered a hexafoil on it using tiny beads. Gwyneth drew a pack of cards from the enclosure. The cards inside were old—but not as ancient as the one she'd sent me through the mail.

"These belonged to my granny Elizabeth Proctor," Gwyneth explained, shuffling them between her fingers.

"She was a teacher, like Gwynie," Julie said. "Granny Elizabeth was the head of magical education here in Ipswich."

"Hush, Julie." Gwyneth's eyes were foggy, like Goody Wu's had been at The Thirsty Goat. "I can't formulate a decent question with you yapping."

Julie made the gesture of locking her lips and throwing the key over her shoulder.

We waited in silence while Gwyneth considered her possible queries, all the while shuffling the cards.

The cards became uncooperative and flew from Gwyneth's hands into the air. I gasped, prepared for them to rain down on all our heads. After a few seconds of suspension, however, they fluttered down onto the table where nine of the cards arranged themselves into a pattern, face up. The rest of the cards were clumped to the side, face down.

Most witches laid out their cards one at a time. But Gwyneth's cards sorted themselves out.

The Proctors had enchanted oracle cards.

"Ooh," Julie said, peering at the cards. "The Two Paths spread. If you read the cards clockwise, the oracles will help you determine a logical course of action. If you proceed widdershins, their guidance will reveal a more intuitive path."

I was for logic at this point.

"Gwynie always uses the widdershins technique," Julie continued, dashing my hopes. "She believes the answers are more reliable."

We fell silent once more so that Gwyneth could get on with the difficult work of interpreting the cards' message.

"You're being pulled backward in every direction and struggling to move forward at the same time, Diana." Gwyneth sat back against the carved chair. "At the moment, it's still possible for you to return to your old life and the bright, familiar roads that have brought you this far."

Vivid visions of New Haven and the Old Lodge, of a summer spent in the Bodleian and visiting family, shot through my mind like blazing stars. But Gwyneth was right; I was always caught between what would be best for the children, Matthew's interests, and my own desires.

"Or?" I asked quietly.

"You can take another step, and then another, until the direction of your own path becomes clear," Gwyneth replied. "*Your* path, Diana—one not mapped out for you by someone else."

Something undeniably powerful had called me to Ravenswood, opening up new worlds that had been hidden for far too long.

"Stay for dinner." Gwyneth's face looked drawn. She was exhausted by the excitement of the afternoon. "I've readied a room for you at the farm, in case you'd rather sleep at Ravenswood tonight than the Squid and Anchor."

How did Gwyneth know that Matthew had made a reservation for me there? It had been the only bed-and-breakfast with a last-minute weekend vacancy.

"A lot of bad blood between the Proctors and the Perleys," Julie muttered. "I wouldn't sleep there, if I were you."

After the reception I'd received at The Thirsty Goat, I'd been inclined to cancel the booking and stay in Boston—and that was before I knew of the family feud between the Proctors and the Perleys. I hesitated, then nodded.

"Thank you, Gwyneth." Agreeing to remain at Ravenswood, even for one night, felt like a monumental commitment.

"It's just one step, one meal, one night," Gwyneth said, drawing her hand across her forehead.

"I'll get Diana settled," Julie told my aunt, grabbing two muffins for the road. "You need to rest, Gwynie."

Aunt Gwyneth acquiesced, an indication of her fatigue, for I was sure that my aunt wasn't the type who liked being coddled and fussed over. She disappeared into another room, leaving her cards scattered on the table. With a cluck of disapproval, Julie gathered them and returned them to their bag.

"If you leave them out, oracle cards can get into all kinds of mischief," she explained. "Let's get you settled at the farm. You probably need a rest, too."

Julie guided me out the back door—which was really the front door, a rather grand affair with sidelights and carved molding—and past a small vegetable patch enclosed within four black iron posts and some chicken wire. It was immaculately kept, with straight rows of seedlings all neatly marked so you could tell the carrot sprouts from the radish, and not a weed in sight. The same orderliness was evident in the perennial borders, which were filled with irises and delphiniums at this time of year. The peonies were still in tight balls but would blossom in the coming weeks.

"My uncle Tally—your grandfather—loved the early summer here on the marsh," Julie said. "He said it was like watching the flesh grow on Ravenswood's bones, when the trees leafed out and the vegetables sprouted."

"Did my dad grow up here?" I asked.

"At Ravenswood? Yes. Not in the Old Place, though. We all grew up in the big house." Julie looked fondly at the spacious white farmhouse peeking out from the small apple orchard just past the garden, the curtains billowing out from the open upper windows.

"Orchard Farm has better plumbing. You need that with teenagers," Julie continued. "The Old Place was the original house on this parcel of land, and it depends on magic to keep it going rather than electricity and sewers."

A large barn was tucked into a rambunctious hedge between the two houses. Its sliding wooden doors were tightly shut, and the whole structure was clad in magic, from alarm spells to wizard bolts. Like the witches' marks in the house, the magic was surprisingly robust and intricate. I frowned at the sheer number of preventive spells.

"Is it safe for Aunt Gwyneth to be here alone?" I asked Julie.

"Oh, those wards are just to keep the local teenagers out," Julie explained. "Witch, daemon, or human, kids turn sixteen and they dare one another to try to get inside the Proctor barn. It's an Ipswich rite of passage."

"What do they think they'll find in there?" I wondered. *The Ark of the Covenant? The Holy Grail?*

"Wonderful things," Julie replied, a twinkle in her eye, *as though she had heard my thoughts.*

My cousin opened a screen door into the passageway between the farmhouse proper and its attached carriage house. Gardening trugs and tools, galoshes and hip waders, folded brown paper bags for the grocery store and kindling for the stove, indicated that this was the main artery of the house.

Julie led me to a room painted a vivid turquoise. The color clashed with the softer blues of the massive Blue Willow teapot resting on the shelves of an old Welsh dresser. Tins and bags of tea were tucked in among the plates and cups. The mystery of my beverage of choice was solved; tea was a Proctor preference. The Bishops all loved coffee.

The kitchen was anchored by a round table that had been scoured clean so many times its wooden edges were now soft. A ring of mismatched chairs of varying heights and styles surrounded the table, including a black Windsor chair embellished with a college seal—Mount Holyoke, of course. A large farmhouse sink, a small stove, another vintage mint-green icebox, and an old jelly cupboard with pierced tin panels in the doors completed the room's furnishings.

I examined the items on the dresser shelves more closely. Family photos were tucked amongst the tea and crockery. As an only child who had grown up with a meager handful of images of my parents (some of them violent and horrifying), these were unexpected treasures. My father's face—younger than I had ever known him, dusted with freckles, his eyes squinting against the sun as he stared into the camera—smiled out from one of the frames. He was standing by a giant boulder, and his arm was slung around the shoulders of a laughing woman who looked just like—

"Wow. You look like Ruby," Julie said. "The boys all swarmed around her in high school, like bees to a flower. Your grandmother wasn't a witch, but she could certainly cast a spell with her hourglass figure."

I spotted another snapshot of Ruby on the shelves, this one a formal wedding portrait. The man standing next to her, in a white suit with a black tie, must be my grandfather—Tally Proctor. Ruby was wearing a slinky satin gown of the sort familiar to anyone who had seen pictures of the marriage of Wallis Simpson and the Duke of Windsor. A veiled, halo-shaped hat was tipped at a jaunty angle over her right eye.

"When was this taken?" I asked, pointing to the photo.

"In 1939. By all accounts, Tally and Ruby were Ipswich's golden couple, and quite dashing," Julie said. "They followed their own moral code, and to hell with convention."

"They look pretty traditional here," I said, noting the bouquet of white lilies Ruby carried and the row of bridesmaids in prim gowns holding sprawling baskets of blooms. It didn't look like a winter wedding, but it must have been. My dad had been born that October.

"Well, they weren't." Julie's voice dropped to a confidential whisper, as if someone might overhear. "Mama told me that all of Ipswich knew they were having sex months before the wedding. It was a huge scandal. They finally married in May. Your grandmother's bouquet had to be that large to hide her baby bump."

Taliesin Proctor and Ruby Addison. Though I'd never heard them before, the two names rang when I whispered them to myself, like the chime of crystal glasses in a wedding toast. Why hadn't I ever noticed their complete absence from my life?

"Poke around, find what you need. We put you in Tally and Ruby's bedroom. You'll know which one it is. Dinner is at five o'clock sharp," Julie said, glancing at her watch. "Don't be late, or the lobster will be tough as old boots."

The screen door swung open on its rusty hinges as Julie departed. There was a sharp thwack when it closed.

Alone in Orchard Farm, I sank into the Mount Holyoke chair and wondered where my next step would take me.

Chapter 5

It didn't take me long to figure out that it involved finding the toilet. I prowled around the ground floor looking for evidence of the prized Orchard Farm plumbing. I found not one toilet, but two, on opposite ends of the range of ground-floor rooms.

I also located a parlor with stiff, formal furniture and a single vinyl-covered recliner from circa 1965. A mason jar full of feathers sat on the table next to it, and a cheerful bouquet of freshly cut daisies stood in the fireplace. They lent a bright note to the otherwise brown room, and breathed life into the place.

Past the parlor was a room filled with a bulky oak desk, circa 1940. Its swiveling metal office chair, with a cushioned green vinyl seat and back, looked like it could withstand a direct bomb strike. Shelves ringed the room, which held a wide variety of books and magazines as well as a complete set of *Encyclopædia Britannica*. Once, the room had been the domain of Taliesin Proctor. I knew this before I saw the burnished metal plate that read TALIESIN PROCTOR, EDITOR, *THE IPSWICH CHRONI-CLE.*

More family photos were here, framed in gleaming silver and Popsicle sticks. One was a glamorous portrait of Ruby. Another showed my dad around the age of eight with a girl of the same age. Both wore rain slickers, boots, and wide grins. There were professional pictures, too, of Taliesin accepting a journalism award, and one of him at a desk in a newspaper office, puffing on a pipe while he studied a page from the latest edition. My grandfather may not have been an academic, like his sister Gwyneth, but he was a man of letters, nonetheless.

I found a snapshot of Tally and Gwyneth's sister, Morgana, taken in her twenties. She was dreamy-eyed and pensive, sitting on the porch of the Old Place with a starchy old woman in a Victorian dress that was decades out-of-date based on Morgana's cinched-in waist and fluffy, knee-length skirts. In the door to the Old Place, just visible in the background, was a slip of a girl who might have been teenage Gwyneth.

There were other rooms on the ground floor, but it was upstairs, where I found five bedrooms arranged around the landing, that the mystery surrounding my father and his family deepened. The largest had a freshly made bed, and fluffy towels waited in its adjoining bathroom. Two of the rooms were sterile and empty, guest rooms devoid of personal touches with sprigged wallpaper in spring hues. The beds were unmade, but towels and sheets waited in case any more unexpected visitors turned up.

The final rooms were a different story, however. They still bore the signs of their previous occupants, literally and figuratively. Wooden letters painted in red, yellow, and blue spelled out S-T-E-P-H-E-N on one door. I stood before it, the knob heavy in my hand. I was reluctant to twist it, for I didn't need the widdershins guidance of Gwyneth's oracles to tell me that what I discovered inside would forever change my sense of my father.

I turned the knob and pushed the door open, revealing a time capsule of his life before he left for college. The navy-and-red-plaid bedspread was smooth, which had never been Dad's strong suit. Usually, he popped out of bed and left everything rumpled and straggly. Apart from that, there was plenty of evidence that an active, curious boy had grown toward manhood here.

I picked up a Magic 8 Ball and shook it. When I turned the ball over to see the message in the window it read *Ask again later.*

I put the toy back, and noted the Slinky, the Etch A Sketch, and the pair of Mouseketeer ears embroidered with my father's name. These were iconic toys of Dad's youth. So, too, were the Hardy Boys mysteries piled up on the floor. Unlike Grandpa Tally, Dad preferred his books in an unsystematic heap rather than a curated collection. His study in Cambridge had always been a maze of stacked books and mounds of paper.

At some point, my father had been passionate about model airplanes. Several flew across the room, suspended on a pale blue fishing line. Becca and Pip loved working on models and puzzles, their vampire blood giving them unusually deft and agile hands.

I shut my eyes tight against the image of my dad—who would be in his late seventies were he still living—sitting on the floor with his grandchildren and gluing together a car, or building an elaborate structure out of Legos. The twins were missing out on so much by not knowing their grandfather.

I opened the drawers, which held a jumble of T-shirts, and the closet, where a few crisp oxford shirts remained. Jeans, like books, were piled on the floor underneath the hangers that Ruby had no doubt purchased in a futile attempt to encourage Dad to take better care of his clothes. My mother had done the same, but to no avail.

A bulletin board hung over a small desk. I switched on the metal desk lamp so that I could see what was posted there. Most of the space was covered with photos, and all of them showed my father, taken at different ages, with the same girl I'd seen in the picture downstairs. They looked as though they'd all been snapped in the same spot, with the same view of the harbor and the seas beyond, and the same lump of granite over Dad's shoulder. Carefully, I removed one of the photos and carried it to the window that overlooked the marsh, searching for the boulder.

It was easy to locate, given its size and position. I turned the photo over. On it was the date *November 1944.* My dad had been just five then, and World War II was still raging across Europe, Africa, and the Pacific.

I was always surprised by the realization that my father had lived through those horrifying years. He was older than Mom, but in my mind they were both the same age. Maybe my father had been more conservative at the start of their marriage than he had been later when he participated in political protests and volunteered his time with the homeless in Boston.

But simple conservatism couldn't explain the long list of conditions he'd put on my mother and their relationship. I returned to the desk and scanned the photos, following along as my father grew taller, then chunkier, then lean and strong. His hair changed, too: short at first in a military buzz cut, and increasingly shaggy as he entered his teen years.

One of the most recent pictures was in color. It showed Dad in a Harvard T-shirt. The girl in his arms was a woman now, no longer pigtailed but sporting bobbed hair, ankle-length cigarette pants, and dark red lipstick. The woman held a Mount Holyoke College mug emblazoned with a green griffin. My dad's usual wide grin distracted the viewer's attention from the worried furrow between his brows. His grip on his companion was tight, as though he wanted to shield her from danger.

The young woman's resemblance to Ruby Addison was undeniable.

She was not one of my dad's childhood friends but his sister. It was impossible to believe that Dad had a sister I knew nothing of, and yet . . .

I went to the adjacent bedroom, with its chalkboard reading *Naomi's Room NO BOYS!* Inside, the room was painted a deep lavender, and had the female equivalent of all of Dad's childhood bric-a-brac: a well-furnished dollhouse that resembled Orchard Farm; an old-fashioned pram for dolls; Nancy Drew and Cherry Ames, rather than the Hardy Boys. Naomi had been an athlete, and there were high school trophies for pole vaulting and hurdles on the bookshelves. She was a music fan, too. A guitar rested in the corner, and a faded advertisement for *The Biggest In Person Show of '56* at the Boston Garden hung on the wall. A faint whiff of patchouli and incense among the childhood items suggested that, unlike Dad, Naomi had spent time here well into the 1960s.

The top drawer of Naomi's white desk, ornamented with Flower Power stickers and peace signs, held another clutch of photographs. I riffled through them, my fingers moving as swiftly as Gwyneth's did when she worked with her oracle cards.

I found a picture of the same girl with the same fashionable hairstyle.

She was with my grandfather in a place I knew well: the cloisters at the heart of the Congregation complex on Isola della Stella. The pictures fell from my nerveless fingers to the floor. They all landed face down—except for the picture of my grandfather and Naomi in Venice.

I swayed on my feet, the shock overwhelming. Reaching out a steadying hand, I gripped the edge of the desk.

In my pocket, my phone buzzed and rang. I jumped at the sound, then went to the lavender-and-white-gingham–covered bed to answer the call.

It was Matthew. I'd texted him when I got gas before turning off for Ipswich, so he knew I had arrived. My silence since then must have been difficult.

"Hello." My voice shook, and I tried to steady it.

"What's wrong?" Matthew's question was as quick as the lash of a whip. "Are you at Ravenswood?"

"Yes." I cleared my throat. "I've met Gwyneth, and a cousin called Julie."

Matthew sighed with relief. "Thank God. I was worried you'd been in an accident."

That was my Matthew. Always prepared for the worst.

"I'm supposed to be the worrywart, not you." I sounded more like myself now that the initial surprise of the photograph taken in Venice had passed. "How are the kids?"

"They're roaring around in the backyard," Matthew said, an unmistakable note of fond pride in his tone. "Rebecca has expressed a desire for a tree house, so that she can keep on the lookout for more birds."

"Ah." I thought of Ravenswood's witch's tree. It would make a good site for a tree house, though there might be even better prospects in the forest that I'd been forbidden from entering.

"How's the inn?" Matthew asked. "Comfortable?"

"I'm not staying at the inn." I let that piece of information sink in before continuing. "Gwyneth thought it would be better if I stayed here, in the farmhouse. She lives in a small saltbox across the meadow."

"You're still at Ravenswood?" Matthew's tone was low and measured—a sure sign that he was grappling with his temper.

"Gwyneth asked me to stay for dinner, and I don't want to make the trip home in the dark," I said. "Don't worry. I'm still planning on coming home tomorrow."

Matthew made a noncommittal sound.

"Gwyneth is answering my questions," I continued, wanting to soothe my husband's ruffled feathers, "but there is a lot of ground to cover. It seems that the letter from the Congregation isn't just about the twins' future. The past is wrapped up in it, too."

"It always is," Matthew said grimly. As a vampire, my husband knew this better than most.

"Dad had a sister, Matthew. I think they were twins." My glance traveled to the photo of her and Tally. I got up to look at it again. When I flipped it over, I found the date *Summer 1957* written on it, and *Full circle! Naomi is delighted. See you soon. XX Tally.*

"Her name was Naomi. She and my grandfather were together at Isola della Stella in the summer of 1957," I said.

There was complete silence on the line.

"Matthew?" I asked, worried we'd been disconnected.

"I'm here," he said.

"There's more." I struggled to speak around the lump in my throat. "Dad made Mom promise not to do higher magic. Aunt Gwyneth calls it their *prenup*. No practice of higher magic, no involvement with the Congregation, no passing her knowledge of higher magic on to me. He put *conditions* on their relationship." My voice had risen, and I was close to tears.

"Stephen didn't strike me as the kind of man who issued ultimatums." Matthew and my father had met in London, during our timewalk. My father had traveled back to the past, too, in search of clues about the mysterious manuscript Ashmole 782.

"And Mom never struck me as the kind of woman who would succumb to the pressure of them!" Not only was my image of my father shattered, my memories of my mother were also in tatters.

"Creatures do unexpected things for those they love," Matthew said. "Are you sure you want to spend the night there?"

"I need to know more about Naomi, and if she was my father's twin. And why he kept her existence from me!" I was angry and frustrated. "Did Naomi do higher magic, too? Did she refuse to give it up, so Dad cut her out of his life?"

My mind took an uneasy turn as something niggled at me. I was missing something—something that would help me to see a pattern in all of this.

"Perhaps the distance between Dad and Naomi had something to do with the Congregation," I said, giving voice to my jangled ideas. "Maybe the Congregation's interest in Pip and Becca is related to it, too."

I spotted a large earthenware crock filled with dark feathers. It was a gloomier assortment than what I'd seen stuffed into the mason jar downstairs.

"And the ravens," I said.

"Maybe there was a good reason why Stephen didn't want you to know the Proctors," Matthew said, his suspicious brain on high alert.

"Are you questioning Gwyneth's motives in sending for me?"

"Of course I am," Matthew retorted. "Ravens falling out of the sky? Missives from the Congregation? Secret twins?"

He had a point.

"The one thing I'm sure of is that Gwyneth wants what's best for me and the family," I said.

"Whose family?" Matthew asked pointedly. "Ours? Or the Proctors'?"

This was a question I couldn't yet answer. But I knew who could.

The prospect of a lobster dinner was reason enough for me to return to the Old Place, but it paled in comparison to the opportunity for me to have an honest exchange with my great-aunt.

"I'd like to speak to Naomi."

I was so intent on answers that I forgot basic good manners and was now standing at the threshold of the parlor. Gwyneth looked at me with raised eyebrows.

"Good evening to you, too, Diana." Gwyneth held up a fine-stemmed glass. "You're early. Wine?"

"How can I get in touch with her?" I asked.

"I don't know." Gwyneth filled my glass with a generous pour. Hers was more measured.

"What was her last known address?" Between Baldwin and Jack, I was sure that I could find Naomi's present whereabouts, given their access to every legal and illegal method of tracing people across the globe.

"The Old North Cemetery in Ipswich." Gwyneth handed me the glass. "She's dead, Diana."

"Dead." I sat down with a thunk.

"Didn't your father mention his twin sister, Naomi?" Gwyneth looked as shattered by this possibility as I felt.

I shook my head. "Dad told me he was an only child."

My revelation sparked Gwyneth's anger. "I'm not surprised. I am, however, extremely disappointed. Naomi doesn't deserve to be erased, a blot on the Proctor family lineage."

"When did she die?" The wine sloshed around in the bowl as I lifted the glass to my lips for a steadying sip.

"August 13, 1964." The date sprang easily to Gwyneth's tongue. She had never forgotten the particulars of her niece's death.

"My birthday." An eerie sensation crept across my shoulders. What must my dad have thought, when I was born on the same date that his sister had died? Had he worried I was a replacement sent by the goddess to fulfill Naomi's interrupted destiny?

I performed some quick mental calculations.

"If Naomi died in 1964, that means she was only twenty-four." Horror swept over me. What must it be like to lose a beloved child at that pivotal moment, when their future life was filled with possibilities on the cusp of being realized? As for my father, the death of his sister would have cut to the bone. To lose a sibling was traumatic enough. For a twin, it meant losing part of yourself.

"Your father was in his first years of graduate school then," Gwyneth said, "and hadn't yet met your mother."

"Was Naomi in an accident?" There was no other reason for the strong, healthy woman in the photographs to die so young.

"Naomi took her own life, Diana." Gwyneth put her wineglass down with exaggerated care, as though she didn't trust herself to complete the simple gesture without catastrophe.

The cumulative effects of this afternoon's shocks were beginning to take their toll. My fingers and toes went numb, and I had the odd sensation of being outside my body looking down on what was happening below, connected but detached, like a member of the audience at a play.

"Naomi was on the Congregation's higher magic track—the same one the twins will be tested for in September. The same program that you were tested for when *you* turned seven," Gwyneth said.

I'd never heard the faintest whisper about any "track" for witches on Isola della Stella.

"I found a picture in Naomi's room of her and Tally in 1957. They were in Venice, at the Congregation's headquarters." I was ashamed to be caught snooping, but Julie had told me to poke around.

"In the cloisters outside the meeting chamber." Gwyneth nodded. "It was taken during the witches' annual training exercises in July. Tally was one of the instructors. Usually, they avoid having members of the family involved in the examinations, but they were shorthanded that year and had to call on Tally at the last minute."

"You're no stranger to Isola della Stella," I said sharply. Only someone who had been to the island would know where the cloisters were relative to the Congregation's main chamber.

"I was in the Congregation's 1948 class of initiates," Gwyneth replied, "the first to form after the end of the war. I took a break to finish my undergraduate degree, and was made an adept in the summer of 1952."

"An adept?" I frowned, unfamiliar with the term in this context.

"There are three levels of mastery in higher magic," Gwyneth explained. "Novitiates, who are taking their first steps on the Dark Path. Initiates, who have been tested at the Crossroads and chosen to continue on the Dark Path. The top rank is reserved for adepts, who have passed through the witches' Labyrinth and been recognized by the Congregation as skilled practitioners of higher magic."

"There's no maze on the island," I said with a frown.

"How much time have you spent in the witches' precinct?" Gwyneth asked, cocking her head.

Not much. The witches had been reluctant to admit a member of the de Clermont family to their hallowed halls, even though I was not a vampire.

"Many members of the Proctor family have been tested on Isola della Stella. Tally's examination was in the summer of 1936," Gwyneth said, her expression proud. "An astonishingly talented bunch of witches that class turned out to be. Morgana was in the class of 1939, but the invasion of Poland brought a halt to the program. She was happy with her oracles, and didn't seek advancement to the level of adept after the war ended."

Gwyneth's face crumpled with grief.

"As for Naomi, she made it through the first two levels of training and was awarded the rank of initiate," she continued. "Naomi was invited to attempt the Labyrinth, but got lost somewhere along the way. She was devastated, and ashamed of failing to live up to Tally's legacy."

I was familiar with the peculiar predicament faced by daughters who wanted to make their fathers proud. It was impossible not to feel you were falling short.

"Naomi broke under the strain. She took a whole bottle of pills, drank a fifth of tequila, and dove off the meetinghouse spire. Stephen never got over it," Gwyneth continued. "He blamed the family for allowing Naomi to enter the Congregation's program, even though she didn't have the strongest talent for higher magic or the self-confidence to brazen out her failures. Stephen blamed the Congregation for not intervening at the first sign of trouble, when something might have been done to save her. And he blamed higher magic itself for her death."

My father's antipathy toward this branch of the craft made more sense now, as did my aunt Sarah's insistence that higher magic was something to be feared.

Though my mother and Em had both experimented with the darker arts, when I questioned their interest Sarah wrote it off as a moment of teenage rebellion rather than a path to higher mysteries. I had long suspected Sarah might have been wrong on this point. When my hands absorbed my weaver's cords soon after returning from the sixteenth century, and Sarah had glimpsed the colors of higher, darker magic on my fingers, she had conceded that their power was only as evil as the witch practicing it. To this day, however, Sarah retained her conviction that higher magic was dangerous.

"Mom was an adept, too." Another piece of the Ravenswood puzzle slid into place. Mom had been drawn to Ravenswood because it supported her higher magic. Sarah didn't want me to know of its existence because of my mother's experiences as well as the tragic circumstances of Em's death.

"She was." Gwyneth's glance softened. "And your grandmother. Joanna Bishop was in the class of 1936, with Tally."

As the synchronicities mounted, I felt the hand of the goddess at work. But the pattern and purpose of her complicated weaving remained beyond my grasp, though some of the stitches were now visible. It was clear that the threads between the Proctors, the Bishops, and the Congregation were knotted and tangled around a dark strand of higher magic. No wonder the witches were interested in gauging the twins' powers.

"There's no way to prevent Becca and Pip from being examined by the Congregation, is there?" I buried my head in my hands.

"No," Gwyneth said. "The truth is on their side, after all. There is nothing Matthew Clairmont can do, either, except declare a bloody interspecies war he won't win."

My eyes rose to meet hers.

"But you might be able to help them when it's the twins' turn to choose their life's path. At the moment, you're only a fraction of the witch you were born to be." Gwyneth folded her hands and let them rest on the table.

I foresaw where her argument was leading and shook my head.

"If you're suggesting I walk the Dark Path and become an adept in higher magic, you're going to be sorely disappointed," I said. "I saw what that kind of magic did to Satu Järvinen and Peter Knox. They were both highly talented witches—adepts, too, no doubt—and they couldn't avoid turning to the darker side of higher magic. Emily Mather, Sarah's life part-ner, might still be with us if she hadn't returned to it. Dad lost his sister to that kind of magic and did everything short of locking my mother up to keep her from the same fate. And my parents died to prevent me from being marked as a potential magical asset for the witches to exploit. I'm a skilled witch, and a trained weaver. I have enough power, thank you very much. Higher magic isn't for me, Gwyneth."

"That's not your choice," Gwyneth replied with the patience of an ex-perienced teacher. "The goddess gifted you with these talents. Now you are faced with a decision, Diana. Will you refuse the goddess and the Dark Path?"

I hesitated. The goddess didn't like it when witches turned down her overtures.

"Will you let Pip or Becca walk the Dark Path alone?" Gwyneth saved the thorniest question for last.

I would never abandon either of my children. My expression told Gwyneth as much.

My aunt leaned forward. "Or will you, like so many of your ancestors—maternal as well as paternal—have the courage to face your fears and claim your birthright?"

"I don't know enough about higher magic to decide!" The truth burst forth in a loud rush. "Not with the children's futures on the line."

"Oh, no. This is about *you*." Gwyneth's finger pointed at my heart, the tip glowing just like Becca's had in New Haven. "This is *your* choice, which you must make without regard for anyone else's fears or desires. When they're ready, Becca and Pip will make their own decisions about their own magic."

"But Sarah—" I protested, thinking of my aunt's strong aversion to higher magic.

"Sarah is eager to tell you what you shouldn't do," Gwyneth said. "What if I taught you what you *can* do?"

Gwyneth made it sound so simple, as though what I wanted was all that mattered. But I was part of a large, complicated family and the time for acting unilaterally was behind me. Still, the prospect of greater knowledge beckoned, as alluring to me as it had ever been, even during the years I'd tried to deny my magical heritage.

"How would you do that?" I asked, wary.

"Carefully, just as I have done with generations of witches for the past half a century." Gwyneth's voice was tart.

"I need to get back to New Haven." I bit the corner of my lip. "We're going to England for summer break."

"A few more hours won't make much difference," Gwyneth said. "Meet me in the barn tomorrow morning. I think you'll find that higher magic is neither as terrifying nor as dark as your father and Sarah made it out to be."

After dinner, I went back to the farmhouse and shared my updated plans with Matthew. The conversation with Gwyneth had revealed the neat hole in my life where the Proctors and their history should have been. Like the space left by a missing piece of a jigsaw puzzle, the outlines of the Proctors' absence were sharp and unmistakable. As a historian, I knew that such a neat hole was never accidental. Such lacunae appeared only when something had been deliberately excised.

In this case, it was my father who had made the surgical cuts to the Proctor family tree. Perhaps tomorrow I would better understand why he had gone to such lengths to keep me away from Ravenswood and my own kin.

Chapter 6

I woke to a chilly late-spring morning, with bright blue skies and fluffy white clouds sailing past the sun. Pulling up the neck of my fleece jacket, I wended my way through the perennial borders that lined the paths between Orchard Farm and the barn.

From the vantage point of the farmhouse, most of the barn's rectangular bulk was tucked into the thicket of surrounding shrubs, making it look smaller than it really was. The barn's tall roofline was also masked by the lower branches of ancient hemlocks and chestnut trees that grew into a protective shell around the structure. A crumbling stone wall hid in a brambly hedge behind the barn, creating an impenetrable barrier of twining grapevines, barberries with their vicious thorns, and the rambling branches of wild roses. Nothing was in flower yet, but soon the hedge would be adorned with splashes of white, pink, red, and purple.

As I approached the barn, I had the uncanny sense I was being watched, but there was no witchy tingle to indicate it was Gwyneth. Drawing nearer to the barn's stout wooden doors, I noticed hundreds of white eyeballs staring back at me. Each bobbed on a blood-red pedicel, a black spot like a pupil on the end. This was baneberry, the poisonous plant that Sarah had warned me never to touch or eat, though she kept a single specimen in her witch's garden and used it in minute amounts for some of her charms and cures. No witch I'd ever encountered would plant a hedge of the dangerous stuff. And the berries didn't usually appear until the end of summer. The shrubs, like the barn, must be covered with enchantments.

Gingerly, I touched the heavy handle on the barn's sliding door, expecting opposition from the wards and bolts I'd felt around the place yesterday. Gwyneth must have lifted them in preparation for my visit, for there was no resistance now. I slid the door aside on its well-oiled tracks.

I gasped in wonder as the barn's interior came into view. Magic had been used on the beams and clapboards so that there was more space inside than the building's footprint suggested. It was crammed with a wizard's workshop of magical objects and supplies. Bookshelves held more dusty tomes than John Dee's Mortlake library, and Mary Sidney would have been thrilled to work in the laboratory located along the back wall, where two brick-faced charcoal stoves topped with gleaming distillation equipment flanked a potbellied wood-burner.

A worktable was centered in the middle of the room over a pentacle painted on the floor—the star surrounded by a circle that was so often included in human horror films and pulp novels about magic. A few old rocking chairs and the baskets, bottles, and boxes that filled the spaces between books completed the barn's furnishings. High shelves extended up into the exposed roof beams. Drying racks laden with herbs were suspended from them on long ropes. A narrow range of clerestory windows just above the shelves let in the raking sunshine.

An old woman sat in one of the rocking chairs by the fire. She wore dark, simple clothing, and a woven blue-and-white blanket covered her legs. Her disordered silver hair was streaked with darker strands and one long tress extended over her shoulder and snaked across her lap.

Gwyneth hadn't mentioned anyone would be joining us.

Puzzled, I waved hello.

Merry meet, daughter, she said, puffing on the pipe that was held firmly in her worn and stained teeth. *Gwyneth is on her way.*

"Good morning," I replied. "Are you a member of the Ipswich coven?"

The old woman rocked and wheezed, doubled over with laughter. She kept drawing on her tobacco while she did so, wreaths of smoke forming around her head.

A member of the coven, the strange woman repeated, gasping for breath. *What need have I of covens?*

"Are you family, then?" I'd only met Gwyneth and Julie, but I was confident that dozens more Proctors were in the wings.

"You should have waited like I asked, Granny Dorcas," Gwyneth said from the threshold. "Suddenly appearing like that would frighten most people to death."

I only frighten those who wish me ill, Granny Dorcas replied. *Never family, Gwyneth.*

"Morgana lost three years of her life when you appeared on her date with Bobby Williams," Gwyneth said reprovingly.

Gwyneth was eighty-seven. She'd told me so yesterday. If this woman was her grandmother, then she would be well over a hundred years old. But Julie called Gwyneth's grandmother *Granny Elizabeth,* not *Granny Dorcas.* Unless—

No. She couldn't be a ghost. Ghosts were hazy and green, fading away at the edges and disappearing whenever you asked them a question. This woman was in full, albeit muted, color. Her edges, like her tongue, were sharp. And she hadn't faded away when I quizzed her.

"Are you a ghost?" I whispered.

I prefer to be called a specter. Granny Dorcas let out another cackle. *Spectral evidence. That's what they claimed they had against me in 1692.*

"Granny Dorcas is your direct ancestor, back eleven generations," Gwyneth said. She was carrying a scroll and waved it at Granny Dorcas. "I was going to show Diana the family tree before introducing you."

My mouth dropped open in astonishment. Eleven generations?

Bah. Granny Dorcas removed her pipe long enough to direct a stream of spit at the woodstove. *We've not got time for fripperies and paper fancies. Let's get to business.*

"This is my classroom, Dorcas." Gwyneth had dropped the reverential designation of "Granny" to assert rank. "I told you last night, you're welcome to join us, but only if you don't interfere."

Granny Dorcas responded by breathing smoke out of her nostrils like a firedrake.

"That's better." Gwyneth nodded. "I think tea and a tidy are in order."

Aunt Gwyneth waved her hand and a barely audible hum filled the air.

Brooms danced across the floorboards, whisking away some ashes that had fallen from the stove. A mop swirled in front of the chemistry bench. Water rushed into a dry sink near the distillation equipment from an old pump hanging in midair. A flame burst forth from the banked coals under a three-legged stand in the laboratory.

"The older I get, the more magic I use," Gwyneth said with a sigh. She went to the sink and peered inside. "The kettle is full. Do you mind lifting it, Diana?"

I skirted by Dorcas and lifted the heavy kettle onto the tripod with care. I didn't want to spill a drop and extinguish the flame. But I needn't have worried. As soon as the kettle was in place the flames increased to boil the water.

"Let me give you the grand tour." Gwyneth took me by the elbow. "I suppose we should start here, with the laboratory."

"Who did these belong to?" I examined the delicate shapes of the pelicans and retorts, and the heavy crucibles and mortars that were arranged around the stove. This was not the apparatus of a modern chemist, but an alchemist.

"Me." Gwyneth's eyes twinkled. "Doesn't the Bishop House have a stillroom?"

"It does," I said, thinking of the small, cramped room off the kitchen. "But Sarah uses a Crock-Pot and a coffee maker to brew her concoctions."

"We're old-school at Ravenswood," Gwyneth replied. "Besides, I haven't found a Crock-Pot particularly useful when it comes to dissolution and conjunction. There's no way to see the color changes."

Gwyneth *was* talking about alchemy—not just making love potions and valerian tea.

"I've read your work, Diana," Gwyneth said gently. "It must be something of a shock to learn that alchemy is a part of higher magic, despite your arguments to the contrary."

My first book had presented painstaking evidence that alchemy was an early form of modern chemistry, and not the stuff of deadly poisons and life-extending elixirs. Working alongside Mary Sidney in her laboratory at Baynard's Castle had confirmed this view. Gwyneth's words were forcing me to reconsider.

"Potions, poisons, medicinal concoctions, the philosopher's stone— I do it all." Gwyneth gestured toward the nearby shelves, where jars of dried plants and roots were arranged in alphabetical order, along with brightly decorated earthenware apothecary jars whose Latin labels identified their contents. Scorpion oil, wolf oil, aconite, basil unguent, mercury, marshmallow root water—Gwyneth possessed an array of precious substances that John Hester would have been proud to display in his shop at Paul's Wharf. I stepped closer, intrigued.

"You'll be interested in the family's scientific instruments, too." Gwyneth led me to a display of brass, ivory, and wooden instruments.

It was an assortment that would have been familiar to any seventeenth-century practical mathematician: a tarnished Gunter's chain, used to measure distances; a circumferentor to gauge horizontal angles to make a map or plan; a plane table compass, which might have been used to draw a chart of the Massachusetts coast; a mariner's astrolabe for navigating the open seas and calculating the height of the stars; a compass to create the arcs and circles that were used in apotropaic marks like the hexafoils on the keeping room door.

"Our John Proctor was an expert geometer as well as a farmer, and interested in all kinds of science," Gwyneth said with pride. "His passion was passed down in the family blood—through my veins and yours. You can see his brass sundial at the museum in Salem, but these items remained in the family, along with his books."

Owning a brass sundial in Puritan New England would probably have been sufficient to get you accused of witchcraft in 1692.

"It was John Proctor who designed the first protective sigils for the Old Place," Gwyneth continued. "He sketched them in the Boston gaol and passed them to the Proctors on the outside to make sure his mathematical legacy lived on after he was gone. His children taught their children how to cipher and sigil and draw the geometrical symbols we still use today in our wards and spells."

"And was it really John Proctor's ghost I saw walking toward Ravens-wood?" Now that I knew the family ghosts were in Technicolor and sub-stantial, Julie's conviction that I'd seen our shared ancestor was more plausible.

"I don't know," Gwyneth mused. "He's never appeared to me."

I reckon it was John. That boy was always a wanderer. Granny Dor-cas tapped the bowl of her pipe against the sole of her shoe, displaying a length of moth-eaten wool stocking that had seen better days. Tobacco rained down on the floor, some of it still alight. Dorcas rummaged in her skirts, found her stash of leaves, and packed the pipe with practiced swiftness. Then she set the tip of her finger aflame and touched it to the contents of the bowl.

"I've repeatedly told you not to smoke in here," Gwyneth said, clicking her fingers. The fire shovel and broom clattered to attention and swept up the remnants of Granny Dorcas's last smoke before they set the barn on fire.

"When were you born, Granny Dorcas?" As soon as the words were out of my mouth, I regretted it. My ancestor drew back, indignant.

Long ago, miss, when you didn't ask for the age of your elders. Back then, birthdays were often followed by burials. So were weddings. Granny Dor-cas's flare of temper fizzled out. *My mam told me I was born under a wan-ing winter moon when Massachusetts Bay was filled with pox and hardship, when the first Charlie still had his head on his neck.*

"Before 1649, then?" Granny Dorcas was a very old ghost indeed.

Granny Dorcas shrugged. *I suppose. I know the day I died well enough—and it wasn't September 1692 when the court killed me on paper.*

"Dorcas . . . Hoare?" When I was ten and Sarah was trying to instill a sense of family responsibility in me, she'd made me memorize all the witches executed in the Salem panic. When I was thirteen, my aunt drew up a list of all the accused witches who had survived. Dorcas Hoare had been among them. She'd confessed and pointed an accusatory finger at some of her neighbors, which earned her a temporary reprieve. There had been no hint that she was connected to the Proctors.

Granny Dorcas will do. Dorcas fingered the lock of hair over her shoulder.

"This all would have been so much easier if you'd been patient, Dorcas." Gwyneth produced a teapot and spooned loose leaves out of an apothecary jar that had once held dried bergamot but was now being used to store Earl Grey. She held the pot under the spout and invisible hands tilted the kettle, releasing steaming water that filled it to the brim.

I watched with curiosity, amazed that there was no spillage. How did it know when to stop?

"Overflow spell. Very useful when you live on the edge of a marsh, and cheaper than flood insurance." My aunt poured the tea, then added a splash of milk from an apothecary jug labeled MALLOW SYRUP. I reached for one of the mugs, eager to get the restorative elixir into my body. Gwyneth looked pleased that I was not politely waiting to be served.

"That overflow spell could conserve gallons of water," I said after taking a sip of my tea. It was excellent, just like every cup I'd had so far at Ravenswood. "It could save Yale thousands of dollars, given how distracted the students and faculty are." Everywhere I went on campus, someone had left a tap running.

"Magic? At Yale?" Gwyneth's eyebrows rose. "Dear me, Diana. It's one thing for the faculty to cast a spell at one of the Seven Sisters—goddess knows it wouldn't be the first time or the last—but I don't imagine Elihu Yale or Increase Mather would approve of a witch doing so in their hallowed halls."

"The faculty practice magic at Mount Holyoke?" How strange it must be to teach in a small liberal arts college surrounded by witches casting spells.

"Certainly," Gwyneth said. "We had a real ghost problem until the class of 1900 decided to collect all the specters and deposit them in Wilder Hall's attic as part of their class gift. And there's a spot on the hill behind the Mandelles where Emily Dickinson left scraps of magic and poetry—some of it quite beautiful. Whenever there's a storm one of the senior witches in English Lit goes out and gathers whatever the wind has brought to light. It counts toward her department service and is a lot more pleasant than serving on the curriculum revision committee."

We both shuddered at the thought of such a thankless assignment.

"Let's look at a file from the family archives," Gwyneth suggested. "It should help you understand the Proctor family's higher magic and give you a sense of our history with the Congregation."

"And the family tree?" I said, taking another sip of tea as I followed her to the worktable.

Gwyneth laughed. "Yes, we'll have a look at the family history, too. Are you coming, Granny?"

No need, Granny Dorcas replied. *I am* the family history.

"Suit yourself," Gwyneth said with a shrug.

"What are those?" I pointed to a dozen carved wooden paddles. Each hung from a heavy nail pounded into the wall. They looked like enormous butter pats, except for the pieces of faded ribbon that clung to some of the frames.

"Spell-looms," Gwyneth explained. "They're the traditional way families in this part of the world preserve the power of their magic. We don't rely solely on written spells. They—"

"Deteriorate over time." This was why weavers like me were so essential in a magical community—and why their deliberate extermination centuries ago had led to a decline in our communities' powers. "The old gramarye no longer has the same resonance it once did, and the spells fray and twist out of shape."

"Exactly." The skin between Gwyneth's eyes puckered as she frowned. "Rebecca thought you might become a knotter, like Stephen. Who taught you to translate your newly knotted spells into words? Not Sarah."

"A weaver called Goody Alsop." I smiled at the memory of sitting in her London house and learning how to weave magic. "Matthew and I timewalked to London in 1590 to learn more about my powers. Thankfully Goody Alsop was still alive—one of the last of her kind."

"And a great witch, too," Gwyneth said. "I'm surprised she didn't notice your predisposition for higher magic."

"Perhaps she did." I was not yet ready to tell Gwyneth about the tenth knot, which could be used to construct spells of creation—and destruction. I wondered whether my ability to tie the tenth knot was woven into my inheritance, along with higher, darker magic.

Gwyneth watched me closely. She knew that I was keeping something from her. After a long silence, she returned to the matter at hand.

"Right," my aunt said briskly. "Where are the Congregation files, Granny Alice?"

I'd suspected there was an enchanted retrieval system to go with the tea-stirring and mop-swirling spells. I hadn't anticipated it would involve another ghostly ancestor.

"Granny Alice's shelving system is rather eccentric, I'm afraid," Gwyneth apologized. "If you're looking for something, you'd best ask for her help. She's the one who devised the Byzantine classifications. It will save you hours of fruitless searching."

A rolling ladder shot toward us, the wheels whooshing along the floor. When it reached the table, a middle-aged woman with an impressive bustline and brown hair knotted at the back of her skull climbed down the rungs. Based on her garments, Granny Alice was another great-grandmother—this one from the nineteenth century rather than the seventeenth. She held a clutch of manila folders, the edges brown.

Granny Alice slapped the files down, looking reproachfully at Gwyneth. *The barn's organization scheme is neither eccentric nor Byzantine. Melvil Dewey based his system on Francis Bacon's* Advancement of Learning. *He thoroughly approved of my modifications to it.*

"Modifications? You totally gutted the technology classification!" Gwyneth gathered the files closer.

Magic is an art, a science, and, yes, it is above all else a technology, Granny Alice retorted, swishing her mauve skirts in irritation. They were accented with black braid, as was the bodice. *We can debate the merits of my interventions later. No doubt Diana will bring a fresh perspective to our argument, given her familiarity with Bacon's ideas. Right now, you have more pressing concerns.*

Granny Alice flounced back to the ladder and vanished on the third rung. Dorcas chuckled and Aunt Gwyneth sighed.

"Here. Have a look at these," Gwyneth said, pushing a file toward me.

I opened the brittle folder. Inside were letters from the Congregation, most of them written in pen and ink on the paper that was still used on Isola della Stella. Their dates ranged from the 1870s to the present. Flipping through them, I encountered Proctors and Easteys, Dickinsons and—

"Mather?" I looked up from the letter dated 1925 that informed Jonathan Mather and his wife, Constance Proctor Mather, that their son, Putnam Mather, would have his magical talents assessed that summer. Sarah's partner, Emily Mather, came from New York, not Massachusetts. Even so, the possibility that one of the women who had raised me might be a Proctor relative sent a chill up my arms and lifted the hair on the back of my neck.

"Your mother's friend Emily descended from Cotton Mather's son Creasy," Gwyneth explained, once again seeming to read my thoughts, though I felt no intrusive touch in my mind.

Reverend *Cotton Mather.* Granny Dorcas spat and forked her fingers in the traditional gesture to ward off evil. *He touched us all, you know, looking for places their devil might suckle. The minister's son was just the same, lascivious and disordered.*

"And the mother?" My witch's third eye prickled in warning.

Tituba. Dorcas's steely gaze locked with mine.

"Impossible. She was an old woman in 1692," I protested.

Says who? Dorcas demanded. *Tituba was still a girl when Reverend Parris bought her in Barbados, and just turned a woman when she arrived in Salem. By 1692 she had been laboring for wealthy men for more than a decade. That will age you, quick enough.*

I knew that the old, haggard witch was a human stereotype, and that thirty was considered a ripe age in the seventeenth century, even though people could go on to live for decades more. Those few who reached the promised biblical age of seventy were considered very holy, very lucky, or both.

When Governor Phips shut down the trials, Tituba was free to leave the gaol—so long as Parris paid the colony what was owed for thirteen months of housing and feeding her. Dorcas's puffing became agitated, and she rocked back and forth. *That devil Parris refused the charges. It was Lady Mary who took pity on the poor creature and paid her fees. Then she took Tituba to Boston to serve in her household.*

"The governor's wife?" A pattern was beginning to emerge. "Wasn't she accused of being a witch herself?"

Granny Dorcas nodded.

"Tituba was safe in Boston, for a time," Gwyneth said, continuing the tale. "When Lady Mary died, the Phipses' adopted son kept Tituba. According to Tituba's story, Cotton Mather spotted her one day when she was out on family business. He followed her back to the Phips house and then returned to his own, afraid for his life. He babbled to his wife and children that there was a witch with the Phipses who wished him ill, and that he'd seen her devil's teat with his own eyes. Creasy Mather was a curious, wayward boy desperate for his father's approval. He decided he would examine this witch himself."

Examination turned to rape, Dorcas said bitterly. *Tituba was at the end of her child-bearing years, and the pregnancy put her poor body under great strain. Master Phips sent her to the family's farm in Maine for the end of her confinement. She gave birth to a girl she named Grace Mather.*

"That's when Tituba became entangled in the life of the Proctors and the Hoares," Gwyneth said. "William Proctor fled to Maine when he was released from prison, like others who had been touched by the hanging times. Granny Dorcas was there, too, along with some of her children. Soon there was a small community of Salem outcasts, bound together by shared tragedy."

The Maine woods were full of magic then, Dorcas said. *My Tabby used what spells she could to mend Will's broken heart, but he longed for Ravenswood.*

"William didn't live to see the place again, but his wife, Tabitha, honored his last wish and returned here with their twin girls, Margaret and Mary." Gwyneth unfurled the scroll she'd carried into the barn.

I bit back a gasp as I saw the Proctor family tree for the first time. The tree focused primarily on my direct lineage, rather than including detailed branches and leaves for every family member. Gwyneth directed my attention to the top of the scroll, where the names DORCAS GALLEY, JOHN PROCTOR, and TITUBA were enclosed in boxes with green borders. Next to each was the name of the father or mother of their children: William Hoare, Elizabeth Bassett, and Creasy Mather.

"Tituba and Grace traveled with them. Tituba died on the journey, and Tabitha raised her daughter as one of her own," Gwyneth continued. "She was a gifted child, intelligent and quick like her grandfather Cotton Mather. Grace was determined to remind people of what had happened to Tituba during and after the hanging times. She never dropped the Mather name—not even after she married and had children of her own. Her eldest daughter was called Tituba Mather, after her mother."

Below the three names at the top of the tree were the children from whom my branch of the family was descended: TABITHA HOARE, WILLIAM PROCTOR, GRACE MATHER. I followed the line of descent until I reached a box at the bottom of the tree that was outlined in gold with my own name inside it. On the branches above were my parents, Rebecca Bishop and Stephen Proctor. Next to my mother's box were two more boxes: one for Sarah, and one for her beloved Emily, a direct descendant of the enslaved Tituba.

Emily was doubly part of my family, and my eyes filled to see her and Sarah recognized alongside my parents. My ancestors had raised her ancestor, just as Emily had raised me.

"As you see, you were always connected to the Proctors," Gwyneth said, squeezing my arm in a reminder that I still had living family here, not just ghosts, "and to Ravenswood."

I nodded, sniffing back the emotions that had stirred the branches of my family tree. Once I was in control of them, Gwyneth continued.

"What's clear from the family history," she said, "is that the Proctor family's talent for higher magic came from Granny Dorcas. John Proctor was a knotter—a weaver, as you call it—and there had been others so blessed in his family line. No one understood why their powers manifested in strange, undisciplined ways. Back in John's day, people believed that designing and casting your own spells was a sign of stubborn pride, bad blood, or some magical malformation in a witch's character."

The way Gwyneth explained it, the seventeenth-century attitude toward weaving was a bit like the vampires' views on blood rage: It was a scourge that had to be stamped out and contained.

"To add to the mysteries of his magic, John worked geometrically, building sturdy spells shaped like Platonic solids, with intricate knots where the planes met that could withstand the ravages of time. He passed those spells on to William, who married Tabitha Hoare." Gwyneth paused to gather her thoughts. "Something happened when the blood of the Hoares and the Proctors mixed, joining weavers who knotted new spells with witches who followed the Dark Path."

My aunt pointed to two silver-filled boxes below the couple's name. One was edged in black, the other in gold.

"Twins." Their two girls, Mary and Margaret, had the same birth year.

Gwyneth nodded. "Since then, twins have appeared in every other generation of Proctors. One twin became a weaver, the other an adept in higher magic. It's as though the goddess didn't want too much power in any one witch's hands, so she divided the ability to knot spells and the talent for higher magic between them."

"And then came you," Gwyneth said, running her finger down the length of the page and touching each set of silver boxes in her path. "An only child, a single witch."

But there were two witches inside me.

"I was a twin, too," I confessed. "My brother's embryo died in the womb. Mine absorbed it, along with his DNA. They call it vanishing twin syndrome. I'm a chimera, Gwyneth."

Gwyneth let out a slow breath of understanding. "That would help explain why Rebecca's first trimester was difficult. We worried she might miscarry."

"Mom did miscarry, in utero." I rested my head in my hands. "My brother was meant to be the timewalker—and the one to carry on the Proctor tradition of weaving new spells, it seems."

And I must have been the twin destined for higher, darker magic. The call of the Dark Path came not just from my mother but from my Proctor heritage, too.

"Had Rebecca given birth to twins, she would have broken a centuries-old pattern in the Proctor bloodline," Gwyneth said, understanding the significance of my being a chimera. "The goddess was forced to abandon one of her rules. She could repeat a set of twins in successive generations, or she could allow a single witch to possess dual powers. She chose the second option. The goddess chose you."

"I never wanted to be chosen," I said, anger flaring. "My family has given enough in the goddess's service. My father—gone. My mother—gone. Emily—gone."

And I am not done with you yet. The goddess's eerie voice echoed through the barn.

Dorcas's jaw dropped, the pipe falling from between her teeth. Gwyneth's eyes swept heavenward, then gently closed. She nodded.

"So must it be," Gwyneth replied. "Whether you want these blessings or not, Diana, is beside the point. The goddess has bestowed them on you, for some purpose of her own."

Aye, Dorcas said, eyeing me through narrowed lids. *It's no wonder the oracles called you home. Besides, no witch should refuse the Dark Path of higher magic—not before she's taken her first steps.*

"What about your twins?" Gwyneth asked. "Do they exhibit a talent for weaving or higher magic?"

"Pip has a familiar," I replied, "a weaver's companion. When he was younger, he played with the strands of time. He hasn't done so recently, however." So far, Pip seemed to be following in the footsteps of my vanished brother.

"That must have been terrifying. And Rebecca?" Gwyneth was nudging me to admit something I couldn't bear to say out loud.

"Becca talks to ravens," I said shortly. "I don't know enough about higher magic to know what that foretells. She's always been more vampire than witch, and takes after Matthew, not me." What happened with the ravens had planted a seed of doubt about which parent Rebecca favored, however. My head told me to run back to New Haven, but my instincts and heart insisted I remain at Ravenswood.

"I need to know everything you can teach me about higher magic," I said, my decision clear, "and quickly, before the Congregation can examine Becca and Pip."

"There's nothing hurried about higher magic," Gwyneth cautioned. "It's not something you can bone up on in a few days. Higher magic requires patience and daily training. You have to follow a standard curriculum, and it takes years."

But I was one of the impatient Proctors, and time was in short supply. I pressed my lips tight, not wanting to erupt into a panicked gush of molten resentment and fear over what had already happened, and what might occur in the future.

"You need a break before we go any further," Gwyneth said, gauging my mood.

"I need to understand what is going to happen when the Congregation witches examine my daughter and son!" I cried.

"I suggest you go for a walk," Gwyneth said, undeterred by my strong reaction. "The wood is cool on warm days like this."

"I thought the woods were off-limits."

"Ravenswood has had a chance to know you. You'll be safe there now." Gwyneth looked to Granny Dorcas for confirmation. She grunted in assent.

Class was dismissed.

* * *

After taking a few measured steps out of the barn, I ran across the warm meadow humming with dragonflies. As soon as I entered the wood, the sound quieted and a cool greenness enveloped me. A scrubby understory of pepperbush and blueberry surrounded stout trunks of oak, alder, white pine, hemlock, and rowan. Here and there I spotted greenbriers, a patch of ferns, a clump of starflowers, the twining branches of a wild rose. I stooped to pick up a fluffy gray feather left by one of the airborne inhabitants of the wood.

I drank in the green air, and with it some of Ravenswood's steadying power. Here, among the towering trees and shrubby thickets, pulsed something ancient and sacred.

I wandered at a slower pace through a clearing with the remains of a fire and past a grove of tree houses, all of them ramshackle. A tattered Jolly Roger flew from one of the more robust structures.

Gradually, my frazzled brain found peace, and my heavy heart rose despite the burdens that had been placed on it this morning—the weight of my ancestors, the responsibility of new knowledge, my children's unseeable future.

Canst thou remember a time before? The line from Shakespeare whispered through the wood once more.

"Mom?" I turned around, looking for her among the trees.

Canst thou remember, Diana?

My mother knew better than to ask me that.

"No!" I screamed, venting the hurt and anger that I was still not prepared to face. "You and Dad made sure of that. I've lost most of my childhood, thanks to you!"

I sobbed, the tears coursing down my cheeks, crying like my seven-year-old self had done when told that her mother and father were never coming back. I wiped the tears away from my clouded eyes.

My mother's ghost stood before me, only a few feet away.

If you've lost something, and can't find it, maybe you're looking in the wrong place. Mom blew me a kiss.

I blinked at the surprising sensation of her lips pressing against my cheeks. When my eyes opened again, she had vanished.

My heart was a moth trapped in a cage, fluttering and banging against the bars of my ribs. Mom was trying to tell me something—something important. I racked my brain, looking for a hidden pocket of memory that I'd overlooked, but found none.

I retraced my steps to the Old Place, determined to learn all that I could about higher, darker magic and its place in my family's past, present, and future—no matter how long it took.

PROCTOR FAMILY TREE

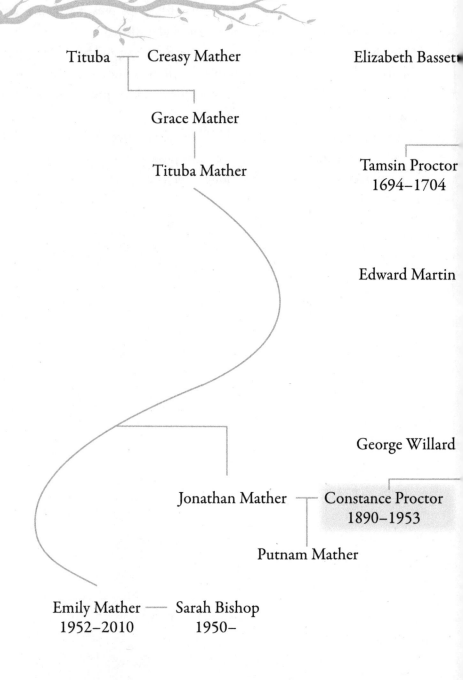

Tituba ── Creasy Mather

Elizabeth Basset

Grace Mather

Tituba Mather

Tamsin Proctor
1694–1704

Edward Martin

George Willard

Jonathan Mather ── Constance Proctor
1890–1953

Putnam Mather

Emily Mather ── Sarah Bishop
1952–2010   1950–

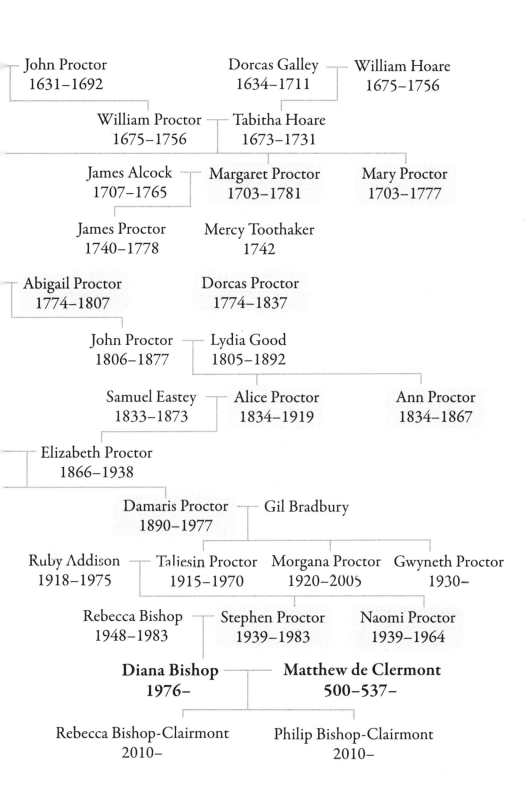

John Proctor
1631–1692

Dorcas Galley
1634–1711 ┬ William Hoare
1675–1756

William Proctor
1675–1756 ┬ Tabitha Hoare
1673–1731

James Alcock
1707–1765 ┬ Margaret Proctor
1703–1781

Mary Proctor
1703–1777

James Proctor
1740–1778

Mercy Toothaker
1742

Abigail Proctor
1774–1807

Dorcas Proctor
1774–1837

John Proctor
1806–1877 ┬ Lydia Good
1805–1892

Samuel Eastey
1833–1873 ┬ Alice Proctor
1834–1919

Ann Proctor
1834–1867

Elizabeth Proctor
1866–1938

Damaris Proctor
1890–1977 ┬ Gil Bradbury

Ruby Addison
1918–1975 ┬ Taliesin Proctor
1915–1970

Morgana Proctor
1920–2005

Gwyneth Proctor
1930–

Rebecca Bishop
1948–1983 ┬ Stephen Proctor
1939–1983

Naomi Proctor
1939–1964

**Diana Bishop
1976–** ┬ **Matthew de Clermont
500–537–**

Rebecca Bishop-Clairmont
2010–

Philip Bishop-Clairmont
2010–

Chapter 7

That afternoon, Gwyneth wasted no time in picking up where we'd left off. She drew a long stick from a box on the worktable. Its tip was pointed, and there was a knob at the base. Halfway up the length the wood bent crisply to the left.

"Is that a—" I began, my eyes darting back to the box of sticks.

"Wand." Gwyneth held it out for me to admire. "James Proctor fashioned it from an oak branch found in the Ravens' Wood. It's exactly eleven inches from base to tip and the top half is bent at an eleven-degree angle. Perfect for higher magic."

My worst nightmare came to life. Unlike the humble branch of the craft, higher magic was filled with rituals and props familiar to fans of television and film. I feared crystal balls would be next.

"As you know, magic has two branches: the craft and elemental magic." Gwyneth's tone was brisk and direct, the pitch and cadence those of an experienced teacher who knew how to snare my wandering attention and bring it back to the subject. "Both the craft and elemental magic have higher, more potent expressions. For elemental magic it's knotting spells—what you call weaving. For the craft, it's higher magic—what the ignorant call dark magic."

Gwyneth made it sound as though dark magic was a superstitious illusion, not a real threat. But I had been on the receiving end of it and disagreed. I frowned.

"All branches of magic have elements of darkness in them that can be exploited for personal gain," Gwyneth said, noting my skepticism. "But it's the witch, not the magic, that's at fault. Let me explain."

My aunt directed her wand toward the center of the room. With a twist of her wrist a canvas unrolled from the rafters. I wondered what kind of concealment spell had been used to cloak its presence, for it hadn't been visible before.

"Abracadabra! One of the world's first PowerPoint slides." Gwyneth's lips curved into a smile. "This should help you understand the relationship between Light, Darkness, and the Shadow that lies between."

Someone had painted THE POWER OF HIGHER MAGIC on the canvas in a swirling nineteenth-century copperplate. Underneath the title was a Venn diagram of three circles arranged in a horizontal line, rather than the traditional pyramid shape. One circle was black. One was white. In the center, a gray circle lay across portions of the black and white orbs.

Gwyneth directed the tip of her wand toward the gray circle. It floated off the canvas. I blinked, thinking it was an optical illusion produced by staring at a black-and-white image too long. When my eyes opened, however, the gray circle was suspended before me. No longer two-dimensional, it had become a sphere of mist. A dark storm burst forth in one hemisphere, followed by a brightening streak in the other. Swirls of charcoal snaked through it, darker veins of pulsating power.

"Higher magic resides here, in the depths of Shadow," Gwyneth said.

I reached out to touch the misty sphere, wanting to know this grayness better. A fraction of an inch before my fingertip touched the orb's surface, I hesitated.

Higher magic is dangerous. Sarah's voice echoed through my memories. *Stay away from it, Diana.* Although Sarah had softened her firm stance briefly, I had little doubt that she would be opposed to me exploring higher, darker magic with Gwyneth.

The orb of Shadow collapsed in on itself. What emerged in its place was a shimmering black globe. I glanced at the Venn diagram, where the flat gray circle was back in its place and there was only blank canvas where the black one had been.

In its three-dimensional form, the circle was no longer merely black.

Sparks of rich midnight blue and aubergine glimmered in its inky center. Darkness seemed to absorb the light around it, growing thicker and more intense.

"You gave in to fear," Gwyneth said. "Fear has no place in higher magic. It's the crack through which Darkness enters a witch's soul. Once it takes root, it's difficult to weed it out."

How could I not be afraid? Coming so close to pure Darkness went against everything I had been taught. Gwyneth would have to find another way to teach me about higher magic. If she refused, I would go back to New Haven.

The black orb swelled with satisfaction.

"Now you've given in to anger." Gwyneth went to the stove and calmly poured two fresh cups of tea. "Anger and fear live in Shadow, and you must face them every day if you want to practice higher magic."

Who wanted fear and rage to be their constant companions? I wanted life to be light and hopeful, filled with my children's laughter and Matthew's love. I wanted to be consumed with passion for my work and make a difference through my teaching.

"And if I don't?" I snapped.

"Then Darkness wins," Gwyneth replied.

Dissatisfied, I drew on previous tactics that I'd used against dark adversaries. I summoned a handful of witchfire and threw it straight at the murky round. Darkness had chosen the wrong witch. I wouldn't let it best me.

My witchfire shot toward the black orb, a flaming meteor approaching a dark sun. The flames glowed orange when they hit the sphere's surface. They turned a venomous green as Darkness latched onto their Light, creating a cancerous bump on the surface that hissed and shot malevolent sparks into the air until the flames went out.

"You shouldn't have done that." Gwyneth put a mug of tea before me and lifted her own to her lips. She was behaving as though we were at a tea party rather than waging an existential battle with evil.

The inky sphere grew again, surpassing its former size. Its edges were jagged, forming tendrils that reached out in all directions. My mouth filled with bitterness.

"You can't attack Darkness with Light," Gwyneth said. "All you've done is increased its hunger."

"Of course you can," I shot back, swatting at a creeping black vine that was making its way toward my tea. "Everybody knows that."

This tenet was central to the plot of every book I read to the twins at night.

"Light isn't a weapon, Diana. It's a resource." Gwyneth cupped her palm as though she held a baby chick. "You want to hold it gently, not turn it into a missile."

Darkness inched closer.

I stepped back, hoping to put distance between me and the black vines.

Darkness kept coming toward me.

Maybe I could make a run for it and escape into the sunshine of the meadow. It was an inhospitable place for Darkness, caught between sea and sky. I was headed for the exit when Gwyneth put an end to my escape plans.

"Stop. Immediately." Gwyneth gestured toward the open barn door, and it slid shut with a bang. "You can't outrun Darkness, either, Diana. If you try, it will follow you into the world and contaminate everything it touches."

"What am I supposed to do?" I was in a panic, my breath rapid.

You must stand firm, daughter. Granny Dorcas heaved herself out of the rocker. She put her hands on her hips and marched toward the Darkness, her elf lock swinging and rusty black skirts swishing around her ankles. *Look it in the eye and don't flinch. Darkness has a low cunning, and you must not allow it to slip past your defenses.*

"My defenses?" I laughed, and the bitter taste returned. "I have no defenses, Granny Dorcas. I know no curses, or spells to turn the tide. My wards are weak at best."

"Think about the people you love, the satisfaction you feel when one of your students achieves a new level of understanding, the curiosity that drives your research," Gwyneth said, ticking off other options. "Draw on these feelings. Be specific. Your secret desires are your real weapons—not a bolt of fire or a spell."

It sounded simple, almost Pollyannaish.

You'll find it's fiendishly difficult, my girl, looking on the bright side morning, noon, and night. Dorcas paced back and forth in front of Darkness with her hands clasped behind her back, giving it a basilisk stare while she did so. *It drove me mad.*

I closed my eyes and focused on Matthew's lopsided smile and the spark in his eyes when I walked into a room. I recalled the night we met, and the night the children were born. I envisioned Becca and Pip, playing in the backyard and fighting imaginary battles with monsters and wizards. I conjured up the sensation of wonder I'd had in the Bodleian when I cracked open the cover on Ashmole 782.

The black ball shrank, frightened—though of what, I couldn't imagine.

"What are *you* afraid of?" I whispered to Darkness.

Darkness answered with a pop and a fizzle as it slowly disintegrated, only to reappear on the canvas where it belonged.

"Well done, Diana." Gwyneth beamed with satisfaction. "Curiosity and wonder are often all it takes to keep Darkness at bay. They, too, reside in Shadow, where promise and potential disaster can be found in equal measure. It was that ambiguity that really terrified your father."

Black and white, good and evil, right and wrong. Dorcas was agitated and continued her pacing even though Darkness had been put back in its place—for now.

"It's so tempting to pick sides, so difficult to center oneself in the in-betweenness of higher magic, caught betwixt here and there, perpetually at a crossroads, needing to choose the best path, knowing it might be treacherous and steep." Gwyneth's tone was somber. "Stephen couldn't bear the uncertainty, or watching Naomi make one mistake, then another."

"*You are a child of the crossroads,*" I whispered, repeating the words that Bridget Bishop had uttered to me years ago, "*a child between, a witch apart.*" I'd had a choice to make then, too—one involving Matthew and our future life together. I had put my feet irrevocably on the road forward that had him in it—even though everything I'd been taught about creatures screamed that I was making a mistake—and never looked back.

'Tis a dangerous place to be, Dorcas said.

"But a witch is not without guidance on the Dark Path," Gwyneth said. "Isn't that right, Granny Dorcas?"

Granny Dorcas nodded and reached into her skirts. She drew a knobbly lump of cloth from the folds. The parcel looked as though it contained mad frogs, their joints poking against the fabric in spiky points as they tried to escape confinement.

A warm hum like a bumblebee filled the side pocket of my leggings. I'd slipped The Dark Path card in there along with my phone when I left the farmhouse.

Granny Dorcas put the rectangular bundle before me on the table. *These belong to you now.*

I touched the homespun enclosure, and the contents of the parcel sprang out. Cards danced in the air before me, delighted to be free. In my pocket, the bumblebee sensation intensified into an agitated swarm.

"The cards will keep doing that until you reunite them," Gwyneth said. "Oracles are very sensitive, and if one of their cards is missing they won't rest until it's found."

I reached into my pocket and The Dark Path leaped out to join her sister cards. Their swirling and twirling grew more animated as they were overtaken with the joy of reunion. They slowed and fell to the table, just as Gwyneth's had done in the parlor of the Old Place. When they came to rest, six cards snaked over the worn wooden surface in a vertical, wiggly line, leaving the rest of the cards gathered into a tight stack.

"Ah. The Dark Path spread." Gwyneth smiled with satisfaction. "I knew there had to be a reason why the black bird oracle selected that particular card to send on to New Haven."

It was an omen. Granny Dorcas tapped the card closest to me. *The Book. You were embarking on a journey that would bring you great knowledge and success.*

I was glad to hear that the signs surrounding my forestalled trip to Oxford were auspicious.

The Owl Queen changed all that. Granny Dorcas's words flattened my sails. *You have knowledge, but you need wisdom—and change.*

Gwyneth nodded and made a note on a nearby pad. "Female wisdom, and an initiation into the higher mysteries."

"I thought oracles only spoke in answer to a question," I said, eager to find a reason to ignore this last message.

"A witch's life is filled with questions," Gwyneth said. "When you touched the cards, some inquiring thought was doubtless going through your mind. Often the queries we don't utter are the most important, and the most profound."

And this spread only appears when a witch is questioning her next step, Granny Dorcas said.

"I know my next step," I retorted. "I came to Ravenswood to see if Gwyneth knew anything about the Congregation's intention to examine Becca and Pip. Now I know why they sent their letter—because of the history of Proctor twins and higher magic. As soon as I can, I'm going back to my family in New Haven."

Family! You can't think straight with them all squawking around you. Granny Dorcas held up the card that bore the image of a group of birds gathered in conversation. *Too many opinions obscure your path.*

I glanced at the next card: The Skeleton. If that was what awaited me, I preferred to remain where I was.

You must use your intuition to find your way, daughter, Dorcas said. *Seemingly worthless signs will light your path. There are new possibilities waiting for you—but only if you become one with Shadow.*

"Blood." Gwyneth pointed to the fifth card of the spread. "It always signifies a sacrifice of some kind. Dorcas is right, Diana. It won't be easy, but you must stop clinging to the Light, and embrace your desire for Darkness."

Push and pull. Here and there, Granny Dorcas murmured. *Blood and A Parliament of Owls in the same reading foretells contention and strife.*

The Dark Path was the final card laid out on the table.

After you take your first step on the Dark Path, all will become clearer, Granny Dorcas promised.

"Fascinating," Gwyneth said. "The black bird oracle never disappoints, Granny Dorcas."

My mam's family always relied on birds for their auguries, Granny Dorcas replied. *When we came to Ipswich, there were owls and ravens, vultures and herons, all of them black, or white, or gray—the colors of Darkness, Light, and Shadow. It was a sign that we were on the right path.*

I fanned through the deck, locating The Owl Queen, The Raven Queen, The Heron Queen, and The Queen of Vultures.

"Couldn't you consult the birds directly?" I asked, wondering why the cards had been necessary, given the number of avian species in this part of Massachusetts.

I was confined to that stinking jail for thirteen months, Granny Dorcas retorted, *unable to wander the marshes and woods in search of guidance. When I got out, my body was feeble, and I made the cards you hold in your hands so the birds could always be with me. The Queen of Vultures uncovered many secrets that might have caused me harm. The Owl Queen was at my side when I required deeper wisdom. When prophesying and consulting the ancestors, I spoke to the Heron Queen and the Raven Queen.*

It was ravens who had brought their message to Becca.

"Did you send the ravens to New Haven, Granny Dorcas?"

Only the goddess has such power, Granny Dorcas replied. *I sent the card—though Gwynie had to help me get it to you.*

I sifted through the deck. While there was a raven prince as well as a queen—and princes of vultures, owls, and herons, too—most of the cards had little to do with birds. The five elements, magical equipment such as cauldrons, and alchemical substances and processes were represented as well.

"What do they all mean?" I had never been a student of tarot, and refused to let Em read my cards, though she had been eager to do so.

"Only you can know for sure," Gwyneth said.

"There must be a guidebook." Every deck in Sarah's Madison shop, Be

Blessed, came with an accompanying booklet that laid out their meanings along with recommended spreads.

"There isn't one." Gwyneth blinked, solemn as the members of A Parliament of Owls. "Every oracle deck in the barn was made by one of our ancestors, according to their own inner mythology and magical talents. Granny Dorcas can share the meanings the cards had for her, but you'll have to figure out what the cards mean for you."

To do that, you'll have to venture deeper into Shadow, said Granny Dorcas. *I don't have time to hold your hand, child. You must do the work yourself.*

"And if I do choose the Dark Path of higher magic, will I be able to keep Darkness away from my children?" I asked, blunt and to the point.

"You cannot prevent Darkness from touching the lives of others. Everyone must find a way to do that for themselves, no matter what type of creature they are," Gwyneth said with a touch of regret.

The cards winked at me. Did I have the courage to face my own Shadow, and walk in my mother's footsteps? Could I leave a trail for my children to follow so that they would not be lost in the dark, as I had been?

See what the cards say about the choice before you, Granny Dorcas suggested.

I gathered the black bird oracle cards and shuffled them again, focusing on which path I should take going forward. A card quickly rose from the deck as though it had been eagerly awaiting my call: The Dark Path. Then another, depicting a weeping woman standing at a crossroads with a castle in the distance: The Crossroads. Finally, the corner of The Labyrinth card emerged with its twists and turns and a tiny figure standing in the center.

Well, well, Granny Dorcas said.

"Stars and moons." Gwyneth's mouth widened into an O of amazement.

The goddess wants you to proceed on the Dark Path through all three levels of higher magic, Granny Dorcas said, puffing on her pipe. *Bad things happen to witches who turn their back on the Dark Path when it opens before them.*

I was more worried about the consequences that might befall me if I continued. Gwyneth's next words gave me a more immediate cause for concern.

"Given the black bird oracle revealed its mysteries to you today, I'm obligated to notify the coven's chair of divination and prophecy."

I made a sound of protest. My aunt raised her hands to silence me.

"It must be, Diana. And you have nothing to fear from Katrina," Gwyneth said. "Goody Wu is a great seer, with an open heart, a curious mind, and decades of experience. She's trained oracles from all over the world."

But I was not sure I wanted to be among her acolytes. The specters of Naomi, Mom, and Em haunted me—all victims of higher magic.

"You aren't Naomi." Gwyneth's bright blue eyes locked on mine. "Nor are you Rebecca Bishop. You are not Dorcas, or Emily, either. You are the latest in a long line of Proctor oracles, but your path is your own."

"The cards are the oracle—not me." My response was quick.

"Without a seer to interpret them, the black bird oracle is nothing more than a deck of cards," Gwyneth replied.

The black bird oracle has chosen to speak through you, girl. Granny Dorcas beetled her brows in warning. *Turn a deaf ear to it at your peril.*

I dreaded having to call Matthew again, but between the Proctor family tree and Dorcas's oracle cards, I was not yet finished at Ravenswood.

When I told him about the illuminated scroll that showed my line of descent, Matthew was quick to express interest.

"I'd like to see it," he said. "Before we knew about DNA and learned how to decipher the human genome in the laboratory, the passing down of bloodlines was captured in documents like yours."

"I'm not sure you'll be able to squeeze much more information from it," I said. "The tree wasn't the only Proctor relic I saw today, however. I met Dorcas Hoare."

"Who's that?" Matthew wondered.

"One of Salem's accused witches," I replied.

"You *timewalked*?" Matthew was furious. "How could you? What if you were lost? What if—"

"Granny Dorcas is a ghost," I said, trying to reassure him. "Proctor ghosts are different. They're three-dimensional, and less smudgy than Bishop ghosts. They're open to questions, too. When I saw her, I thought the old woman was a vagrant who'd wandered down the carriage road and into the barn."

"Granny?"

"I'm her direct descendant," I explained. "Tabitha Hoare married William Proctor. After that, twins and weavers appeared regularly in the Proctor line."

As well as witches with a talent for higher, darker magic, my conscience whispered. I brushed the words aside.

"So that marriage was the crucial genetic moment," Matthew said, thoughtful. "Perhaps I should come to Ipswich."

"It's not a good idea, Matthew," I said firmly. "I'm on thin ice with the local witches, and Gwyneth and I are just starting to trust each other. I need to stay here and learn more about the black bird oracle."

Matthew drew in a sharp breath. "Oracle?"

I told him about Granny Dorcas's cards, and the guidance they could provide about events that were still to come.

"Knowing what the future might hold for the children—for us— could be important," I said.

"Do you have reason to believe these oracle cards are accurate?" Matthew had been intrigued by the connection between traditional auguries—with which he was familiar from his earliest days—and Dorcas's cards.

"Gwyneth and Dorcas are sure, and until they're proven wrong . . ." I let my words trail off into silence.

Matthew sighed. "I can't help but feel you're going somewhere I can't follow, *mon coeur*. Omens, family traditions, Proctor legends—there's no place for me in them."

Your path is your own. Gwyneth's words echoed in my ears.

"But I trust your instincts," he continued. "If you feel staying at Ravenswood is the right action to take, then of course you must remain where you are."

"Thank you for understanding," I said, relieved to have settled the matter. For now.

I was ready to say good night, but Matthew had more to say.

"Diana?"

"Yes?"

Matthew hesitated.

"You would tell me if there was reason for concern," he said at last.

"Of course," I said promptly. There was no reason for Matthew to worry about the Dark Path of higher magic, not before I took my first step down it.

He considered my reply. "Keep in touch tomorrow, and let me know how you are. I'll do some research into Dorcas Hoare and her descendants, and see what I can discover myself."

Matthew was no good to himself or others if he wasn't hunting something down.

"Good night, *mon coeur*," he said, voice husky with longing. "I'll be waiting for your call."

Chapter 8

I pulled the car into a vacant spot outside The Thirsty Goat. Its wooden sign swung on an iron bracket, moving with the breeze blowing off the water. The gentle creak took me back to sixteenth-century London, and the similar sounds on our street in the Blackfriars. I sat for a moment, gathering my strength to enter the café and meet Goody Wu. Though Gwyneth had warned me the summer tourists would begin to descend on the place any day now, the street was quiet and only a handful of people were enjoying the fresh air and sunshine. I peered through my windshield and the café windows, trying to see who was inside, but the doubled reflections and bright light made it impossible.

There was no choice but to go in and face whichever members of the Ipswich coven might be gathered inside.

Though there were a few curious looks from customers, the only familiar faces were behind the counter, where Ann and Meg were readying themselves for the late-afternoon rush.

Meg was waiting for me at the till when I approached the counter.

"Diana. What can I get for you?" Meg's strange eyes were a bit less alarming than they had seemed on first meeting.

I glanced over the menu. "How's the oolong?"

"Delicate," Meg replied shortly.

"I like something heartier," I replied, looking for another option.

"We have our own Thirsty Goat blend," Meg suggested. "It's malty and stands up to milk."

"Perfect," I said.

The bell hung by the door tinkled and Goody Wu entered the café. Her signature round tinted glasses (today their hue was amber) were perched on her nose and she was carrying a lightship basket along with a violet parasol.

"Your tea's waiting, Katrina," Ann said, nodding toward a secluded table in the corner.

"We'll need a bigger pot, Ann," Goody Wu replied. "And another cup."

"Sorry," Ann said, bustling behind Meg. "I got the message you would be here at two-nineteen sharp, but I missed that you were expecting a guest."

"The ether doesn't always transmit such subtleties," Goody Wu said.

Katrina studied the paper cup filled with black liquid that Meg put before me, reading the name of the tea off its tag. Goody Wu shuddered.

"Tea from a *bag*? In a paper cup?" Goody Wu was incredulous. "That's no way to treat a fellow witch, Margaret Skelling."

"I assumed she wanted it to go," Meg replied.

"She?" Goody Wu's delicate eyebrows shot skyward. "What is it you are always saying in coven meetings—*She is the cat's mother*? Leave that dreadful concoction where it is and come with me, Diana."

Meg's eyes narrowed to speculative slits.

"If you would bring a fresh pot, Ann?" Goody Wu folded her parasol and directed me toward a waiting table. "And a proper cup for Diana."

My knees felt bowed under the weight of the other witches' curiosity as I walked the short distance to Goody Wu's table, grateful that there weren't more witnesses when my legs wobbled. Goody Wu sat opposite, inspecting me as if I, too, were a type of tea.

Ann brought the fresh pot, along with some milk and a sticky jar of local honey. She plopped a teacup before me. Goody Wu preferred her tea served in the Chinese fashion, in small cups that you cradled in your hands.

"We won't be needing them," Goody Wu said, waving off the milk and honey as though they were annoying mosquitoes. She emptied the small clay pot into our cups and handed it back to Ann. "You don't adulterate the perfection of Iron Goddess."

"Anything else?" Ann said, clearly wanting to linger, hoping that she might learn why Goody Wu had invited me here today.

"We have everything we need, Ann," Goody Wu said. "Don't let your tea get cold, Diana."

Ann obediently whisked away the honey and milk. Just as obediently, I picked up my cup and gave it an inquisitive sniff. Warm, slightly toasted floral and nutty aromas met my nose. I took a cautious sip. My eyes widened in surprise.

Goody Wu smiled with satisfaction. "It's very good, isn't it? My sister sends it from China. It comes from the mountains of Fujian. This one is not baked as long as many you find that are imported from Taiwan. I prefer it that way."

The tea was surprisingly flavorful and robust. I took another sip.

Goody Wu lifted the lid of her basket and removed a red satin bag embroidered with golden dragons.

"Meg's energy can be a bit intense for an oracle like you or me," Goody Wu said. "My cards find it disruptive, but a good shuffle helps them settle."

I choked on my tea. "I'm not an oracle. I just have a deck of old cards."

Goody Wu drew her deck from their bag and moved the cards slowly between her fingers. They were longer and narrower than the cards Granny Dorcas had given me, with faded red brushstrokes spelling out a mystery on one side and a painted network of fine lines on the other that resembled the crazed cracks in a piece of old porcelain.

"As a historian of magic, you know that oracles can be people and places, as well as things," Goody Wu said.

"I'm a historian of science," I replied, quick to correct the witch.

"Hmm. Why don't you take out your own deck?" Goody Wu suggested, looking at me over her amber lenses. "I find the oracle is most cooperative and has the greatest clarity when I'm not ordering it around."

"I left it at home," I said hastily, "for safekeeping." The last thing I wanted was the black bird oracle rising like a murmuration of starlings and flying about The Thirsty Goat.

"You'll find them in that giant bag of yours." Goody Wu stopped shuffling and turned over the top card. She smiled with satisfaction. "You should reconsider toting that thing around. It's terrible for your back and shoulders, and it's the root cause of your headaches."

Lately, the list of contributing factors to my recurring evening headaches had been lengthy: department politics, research funding deadlines, graduate student assessments. Coming to Ipswich and meeting the Proctors hadn't shortened it.

"I'm sure they're in the spellbox on my bedside table, Goody Wu." I'd secured them before I left, turning the small key in the lock to keep them from wandering.

"Call me Katrina," Goody Wu said in reply, her eyes glittering with amusement behind her tinted lenses. "I've used it since coming to Ipswich, to keep the other witches from mispronouncing my real name, Siyu." She fixed her gaze on my bag.

I sighed and lifted the Bodleian Library tote from the neighboring chair. I'd rummage through it, just to show Goody Wu—Katrina—that she was wrong.

My fingers brushed against one soft edge, then another. The precious Proctor oracle cards were strewn all over the bottom of the bag, mixed in with my car keys, some old receipts, and the pair of sunglasses I thought I'd lost last week.

"Oh no!" I scrabbled them out to see if they were damaged.

Goody Wu slid a turquoise silk bag toward me. It, too, was embroidered with a dragon in brilliant greens and silver, and it had a thin ribbon tie at the top.

"Thanks, but I have a box for them at Ravenswood." Not that my efforts to keep them there had been successful.

"You'll find bags more useful than boxes, and less likely to be searched when you go through airport security," Katrina commented.

The thought of the cards tumbling out of my tote when I was searching for my passport was alarming. I shook my head.

"I'd rather not carry them around. They're so old—a family heirloom," I said. Katrina meant well, but she couldn't imagine what the children stuck in my tote bag over the course of a day.

"The black bird oracle won't tolerate being left at home," Goody Wu said. "The cards will find a way to be with you—some of them inconvenient. It's best to keep them with you, and in their own bag, from now on."

I picked the last cards out of the tote and gathered them together in a neat stack. Goody Wu was right about their mood, just as she had been about their location; they were agitated and unhappy. Gently, I moved them through my fingers to calm them.

Katrina flipped one of her cards over. This time the card was met with a low sound of disappointment and she returned to her shuffling.

"More hot water?" Meg was back with a steaming kettle. "I know how you like a second steep."

"And a third, and a ninth." Katrina squinted up at her. "If I need anything, I will call. If I don't call, I would appreciate some peace and quiet."

Meg's eyes were fixed on the cards that were shuttling between my hands.

"Which deck is that?" Meg asked, bending closer to make out the details. "I don't think I've seen it before. Is that a Bishop oracle?"

Card 17, The Siege, snapped out of the deck and swatted Meg across the nose.

"Dorcas Hoare and her daughter, Tabby, made them," I said, retrieving the card with its image of a castle ringed by cannons and explosions.

"The black bird oracle." Meg looked aghast—and envious. "It's been lost for generations. Where did you find them?"

"They found me," I said, glancing at Katrina, who was now bright pink with the effort to suppress her laughter.

"Which is why I'm meeting with Diana now," Katrina said. "As chair of the coven committee on divination and prophecy, it's my responsibility to register all the oracle decks in current use. Remember what happened in 2000?"

Meg's skin was greenish.

"Too many oracle cards were out of their bags and being handled by unskilled witches," Katrina said severely. "They bickered and squabbled until we had a magical version of the Y2K panic, and we mustn't let that kind of trouble brew again."

"I'll leave you to it, Goody Wu." With a final backward glance at the cards, Meg returned to the counter. Once there, she launched into a long, whispered conversation with Ann.

Katrina muttered something in Chinese.

"What was that?" I suspected that one should pay close attention to Katrina's words, whatever the language.

"Before you embark on a journey of revenge, dig two graves." Goody Wu's expression soured. "I am often reminded of it around Meg. Without an enemy, Meg isn't fully alive. It's a pity. She would be a great witch if only she could give up her belief that the goddess's deck was stacked against her."

I'd given in to the urge for vengeance years ago, when I decided to spellbind Satu Järvinen in retaliation for how she'd tortured me to learn the secrets of my magic, and for being in league with Peter Knox and Gerbert D'Aurillac. But I'd been motivated by more than righteousness; there had been anger, too. Without knowing it, my spellbinding had been stained with Darkness. Perhaps I needed to acknowledge that before continuing with higher magic. If I didn't, the second grave I might unknowingly dig could be my own. Or Becca's.

Meg's presence in the café, and the interest she'd taken in the black bird oracle, felt more threatening when I thought of my daughter. I gathered the cards together, ready to make my apologies and return to the safety of Ravenswood. But Katrina was attuned to shifts of energy in ways that I was not. She sensed my restlessness, and the reason for it, too.

"Stay where you are," she commanded, "and keep the cards moving. The oracle needs to be grounded, not flitting around Essex County in your gas guzzler. You need to rethink that, too. Witches should know better than to abuse Mother Earth by wantonly consuming her resources."

It was the second time a witch had reprimanded me for Matthew's choice of transport. I couldn't imagine what they would make of Baldwin's jets and helicopters.

"This witch is married to an overprotective vampire with a pathological fear of car accidents," I replied.

A card dropped out of my hands.

"A Wake of Vultures." Goody Wu's mouth twisted into a sardonic smile. "Your husband needs to change his attitude."

Good luck with that, I thought, returning the card to the deck. It responded with immediate tension and three cards flew out of the deck with an audible pop, like slices of bread springing from a toaster.

"The Cauldron. Sulfur. Mercury." These were alchemical emblems and easier for me to interpret. According to the oracle, Matthew *was* going to have to change. "The vessel of transformation. Spirit and soul. Judgment and desire."

"As I told you, oracles don't always respond well under the pressure of direct questioning. Sometimes, it's better to let the messages drift into your life and suggest small changes, rather than demanding they blow on a trumpet to proclaim matters of enormous import." Katrina's mouth widened into a smile. "And it's much more pleasant than dragging your cards out after the alarm clock rings in the morning, in a daily ritual like brushing your teeth. The oracles like a bit of wildness."

This was an entirely different way of using the cards than the regular consultations recommended to me by Granny Dorcas and Aunt Gwyneth. I was intrigued by Katrina's alternative and its flexibility, which suited my temperament—and schedule—better.

"Aunt Gwyneth said you could help me understand the connection between higher magic and the black bird oracle." I kept my fingers moving, the cards shuffling. "I understand that higher magic resides in Shadow, though it touches on Light and Darkness, too. But where do the cards fit in?"

Before Katrina could answer, the cards thrummed between my fingers and the edges of two cards poked out from the deck. I froze, not knowing what to do next.

"When the goddess takes our call, we usually pick up on the first ring," Katrina said wryly. "Go ahead. Your answer awaits."

Gingerly, I removed the two cards and placed them face up. Card 19, The Key, and card 22, The Mirror.

"Restate your question," Katrina instructed. "Then look at the cards and tell me the first thing that comes to mind."

I closed my eyes to concentrate. "Where do the cards fit into the practice of higher magic?" I whispered.

My witch's third eye flew open.

"They're the key to greater knowledge, as well as greater mysteries. The cards open the doors to new possibilities and provide fresh solutions to old problems. They will grant me freedom but carry with them the weight of responsibility." I was amazed by the words tumbling out of my mouth. "The cards help to differentiate between truth and deception."

"I couldn't have said it better myself." Katrina nodded. "Gwyneth told me that the black bird oracle chose you for a reason. You show promise as a seer, Diana Bishop."

Katrina's blessing fell on me with the gentle warmth of an eiderdown cloak. My shoulders, which had been hunched up around my ears in self-defense, lowered, and my chin rose in pride.

"And will you help me, Katrina," I asked, adding hastily, "if I do decide to walk the Dark Path?"

"It would be my pleasure." Goody Wu gathered her cards and slipped them into their bag before tucking it under the lid of the lightship basket. "I'll meet you here next week. The exact timing will be up to the portents and signs. When I know what they recommend, I'll call you."

"Until then?" I asked, putting the black bird oracle in the bag Katrina had provided.

"Carry the cards with you. Follow Gwyneth's advice, of course, but remember the cards don't know you yet. If you feel them stirring, be sure to handle them so that they know you're paying attention."

"All right." This sounded doable. Matthew wouldn't mind if I stayed at Ravenswood a bit longer.

Katrina and I left the café together. As we walked out onto the sidewalk, Meg's malevolent stare bored into my shoulder blades. I shivered.

"What was that?" Katrina asked.

"Meg Skelling isn't happy that you and I met," I replied. "I have a feeling she might cause trouble."

"Trouble is Meg Skelling's *modus operandi*." Katrina waved her hand dismissively, as though Meg were an unnecessary milk jug. "Don't let her

Darkness follow you back to Ravenswood. Leave it here, where it belongs." She pointed to the garbage can overflowing with used coffee cups and sticky napkins.

I laughed. "I'll give it a try."

When I returned to the car, a raven's feather was lodged in the door's handle. I hesitated, then tucked it into my tote bag. The black bird oracle jumped and hopped with excitement.

I'd ask the cards what the feather signified later, when I was home.

My fears about Meg's malevolence were realized two days later when Ann Downing paid an unexpected call.

Aunt Gwyneth and I were in the barn, where I was working with the black bird oracle. Within a few shuffles the cards rose up, agitated and fluttering. When they settled down on the table, six cards faced me, arranged in a rough triangle.

"The Raven's Wing spread," Gwyneth said, peering at the cards. "You'll have to confirm it with Granny Dorcas when she wakes up, but as I recall that's a spread about what the future holds, what resources you will need, and the challenges you will meet along the way. A useful spread, although not always terribly precise."

Granny Dorcas was napping in her rocking chair, her snores regular and sonorous. There wouldn't be help from that quarter anytime soon.

My aunt's spine stiffened and she looked toward the barn door. It was partially closed, as a storm was bringing cooler temperatures to the area.

"Ann Downing is here." Gwyneth put out a restraining hand. "Stay where you are. I'll see what she wants."

Gwyneth stepped outside and drew the heavy door across the opening. She left a small gap, and I could hear their conversation.

"Good morning, Ann," Gwyneth said. "What brings you to Ravenswood?"

"Nothing good," Ann replied, her tone dour. "Is Diana Bishop with you?"

"Yes," Gwyneth said. "But I don't see why that's any concern of yours."

Ignoring my aunt's instructions, I left my stool and heaved the door open.

"Looking for me?" I said, meeting Ann's surprised gaze with a steely resolve that would have made Granny Dorcas proud, had she been awake to witness it.

"Let me in, Gwyneth." Ann was at the end of her rope. "I need a cup of tea before I deliver the bad news."

Gwyneth ushered Ann past the table where the cards were splayed out, and deposited her in the rocker opposite Granny Dorcas. My aunt sat next to our ancestral grandmother, gently rearranging the woven coverlet that had slipped from the old woman's knees.

I filled the kettle without any trouble. The automated magic in the barn didn't require a single spell, which was a blessing since I couldn't use other witches' magic and might flood the place. By the time the water boiled, I'd arranged three mugs, some milk, and a pot of sugar on a tray and spooned the leaves into the teapot. I poured boiling water over them. The tea would need to steep for a few minutes, but then we would have Ann's bad news.

"Well?" Gwyneth demanded the moment I deposited the tea tray on a nearby stool.

But Ann was in no mood to negotiate. "Tea first."

Impatient, I monitored the five-minute countdown on my watch. When the bell dinged, I sprang into action.

"Sugar, no milk," Ann instructed, rubbing her hands together in anticipation. "Goddess bless me, I'm parched."

I put a generous amount of sugar in her cup and added milk to Gwyneth's and mine. The stirring spells went to work as I delivered the drinks to the waiting witches.

"Thank you, Diana." Ann took a deep draught of the hot brew then sighed with satisfaction.

"What happened in town, Ann?" Gwyneth held her cup between her hands, as though she needed the tea's comforting warmth more than she needed a drink.

"I didn't want you to hear the news secondhand," Ann began apologetically. "You know how quickly the phone tree starts buzzing."

The coven phone tree was the blessing—and curse—of every witch. Quick to respond in an emergency, real or imagined, witches relied on it for gossip, exchanging recipes, and arranging childcare, too.

"Meg's asked for a meeting of the coven next Friday," Ann said in a rush. She took a hasty sip of tea. "I had no choice, Gwyneth."

"We don't usually meet under a full moon," my aunt commented. "Emotions will be running strong."

Ann sighed. "I know. But Meg insisted, and according to Hitty Braybrooke she has a right to be heard immediately."

As I suspected, Hitty was the coven parliamentarian. Every gathering needed witches to arbitrate disputes and govern procedures. Coven meetings deteriorated rapidly into gripe sessions without someone keeping a tight rein on the proceedings.

"We must hope that harmony and balance prevail," Ann said. "Full moons are a good time to manifest those energies."

Gwyneth looked skeptical. "What is Meg's grievance this time?"

"Me. And my custody of the black bird oracle." I'd felt Meg's malice at The Thirsty Goat as she watched every move Katrina and I made.

"Diana's right," Ann said, "but Meg's concerns extend to you, too, Gwyneth. She's accused you of flouting our protocols with respect to training novices in higher magic. All pupils, Hitty confirmed, must be presented to the coven membership before any lessons begin."

"That rule only pertains to outsiders," Gwyneth said. "Diana is my flesh and blood—a Proctor. The coven didn't interfere when the Greens and the Vinsons embarked on their own course of higher magic training, not even when it brought down the Ferris wheel at the Topsfield Fair and loosed the carousel horses on the crowd."

Ann winced at the memory.

"Meg has claimed that Diana *is* an outsider, and that the Bishops' decision to abandon the community and move west trumps her Proctor bloodline," Ann replied. "I'm sorry, Gwyneth. Hitty has ruled in Meg's favor. There's nothing for it but to meet."

"Even though it will be the three hundred and twenty-fifth anniversary of Bridget Bishop's hanging?" Gwyneth let out a small sound of disbelief and her mouth twisted into an expression of distaste. "A bit heavy-handed, even for Meg."

Tea sloshed over the lip of my mug.

"Sorry." I wiped my dripping hand on my leggings.

"Summer is always difficult for our gathering as we remember the hanging times." Gwyneth snapped her fingers twice. She handed the napkin that materialized over to me. "This will only make things worse."

"Other witches go on vacation in the summer," Ann explained, my confusion evident. "We stay in Essex County and mark the names of those who lost their lives during the panic, no matter if they died by the hangman's noose, or were pressed to death, or perished because of neglect and heartbreak. We begin by keeping vigil for Bridget Bishop on the eve before her execution, and continue until we reach Mabon, when the last of our sisters and brethren were murdered."

Sarah usually forgot it was the anniversary of Bridget's hanging until weeks after the fact. Then, she lit a candle and put it in the window. What Ann was describing was far more elaborate.

"You look surprised," Ann said.

"I am," I replied. "The Bishops don't seem to be very popular in this part of Massachusetts." Before Ann could respond, my aunt spoke.

"Well, if Meg and the coven want to question my teaching methods or how the Proctors pass their legacy from one generation to the next, they can do it here." Gwyneth's expression was forbidding.

"What's wrong with the meetinghouse?" Ann asked, careful to keep her tone just short of an accusation.

"You know how restless the ghosts are during the anniversaries," Gwyneth said with a shake of her head. "Some of the old families fail to keep their kin close to home, and I don't want them latching onto Diana."

"I've already been around to the Redds," Ann said, trying to reassure my aunt. "They won't leave the attic door open this year."

"They're not the only ones, Ann." Gwyneth shook her head again. "Diana will not face the coven under a full moon, on the eve of Bridget

Bishop's hanging, at the site of the old gaol. Diana will be at Ravenswood that night, with her family."

The room fell silent except for the snap and hiss of the logs in the stove.

"Very well, Gwyneth. We'll gather here at eight o'clock," Ann said at last. "The sun sets at—"

"Eight-twenty," Gwyneth said. "I look forward to welcoming our sisters and brothers then."

Later that evening, I pressed the buttons on my phone that would connect me to Matthew. I wasn't the goddess, but he picked it up on the first ring nonetheless.

"Diana." The syllables rolled in his mouth and over his tongue, as though he were savoring the relief of being connected once more.

"It's good to hear your voice." Being at Ravenswood without Matthew and the children had been my decision, but the nights were especially lonely.

"You sound rattled," Matthew said. I could imagine the worried frown that accompanied his words.

"Not rattled, exactly." How was I going to explain what was happening in Ipswich without Matthew racing to my rescue? "Coven politics, that's all."

"Ah." As a veteran of numerous academic departments, Matthew was well versed in the bitterness that could linger in small communities.

"My presence at Ravenswood has been noted, and now I have to be formally presented to the coven," I said, clinging as closely to the truth as I could without unduly alarming him.

Of Meg Skelling, and her charges against Gwyneth, I made no mention.

"It sounds positively biblical," Matthew murmured.

I laughed. "Hardly. They've picked next Friday for the event."

"June ninth?" Matthew had been reading about Salem and the witch trials. "That's the day before Bridget Bishop was executed. You'll be staying with Gwyneth a bit longer, then."

"I'm sorry, my love, but I can't very well walk out and leave her without responding to the coven's invitation," I explained. "The anniversaries are a big deal here, and emotions are running high."

"Do you want me to come?" Matthew said. "Rebecca and Philip would be fine with Chris and Miriam for a few days."

"That wouldn't be wise," I said hastily. "It's not any old anniversary of the hangings, but the three hundred and twenty-fifth. Usually, a few members of the coven go to Proctor's Ledge and leave offerings where the gallows stood, but this anniversary is turning into a special remembrance because of the opening of Salem's new memorial."

"I read about it in the news," Matthew said thoughtfully.

"The site doesn't officially open until the nineteenth of July," I said, "but the authorities have invited the area covens to visit next week."

"Bridget deserves to have her family present," Matthew agreed. "I know you don't want me there for the coven meeting, but should I come for the public ceremony, and bring the children?"

I was torn. Part of my heart remained in New Haven, and I missed my own family despite all the excitement surrounding the Proctors.

"I don't want their first meeting with the family to take place at a time of sorrow and grief." This was entirely truthful, and my fingers relaxed slightly on the phone. "I know it's another change of plans, but I've been learning a bit more about the oracle cards, and Becca's ravens. Granny Dorcas didn't send the birds, by the way. She said that only the goddess could command them."

"I don't know if that makes it better or worse." Matthew had experience with the goddess's crafty agreements and clever invitations.

"At least we know the Proctors had nothing to do with it," I said, hoping this would please him.

"If you change your mind about Proctor's Ledge, let me know." Matthew was disappointed—even hurt. He was making every effort to put some slack in the silver chain that bound us, witch and vampire, but it was not easy for him.

How long would it be before Matthew's protective instincts made it impossible?

"It's just a little while longer," I promised. "For now, it's better if you stay away. The coven is struggling to accept a Bishop in their midst. I can't imagine what they'd do if a vampire came to town."

After we said good night and the line was disconnected, I held the phone a few moments longer, as though I could maintain my connection to Matthew.

"Nine more days," I whispered, putting the weight of all my magic into my words so that they had the power of a spell.

In my side pocket, the black bird oracle hopped and danced. I drew out the bag Goody Wu gave me. One of the cards was threatening to burst through the fabric.

The Crossroads.

It suggested I'd made another step down the Dark Path by agreeing to stay at Ravenswood.

Shadow crept from under the bed, dimming the light of the waxing moon and shrouding me in doubt.

Had I done the right thing? My finger hovered over the screen of the phone. Should I call Matthew back, and tell him about Meg Skelling?

"*Sufficient unto the day is the evil thereof,*" I said, uttering the traditional prayer to protect a witch's sleep before turning out the light.

Chapter 9

The days between Ann's appearance at Ravenswood and the coven meeting were fraught and difficult, not just for me but for Gwyneth, too.

With more than one hundred witches on the Ipswich coven membership scroll, Gwyneth doubted they would all show up. Julie, however, predicted that the spectacle of a Proctor charged with misconduct would draw witches like honey did flies.

"You're underestimating the level of curiosity that Diana's sparked in Ipswich, too," Julie warned, "not to mention the resentment some families have about the Proctors' influence over local affairs."

Despite Julie's ominous forecast, Gwyneth strictly limited the number of chairs she would allow to be hauled over to Ravenswood.

"Seventy-eight is my absolute limit, Julie. Six times the witches normally present at a monthly coven meeting seems plenty," Aunt Gwyneth said sharply, her nerves frazzled and temper short with all the arrangements.

A gleaming black van decorated with a goggle-eyed clam wearing a pointy hat trundled down the hill shortly thereafter. IPSWITCH SEAFOOD and the legend SO FRESH IT'S MAGIC! were painted on the side in white and gold. Two women roughly my age climbed out of the vehicle, one fair with curly brown locks caught up in a loose knot and the other ginger-haired and freckled with a muscular physique.

"You must be Diana. I'm Tracy Eastey," said the witch with the updo. "Julie's niece."

Tracy's eyes were not the pale sea-glass green or blue I'd grown used to seeing in Ipswich witches. Instead, they were a luminous brown, like a decanter of sherry sitting on a windowsill in the sunshine, sparkling with life and light. Her coloring suggested Irish ancestry, but those other-worldly eyes told me there was plenty of Proctor blood in her, too.

"I'm Grace." The other witch's pale green eyes rimmed with blue crinkled at the corners, the fine lines spreading across her cheeks to tell the story of a lifetime spent on the water. "I come from the Mather branch of the Proctor family tree."

"There you are!" Julie bustled forward, the orange and white stripes on her shorts flashing in the sun. "Did you bring the chairs?"

"Did you ask us to bring the chairs? Then we brought the chairs." Tracy reached into the back of the van and pulled out a plate of cupcakes, handing them to Julie. "Here. Take these."

"Tracy's famous for her baking—and her lobster rolls." Grace swung open the door on her side of the van and removed a tub full of ice nestled with an assortment of clams and oysters. The combined weight of the ice and the shellfish must have been considerable, but Grace carried it easily, her arms taut and athletic. I spotted *Mount Holyoke College Class of '86* printed in red on the front of her white T-shirt, along with a cartoon figure of a smiling pink-and-red Pegasus on the back.

Heaven help Becca if she wanted to attend my alma mater, Bates College, or one of her father's colleges or universities. A tingle in my pocket suggested that the oracle cards had wisdom to share on this subject, but this was one message from the goddess and her oracle I refused to pick up.

Tracy was busy at the rear of the van and emerged with folding chairs draped over her shoulders like an oxen's yoke.

"Let me help." I grabbed my own fair share of chairs and followed the procession to the barn.

"We brought clams, Aunt Gwynie!" Grace called as we drew near.

"There's dinner sorted," Aunt Gwyneth replied. She shielded her eyes to get a better look at the plate Julie carried. "Are those cupcakes vanilla?"

"I wouldn't dream of bringing you chocolate." Tracy gave Gwyneth a smooch on the cheek as she passed by. "I put a bit of blackberry puree in the icing."

"Yum." Gwyneth licked her lips in anticipation. "Tea's ready. Let's have a cupcake before you bring in the rest of the load."

It was not difficult to agree to Aunt Gwyneth's plan, given the mouthwatering pastries. We sat around the worktable, which today doubled as a lunchroom counter and a packaging station for dried herbs. Gwyneth gathered sticks of mullein to clear a space for Tracy and Grace. They were a gift for Katrina, who used them in her divination.

We tucked into the cupcakes and tea. Grace was right; Tracy's baking skills were very good indeed. The cupcakes were moist yet light, and not too sweet, allowing the vanilla and the blackberry to take center stage. Aunt Gwyneth, as always, concocted a divine pot of tea. It was dark and rich, with notes of lemon and mint.

"My own blend of Golden Tips from Hunan, lemon verbena from the garden, and fresh mint," Gwyneth told Tracy after she inquired about the ingredients. "It's as close as I'll ever get to iced tea."

"Not me. It's so damned hot I'll take all of the ice I can get." Julie conjured a heap of cubes into her mug and then poured some of the hot brew over them.

The four of us chatted companionably. I asked about Tracy's family, and Grace shared pictures of her two daughters. I passed my phone around so that they could see the twins with their father, their faces painted blue and white, at one of Yale's spring picnics. Once we were on a proper family footing, the conversation turned to more urgent matters.

"What are you going to do with the ghosts when the coven arrives?" Grace asked, taking another bite of her cupcake.

"Keep them locked up where they belong." Gwyneth's attitude toward the dearly departed was draconian. "We are not like the Redds or the Toothakers. Deceased members of the Proctor family do not roam about, willy-nilly, apparating and disapparating at whim, frightening children, then moping and moaning in cemeteries. It's a wasteful expenditure of energy, not to mention a source of friction between neighbors." Gwyneth turned to me. "We keep them in the attic of the Old Place, Diana, where they can rest and recharge in peace."

This must be why the ghosts I'd seen at Ravenswood were so clear and colorful, unlike the blurry smudges of my ancestors in the Bishop House, which were barely discernible.

"They're stuffed into trunks!" Julie didn't seem to approve of incarcerating the dead any more than I did. "I think that's against the Geneva Conventions, Gwynie."

"It's *Proctor* conventions that hold sway at Ravenswood." Gwyneth looked at me sharply. "Let me guess. Sarah lets the Bishop ghosts do what they please, when they please."

"She definitely doesn't lock up relatives," I admitted. "Sarah's approach to ghost-keeping has always been free-range."

"My mother was the same, letting the ancestors form packs and scare the postman." Gwyneth sniffed, looking down her long, elegant nose. "The dead are always with us, but I find more than a dozen dearly departed a real nuisance."

I let my aunt and cousins discuss the vexed questions surrounding refreshments, assigned seats, and how Gwyneth could get the membership to leave promptly at the end of the meeting. Their words passed in one ear and out the other. My thoughts were elsewhere: on my next meeting with Katrina at The Thirsty Goat. It was scheduled for Thursday, the day before the coven met.

I'd been working regularly with the black bird oracle cards, as Katrina had suggested, and had a stack of queries that I hoped she could answer. But I was reluctant to go into town and be on public display at the café for a second time, especially after the charges Meg had leveled against Gwyneth and me. Doing so sounded like a prescription for disaster, but Katrina had insisted that I could not cower all week at Ravenswood.

"Far better for Diana to meet you right under Meg's nose," Gwyneth agreed, when Katrina rang Ravenswood to arrange the details.

"Thursday morning should be safe," Katrina had replied. "The full moon energy will be near its peak, but I think Diana can manage it so long as we meet early in the day."

"I don't suppose we'll be joining the rest of the coven in the town cemetery after the meeting," Grace said, drawing my attention back to the present. "My stash of graveyard dust is running low, and I was counting on spending a few hours there on Friday night to replenish my stock."

"I hate coven politics," Julie said, reaching for another cupcake. She peeled off the pink, ruffled paper and took a bite. "They're so petty."

This was one of the many reasons I had never belonged to any official gathering of witches.

"We could always gather dust here in the wood," Tracy suggested. "Go old-school, and return to Proctor tradition."

"You mean go rogue," Julie said, visibly excited at the prospect. "That's an excellent idea. Can we, Gwynie?"

"A lot of witches were put to rest in the Ravens' Wood," Gwyneth cautioned. "And not just Proctors. Most of the old families have kin buried here. The town cemetery was off-limits to witches then."

"Thorndike Proctor opened the wood for burials, and promised to maintain it as sacred space," Julie explained. "That's why we never cut down trees, and only gather herbs and plants when the moon allows."

No wonder the wood was filled with power. It was storing not only Proctor magic, but the magic of other witches, too.

"We welcome the families on anniversary days," Gwyneth said. "July, August, and September are busy months at Ravenswood, filled with rituals and ceremony."

"Now June will be, too," Julie said, finishing off her cupcake and dusting the crumbs from her hands. "Right. Let's get the rest of those chairs in. Then I'll start the phone tree to ask for volunteers to bring treats. A coven meeting without cookies is downright unmagical."

Katrina's tinted lenses were lavender when we met at The Thirsty Goat, and she wore a high-necked sleeveless dress that extended to her knees and buttoned up the front. It was made of ivory silk, and embroidered with wisteria reminiscent of the vines that sprawled over the porch at

Ravenswood. Her black hair had a sheen of blue when she turned her head toward the light.

"Am I being paranoid about Meg?" I blurted as soon as we were seated with our tea.

"What do the cards say?" This was becoming Katrina's standard response.

"Not much," I said, shuffling the cards between my fingers as Katrina had taught me. "They're quite fulsome on the subject of how I can support Gwyneth and help her get ready for tomorrow, however."

I'd replenished the wood stack next to the stove when the Fire card appeared in my teacup at breakfast, and gone to town for more salt when the cards advised that Gwyneth had run out and still had windowsills she needed to protect with a sprinkle of the magical stuff.

"Perhaps the oracle doesn't know." Katrina turned over one of her cards and blinked. She never shared their interpretation with me, but this time the card was met with a sigh.

"What good is an oracle if it doesn't know the future?" I demanded, slamming my cards on the table in utter frustration.

"Manhandling it isn't going to help," Katrina said, gathering her own cards together. "A coven meeting is a place where wits are sharp and unexpected questions are posed. I'm not surprised the oracle can't divine what's to come, or what the final decision will be."

"What does Meg have against me?" I felt victimized.

"Try the cards again," Katrina instructed. "Pick them up—gently—and ask them—respectfully—if they have any insights into what lies in *your* path. Leave Meg and the coven out of it, and give the oracle some room to maneuver."

I did as Katrina suggested, moving gently and respectfully, spending a few moments with the cards cradled in my hands to atone for my rough treatment. When my fingers began their shuffling movement, the cards held less tension. They were still shy, but over the course of the next few minutes they loosened up to such an extent that I thought they might be willing to converse with me. I closed my eyes and whispered the question exactly as Katrina had formulated it.

"Do you have any insights into what lies in my path?"

As was usually the case in matters pertaining to divination and prophecy, Katrina's advice had been excellent. The cards moved of their own accord and I let them fall on the table. They continued to shift and rearrange themselves, then pause, only to shift and shuffle some more.

When they stopped moving, the oracle had arranged six cards before me. Four of them were stacked vertically in a straight line. Slightly beneath and to either side of the top card were two more cards. The overall effect was that of an arrow flying toward its target.

"I've never seen this spread before," I said. "Do you know what it means?"

Katrina shook her head. "You'll have to listen to your intuition."

Thanks to the time Aunt Gwyneth and Granny Dorcas had spent poring over the deck with me, I was more experienced with the black bird oracle and the interpretation of its messages. I knew that it was best to start with the closest card, which undoubtedly represented the querent— me—now, and then move up through the spread.

Darkness.

"My fears are getting the better of me," I said glumly. The next card was no better. "Blood." Sacrifice, longing, and revenge were some of the meanings associated with the card.

"The Parliament of Owls must signify the coven," Katrina said, pointing to the next card, "although in what context, I'm not sure."

The card directly above it was The Crossroads. To the left was The Box—a rendition of Pandora's casket releasing chaos into the world. On the right was The Unicorn, serenely sitting in a garden.

"Chaos or calm." I didn't need an oracle to tell me those were the two possible outcomes of Friday's gathering.

"Let Gwyneth and Dorcas help you explore the cards' message more fully." Katrina put her own deck away. "And get some rest. Tomorrow will be a long day."

* * *

On the eve of Bridget Bishop's hanging, I followed Granny Dorcas toward the barn.

Remember what I told you, daughter. Fear is natural but you must not let them see it. She elbowed her way through the throng of waiting witches, casting a baleful stare over the assembly.

Hold yourself proudly, Granny Dorcas continued, still barking out instructions. *You're a Proctor, and my kin. Never let these witches forget it. Make no apologies for who and what you are.*

Gwyneth waited at the threshold with Betty Prince, the coven elder I'd met on my first day at The Thirsty Goat. Tonight she was sporting neon-pink clamdiggers embroidered with starfish, and had topped them off with a matching twinset and pearls. Her white hair had been freshly rinsed and set, resulting in a cloud of violet. She held a clipboard covered with tiger stickers, in honor of the local high school mascot.

"Let's check you in." Betty's eyes traveled down the length of the paper attached to her battered clipboard. "Gwyneth Proctor, present. Diana Bishop—"

"Guilty." I covered my mouth in horror at the unexpected toad that had leaped from my tongue.

Betty gave me a reproving glance. "Everyone's present and accounted for. Time to go in and get settled."

She conjured a large bell. It hung in the air, its rope pooling on the ground at her feet. Betty tugged on the rope, and the bell tolled a mournful dirge.

Cousin Julie appeared with a Boston Red Sox megaphone. She lifted it to her lips.

"This meeting is called to order!" she hollered over the clanging of the bell.

Inside, the mood was somber, and low waves of conversation crested and fell. Candles brightened the space, casting dark shadows in the corners where the light did not reach. The barn doors remained open to the quiet music of the owls and herons, the soft lapping of the tide against the edges of the marsh, and the glow of the full moon. Two rings of chairs occupied the center of the barn. The inner circle was reserved for coven officers. The large outer circle was for the rest of the coven membership. As Julie had predicted, it was standing room only.

I spotted some familiar faces in the crowd: Ann Downing, Hitty Braybrooke, my cousins Tracy and Grace, and of course Meg Skelling. The rest of the assembly represented a cross section of the town's population—young and old, male and female (though the latter far outnumbered the former), of European, Latin American, African, and Asian descent. One elderly wizard slept in his wheelchair. Had I not known better, I would have thought elderly members of the Junior League, Goths and Bohemians in their forties and fifties, young mothers, and millennials with nose rings and cellphones had mistakenly wandered into the same meeting.

The coven officers wore name badges like those I'd seen at The Thirsty Goat. The assignments ranged from the membership committee (Meg) to the education committee (Gwyneth), the divination and prophecy committee (Katrina) to the young witches activity committee. The badges also included the coven parliamentarian (Hitty), spellmaster, historian, secretary (Betty), mistress of coven ceremonies, and treasurer. As for the names on the badges, they represented a who's who of the Salem trials: Proctor, Jackson, Perkins, Varnum, Green, Skelling, Braybrooke, Wildes, Prince, and Eastey.

There were few empty seats, and I was about to perch on the woodpile with Granny Dorcas when Gwyneth hooked me by the elbow.

"Come, Diana," she said. "They've put you next to me."

We processed to our places, neither of us meeting the curious glances of those around us. Once we were seated, Gwyneth looked into the barn's rafters. Her mouth tightened into a line of displeasure, and I followed her gaze to where a row of ghosts sat on the central crossbeam, looking down over the proceedings. Their clothing ranged from the seventeenth century to the twentieth. One dashing young woman with bobbed hair and rouged knees blew us a kiss.

"My mother," Gwyneth whispered, grim. "Not only did she find a way to escape from the attic, she's released all the family's other black bird oracles, too. Look at them, preening and posing."

I glanced over at Julie, who had a mischievous twinkle in her eye and an innocent expression plastered over her face. Gwyneth pursed her lips, her cheeks pink with suppressed irritation.

"I call this special meeting to order," Ann proclaimed, rising to her feet. "Before turning to our first item of business, we will, as is our custom, mark the beginning of the hanging times by remembering our sister, Bridget Bishop, whose descendant is with us tonight."

Ann waited while the muttering and sharp looks of the coven members subsided.

"On the eve of the ninth of June, three hundred and twenty-five years ago, Goody Bishop awaited her execution. She was not the first person accused of witchcraft in this part of Massachusetts, nor was she the last," Ann continued. "Her death fractured the wider community and caused division and dissension among witches as false allegations brought hundreds of innocents into the snare of the courts."

Meg's glance touched me with a dark, cold pressure, then moved away.

"Let us join together in a moment of silence to reflect upon the past, when Darkness took root in this community and we lost our way," Ann concluded.

The birds stopped chirping, the waves quieted, and the moon hung heavy in the sky.

"We humbly entreat the goddess to keep us united and dedicated to her path in the years to come," Ann said, bringing the silence to an end. "We will follow our customary calendar of observances at the other summer gatherings, reading aloud the names of all those accused, imprisoned, dead, and executed. This sacred season of remembrance will culminate with our Mabon ritual marking the end of the hanging times."

The witches murmured spells to remind them to reserve the dates.

"In the interest of time, I've requested that the committee reports be filed with the secretary, who will distribute them by email," Ann said, nodding at Betty. "If there are no objections, I turn the meeting over to Goody Eastey."

Julie rose, casting an apologetic glance toward Ann.

"Sorry," Julie mumbled. "I forgot to make copies of Meg's charges."

A few groans erupted. Meg straightened in her chair, visibly agitated by this slip.

"Another example of the Proctor conspiracy," someone in the barn hissed.

"Most of you know what the charges are already, so I'm not sure why we need to kill more trees," Julie said. "Don't worry. I remembered Mama's document manifestation spell. She used it whenever she forgot to sign our permission slips and report cards."

"It's a good piece of magic," Betty Prince commented, hoping to assuage the disenchanted. "Julie shared it with me when I misplaced my passport."

Other testimonies concerning the value of the spell were offered, proving that her lapse had been forgiven, perhaps even forgotten. Only Meg continued to fume.

"You and Harold had a wonderful cruise, as I remember," Julie said with a grateful smile at Betty. Without preamble, she directed her wand into the air and swirled it around. A flurry of white paper rained on the coven, the pages sailing into the laps of the gathered witches.

Except for me. I was not a member of the coven, and, though I stood accused with Gwyneth, I had not been included in this special delivery.

"Excuse me, Julie." Gwyneth raised her hand. "Diana doesn't seem to have received a copy. I've never studied the law, but this seems out of order."

Debate erupted on the floor and Julie, instead of being flustered by it, looked pleased.

"I was told only coven members should be privy to the charges," Julie said, voice sweet and expression wicked.

"Order!" Hitty Braybrooke stamped her high-heeled foot several times as if it were a gavel. She had come to the meeting straight from work in a gray suit and pink blouse. "The lady from Ravenswood was not recognized by the mistress of ceremonies before she spoke."

"Oh, for Pete's sake, Hitty," Julie said, hands on hips. "Lighten up. You're not presiding over the Massachusetts General Court tonight."

"If I may interject," said the coven historian, James Perkins, whose button-down collar and khaki trousers suggested he may be an academic, "we haven't followed Robert's Rules of Order since 1972. We voted them down as a patriarchal form of governance that privileges elite, white men and puts marginal voices at a disadvantage."

There were murmurs of agreement.

The Ipswich coven gathering was turning into a nightmare version of the monthly PTA meetings held at the twins' progressive school, complete with officiousness masked in deference, and unresolved resentments cloaked in virtue.

Agitated chatter broke out again following James's remarks, and Julie lifted her megaphone in warning. The rumbling quieted.

"Diana Bishop is not a member of the coven," Meg said, piling fuel on the fire.

"I move that an exception be made in this case," said a quavering voice. I traced it to the old man in the wheelchair.

"Seconded," said a tall male witch standing by the shelves, his tattooed arms crossed over his Harvard T-shirt. "If this coven follows the U.S. Constitution in its procedures, Diana has a Sixth Amendment right to know the charges."

"Thank you, Junior. All in favor?" Julie asked.

There were a handful of holdouts, but most of the room agreed, albeit grudgingly.

"The ayes have it," Betty noted for posterity.

A single piece of paper slowly fluttered down into my lap.

"I guess it's time for Meg to make her formal declaration." Julie was determined to keep the proceedings casual and low-key, despite Hitty's emphatic stamping. "Take it away, Meg."

Meg took her time rising to her feet and moving to the center of the inner circle. She was relishing her moment in the spotlight. My pocket buzzed and swelled as the black bird oracle cards took note of the proceedings. I patted them through the fabric, reassuring them that I had this covered.

"I charge Gwyneth Proctor with abusing her position as headmistress of this coven, and ignoring our established procedure regarding witches who seek the Dark Path." Meg took a brief pause for dramatic effect. "Furthermore, I charge her with divulging Ipswich coven knowledge to Diana Bishop, who is not a member of this assembly."

Meg deliberately pointed her finger at me. There were gasps from every direction. To be singled out like this by a witch was not something to be taken lightly, for a pointing index finger showed the direction in which your magic would be unleashed. All witches were schooled from an early age not to point a finger unless they intended to use it.

"Since this stranger arrived in Ipswich, she has been seeking advice and expertise without the consent of the coven leadership. Gwyneth Proctor has aided and abetted her, putting her own interests and those of her family above the community." Meg's finger was still extended, quivering with rage. "Goody Proctor has knowingly led Diana Bishop down the Dark Path—Bridget Bishop's kin, whose irresponsible actions, and their deadly consequences, we remember this night. Goody Proctor has done so with unreasonable haste and a profound lack of judgment, jeopardizing the lives of herself and others."

Darkness entered the barn, feeding on old terrors and jealousies, snaking through the room, charging the atmosphere with vitriol.

"A *Bishop* has returned to Ipswich." Meg's glance swept over the coven, lingering on those who were nodding in agreement with her. "Do you feel it? Gwyneth Proctor has allowed Darkness into Ravenswood and polluted our community."

Gwyneth's spine stiffened, but she remained silent.

"I humbly submit these charges to the coven for full consideration, Goody Eastey," Meg said, returning to her seat. "Whether I am in the right or in error will be the coven's decision, and I will abide by it. So must it be."

"So must it be," the coven intoned.

"Well. My goodness. That was quite an opening act." Julie's sharp gaze flickered to me and Gwyneth before she faced the coven. "Anyone else want to speak?"

Most hands went up.

"Oh-kay." Julie pinched the bridge of her nose and regrouped. "Betty, can you keep a list? And please observe the three-minute rule with respect to comments or we'll be here until Midsummer. The bell will ring in warning if you go over your limit."

"Goody Varnum is first, then Goody Jackson." Betty's formal address took the gathering a step further back in time to Salem and 1692. "Then Goody Wildes."

One after the other, the witches dredged up old grievances against the Proctors in general, and Gwyneth in particular. Gwyneth had refused to educate her niece, Hannah Varnum stated, simply because she resided in New Hampshire. Why had she made an exception for Diana Bishop? For Phoebe Wildes, the issue was the speed of Gwyneth's lessons, and the young mother of two dredged up her own slow progress with higher magic, which was, she claimed, a direct result of Gwyneth's unfair judgment of her skill. Would her children enjoy the same fate at Goody Proctor's hands? Grudge by grudge, slight by slight, Gwyneth's reputation was brought into question.

And the disgruntled accusations didn't stop with Gwyneth; they extended to past generations of Proctors as well. Tales of Granny Alice's tyrannical methods of instruction and strict observance of tradition were held up as beacons of light, while legends about Gwyneth's mother's lax requirements, and how they had contributed to Naomi's downfall, bubbled to the surface.

Objection! Granny Dorcas cried to no avail after each accusation. *Objection!*

Gwyneth and I were already guilty in the eyes of the coven. Only a few members approached the matter impartially: Katrina, James Perkins, and Betty Prince. Their probing questions were concerning, however apologetically they were delivered.

Katrina asked why Gwyneth felt compelled to deviate from her own traditions.

Was Gwyneth under some kind of compulsion spell? Betty Prince wondered.

Had I threatened her? James demanded of my aunt.

Gwyneth sat silently as her friends and colleagues vented their fears of the future and their resentments from the past. After every member of the coven who wanted to had spoken, Gwyneth raised her hand.

"Might I respond?" my aunt asked, her tone mild.

"Yes," Julie said with a sigh of relief. "I recognize Goody Proctor."

In a steely but quiet voice, Gwyneth spoke to the accusations leveled against her.

"My lessons with Diana did not fall under my role as coven headmistress of education. It is my right, as one of the senior members of the Proctor family, to guide successive generations in their study of higher magic as I see fit, without interference, according to the traditions of the Ipswich coven," Gwyneth said. "Diana's lessons took place on Proctor land, as is customary whenever a family undertakes its own program of instruction, to limit any damage to the community."

Several witches shifted in their seats, uncomfortable. James Perkins nodded vigorously.

"True," he said. "That's true."

"My niece, Diana, has just as much Proctor blood in her veins as she does Bishop blood," Gwyneth said. "She is, without question, a member of the Proctor family. Putnam Mather was aware of what was happening at Ravenswood, and fully approved of it."

All eyes turned to the aged man in the wheelchair. He was looking more sprightly than he had earlier.

"So I did, Gwynie," Putnam said. "This is a Proctor family matter. I still don't know why we're meeting tonight. I'd rather be in bed."

Grace, who was sitting beside Putnam, beamed at him and patted his hand.

"So, too, did the Easteys," Gwyneth said, directing her attention across the room where a slightly older version of Julie sat, Tracy at her side.

"Furthermore, I notified our chair of divination and prophecy that Diana had been chosen by the black bird oracle, as our bylaws require."

The assembly gasped, and whispers broke out once more.

"Goody Wu met with my niece at the café, as Ann and Meg well know, and approved Diana's use of the cards," Gwyneth continued. "My niece's training in higher magic, and my supervision of it, will continue unless and until her path crosses the Ravenswood boundary."

Gwyneth had hoisted the Ipswich coven by their own petard, using their customs to mount an inspiring defense.

Concerned by the shifting mood in the barn, Meg changed tack.

"Diana Bishop is married to a vampire!" Meg cried. "Do we really want our secrets known to the notorious de Clermont family? How can we allow Matthew Clairmont to understand the subtleties of higher magic, given what Ysabeau de Clermont did to our people?"

I shut my eyes and swore silently. The Ipswich witches knew my mother-in-law's checkered past.

"Everyone in this room has done something that they're ashamed of," I interrupted, appealing directly to James for support. "History is full of misdeeds and atonements, isn't it? Ysabeau would be the first to admit that her prejudices and fears got the better of her during her darkest days."

Howls of protest accused me of being complicit in the actions Ysabeau had taken centuries ago, simply by extending an olive branch of compassion to my mother-in-law.

"Order! Order!" Hitty Braybrooke tried to bring the assembly under her control, banging her foot against the floor.

The tide of opinion in the barn had changed again—and not in Gwyneth's favor.

"And what about Diana Bishop's children? They are unnatural, of mixed witch and vampire blood." Meg glowed in triumph. "We cannot let that Bishop woman pass an understanding of higher magic to them, either."

"No matter how vivid Meg's fantasies, or this gathering's eventual determination, I will continue to share Proctor knowledge and traditions within the family." Gwyneth's voice rang through the barn. "The coven can strip me of my position, expel me, and report me to the Congregation, but I will not be bullied into submission."

"You have betrayed this coven and everything we stand for, Gwyneth," Meg spat. "You have given Darkness shelter. No good will come of it."

I'd had enough. Without asking for recognition from Julie, and though I was a guest and therefore had no right to speak, I faced Meg squarely.

"You have an issue with me, Meg?" I demanded. "Why don't you leave the protection of the circle and step outside. I'm sure we can settle this. Just the two of us."

Meg's satisfied smile told me that she'd been waiting for just such an outburst. I'd fallen into her trap.

"Very well," Meg replied. "I challenge Diana Bishop to prove herself fit for the study of higher magic at the Crossroads."

The coven's answering silence was more unnerving than all the previous hullabaloo.

"A challenge has been issued. Do you accept it, Diana?" Ann asked.

The Crossroads card shimmered in my memory. My pocket warmed with satisfaction. Meg was not the only one whose expectations had been met this evening. The black bird oracle had been proven right, too.

"Yes." I had no idea what this meant, or why Gwyneth looked so alarmed at the prospect, but, like my aunt, I would not back down from Meg Skelling.

"Is Diana ready for such a challenge?" Goody Wu asked Gwyneth, an edge of concern sharpening her voice.

"More than ready," Gwyneth confirmed.

"So must it be," Ann Downing said with a sigh.

"So must it be," the coven murmured in unison.

"So must it be," I said, adding my voice to the rest.

Chapter 10

"I don't think there's time for me to embark on your higher magic course, Gwyneth." I sat by the fire in the Old Place, gripping a cup of tea and reeling from the meeting and its outcome. "They've given me just a week to prepare for the Crossroads. According to your syllabus, we will still be covering the basics of ritual and preparing ceremonial spaces and magical inks."

"Oh, that's just the intro," Julie said, consulting the six-page document. "We can skip that, along with prognostication, oracles, and omens, and even basic spellwork. That puts us at unit three: 'Protection Spells and Basic Wards.'"

"That would be useful for a normal witch," I said, curbing my panic, "but I'm a weaver. I can't use other witches' spells for more than inspiration. I have to make my own. The curriculum allots three weeks for witches to perfect the use of old spells. I've got one."

What awaited me if I advanced to the status of initiate after the Crossroads was even more daunting—and alluring. A week keeping Light and Dark in balance, followed by classes on the use of wands, the magic of locks and keys, how to make poisons (and their antidotes), living with the dead, and even a unit on mnemonics and mind reading.

I'd borne silent witness to how the Proctors practiced the higher branch of the craft. It was not done with complicated ceremonies or a daily hour of spell-casting. Instead, they wove magic into daily life. When Gwyneth adjusted the windows to let in the breeze, she sprinkled salt on the windowsills. When she crossed a threshold, her lips moved in silent blessing. Each morning, when she made her first cup of tea, my aunt tucked a sprig of rosemary into the frames of the ancestral portraits. Gwyneth collected feathers wherever she went, arranging them in the already overstuffed jars found in every room of the Old Place and Orchard Farm. I, too, had been collecting the feathers that seemed always to be in my path. They'd appeared at The Thirsty Goat, on my regular walks along the shore, and even inside the farmhouse on occasion.

Then there were the oracle cards, the sigils, and the ghosts—all signs that witchcraft was constantly afoot at Ravenswood. Gwyneth told time by the rising and setting of the moon, not the sun, her hours tied to the goddess's rhythms. Her most active periods sometimes began in the morning, at other times in the afternoon. During my first few days at Ravenswood, I'd wake after midnight and she would be out, walking the meadow, staring out to sea.

Higher magic wasn't a bag of tricks the Proctors pulled out at Halloween. It was their way of life.

Could I sustain such a magical routine, attuned to forces that didn't care about university calendars or deadlines set by humans? And what if Matthew issued an ultimatum and demanded that I not continue to study higher magic, like the one my father had given to my mother?

"I can't just dive into higher magic without telling Matthew what's happened at Ravenswood," I said. "I've been keeping things from him for weeks. Small things. But this—" I shook my head. I fell silent, brooding over my options.

Gwyneth waited with me while I considered my dilemma. Finally, she weighed in on the matter.

"Call Matthew and invite him and the children to Ravenswood," Gwyneth urged. "Trust him, Diana. Put it all in the goddess's hands so that your path can become clear."

I remained unconvinced. I needed to talk to someone, but I couldn't call Sarah for advice. She had just returned to Madison after spending time with Agatha in Melbourne. So far as Sarah knew, we were settling into the Old Lodge. Given the questions I had for her, and the anger I felt after Gwyneth's revelations, now was not the time to update her.

I called Ysabeau instead. It was early in the morning in France, but my mother-in-law, like most vampires, seldom slept.

"What are your witches up to now?" Ysabeau demanded.

I might not have told Sarah about Becca's ravens and our change of summer plans, but Matthew had kept his mother apprised. Ysabeau would never have forgiven us if we failed to disclose such important news. She was a protective grandmother, and deeply involved in the children's lives.

"I'm in over my head." There was no point in prevarication or social niceties. "The Ipswich coven met today. I've been challenged by another witch, and I either have to back down and leave Ravenswood or stay here and formally commit myself to the study of higher magic."

"Ah." Ysabeau was silent for a few moments. "And Matthew doesn't know."

"Yes. No. It's complicated." I was reluctant to bring the extent of my half-truths to light, but Ysabeau needed to understand my conundrum if she was going to give me advice. "Matthew thinks I stayed here for the anniversary of Bridget Bishop's hanging. That's true—the coven will go to Gallows Hill tomorrow to mark her death. But one of the witches charged my aunt Gwyneth with flouting coven rules. She said I should have been presented to the coven before launching on a course of magical study. I haven't even mastered the basic theory of higher magic yet, but a special meeting was called, and I couldn't abandon my aunt to face their tribunal alone."

"You have attracted the attention of a powerful enemy." Ysabeau sounded delighted at the prospect. "What is this creature's name?"

"Meg Skelling," I replied. "Her animosity toward me was immediate."

"You already stood up to the witch." Ysabeau made a contemptuous sound. "Good. Being *une carpette* is not in your nature, Diana. If it were, you could not be with Matthew. Now this Skelling creature knows you are a worthy adversary."

"Meg is powerful, Ysabeau," I confessed, not feeling worthy at all. "And influential."

"As powerful as you?" Ysabeau asked. "No modesty, Diana. When faced with such an opponent, it is important you are honest about your strengths as well as your weaknesses."

This was the advice of a battle-tested warrior who had survived challenges far more daunting than the one that was facing me.

"I'm not sure," I confessed. "But Meg has walked the Dark Path herself, and has risen through a series of tests to become an adept in higher magic. Her practice of it has the blessing of the Congregation. I'm just a novice."

"Then you have no choice but to educate yourself until you are her equal in skill," Ysabeau replied. "Your aunt is helping you on this Dark Path?"

"My great-aunt," I replied. "Her brother, Taliesin Proctor, was my grandfather."

The line went silent and I was afraid we'd been disconnected.

"Ysabeau?"

"I am here."

It was the same response that Matthew had given me when I first mentioned my grandfather's name. My suspicion that my grandfather's path had crossed the de Clermonts' grew.

When she was ready, Ysabeau broke the silence.

"Lieutenant Taliesin Proctor notified me that Philippe had fallen into the hands of the Nazis," Ysabeau said, her voice quiet. "The Americans' unit was operating in the mountains of the Gothic Line near San Marino. Neither he nor I knew that Philippe had put himself in harm's way to save Janet."

Janet was a Bright Born descendant of Matthew, his great-granddaughter through Benjamin Fuchs. She, too, was part witch and part vampire—though not an equal blend like the twins. The Nazis had rounded her up in Romania and taken her into the concentration camps.

Philippe had managed to liberate Janet, along with several others from Ravensbrück, before he was captured by the Nazis. Given what I knew about Ysabeau's state of mind while Philippe was in enemy hands, it was a miracle that my grandfather had survived to become the editor of *The Ipswich Chronicle*.

"He brought a British soldier with him to break the news of Philippe's capture, a Captain Thomas Lloyd. I knew immediately they were both witches," Ysabeau continued. "What I did not know was that they were agents for the OSS and the SOE as well. They warned me that Philippe may not survive Nazi captivity, vampire or not."

My mind was bursting with questions.

"Lieutenant Proctor offered to help me locate Philippe and remove him from behind enemy lines. But I refused." Ysabeau's tone lowered with regret. "He was a witch and a member of the Congregation. How could I trust him when your kind had played a role in Philippe's capture?"

I scrambled to put these new pieces of information about my family into the puzzle of my life.

"I always wonder, when I am grieving and cannot find peace, if Lieutenant Proctor could have succeeded where Matthew and Baldwin failed." Ysabeau's voice sounded far away, carried on the tenuous strands of memory. "We shall never know, but I have struggled with my decision, especially after you and Matthew were mated, and the children were born."

The enormity of what might have been had Ysabeau agreed to Grandpa Tally's offer threatened to take me under. Philippe might be alive still, had Ysabeau only been able to trust the sincere offer of help from a witch.

"You must stay where you are, Diana. At Ravenswood." Ysabeau's tone returned to its usual warm steeliness. "Be firm with Matthew when you tell him. Whether or not to study higher magic is *your* choice. He can be part of it or not. That is his choice."

The vampire's advice was much the same as what Gwyneth had offered me during my time at Ravenswood.

"And the children?" I demanded. "What happens to them if Matthew can't accept higher magic into our lives?" My father's ultimatum to my mother was uppermost in my mind.

Ysabeau made a dismissive sound. "Matthew could never leave you for long, Diana. His mating instinct is too strong. As for Rebecca and Philip, Matthew won't deprive them of their mother's presence. Philippe would have done so without a second thought. Matthew? *Non.*"

But I was still concerned. Matthew would fight me at every step if he believed the twins were at risk.

"Matthew must have told you about Becca and the ravens," I said. "My choice will affect her future as well as my own."

"He told me of the curved one's message, yes," Ysabeau said. "Poor Coronis, buried in your backyard under an elm tree. But that is a tale for another day."

This was Ysabeau's response whenever conversation drew too close to her ancient history. I made a mental note to look up the legend of Coronis for further insights into my mother-in-law's past.

"As for Matthew, he is a knight and must have a quest," Ysabeau continued.

"He's been researching Salem," I told her.

"That won't engage him for long," Ysabeau said. "You must find him a better one. If not, he will make you the sole object of his attention and become a liability. Your goddess will have no more patience with you than mine did when I dithered and wasted her time."

"Which goddess is that?" I was on thin ice already when it came to learning Ysabeau's secrets, but I took the risk of probing further.

"Nemesis."

I was mute at the honor of being entrusted with such an important piece of information.

"I thought you might have guessed," Ysabeau said, drawing the cloak of her mysterious origins around herself once more. "That, too, is a tale for another day. Do not worry about Matthew. Be attentive to Rebecca and Philip, for they will have to adjust to your new power and priorities. This is a lesson best learned sooner in this family, rather than later. Look after your own desires and needs. All de Clermont women must do so. If we left it to the men, we'd be ruined."

Ysabeau ended our call with the same abruptness with which it began. The sigils and hexafoils carved into the keeping room doorways shone softly in the dark. Someone had switched on all the magic in the Old Place.

The black bird oracle warmed in my pocket, reminding me that I had other sources of advice at my fingertips. I drew the cards out and shuffled them while I wondered how to tell Matthew my news.

The cards arranged themselves in the same pattern I'd seen earlier in my visit. This time, a shimmering thread of blue connected the outer cards, while an amber one did the same for the inner cards. Another shot of blue thread ran vertically through the first, third, fifth, seventh, and ninth cards. An amber thread provided a horizontal axis through cards two, four, six, eight, and nine.

Gwyneth stole into the keeping room, drawn by the oracle's magic.

"The cards are awake," she said, easing her old bones into one of the tall-backed chairs.

Gwyneth lowered her spectacles from the crown of her head so that they were perched on her nose. "The sunwise/widdershins spread offers two different readings, depending on whether you move clockwise— what we used to call sunwise—or widdershins, moving anticlockwise. And you can read them down the vertical axis, or across the horizontal axis, too."

The circles contained a crossroads, too. That couldn't be an accident, given its significance in a witch's progression to the level of adept.

"What does the center card mean?" It was The Unicorn nestled at the heart of a maze, a crescent moon overhead and sprigs of flowers all around.

"It's the signifier," Gwyneth said. "The Unicorn represents you, standing in the middle, bathed in Shadow."

I was neither a healer nor a virgin, two of the traditional attributes of a unicorn, but I supposed the black bird oracle knew what it was doing. I assigned a number to each card, starting at the top of the outer circle and proceeding through the inner circle, in the order in which they had arranged themselves. I reversed course and assigned them another number.

"This spread typically presents itself only when someone faces a difficult impasse," Gwyneth explained. "The card at twelve o'clock represents your dilemma, the card at six o'clock represents your first option to solve it, and the card at the top of the inner circle represents your second option. The bottom card in the inner circle indicates which option would serve the highest good."

"How do I choose whether to read the cards sunwise or widdershins?" I wondered.

"Usually, the cards indicate which way to proceed," Gwyneth said.

The air in the keeping room was heavy with anticipation. Nothing happened.

Gwyneth made us cups of tea, and we waited some more.

Finally, the top card—the one that stood for my dilemma—moved left and down.

"Widdershins it is," Gwyneth said.

I was not surprised. Ravenswood was a logic-free zone, and my experiences here had been anything but linear.

Now that I knew I was reading to the left, I could try to decipher the oracle's message.

My dilemma was represented by The Alchemical Wedding, depicted here as an interlocking serpent and firedrake, one with wings and feet, and one with smooth scales.

"The double ouroboros," Gwyneth said. "Isn't that a de Clermont family symbol?"

"The single ouroboros is used by the whole family. This double version is the official emblem of the Bishop-Clairmont scion—our family," I explained. Matthew's grandson, Jack, had designed it for us. Or so I had thought. How had it ended up on a seventeenth-century oracle card?

I moved to the next card in the spread—The Prince of Vultures. The bird sat on a dead tree branch overlooking a barren landscape, his neck ruffled with downy white feathers and his body black. The vulture held a piece of carrion, dripping with blood.

"The Prince of Vultures represents what's shedding Light, or casting Darkness, over your dilemma," Gwyneth reminded me.

"Picking over the dead?" I frowned. "Does that mean I should question the ghosts?"

"Perhaps. But vultures aren't only a symbol of death and cannibalizing ancient wisdom. They also symbolize silence," Gwyneth said.

There were all sorts of silences in my life—my own, Matthew's, my parents' secrets, Ysabeau's untold tales. They cast a deep shadow over everything that I did.

As I gazed over the cards, I recognized that The Box, The Key, and The Death's Head all symbolized great mysteries. The Box's image of chaos unleashed into the world was one option facing me. The Key, with its dual messages of opening doors and locking away secrets, and new possibilities as well as solutions to old problems, felt like a better second choice. But the oracles were suggesting that The Raven's Head would lead to the best possible outcome.

I sat back in my chair, reflecting on why the black bird oracle had chosen The Raven's Head rather than one of the other raven cards. The image was specific to alchemy, representing the *nigredo,* or blackening phase, of the philosopher's stone. Alchemists likened it to death, as the substances in the crucible were subjected to heat until they were reduced to ash, then put through other chemical processes to separate the charred substance from its inner spirit. The Raven's Head was thus a symbol of rebirth, too.

"The end of one stage of being, and the beginning of another," I mused. "Shedding what's not necessary to make room for something new."

I studied the cards that provided a horizontal axis for the spread: The Vulture Prince, The Heron Prince, The Owl Queen, Quintessence.

"Matthew, Dad, Mom, and the children," I said, running my finger across the cards to confirm that my reading was correct. They tingled and sparkled, the firelight catching the surface in glints of amber and blue.

And I was The Unicorn caught in the maze of their conflicting desires. My confusion stemmed from the concerns and priorities of those I loved. How could it be otherwise, when the Bishops and Proctors were tied up with the de Clermonts, my magical talents, and Matthew's blood rage?

Somehow, Matthew and I had to do a better job keeping these threads untangled. Secrets and lies clogged the back of my throat and made my eyes stream with frustration as I contemplated what a difference it would have made if the important people in my life had chosen a different path.

If only Dad hadn't made my mother give up higher magic.

If only my mother had stood up to him.

If only Philippe hadn't been such a good chess player.

If only Ysabeau could part with her prejudices and secrets.

If only I could center myself, quiet the constant chatter of guilt and responsibility, and choose—

"What do *you* want to do, Diana?" Gwyneth inquired. "Don't overthink it. Just say the first thing that comes to mind."

"I want to best Meg at the Crossroads," I said, surprised by my own vehemence. "And then I want to study higher magic until I am an adept, like my grandfather and mother before me."

The echo of my words filled the air. The hexafoils and sigils indicated that I had uttered a powerful truth, flickering in joyful pinpoints. The ancestral portraits reacted next, nodding their heads on stiff necks. The besom resting against the fireplace spun into the air and hung over the table, as if offering to take me on a wild ride through the stars.

For the first time since coming to Ravenswood, I felt connected to the true spirit of the place. It may be shadowed in power and heavy with legacy, but at its core was the pure exhilaration of being true to one's self.

Gwyneth reached over and clasped my hand in hers. "Never forget the feeling of being aligned with your purpose. It will steer you through Shadow and illuminate your path no matter where it leads."

Right now, it was telling me that my husband and children belonged on the Dark Path with me.

"I'm going to call Matthew."

Back at Orchard Farm, I put my treasured oracle cards to bed in the carved spellbox that Gwyneth had given me and settled into the armchair in my grandfather's office.

Then I dialed my husband's cellphone.

"You're up late," Matthew said. "The coven meeting must have lasted longer than you expected."

I swallowed around the lump in my throat, unable to say the words my heart yearned to speak.

"Diana?" Matthew's voice warmed with concern.

"Could you come to Ipswich?"

Matthew's breath left his body in a whoosh of relief. "Thank God. We'll be there in four hours."

The drive from New Haven to Ipswich took nearly three hours without traffic, griffins, dogs, and children who needed food, drink, and frequent bathroom breaks. There was no way he could make it here so soon. I glanced at the clock ticking on the desk. It was nearly three o'clock now. Matthew would reach the Boston area just as rush hour started.

"Take your time," I protested. "You've got to pack, and get the twins ready—"

"We've been ready for over a week," Matthew said gently. "The car has been packed since the last time you extended your stay."

"Oh." I reminded myself that vampires seldom slept, and therefore had extra time to prepare for every eventuality.

"You needed space and time," Matthew said. "I understood that, hard though it was difficult to stay away. Rebecca and Philip were less able to see things from your perspective."

The cultivation of empathy had been a focus of our child-rearing since the children could walk (and had teeth), but it was not easy for them to exercise this superpower when they were hurting or lonely.

"We've missed you." Matthew's voice dropped. "Me most of all."

"I've missed you, too," I said. "Ravenswood, Ipswich, Salem—I'm so overwhelmed I can't think straight."

"I was concerned about you facing the crowd at Gallows Hill by yourself," Matthew said. "Now I can be with you. Perhaps the children can stay behind with Gwyneth?"

"No." I was firm. "We can't keep the children from their lineage and its legacies."

Matthew was taken aback by my response. "Of course, *mon coeur.* Let's talk about it when I get there."

He was intending to pressure me into protecting the children.

"I won't change my mind, Matthew," I said, tears springing to my eyes. "I will *not* do to Becca and Pip what was done to me. No secrets. No lies. It all stops here and now." I wiped away a fat, falling tear. My witchwater was rising, as it always did when I experienced strong emotions.

"Besides, it would take more magic than I possess to prevent Gwyneth from attending such an important event," I continued. "The children will have to come with us. They must learn who they are and where they come from—from us, rather than discovering the truth on their own."

Darkness was drawing in and couldn't be kept at bay for much longer.

"Very well," Matthew said at last. "I would have preferred to wait, but in light of the Congregation's letter . . ." His voice trailed off into silence.

"It's time," I said, supplying the words Matthew couldn't yet say. "Don't worry. They'll be utterly surrounded by Proctors."

Matthew didn't know or trust the Proctors—yet. He was used to relying on members of his family for support, not mine. That would have to change, too.

"Drive safely," I said. "Please *try* to obey the speed limit."

"No promises," Matthew replied. "See you soon, my love."

I held the phone to my heart after Matthew hung up. Had I done the right thing? I wanted Matthew to be there when I met Meg's challenge and chose my path. When he found out all that was involved, would he refuse to walk it with me?

I was too exhausted to think about it now, and there were precious few hours of sleep left before Matthew and the twins arrived. I climbed the stairs, flipped on the light at the bedroom door, and sloughed off my shoes.

Nestled into the center of my pillow was a fluffy gray-and-white feather. The horizontal markings resembled those of a barn owl, but the colors were wrong. The size was wrong, too. This feather was far lengthier than would be found on most owls.

I checked the windows, thinking some strange bird must have flown in through a loose screen. They were all secure.

My flesh rippled at the uncanny sight of that single, long feather with its downy fluff and shadowed hue.

Perhaps the Owl Queen had paid a visit.

I plucked the feather from the pillow and brushed its softness against my cheek. Then I crept into bed and turned off the light, the Owl Queen's gift still in my hand.

PART TWO

Chapter 11

Next morning, the slam of car doors and chorus of ecstatic barks and chirrups indicated that Matthew and the children had arrived. I flew out of the Old Place to meet them.

"It tingles!" Becca was already out of her seat, hopping from one foot to the other. Tamsy hung from her arms, eyes wide with astonishment. "See if you can feel it, Pip."

Pip climbed down with more caution. He stood, unsteady, then bent over to put his hands on the earth.

Becca removed her lavender sneakers. "It's even better with bare feet!"

Matthew released the back hatch and Ardwinna tripped out on her long legs, graceful as a ballerina. She gave a good shake and slunk off to the scrubby brush on the side of the property, sniffing to see if there were any creatures hiding there that she might be able to chase.

Apollo stuck one paw out of the cargo area, then slowly released another. Gingerly, he dropped them to the ground so that he was half in the car and half out. Apollo's eyes widened in surprise. As a magical creature, he felt the same tingle Becca had. He slithered until he was fully out of the Range Rover, at which point his Labrador disguising spell evaporated, revealing the splendid griffin underneath. My poor weaving was no match for the power of Ravenswood.

Matthew lowered the hatch and it snicked closed. At the touch of his eyes, the world was set to rights. We met halfway between the car and the house, each of us eager for the reassurance of physical contact.

"I don't like being separated from you," I said as he folded me in his arms.

"I don't, either, *ma lionne*," Matthew replied.

We held each other, my heart beating in a rapid rhythm. Matthew's pulse was equally strong, though slower, and my own quieted to match, reveling in our instant connection.

"Mommy!" Pip thundered toward us, one shoe on and the other forgotten by the car. He barreled into me without regard for the fact that I had no vampire blood to withstand such an enthusiastic reunion.

"Steady, Philip." Matthew stayed Pip's momentum with a firm hand. "*Maman* cannot hug you with broken arms."

"Mom!" The fireball of energy that was Becca plowed into the family hug. "I love it here. The ground is welcoming me. Can we stay?"

"You are always welcome at Ravenswood, Rebecca." Gwyneth had followed me out of the house, leaving plenty of space for the family to come together before she joined in our reunion. "All of you are. I'm Aunt Gwyneth."

"Thank you for having us." Matthew gathered the children closer. It was an instinctive movement, and Gwyneth's eyes flickered as she registered it. "It's a pleasure to meet another member of Diana's family."

My husband's tone did not match his words. It was wary, like his embrace of the twins. Gwyneth pretended otherwise and approached Matthew with her hand extended.

"Matthew de Clermont." There would be no effusive hugging between my aunt and my husband. "My brother, Taliesin, met your mother during the war. She left an indelible impression on him."

So Gwyneth *had* known about Ysabeau's interactions with Grandpa Tally.

"Which war?" Matthew's expression was carefully neutral but his eyes narrowed.

"World War II," Gwyneth replied, without missing a beat. "He was in the Allied intelligence service."

"My mother never mentioned him." Matthew absorbed this piece of information with his usual impassivity, but I suspected that it was not the whole truth.

With a bright smile, Gwyneth turned to the children.

"You must be Philip." She gestured toward the griffin, who was preening in the strong sunlight. "Who's your friend?"

"Apollo," Pip said shyly. "And he's not my friend. He's my familiar."

"I thought as much. Do you see that big rock down by the marsh?" Gwyneth shielded her eyes and directed our attention to the enormous granite boulder that dominated the shore. "That's where your grandpa's heron familiar, Bennu, first appeared to help him learn his knots so he could make spells."

Pip's eyes were round. "Really?"

"Really." Aunt Gwyneth beamed at her great-great-nephew. "You look like your grandpa, you know. All those freckles."

Pip giggled.

"This is Tamsy." Becca, feeling left out, held her doll up for Gwyneth's inspection. The bone ring around the doll's neck shone in the light. "She wanted to come home, too."

Gwyneth drew a sharp breath. "I imagine she did. Where did Tamsy get her ring, Rebecca? It looks very old."

Rebecca shrugged. "It was in the dead raven's beak. I thought she'd want me to keep it."

A gentle buzzing in my pocket suggested that I could ask the oracle about Becca's decision.

Ardwinna was the last to welcome me. She had finished a thorough exploration of the hedge and was panting with all the excitement of new smells and sounds.

"Hello, sweetie." I ruffled her fur and scratched her ear until her back leg thumped in ecstasy. "I trust everything meets your expectations?"

The deerhound's vigorous tail-wagging confirmed it.

"Where are my manners!" Gwyneth clapped her hands. "You've had a long drive, and must be thirsty. Who wants lemonade? And I have blueberry muffins, too."

Becca nodded enthusiastically. Thankfully, her reliance on blood as a major source of nourishment had waned as she aged, and she was less finicky about what she consumed.

"Yes, please," Pip said.

Gwyneth beckoned the twins toward the house. "Let's get out of this bright sunshine and get everybody fed and watered."

Ardwinna, who knew what both *fed* and *watered* meant, loped past Gwyneth to the promised land of the kitchen, the twins behind her. Apollo glued himself to Gwyneth's side, chattering away and letting out the occasional chortle. He spread his wings wide, his feathers ruffling in the breeze.

"Yes, there are a great many birds around here." Gwyneth responded to the griffin as though she understood perfectly what he was saying. "I don't imagine you have anything to worry about, Apollo. You've got wings and a beak. Surely that's all you need to join in their flights?"

Matthew and I remained where we were. A shimmer of awakened power filled the space between us with golden motes that attracted the dragonflies and bees that hummed over the meadow.

My husband searched my face, caressing my cheek and drawing a wayward curl away from my eye. His expression of wonder reminded me of the first time we'd dared to touch each other in love, the power of our connection undeniable.

"You look like you're seeing me for the first time," I said, resting my cheek in his hand.

"Maybe I am," Matthew replied softly.

I kissed his palm and his eyes smoldered with unmet desire. Then he remembered where we were. The moment passed, but we would return to it later. He took my hand and we strolled toward the house.

"We've barely got time for an early lunch and a whirlwind tour of the Old Place and Orchard Farm before we have to go to Salem," I said, knowing how many questions Matthew must have about my experiences at Ravenswood. "Can our catch-up wait until after the ceremony?"

"It sounded urgent last night," Matthew said, frowning. He suspected something was not quite right.

"You'll see why when we get to Gallows Hill," I said. "Essex County is not like Madison County. The witches here are in a league of their own."

Matthew's frown deepened, but he let me lead him into the Old Place to join Gwyneth and the twins.

It was, I knew, only a temporary reprieve.

"Good Lord." Matthew surveyed the cars that were parked haphazardly near the intersection of Bridge Street and Boston Street, a short walk from Proctor's Ledge. It had been cordoned off so that the witches could find a place to park on a busy summer Saturday, when Salem was filled with tourists buying black hats and potion bottles filled with scented oil.

I sighed. "It's a lot. I know."

Matthew was familiar with the close relationship between witches and their modes of transport, be they car or broom. Vampires were the same, although they prioritized raw horsepower over everything else, including fuel economy and the environment. But nothing could prepare you for the sight of a hundred parked cars driven by witches from all over New England on the anniversary of Salem's hanging times.

Curious visitors took pictures of the vehicles to share with the folks back home. The snapshots would no doubt feature the SUV with a flying black witch attached to its roof rack. The bumper stickers Sarah was so fond of were all represented, as well as others that were unique to the area. WE ARE THE DAUGHTERS OF THE WITCHES YOU DIDN'T HANG! proclaimed one popular example. 1692—THEY MISSED ONE! read another.

And it wasn't only the bumpers that carried messages. An ancient VW Bug was covered in pagan symbols and crescent moons. Nineteen nooses decorated the side of a paneled van, one for every accused witch hanged over the summer of 1692. The owner had not forgotten poor Giles Corey, pressed to death under a rock-covered plank when he refused to confess. The rear of the vehicle was embellished with a painting of said wooden plank with Giles's name inscribed in red paint. The other side of the van was dedicated to the five unfortunate souls who had died in gaol: Ann Foster, Sarah Osborne, Lydia Dustin, Roger Toothaker, and Mercy

Good, who was born in prison and died before her mother was hanged. Four large tombstones and one tiny marker for Mercy were silent testaments to lives lived, and tragically lost, centuries ago.

I spotted Grace's Ipswitch Seafood truck pulling into the parking lot, with its enchanting bivalve.

"The family are here." I straightened Pip's collar, and made sure that Becca had shoes on. Since arriving, she had preferred to go barefoot. "Aunt Gwyneth will be with two of Mommy's cousins. We'll walk to the memorial together, and then put Aunt Gwyneth's flowers under Granny Bridget's stone."

"I miss Apollo," Pip said, clutching his long-eared rabbit, Cuthbert, for comfort.

We'd left the animals behind under Granny Dorcas's watchful eye. It was going to be difficult enough to manage the children while supporting Gwyneth. A griffin with a Houdini-like ability to shed his disguising spell and a scary-looking wolfhound with very sharp teeth would have made it impossible.

"Hi, Aunt Gwyneth!" Becca removed Tamsy from the seat belt she'd fashioned from Ardwinna's dog leash. Sadly, we had not succeeded in leaving the doll at Ravenswood. Our daughter trotted off, eager to meet more Proctor witches.

"Do you want to go with Becca?" I asked Pip as Matthew carefully removed a large bouquet picked that morning from the back of the Range Rover. Grace's van was filled with empty crab pots, so she'd carried Gwyneth and we'd brought the flowers.

"I'll stay with you." Pip was still adjusting to his new environment. His clinginess was a departure from his usual roll-with-the-punches approach to life.

Matthew eyed Pip with concern before his features smoothed out into something that was gentle yet determined.

"I could use your help with this vase, Philip, if you have a spare hand."

Now occupied with important business, Pip started to relax. By the time we'd met up with the Proctors, he was even giggling at some of the more overtly witchy car decorations.

"Have you seen that?" Grace asked, picking up on Pip's interest. She pointed to the city's water tower peeking over the summit of Gallows Hill. It was painted SALEM and ornamented with a black witch's silhouette flying skyward on a broom. She gave Matthew a nod and a smile.

"Ri-diculous," Pip said, giggling again. "Everybody knows witches don't need brooms to fly—just spells!"

"Exactly," Grace said. "Tell me about your rabbit."

Pip was quick to abandon Matthew now that he'd met a kindred spirit who appreciated his stuffed companion.

"Thanks for bringing the flowers, Matthew." Tracy took charge of Gwyneth's elbow, making sure our aunt didn't stumble over the broken pavement. "I'm Diana's cousin Tracy. Welcome to Salem."

"It makes quite an impression." His was a classically obscure vampire response.

"You ain't seen nothing yet!" Tracy said. She hoisted a bag filled with snacks and water bottles onto her shoulder. "I thought Julie and the kids might need munchies and some hydration to keep their blood sugar on an even keel."

"Good idea," I said. Matthew might have been reserving judgment, but I was thrilled to have Tracy's eyes on the twins.

We made our way to Pope Street. A knot of witches indicated we were close to the memorial.

Matthew's step faltered.

"From what I've been reading, Bridget Bishop was something of an outcast amongst the witches of the area," Matthew murmured. He checked on Becca, who was skipping next to Gwyneth, and Pip, who was enumerating the family's other pets to Grace. She didn't seem at all surprised that one was a griffin.

"Don't let the crowd fool you," I replied. "They're only here to get a sneak peek at the memorial. And you."

"They're here!" Julie burst out of the throng, her long arms extended, and her legs encased in a pair of hot-pink Bermuda shorts. She picked up one knee. "I'm not a flamingo! You can call me Aunt Julie like everybody else!"

Julie's joy was infectious. Even Matthew lifted a corner of his mouth as she swept toward us like an airplane in flight.

"My goodness, Philip, you're very tall for your age," Julie told Pip, winning his undying love. She cemented a place in his heart by shaking Cuthbert's ear. "Nice to meet you, too."

"And you must be Rebecca." Julie's hand touched Becca's raven-dark head and Matthew tensed beside me. He'd heard my tale of how Peter Knox had tried to invade my mind with just such a touch.

"Look what I found," Julie said, seeming to draw a small black feather from Becca's long tresses. "It told me to give it to you."

"You talk to feathers?" Becca's face lit up. "I do, too. And birds. And sometimes the trees, but they've been quiet lately."

"I talk to the wind, and cast spells for the fishermen to keep their boats from being damaged in storms," Julie replied.

"*Christ Jesu,*" Matthew said under his breath, "*Filia mea custodiat.*" Falling back on medieval Catholicism was a sure sign he was under stress.

"Neither of your children is in any danger," Gwyneth said softly. She was not Catholic, but she knew Latin. "Not with so many Proctors here."

"Who would like to meet Put-Put? He's even older than Aunt Gwyneth." Julie put her hands on her hips and waggled her eyebrows like Tinker Bell.

"I beg your pardon!" Gwyneth said tartly, but Julie's grin only got wider.

Julie led the twins off like the Pied Piper of Hamelin. There was something irresistible about her sparkling web of magic and possibility.

"Should you go with her?" Matthew asked, holding the heavy bouquet in one hand as though it, too, were a feather.

"We'll all go," Gwyneth said firmly. "Together. The moon is near nadir, and they'll be waiting for Diana."

I was surprised. "Who knew I was coming?"

"Everyone within reach of the coven phone tree, of course," Tracy replied. "Come on. Let's not keep the old biddies waiting."

We were yards away when the whispers began. Then came the curious looks. There were a few pointed fingers, too. Pip and Becca, oblivious to it all, had made friends with the elderly man from the coven meeting. Standing next to him was the young lawyer who'd invoked the United States Constitution in my defense.

Matthew took account of every narrowed eye and acid remark.

"That's her," one witch whispered to her neighbor. "And that's her vampire."

"Steady," I murmured. It was the advice Matthew always gave Pip when he forgot he was part vampire and acted on his instincts.

My husband, however, was all vampire. He remained calm, but the ticking of the dark vein in his temple and the set of his jaw revealed that he was on guard, and would move swiftly if anyone made an aggressive move.

"Are you all right, Gwyneth?" Matthew inquired, not taking his eyes off the crowd. His protectiveness had quickly enfolded my aunt.

"Perfectly fine, Matthew," Gwyneth said serenely. "You worry about the flowers. Everything else is under control."

We joined the rest of the family.

"Marvels and magic, you are tall, even for a vampire," said the old man in the wheelchair. "Come closer so I can get a good look at you."

"This is Put-Put," Pip told Matthew, shifting his weight between his feet. "He was a soldier, too, just like Grand-père. But he fought on a ship. So did Uncle Ike, but that was in a different war, and he was a merman."

"A Marine." Ike was the lawyer with the Harvard T-shirt. He had luminous jade-green eyes and high cheekbones, and was as tall and broad as Matthew. He extended a hand to my husband. "Isaac Mather. Put-Put's grandson. Most people call me Junior, but I prefer Ike."

Matthew's eyes widened slightly at the familiar last name, then returned to normal as he clasped Ike's hand. The two men exchanged a look like those I'd seen pass between Matthew and Marcus, and Gallowglass and Fernando. It was the look that soldiers gave one another, a recognition that they were brothers-in-arms no matter which side they fought on, who shared a common code of honor. My husband's shoulders relaxed a fraction more.

"Bend down, young man," Put-Put said testily. "My neck doesn't work that way anymore, and I still can't see you."

Matthew did so. "It's an honor to meet you, sir."

"Sir." Put-Put looked like he'd bitten into something sour. He pointed to his hat. It was embroidered with *USS Essex* and had a badge of three bars, three stars, and a white eagle. "I left the officer corps to Tally. Then my son went to Annapolis, and I was outranked. As for Junior, he enlisted in the Marines and broke his mother's heart."

Put-Put's look of pride indicated that he thought the world of Ike, no matter what he said with his dry New England wit.

"That's Captain Junior to you, Master Chief." Ike grinned down at his elder, who gave him a sharp salute. "Let me take those flowers, Matthew. What on earth were you thinking, Aunt Gwynie? This vase is so big you won't be able to read Bridget Bishop's name on the stone."

Gwyneth had been out in the early hours of the morning, selecting blossoms for the bouquet: white anemones with their dark centers, red roses, white snapdragons, purple irises, bright marigolds, sprigs of azalea from the shrub outside the farmhouse, and the velvety celadon leaves of silver ragwort.

Now that Matthew's hands were free, he was able to gather Becca in one arm and Pip in the other.

"And here is Ann with the rest of the coven. Perfect timing as ever!" Julie said brightly.

She maneuvered into place behind Matthew, linking arms with Tracy and Grace. The three witches were smiling, but steely resolve shone in their eyes. The Proctors were going to present a unified front at today's proceedings, no matter what bombs were lobbed our way.

I swung around to see who had joined Ann today. Meg Skelling's uncanny eyes met mine. She hissed.

Matthew's spine straightened, his teeth bared in a terrifying smile. Ike quickly passed the flowers to Grace.

"Hey, squirt," Ike said to Pip. "You want a lift so you can see better?"

Pip held his arms up. "Yes, please!"

In one smooth move, Ike lifted Pip onto his shoulders. It was an exhibition of controlled strength. Matthew drew Becca closer.

"Come here." Put-Put beckoned the members of the Ipswich coven over to where we stood. "We need to show the Salem witches that we outnumber them."

Ann hesitated.

"I warned you," Meg said, low and venomous as a snake. "I warned you that Diana Bishop would share our sacred knowledge with that creature." She forked her hands in Matthew's direction.

Without a moment's hesitation, I sent a black thread toward her. It wrapped around Meg's fingers. I tightened the lasso's hold and she gasped.

"Don't fork with me," I said, deadly serious. "Not today."

"Dang. You beat me to it, Diana," Julie said, her eyes glowing with amusement and power.

"If you can beat Julie to a spell, you really are a Proctor." Grace's eyes crinkled at the corners.

"What is she talking about?" Matthew murmured, his lips close to my ear. "What sacred knowledge?"

"Later," I replied under my breath. "Ann. You haven't met my husband, Matthew Clairmont. Ann is the high priestess of the Ipswich coven, Matthew."

Ann's name tag proclaimed her position, as did those worn by Hitty Braybrooke, Betty Prince, and Meg. Katrina was there, too, her tinted glasses a mournful gray in honor of the occasion, and her parasol black.

The screech of a poorly controlled microphone split the air, capturing everyone's attention.

"Welcome to this special soft opening for the Proctor's Ledge memorial," a city official said, interrupting the growing tension among the Ipswich coven membership. "We didn't expect such a crowd." The woman laughed, nervous. "But we're delighted that you can all be here on this sunny day."

"She makes it sound like the martyrs' memorial is a new Dunkin' Donuts," Tracy muttered.

"And forecasting the weather is not her forte," Katrina said, twirling her parasol to block the sunshine. "A storm is headed this way."

Everyone looked up in disbelief. There wasn't a cloud in the sky, but we all knew better than to question the chair of divination and prophecy when it came to making predictions. I shrugged off my own sixth sense that a brewing storm was an ill omen and returned my attention to the ceremony, ignoring Meg's fixed stare.

"We are all aware, here in Salem, that today marks the three hundred and twenty-fifth anniversary of the first hanging to take place at Proctor's Ledge," the official continued. "While we will welcome the general public here in July, it felt neighborly and right to give this special community VIP access."

Julie groaned. "Now she's turned it into a movie premiere."

"And I'm told that one of Bridget Bishop's direct descendants is with us today?" chirped the city official.

Pip and Becca raised their hands.

"Three actually," I said, stepping forward.

"It's showtime," Ike said, putting Pip down and taking Gwyneth's arrangement from Grace. "I'm right behind you, coz."

Julie had called me *coz* when I was outflanked by unfamiliar witches at The Thirsty Goat. Was it a Proctor endearment, or a warning to any witches within earshot to back off or face the family's collective wrath?

I gave Matthew a reassuring smile and bent to kiss Becca on the brow.

"Can I come, too?" she asked, her expression full of entreaty.

I hesitated and looked to Matthew. All eyes were upon us, and much depended on everyone remaining composed. He nodded and I took Becca by the hand.

"Do you want to go with us?" I asked Pip.

"No, I want Dad to pick me up like Uncle Ike did so I can see you from here," Pip replied.

"Wise wizard, for one so young." Tracy handed Pip a granola bar as a reward. "Here. You don't want to get light-headed at high altitude."

The crowd parted before us, falling silent as we passed. It was not out of respect, but rather a sign of how amazed the witches were to have

Bishops walking freely among them. Once my back was turned, however, snippets of bile floated to my ears. I heard the words *fault* and *blame,* as well as the distinct phrase *She deserved it.*

I spun around, using my teacher-stare to reveal the identity of the witch who had said those unforgivable words. Ike put himself between Becca and the crowd. He was ready to clobber anyone who laid a finger on my daughter, first with Gwyneth's heavy crystal vase and then with his bare hands.

The guilty party wasn't hard to spot. She was red-cheeked and defiant, but I could smell her fear.

"Don't." My voice was rich with the promise of magic to come and a lock of red-gold hair whipped against my cheek like a lick of fire. For all I knew, my head was ablaze with anger.

The witch's eyes dropped to the ground.

Coward. I used silent speech, sure that most of the witches present would hear me. The gasps told me that my assumption was correct.

A smattering of applause sounded from the Proctor encampment.

"Listen, Mom," Becca said, her eyes wide. "They're clapping for Granny Bridget. She must be famous in this town."

I smiled and nodded, moving her closer to Ike. Together, we went to the curving stone wall of the memorial. The names of the martyrs were arranged in a terrible timeline of executions. Bridget's stone was the first, and the only one to read *June 10, 1692.*

"Ready?" Ike asked.

Becca nodded, thinking the question was for her.

"I guess so," I replied, taking a deep breath.

Ike nestled the vase filled with brightly colored blossoms at the base of the wall under Bridget's name. He stepped back so that Becca and I could approach.

Becca, who was no stranger to memorials and spent hours in the de Clermont chapel whenever we visited Sept-Tours in hopes of seeing Hugh de Clermont's elusive ghost, wasted no time in plucking a single red rose from the arrangement. She kissed its velvet petals and touched the flower to Bridget's name before putting it at the foot of the vase.

"Well done," I said, my heart filled with pride at my daughter's dignified sense of ceremony.

It was my turn.

I rested my hands against the stone wall in silent communion with my ancestor, who had faced the gallows alone. As a historian, I was not surprised that Bridget's fiercest enemies in 1692 had been her onetime friends. It happened all the time, in every century and every culture. But I was angry that such allegiances could be so quickly cast aside. A tear fell from my eye into the vase of flowers. Then another.

The change of barometric pressure, combined with my rage and heartache, was too much for the atmosphere to bear. The heavens opened, clouds roiling in a sudden tempest.

"Wow," Ike said, blinking away the sudden torrent of raindrops.

Many of the witches had umbrellas with them. They, too, had smelled an approaching storm and come armed to Proctor's Ledge. Katrina held her parasol so it would protect Put-Put and Gwyneth from the downpour.

"Woo-hoo!" Julie cried, whipping a bucket hat out of her back pocket and slapping it on her blond head. "There's a new sheriff in town, and her name is Bishop."

Startled by this announcement, I released a lightning bolt into the sky.

"We don't see much ground lightning on the coast," Ike commented mildly, taking Becca's hand. "You might want to follow it up with a bolt from the blue, coz, or a bit of spider lightning, just in case there are any meteorologists among the tourists."

I waved my hand above my head as though I were diverting the raindrops, and a gratifying clap of thunder and a network of silver illuminated the underside of the darkest cloud. I took Becca's other hand and the three of us ran toward Matthew and the rest of the family.

Matthew caught me in his arms. He'd put Pip down at the first hint of lightning, so that our son didn't become an electrical conduit.

"If you intended to make it rain, you should have warned me to bring an umbrella," he said, pressing his lips against my ear in a kiss.

"Weren't you a Boy Scout?" I said, my shoulders shivering in the white shirt that was now stuck to me.

"Hardly," Matthew said, eyeing my body appreciatively.

"I was a Girl Scout," Grace said, handing my husband a large golf umbrella. "And our Mount Holyoke education taught us to be prepared for any crisis."

"Thanks, Grace," Matthew said, holding it over me and the children.

"God, I need coffee," Ike said, releasing the brake on Put-Put's chair. "I bet you do, too, Grandpa."

Matthew's expression turned wolfish and hungry.

"Let's stop at The Thirsty Goat on our way out to the neck," Gwyneth suggested. "We can take our drinks home and steam in front of the fire with Granny Dorcas."

The prospect of dry clothes was enough to get us all moving toward the parking lot.

Our fast retreat was halted by Meg and some of her cronies. They strung themselves across the path, a moat of malevolence that would be difficult to cross. In the thick of the mob, the cowardly witch who hadn't the courage to face me before now did.

"Tss," Meg hissed.

The rest of the witches took up Meg's strange song, until the air filled with the sibilant sound.

"Go back where you came from," Meg said, her strange eyes sparking green and black. "We don't want Bishops or vampires here."

"Why is she mad?" Becca asked her father.

"Because you don't belong." Meg spat at the ground near Becca's feet.

Julie was nose to nose with Meg before Matthew could move. Vampires were fast. But magic? It was always faster.

"All righty, Meg." Julie had a handful of fire in one hand, and a curved blade in the other. "Ike told me never to bring a knife to a firefight, so I brought both."

Meg's eyes flickered with alarm. Julie was more powerful than she seemed.

"Grace. Ike. Get everybody into the cars and then home," Julie said in a tone that didn't welcome negotiation. "We don't want Becca and Pip to get sick on their first day in Essex County. It wouldn't be much of a welcome, would it, Meg?"

"Go," I told Matthew. "I'll stay with Julie." My hands were itching to make more magic.

"I appreciate the offer, coz, but Meg and I need to chat about a few things—nothing that need bother you," Julie said. "We don't want you falling sick, either. Not with the Crossroads in a week's time."

"What crossroads?" Matthew asked, his vampire instincts on alert.

"Let's go home," I said. "To Ravenswood. Where we belong." I swept the line of witches with a deadly stare, daring them to disagree with me.

None did.

"Why the hell didn't you tell me!" Matthew exploded.

We'd been arguing since the children went to bed. First, the twins had demanded answers to at least a million questions while they sipped warm apple cider in front of Gwyneth's fire. My aunt supplied as many as she could, while I remained as quiet and invisible as possible.

Matthew seethed with his own unanswered queries, and after dosing him with a full pot of coffee, Gwyneth resorted to pulling red wine out of a cupboard. Julie and Ike tried to smooth things over, too, but their efforts were in vain.

The agonizing afternoon we'd spent with the family at Proctor's Ledge and the stilted conversation over dinner seemed a positive picnic compared to what was happening now behind the closed door of Grandpa Tally's study.

"Lower your voice," I said. "You know how sensitive their hearing is. Becca and Pip have been through enough today."

Matthew nearly put his fist through Tally's oak desk trying to curb his tongue and his temper.

"You should have told me as soon as this vendetta with Meg started,"

Matthew said. "I would never have allowed you to remain here alone, had I known."

"Allowed me." I was incredulous. "I don't require your permission to live my life, Matthew."

"It's not your life!" Matthew gripped me by the elbows. "It's *our* life. Why can't you see that your magic touches all of us?"

"You mated and married a witch," I retorted. "You knew what you were getting into."

"I thought so," Matthew shot back. "Oracles? Prophetic twins? Higher magic? Dark paths that meet at a crossroads?"

Until now, these had never been part of our life. The Proctors were, as I feared, challenging Matthew's control over his ingrained prejudices and deep Catholic faith. Years ago, I'd confessed that I felt the pull of darker, higher magic and was afraid Matthew might not be able to accept it. He'd reassured me then, saying that there was darkness in him, too.

"What happened to loving my darkness?" I demanded.

"I said I couldn't hate you for it, because I fought against my own every day." Matthew's pupils shot wide, giving him a dangerous, wolfish look to his face. "But not hating you and loving your darkness are two very different things. My God, the children understand that and they're only six."

"The twins have had the benefit of your fine medieval education," I hissed in reply. "I was raised by ordinary witches, not someone who studied philosophy and theology at the University of Paris under Peter Abelard and can use logic to thread a camel through the eye of a needle."

Matthew blinked, taken aback by my vitriol.

"As for Darkness, I'll know more about that once I defeat Meg at the Crossroads," I continued.

"If you fail—" Matthew growled.

"I've never failed a test in my life," I replied. "I just have to hold Meg off until I see the Dark Path."

"I know more about Darkness than you do, Diana," Matthew said. "I don't want it to be part of your life—or the life of our children."

"Darkness *is* a part of life," I cried. "It's only a problem when you pretend it doesn't exist."

"I have never ignored it, or its power," Matthew replied, crossing his arms over his chest. "Darkness has been my close companion for some time."

"Bullshit." I pressed my finger into his chest. "You've experienced pain, trauma, sin, and agony. And you've turned that all inward until you convinced yourself that you are Darkness incarnate. Well, I've faced Darkness here at Ravenswood, and I hate to tell you but you aren't it!"

Matthew's jaw tightened with fury.

"Go ahead. Let it out," I said, my voice as level as one of my grandfather's neatly arranged bookshelves. "I've never been afraid of you, Matthew, or your Shadows, or your anger. But you are filled with fear, and it makes you Darkness's willing prey."

"Everyone fears Darkness," Matthew said. "To think you are immune from it is unforgivable hubris."

"The goddess forgives everything," I told him. "And you don't even have to flagellate yourself to earn it."

Matthew recoiled in shock. Normally his faith was off-limits when we argued, but tonight's disagreement was far from normal.

"Why do you need to do this? Are you unhappy?" Matthew demanded. "Is there something lacking in your life—something I'm not providing you that I should?"

"This is not about you, Matthew." I took his clenched fists in my hands. "My desire for higher magic is innate. It's in my blood, on both sides of my family, and like blood rage there isn't a drug to cure me of it."

My words hit a painful bruise, and Matthew looked away.

"If you take the Dark Path at the Crossroads, I will follow you," Matthew promised. "God help us then. God help Rebecca and Philip. Will they lose both their parents, just as you lost yours?"

"Would you ask me to give up my power—my *self*—like my father demanded of my mother?" I cried.

The farmhouse's screen door creaked open and slammed shut.

"What was that?" I asked Matthew.

"Philip," Matthew said. "He's talking to Apollo."

"Why was he outside?" I'd left Pip upstairs, tucked into bed.

We found him in the mudroom trying to remove his boots. Pip was soaked to the skin, trembling, and carrying a droopy rabbit.

"What's wrong, Pip?" I said, gathering him close. Apollo joined in, enfolding us in a damp, feathery embrace. He clacked and chirped with worry.

"I'm sorry," Pip said before he burst into sobs.

Chapter 12

"Shh, shh," I murmured, rocking him in my arms. "It's all right. It's all right."

"But it isn't!" Pip screamed through his tears. "You were yelling at each other. You're not supposed to yell in the house!"

"That was wrong of us, Philip," Matthew said, crouching before him. "Where have you been?"

"Becca said we should run away." Pip hiccupped. "But I couldn't go in there with her. It made my tummy hurt, and I was scared of the dark."

"Go in where?" I said, my panic rising. "The attic? The barn?" The twins had been told both areas were strictly off-limits unless they were with Gwyneth.

"The trees by Aunt Gwyneth's house," Pip said, sniffling. "Apollo didn't like them, either."

"She's in the Ravens' Wood." I let go of my son and jammed my feet into one of the many pairs of Wellington boots that were stored here, pulling on a bright yellow slicker at the same time. I grabbed a flashlight. It sent out a weak glow, but it was better than nothing. "I have to find her. Ardwinna!"

A crack of thunder and a flash of lightning emphasized Becca's peril. The rain, which had been falling steadily, now came down in watery pellets that made a sharp sound when they hit the ground.

"Can I stay here?" Pip's face was white at the prospect of going back out into the stormy darkness.

"You can stay with Aunt Gwyneth." I'd already lost track of one child. I wasn't going to leave the other home alone.

I raced across the garden, trampling Gwyneth's prized flowers in my haste. Matthew picked up Pip and was already knocking on the door of the Old Place when I arrived on its stolid, granite step.

"Just go in!" I shouted over the rain. "She's probably asleep."

But my aunt was not asleep. Gwyneth was still fully clothed, though her startled expression suggested we'd woken her from a nap.

"Is everything all right?" Gwyneth asked, opening the door wide to let us in.

"Becca is gone." I stood in the pouring rain and swallowed down the lump of dread that was lodged in my throat. "We need to find her, before the storm gets any worse."

"Gone where?" Gwyneth frowned.

"She's in the Ravens' Wood," I replied.

Gwyneth's faced turned milky with shock. "Alone? Under a full moon?"

Another rumble of thunder and flash of lightning lent urgency to my words.

"Can Philip and Apollo stay with you?" Matthew asked, depositing Pip in the Old Place's narrow entrance.

"I didn't like the woods, Aunt Gwyneth." Heavy tears fell from Pip's eyes. "Now Becca's alone in the rain and it's all my fault."

"You were right not to go into the Ravens' Wood." Gwyneth reached for the mackintosh hanging from a peg by the door. "There's no telling what the storm and the moon have awakened."

"I don't want to go," Pip protested.

"We're both going—me because I know the wood, and you because Becca is your twin sister." My aunt took Pip's hand and turned to his griffin familiar. "It's your responsibility to watch after Pip. Understood?"

Apollo thumped his tail, eagle-eyed and serious. There was no idle chatter now.

Gwyneth grabbed her wand and sharp-bladed athame from a basket by the door. She picked up an ancient lantern and murmured a spell to conjure everlasting witchfire. The lantern filled with a glow that was far brighter than what was produced by my flashlight.

Together, we set out toward the dark grove of trees at the end of the meadow to look for our missing daughter.

Lantern and flashlight bobbing, we followed the narrow trail that led from the Old Place into the trees. An eerie green-gray glow surrounded us, and ether-trails of mist crept through the thickets of black huckleberry and wild blueberry, sending fingers of fog deeper into the wood.

"Becca!" I cried out, hoping that my voice would carry through the stout trunks of the hemlock, oak, and pine.

Pip added his voice to mine, while Gwyneth swung her lantern in shallow arcs, using it as a divining rod that might indicate Becca's location. The trees closed around us as we trampled ferns and pushed aside the toothed-leaved branches of summer sweet. Matthew attempted to track Becca's scent, keeping a sharp eye out for freshly broken branches or footprints in the wet earth that might indicate our daughter had passed this way.

"Find Becca," I told Ardwinna. She was familiar with this command and scampered into the darkness.

The gray mist we had encountered in delicate tendrils at the edges of the Ravens' Wood grew thicker, clinging to the hemlocks and swirling around the ancient oak trees.

"I'm still scared," Pip confided in Apollo, who promptly extended a golden wing to shelter him from the gloom.

"Any trace of her?" I asked Matthew, desperate for some indication that we were on the right path.

"I picked up a bit of her scent when we entered the forest, but it faded away." Matthew crouched to be closer to the woodland's floor. He pressed his hands against the mat of fallen leaves and needles that were soaking up the storm's moisture like a sponge. "The ground is so thickly covered with debris that someone as slight as Rebecca isn't likely to leave footprints."

Matthew stood, his mouth arranged in a grim line. The sharp set of his shoulders and the tense muscles in his thighs indicated he was ready to race to his daughter's aid.

Gwyneth pulled her crooked wand from the front pocket of her pants. She held it aloft and murmured a few words. The end of the wand sent out firecracker sparks of gold and green.

"May I borrow your familiar, Philip?" Gwyneth asked. "I'll give you my magic lantern in exchange. It will serve as a lighthouse like the one in the bay, so that Apollo will be sure to find his way back to you."

Pip nodded, his eyes as wide as an owl's.

Apollo spread his wings and cocked his head, awaiting further instruction.

"You know what to do," Gwyneth murmured to the griffin. "Fly, and find your charge's sister spirit."

Apollo's answering shriek cleaved the air as he soared upward, his golden plumage on full display and the lethal claws of his lion's paws extended. The griffin climbed to a height that allowed his eagle eyes to see farther even than Matthew.

Emboldened by the steady light from Gwyneth's lantern, Pip renewed his calls to his sister. Gwyneth, eyes closed, let her wand lead the way. Matthew continued to scan the ground, making methodical sweeps of the area.

"Too slow," I murmured, feeling the urgency rise as we traveled deeper into the Ravens' Wood. I felt useless, unable to do anything more than follow Gwyneth and Matthew in their pursuit.

I realized there *was* something more I could do—something that wouldn't get tangled up with Gwyneth's magic, or disturb the powers of the wood. I had been so caught up in fear for Becca's safety that I had forgotten Apollo was not the only member of the family who could fly.

"Magic is faster," I reminded Matthew, handing him the flashlight. Matthew gave me a small smile that collapsed into a worried frown as he realized that I, too, would soon be out of his sight.

There was no time to reassure him. Becca was out in the storm, angry with her parents and separated from her brother. Determined to find her and put things to rights, I called on the air to lift me into the sky. Apollo saw me flying in his wake and widened his search area in response.

I flew through the tree houses, some recent and others long abandoned by the Proctor children. I passed by a tall sassafras tree, my hands brushing the leaves and releasing their sweet scent. I spied dark patches in a clearing where a fire had been lit, and wondered what higher magic had been worked there.

A flash of phosphorescence slipped between the trunks of two oak trees, about the height of a six-year-old.

"Becca!" I cried, following the faint trail.

I overtook the figure and swept down, hoping to see my daughter's face. But the figure, though familiar, was not Becca.

"Mary Beth?" It was my imaginary childhood friend who I'd played with in the woods near our house in Cambridge. I had forgotten that she wore the long, full skirts and ruffled cap of another era. The girl resembled Tamsy, with her tight bodice, an apron tied around her waist, and a linen kerchief tucked around her neck for warmth and modesty.

Helter skelter, hang sorrow, care'll kill a cat, Mary Beth whispered. *Uptails all, and a Louse for the Hangman.*

I blinked, surprised at this outburst of Ben Jonson from a girl not yet ten.

Mary Elizabeth Proctor! Granny Dorcas had joined our search, though she was less grandmotherly at present and more an avenging angel. Her elf lock whipped this way and that, crawling with fairies. Fire shone from her eyes in an ominous display of power. *If you vex your niece in her need, I will hex you in return.*

Two more ghosts apparated from a low pepperbush. One was identical to Mary Beth—a twin. The other was older and bore enough resemblance to the pair to suggest all three were sisters.

I beg your pardon. Mary dropped into a curtsy. Her sisters joined her, then linked their arms in the same show of solidarity I'd seen from later generations of Proctors at the ceremony in Salem.

Matthew, Gwyneth, and Pip arrived, the magic lantern glowing.

Matthew drew up short at the sight of the ghosts gathered around me.

"Ghosts." He had long wanted to spot one. In the Ravens' Wood, where Proctor power was at its height, the dead were visible even to him.

Thrice-faced imps! Granny Dorcas thundered. *What mischief is this?*

Mary's ghost traced the tip of her stout shoe in a circle, gathering her courage to respond to Granny Dorcas. *I only wanted to watch over little Rebecca, like I once watched over Diana. But Tamsin said I wasn't enough. She said it was her task.*

"Tamsin." I faced the eldest sister. "Tamsy?"

If the ghost of Dorcas's granddaughter had been inhabiting the body of Becca's treasured doll like a homunculus, there was no telling what confidences she'd shared—nor what my child could be doing in this enchanted place.

You told me to watch out for such a one, Granny. Tamsin's chin rose and she met her grandmother's sparking eyes and dark countenance without flinching. *When I learned my spells at your knee, and you taught me the wisdom of the birds and how to read their signs.*

The fire in Granny Dorcas's eyes dimmed, but not enough to spare her grandchild a tongue-lashing.

Tell me where she is, Tamsin, or the fairies will take you away to Elfame to repent your misdeeds.

Rebecca's not gone far, Granny. The other twin, Margaret, spoke up for the first time. She pointed at a dark clutch of trees. *She is Elsewhere.*

Matthew was a blur as he went in the direction that Margaret had indicated.

I'm not done with you three, Granny Dorcas warned.

I followed Matthew, making no effort to muffle the sound as I trampled down ferns and crushed sarsaparilla underfoot, stepping directly on branches to snap them when I could or clambering over them when they were large and covered in lichen. Aunt Gwyneth and Pip followed along the path I was forging, making slower progress and watched over by Apollo, who flew low above them.

As I approached Margaret's trees, the trunks seemed stouter and the canopy of leaves denser than they had appeared at a distance. I sniffed. An unmistakable scent of unfamiliar magic hung in the air: blackberry, honeysuckle, hyacinth, and lily of the valley. Exotic and sweet, there were darker notes of pine, sage, musk, and clove drifting through the mix. I peered into the darkness ahead.

We sometimes who dwell this wild, constrained by want, come forth. The three Proctor sisters skipped into view, unrepentant despite Granny Dorcas's warning. *To town or village nigh, curious to hear, what happens new finds us out.*

It was mangled, but it was recognizably John Milton.

"They were singing that song when Becca decided to go into the woods," Pip said, chin quavering. "I don't like those girls."

Mary stuck her tongue out and Margaret forked her fingers at Pip. Tamsin separated from the group, floating through the mist.

See this trophy of a man, Tamsin said, drawing her hands through the murk as though opening a window, *rais'd by that curious engine, your white hand.*

Though delivered quietly, Tamsin's words had the ring of a spell. The dense mist parted, revealing a large clearing ringed by oaks—trees sacred to the goddess and revered by witches. Becca stood at the center.

"Becca!" I cried, running toward her.

"She can't hear you, Diana," Gwyneth said.

She is Elsewhere, like I told you. Margaret heaved a sigh. *I'm not an oracle, like Mary. No one pays much attention to me.*

The cold finger of premonition tickled along the length of my spine. *Elsewhere* was not an evasive answer to a question, as I'd thought. It was a real place between the worlds. And Becca was trapped in it.

Shadows rose like licks of flame at Becca's feet, and an unkindness of ravens swept over her in waves. A single raven broke from the group, its knobbed black feet and lethal talons reaching for her. Becca shrieked and fell to the ground in a tight somersault before rising, arms held out for balance. Another raven fell, its beak open, and pecked at her hand.

Matthew reached the clearing before me. His hands pressed against some invisible barrier and he swore.

"I can't go any farther," Matthew said, his eyes wild with the need to free his daughter from her tormentors.

I put my hands next to his, trying to understand the spell around my daughter. Every ward had a weakness. If I could find the vulnerable point, I could breach the magic and release her.

Gwyneth, sensing my intentions, held fast to my arm. "You don't have the knowledge or the skill to break Becca's circle. Tamsin taught it to her, and it's strong and pure, as only a child's magic can be."

A quick glance at Matthew told me I was not the only creature in the wood who was battling their inner demons. Matthew's eyes were glassy, a sign that his blood rage was bubbling to the surface as his control slowly unraveled.

"I'm here, moonbeam," Matthew said, his voice cracking on his pet name for her. "*Maman* and I will fix it, I promise."

"It would be better for Becca if you let this play out," Gwyneth advised. "The wood won't let harm befall her, nor will I."

"You already have." Matthew's expression was chilling. "The Proctors have laid claim to Rebecca, with your oracles and shadows and alluring magic. But she is a de Clermont, too, and we won't give her up to your Darkness so easily."

Becca ran in the circle, dodging two ravens who were clawing at her hair and pecking at her head.

"The ravens—they're going to kill her!" I cried, my eyes stinging with tears as the ravens croaked with glee.

Matthew, who was not known for letting matters unfold in their own way, never mind taking advice from witches, decided on a different path. His muscles bunched as he dropped into a low crouch.

"Rebecca!"

The tone of Matthew's voice, or her own awareness that her father was nearby, stopped Becca in her tracks. She spotted Matthew and smiled.

"You can come in, Daddy," she said, waving her hand in invitation.

Matthew passed effortlessly through the once-impervious barrier. I tried to follow, but the circle snapped shut. Her father was welcome; I was not.

"I never foresaw that," Gwyneth murmured.

"Will they be okay, Mommy?" Pip, too, had been excluded from his sister's presence.

"Of course," I said, falling back on Ysabeau's vague words of assurance. In truth, I had no idea what was going to happen now that Matthew—and his Darkness—had entered Becca's arena.

The ravens erupted into an ear-shattering chorus of clacks, chortles, and guttural cries as Matthew wrapped strong arms around his daughter. Bells chimed, filling the air with painful reverberations. Pip clapped his hands over his preternaturally sensitive ears.

Inside the circle, Becca spoke to Matthew with great animation, waving her arms and laughing.

Matthew straightened, an expression of cautious wonder on his face. The largest of the ravens swooped onto Matthew's head, cackled, and lifted off again.

Becca returned to her whirling, the ravens following in her wake while a train of Shadow and starlight formed behind her. Matthew watched the birds sweep past, tumbling above Becca and pecking at her shoulders.

"Why isn't he doing something?" I cried.

"It looks—" Gwyneth paused and reconsidered. "Can it be that the ravens are *playing* with her?"

Matthew turned, following Becca's movements. Two ravens grabbed at the fabric of her raincoat. Becca screamed in delight as they lifted her into the air before releasing her. I stifled a cry as Becca tumbled back to earth.

"Don't worry, Mom," Pip told me. "Becca jumps out the window at home all the time."

I didn't find this particularly comforting, given the lofty position of the second-floor bedrooms in New Haven. Pip was right, however. Becca somersaulted as she hit the ground and was back on her feet once more.

"Come on, Daddy!" she said, her voice barely audible over the cry of the birds.

Wary, Matthew performed a somersault of his own, springing into the air before tucking his head and rolling to his feet. He adopted a crouch—but this one was not a battle stance. He looked like a puppy ready for play.

A memory niggled of a different bird, a different wood. I'd given chase, but she flew before me, elusive and unreachable. I'd laughed, following her into the darker recesses of the woods at the Bishop House.

Canst thou remember a time before? My mother watched with fiery eyes from the other side of the clearing. A huge gray owl perched on her shoulders, a white crossroads marking the space between its brilliant yellow eyes.

Something—someone—else was watching me, too. Becca's doll was propped up against the trunk of a nearby pine tree, forgotten in my daughter's eagerness to be with the ravens. Tamsy's unblinking eyes reflected the gray licks of Shadow that clung to Becca's legs.

When I looked back across the clearing, my mother was gone.

"She's getting tired," Gwyneth said.

But Becca had vampiric reserves of stamina that my aunt could not predict. Her play may have quieted, but magic was still afoot and my daughter wanted to be part of it.

The largest raven whistled at Matthew and his head swung around at the sound. The vampire began a fast lope around the perimeter of the clearing, inviting the bird to follow him.

The raven took the bait. With a mighty flap of its wings, the bird hovered as though about to swoop. Matthew snapped at the air above him like a wolf, his strong jaws closing. The other ravens landed around Becca, rattling their beaks like sabers and watching the standoff between the bird and this strange wolf in man's clothing.

Matthew laughed.

Somewhere in the wood, an owl hooted in joy.

The raven plunged to Matthew's waist and pecked my husband's backside with his powerful, ebony beak.

Matthew rubbed his rump and laughed again. Then he ran, his body a blur as he rocketed around the clearing.

Gwyneth was right. The ravens were playing with Becca—and with Matthew, too.

Matthew's delight at their game was as great as his daughter's, perhaps greater. As he ran and jumped, snapping at the raven without ever touching a feather, the raven parried with talons and beak.

The other birds remained with Becca, bobbing their heads up and down while she whirled to music only she could hear. She was mesmerizing, another wild creature of the forest. Our daughter's laughter joined with her father's, the higher note resembling the bell-like sounds of the ravens in flight.

Matthew tipped his head back and howled. He leaped into the air and tumbled. My breath caught at Matthew's graceful movements.

For the first time since I'd known him, he was free.

I wondered what special magic my daughter had wrought.

Matthew bent over, panting with exertion. Becca's feet stilled and she stood, straight as the meetinghouse spire, her arms outstretched. A raven perched on her slender arm. It rose, only to be replaced by another member of the unkindness, then another, in what looked like a blessing or a ritual of shared power.

Becca saw her brother waiting outside her magic circle and broke it.

"Pip!" Becca ran toward him, her arms wide like a raven's wings.

Her brother and I met her halfway. I buried my nose in her hair and drank in the familiar scent, now sweetened with magic, cuddling her so close I thought my ribs would part so that I could hold her safe against my heart.

"You scared me," I whispered between kisses.

Matthew drew near. His complexion was ruddy, and his breath followed a quicker, warm-blooded rhythm.

"What a night," Aunt Gwyneth said, her face gaunt from the strain. She slipped her wand into the pocket of her mack with a trembling hand. It hadn't left her grip since we entered the gloom of the wood. "Tomorrow, when we've recovered, we will see what we can do to extract the spirit of Tamsin Proctor from Becca's doll and I will bring Becca and Pip back here and introduce them properly to the Ravens' Wood. But first, we are all going back to bed." My aunt drew a weary hand across her brow.

Pip and Becca scampered off, chattering with excitement, Apollo flew above the pair like a guardian angel, and Gwyneth followed with her witchlight, showing them the way home.

Darkness drew close, taunting me with images of Matthew as I'd never seen him before.

"How did it feel, playing with the ravens?" I asked Matthew softly, as our steps slowed and we fell behind the rest of the group.

He kissed me. After our earlier argument, I was reserved and chilly at first. But Matthew was persistent, his tongue teasing my lips until they parted with a soft sigh that he swallowed as though it were water or wine.

My arms locked around his neck, and he hitched my leg until my sex was pressed against the hard lines of his body. An energy that Matthew kept closely confined had been released, here in the Ravens' Wood.

"It felt like that," Matthew said when our lips parted. "Hungry and wild, tinged with sweetness and danger."

I looked deep into his eyes, wordless with wonder at the passion that never failed to bridge the space between us.

"Let's go home," Matthew said, his thumb soft against my lower lip.

Matthew took my hand and we walked through the trees, the moon illuminating our steps and our bearing clear so long as we followed the gleam of Gwyneth's lantern and the happy sound of our children's voices.

No matter what the future held, for now I was exactly where I belonged: at Ravenswood, with Matthew and our children, moving forward on our shared path.

Chapter 13

When I woke the next morning, stiff from being out in last night's chilly rain, the house was filled with the scent of coffee and woodsmoke. Muffled sounds from the kitchen floated up the stairs: pots and pans clattering, snatches of conversation, the gentle clack of claws on the floor. I swam through memories of last night. It took only a few moments for the enormity of what had happened in the Ravens' Wood to get me out of bed.

I peeked into Naomi's room. There was no sign of Becca or Tamsy. As for Pip, he and Apollo were still snoring in my father's old bed, the griffin's wing slung over his charge like a feathered blanket. Usually, Apollo and Ardwinna slept together downstairs, but we'd made an exception last night.

As I descended the staircase, the conversation in the kitchen grew louder and more distinct with every tread.

"Ravens and wolves are friends, moonbeam," Matthew murmured, against a background of whirring and rinsing as he made another pot of coffee. Based on the house's roasted aroma, it was not his first. Based on what had happened last night, it would not be his last.

I paused, my hand on the banister. Matthew and Becca were both light sleepers and early risers. Part of their father-daughter routine was a daily coffee ceremony, which involved Marcus's old French siphon coffee maker and whatever light roast coffee Matthew could find in a town like New Haven that preferred cold brews and espresso. The siphon resembled a chemical apparatus, and from it Matthew drew a pure, delicate brew that made Becca feel grown-up without packing a wallop to her finicky digestive system.

"Have you played with ravens before, Daddy?" Becca asked. The squeak of wheels across the floorboards indicated that she was settling Tamsy into the chipped wooden high chair parked in the corner.

"I have," Matthew replied. "Remember how I worked in the snow so I could learn about wolves?"

Matthew's tales of the wolves and their pack and hunting behaviors had been an important component of the twins' early education regarding what it meant to be a vampire.

"Uh-huh," Becca replied.

"I saw ravens and wolves playing there, dodging and tumbling in the air and on the ground," Matthew explained. "They were friends and shared meals, and sometimes a raven would adopt a wolf. They would spend lots of time together, and even when the wolf left her family to start her own pack, the raven would go with her."

This was a story I had not heard before.

"Like best friends!" Becca said. "Like me and Tamsy."

It was an opportune moment to break the intimate father-daughter bubble. It worried me that Becca felt her closest companion was a doll occupied by the spirit of a dead girl.

"You two are up early," I said breezily, giving Becca a peck on the cheek. I drew back and spotted something more worrying than the doll.

Becca always wore the key to Tamsy's Hadley chest on a coral satin ribbon around her neck. This morning, the raven's ring hung from it, too. The juxtaposition of the coral ribbon, the brass key, and the white-and-dark bone ring sent a shock through me, as though these were signs waiting to be understood.

My fingers itched to consult the black bird oracle, but I'd left the cards in Grandpa Tally's study, locked within their wooden coffer for safekeeping. Katrina was right; I needed to keep them with me. I wondered how Matthew would react when he saw the full deck, and understood their significance. I'd meant to show him last night, but events had overtaken us.

Matthew was at the stove, stirring oatmeal with a wooden spoon. It was a crisp morning here by the sea, and warm food would be welcome. He smiled, and his eyes lit up as they always did when I entered the room.

"Is that for me?" I said, rising on my toes for a kiss. Matthew tasted of coffee and Darkness, the aftereffects of the wood still with him.

"Of course it's for you." Matthew cast his eyes toward the stairs. "And Philip, should he ever wake and join us."

"Enjoy the quiet while you can." Stifling a yawn, I rummaged through the tea stashed on the shelves of the old dresser. Did I want English Breakfast? Pu-erh?

Matthew was ahead of me, as usual.

"Already made." Matthew nodded in the direction of a teapot encased in a crocheted cozy. He ladled oatmeal into a bowl, sprinkling it with cinnamon, walnuts, and blueberries. "Come get your porridge, Rebecca."

Matthew prepared a second bowl for me, with bananas and walnuts and brown sugar. He knew everyone's favorite toppings, and we each got a bespoke bowl. Though the scent of coffee might not rouse Pip, the oatmeal likely would.

"I smell breakfast!" Pip pelted down the stairs. "Morning, Mommy!"

I opened my arms. Pip knocked me back in his eagerness to fill them.

"Gently." Matthew beetled his brows at his son, fixing the third and final bowl of the day.

Pip took two moderate steps in Matthew's direction and then leaped to pluck his breakfast from his father's hands. His generous portion of oatmeal boasted a thick swirl of cream and a heavy dose of cinnamon sugar.

Once it was safely in his possession, Pip inhaled the aroma and sighed with reverence. "Thanks, Daddy."

"You can have a snack, Tamsy. Then we'll get dressed for our hike." Becca put a single blueberry and a walnut on the tray in front of her doll.

"What hike?" I spooned oatmeal into my mouth.

"I thought I'd take the children on a walk." Matthew poured himself a fresh cup of coffee. "I've taken a look at Gwyneth's syllabus and you have a busy day of hexes ahead of you. Ardwinna and Apollo could use some exercise after the long car ride. We will venture forth into unknown lands, and pretend Ravenswood is a map that we must read closely."

Matthew tousled Pip's hair, and our son giggled.

"That's what Tamsy's grandfather did when he came to Ravenswood," Becca said, tracing a ribbon of sugar in her bowl. "It was all new and he had to clear the trees and cut the wood to make the house."

My spoon of oatmeal hovered halfway to my lips. Matthew and I exchanged a worried glance. When the oatmeal finally made it into my mouth, it was difficult to swallow, my throat tight with concern about what information Tamsy was imparting to Becca, now that she was back at Ravenswood.

We chatted easily while the twins finished their meal. Becca was suffering no ill effects from last night's strenuous play, and Pip—who thrived on any amount of sleep—was energized and curious about the prospect of combing the edge of the property for buried treasure.

When the twins went upstairs to change, Matthew and I tidied the kitchen. We'd learned our lesson and kept our voices low and calm.

"I'm worried about that doll," I said, running the water full force into the sink to further muffle my words.

"I'm worried about Ravenswood," Matthew confessed, his expression grim. "Philip is still wary of the place—and with good reason—while Rebecca is already deeply attached to it."

"Gwyneth will make sure that the children come to no harm," I assured him. "She's attuned to everything that happens here."

"Your aunt didn't know Rebecca and Philip had run away," Matthew observed. "Nor that Rebecca had gone deep into the wood, though I suspect that there was nothing she could have done about it."

I thought of the ring around Becca's neck, and the easy way she spoke about Ravenswood's past.

"Becca's coming into her power." I wasn't going to sugarcoat this pill. "She has a talent for higher magic, Matthew, just like me, and Mom, and Dad's sister. The Congregation is going to recognize she's suited to the Dark Path the minute they examine her. We can't prevent that, either."

Matthew put his back to the sink so that he could meet my eyes. He adopted the stance he usually did when faced with an uncomfortable truth, legs slightly bent and arms crossed over his chest.

"Very well. But Rebecca will make her own choice about whether she wishes to study higher magic," Matthew warned. "Neither you, nor her DNA, nor the Congregation will decide for her."

I was stung by his belief that I would force Becca's hand.

"Higher magic may be an inextricable part of Rebecca's constitution, and I won't keep her from it," Matthew continued. "But I won't encourage her to pursue it. Neither should you."

A knock on the screen door interrupted our talk.

"Come in, Gwyneth," Matthew said, pulling himself away from the counter.

My aunt's eyes were sharp. Gwyneth had overheard part of our conversation about higher magic, and she wasn't happy about it.

"I promised the children a tour of the Ravens' Wood," Gwyneth said. "Is this a good time?"

"Thanks for the offer, Gwyneth, but we're headed out on a long walk toward the water," Matthew replied. "Rebecca and Philip require a great deal of exercise, especially when they're under stress."

It was not an ideal way to start the day, with Matthew making pronouncements and building defenses around Orchard Farm and the children. But he was on Proctor land, not his own, and it was Gwyneth who ruled here.

"Excellent," Gwyneth replied. "The quickest way to reach the river is through the woods. I'll show you the way."

Check. I was reminded of the de Clermont family's regret that Matthew was such a terrible chess player. Unlike Philippe, it could be easy to predict my husband's next move, especially if he was wearing his Master of the Universe cape.

"That sounds delightful," I said, giving my aunt an appreciative hug and a kiss. "Did you sleep well?"

Becca and Pip had heard Gwyneth arrive, as had Ardwinna, who let out a sharp bark of welcome and plummeted down the stairs. She was followed by a ball of fur and feathers.

"Hi, Aunt Gwyneth!" Becca came next. "Are we going back into the woods? Can I lead the way?"

Matthew might be able to argue with me, but he could not oppose the collective will of two Bright Borns, a deerhound, a griffin, and my aunt. His plans for a family walk, getting the lay of the land and scouting for small rodents and other edibles, vanished into thin air. Coolly, he accepted Gwyneth's offer.

"We are going back to the wood but this is your aunt's house, Rebecca Arielle, and she will lead the way," Matthew said sternly.

"Okay," Becca replied, slapping a hat on Tamsy's head and putting shoes on the doll's feet.

"Can we go *now*?" Pip asked, his baseball hat askew.

After a liberal application of bug spray, we trooped toward the trees. The green flies were biting, and the children's tender flesh would be irresistible to the persistent bloodsuckers.

We took the same path we'd taken to find Becca last night. Tamsy came with us, and Pip hopped alongside Apollo. Ardwinna, who knew all about pack rules and was fully aware of Gwyneth's position in ours, stuck close to my aunt.

Without the distorting lens of panic, I was able to see the Ravens' Wood clearly, and better feel its magic. This morning the wood was not a place of nightmares but an enchanted forest from a fairy tale, where Darkness and Light were held in perfect balance and anything was possible.

"Look, Pip. That's the tree house I told you about." Becca pointed out a particularly lofty perch with wooden boards that circled the trunk of a stout oak tree like a crow's nest on a schooner's mast. Someone had propped a rickety ladder against the rough bark. It was made from fallen tree branches lashed together with rope, the uprights twisted.

"And this is where I want to build a cottage for the fairies," Becca said, crouching at the base of the tree, where the moss was thickest. She beckoned to her brother. "Come see, Pip. You decide if it's a good place for a house."

Eager to share his architectural skills with his sister, Pip raced to the prospective building site.

"This brings back happy memories." Aunt Gwyneth's eyes were brilliant with unshed tears. "I never thought I'd see any of Tally's great-grandchildren here."

"Becca!" Pip cried in a loud whisper. "I see a fairy."

"Where?" Becca's head swiveled like an owl's.

"There." Pip pointed to an agitated huckleberry bush. "I think she's stuck."

"Let's rescue her!" Becca said, leaping to her feet.

Happily, the fairy—if indeed there had been one—could not be found, and we resumed our progress through the wood. Gwyneth laid out the rules should the twins wish to return, doling them out one at a time so that Becca and Pip would remember them. My aunt might have retired from teaching, but she had not lost her gift for gauging how much new information a creature could absorb.

"The Ravens' Wood prefers you keep to the paths," Gwyneth warned when Becca got entangled with a baneberry bush. The goggle-eyed berries rolled on their bracts in agreement.

"I wouldn't dig the earth up with that stick, Pip," my aunt advised. "It disturbs the trees' roots and they get annoyed."

Overhead, the limbs of an oak tree whipped this way and that. They quieted as soon as Pip put his digger down.

"You'll find the river is this way, Matthew," Gwyneth told my husband when he caught scent of the sea and forged ahead toward the water. "There's nothing but bog and marsh in that direction."

Matthew, who was as eager to bash through things as his son and daughter, paused in his tracks. He turned.

Gwyneth pointed to an old sign in the shape of a manicule that read RIVER THIS WAY. Foiled again, Matthew pressed his lips into a thin line and stalked ahead of us.

"Sorry," I murmured to my aunt. "He likes to be in charge."

"So do I," Gwyneth said, blue eyes glittering.

The path to the river wended this way and that so that we headed north, then west, then south around a clump of trees, then north, then east, until I was bewildered and gave up trying to remember how we'd gotten here.

"Just stick to the path and everything will be fine," Gwyneth said whenever the children asked if we were there yet.

The more often my aunt said it, the more I suspected that there was a deeper meaning to her words.

When at last we reached a bit of solid ground where the Ipswich River touched Neck Creek, we looked out over a complicated maze of estuaries, salt marsh, and streams that ran from inland to the sea. The waterways were crowded with all types of craft from clam boats to sailboats.

"Wow!" Pip hopped with excitement. "Look at them!"

"Your aunt Grace is out there," Gwyneth said. "Can you see a boat flying a Jolly Roger?"

Mount Holyoke women were part pirate, too. This made perfect sense based on the alumnae I had met thus far.

Though we all searched, we couldn't find such a vessel. Disappointed, the children now had a chance to focus on their other wants.

"I'm hungry," Pip said.

"I'm thirsty," Becca complained.

Gwyneth turned to where a small clutch of houses perched close to a road.

"Looks like Betty's home," she said. "We can stop there for a visit before we go back to Ravenswood. And I know another way home, too."

Betty was pleased to entertain a griffin for the first time, and supplied Apollo with a bowl of birdseed. She gave the children lemonade and lavender shortbread, while Matthew and Ardwinna opted for fresh water, and Gwyneth and I had cups of Earl Grey tea. We spent a pleasant hour with the coven secretary before Gwyneth led us home via the road that passed by the entrance to Ravenswood.

Matthew was eager to get away from my aunt and replenish his patience with something stronger than Betty's refreshments, but my aunt had one final ace up her sleeve.

"Who would like to see the barn before I take my nap?" Gwyneth asked no one in particular. "It's where your mom will be studying higher magic."

The children's hands shot into the air. Matthew's lips tightened. His red wine and coffee would have to wait.

"Let's take a peek inside." Gwyneth beckoned the children forward toward the sliding doors. "Can you feel something?"

"Not a tingle," Pip said with a frown. He pushed his finger at the door to be sure. "Ow! That stings!"

"My famous wasp spell. It keeps people from poking their fingers where they don't belong." My aunt's face twisted into a grimace that made both twins laugh. "Make sure you have permission from your mother or me if you want to go inside. If not, you're going to feel like you've stepped on a hornet's nest." The look Gwyneth gave Matthew notified him that he was included in this warning.

"Can you help me with the door?" Gwyneth asked my husband sweetly. "It's quite heavy."

Gwyneth routinely manhandled the door into place, and if that didn't work she used a TNT spell handed down through the Finnish witches and quarry workers of Cape Ann, which blew the doors apart while causing minimal damage to the structure and its contents. She was up to something.

Matthew stepped up, happy to save any damsel in distress, and we filed into the barn.

"Whoa." Rebecca looked around with wide eyes. "There's more old stuff in here than in Grand-père's room at Les Revenants."

Matthew slid the door fully open at that startling announcement, for Philippe's vast personal library at our house in France qualified as the eighth wonder of the world. It was stuffed with uncatalogued bits and pieces that the de Clermont family patriarch had collected over his very long life.

Ravenswood's old barn was neither as large nor as imposing as the library at Les Revenants, but it was impressive nonetheless. I smiled at the children's astonishment and Matthew's surprise as they examined the riches within.

Becca and Pip raced around, finding the spell-looms and the library ladder. Becca squealed when she located the alchemical laboratory. Pip stared in wonder at the enormous mandrake root atop a cake stand, under its domed glass lid. Matthew examined the old instruments, a fond smile on his face as he remembered our friend Tom Harriot and his love of mechanical gizmos.

Matthew and the children were falling under the Proctor family's spell, just as I had.

Thunder and lightning! Granny Dorcas's pipe dropped from her lips, spilling burning tobacco everywhere. She was transfixed by the sight of Matthew and the twins. *Babes. And a blood-letch. I saw them in the wood, Gwynie, but never imagined you'd let them in here.*

Pip came to an abrupt halt before Granny Dorcas and swept a courtly bow. "I am sorry, *Madame,* I did not see you. I am Philip Bishop-Clairmont."

And a very presentable lad, too, Granny Dorcas cooed, disarmed by Pip's fine manners. She motioned Becca forward. *Come here, lass, and greet your old granny. I won't bite, like your pa.*

"Biting's not polite," Becca replied, inching her way toward the rocker. Like Pip, she had been schooled in proper creature behavior by her father and Ysabeau. Politeness was important in the de Clermont family—even if you were stabbing someone in the back, or plotting the ruin of their family.

Then what are you feart of, sprite? Granny Dorcas peered at her granddaughter.

Becca hesitated.

Helter skelter, hang sorrow, care'll kill the cat, girl. Granny Dorcas patted out a small fire smoldering in her skirts. *Spit it out, or it will turn into an evil toad and choke you.*

"I beg your pardon, *Madame,*" Becca began, "but *what* are you?"

Granny Dorcas stared at Becca, wide-eyed. Then she tilted her head back and roared with laughter.

I'm your granny, that's what. Granny Dorcas wheezed and chuckled.

"You smell like a ghost," Becca replied, wrinkling her nose, "but you don't *look* like one."

"Proctor ghosts aren't like Bishop ghosts, honey," I said, putting my arm around her shoulders. There would doubtless be many nighttime metaphysical conversations about the nature of ghosts, why some were nothing but green vapors, and others more substantial. I looked to Matthew for support.

My husband, I saw, would be no help at all. Though he'd seen the ghosts last night, being so close to one again had rendered him mute. He stood, dumbfounded, with John Proctor's very fine brass gunner's compendium in one hand, staring at my great-grandmother.

Matthew crossed himself with his free hand.

A blood-letch and a papist to boot! Granny Dorcas angled her head to see him better, enfolding him in pipe smoke. *Go on, rapscallion. You know you want to.*

Matthew touched her on the shoulder. He pressed a bit farther, poking his long finger deeper until the tip disappeared into Dorcas's flesh. He jumped.

Don't be such a barmpot, Granny Dorcas said. *What did you expect? I'm dead, man. And you better get used to it, for I'm not the only ghostie around the place.*

Pip and Becca listened attentively to this exchange, squirreling away *papist, blood-letch, rapscallion,* and *barmpot* for future use.

Overall, Matthew's first encounters with the Proctors, living and dead, were going better than I'd feared. Gwyneth was turning out to be something of a mistress of ceremonies herself. I could detect her guiding hand in everything that happened today, as she got Matthew and the children feeling safe and secure at Ravenswood. Becca's next words made it clear that she was ready to cross over from guest to summer resident.

"Can we stay with Aunt Gwyneth, Daddy, until *all* the ghosties meet us?" Becca asked her father. She knew better than to wheedle. Instead, she fell back on logic and reason.

"I'd like to play with the ravens again, and pretend I'm a wolf," she continued. "And there are lots of chipmunks and squirrels in the wood—more than in England, even. We could go on an overnight hunting trip and stay in one of the tree houses."

Becca, who already showed signs of a Scholastic bent, was mounting an excellent argument in favor of her proposal. Matthew's efforts to share his medieval education with his children had, like the raven in the wood, come back to bite him.

"I think Philip would prefer to go to England, moonbeam. So would your mother," Matthew countered.

Would I?

"I don't mind. There are woods and fields here." Pip shrugged. "And Ravenswood already has tree houses. We just need to fix them up and make them nice again. Apollo's happy to stay, too. He wants to meet the herons who live out there." Pip used the spell-loom he'd removed from the wall to gesture toward the marsh.

"You mean The Nestling," Gwyneth said. "That's where the herons hatch their eggs. We can walk out there at low tide."

"Tamsy was right, Pip," Becca said. "Aunt Gwyneth does know how to find the herons, and she said Aunt Julie will take us out there on her boat if the water is too high to walk."

A touch of magic washed over me, faint but distinctively Becca's, with its honeysuckle sweetness and blackberry bramble core. With Tamsy in her arms, Becca didn't need oracle cards. She was relying on the spirit of her ancestor to see the future. I thought of Bridget Bishop, and the poppet the authorities had found tucked into her wall. Perhaps training in higher magic began with dolls, then moved to oracle cards. If so, then Becca was right on track.

"Aunt Gwyneth no doubt has her own summer plans," Matthew said. "We don't want to disturb them."

"This was my summer plan," Gwyneth replied, squashing Matthew's penultimate line of defense. "Welcoming you to the family, and showing you the magic of Ravenswood."

"And learning how to sail," Pip chimed in, "so Apollo can meet the herons."

Gwyneth chuckled. "And sailing. And herons. And clambakes. And playing with your cousins. And even going to magic camp, if your parents want some well-earned peace and quiet."

The prospect of magic camp was met with enormous enthusiasm.

"Settle down, or I'll use my mother's troubled waters spell on the pair of you." Gwyneth waggled a finger for emphasis. "She used it on your grandpa Stephen and aunt Naomi. They were twins, too, and as wild as grimalkins when they were your age."

"What does the spell do?" Pip asked, wide-eyed.

"It makes you tired for days," Gwyneth said. "All you'll want to do is nap, and I don't imagine you'd like that one bit. You might miss something interesting."

Matthew laid down what he hoped was his ace.

"Your mother has important work to do in the library," Matthew said firmly, drawing the discussion to a close. The whole family knew that if I didn't get regular boosters of the Bodleian's unique magic, I was no fun at all.

"But I have a whole new library right here," I said, sweeping my arms out, "just waiting to be explored."

Matthew's face darkened like a thundercloud scudding across the marsh.

"I have a lot to learn from Aunt Gwyneth," I said. "We can all be students together. Wouldn't that be fun?"

The twins' nods indicated they agreed. Ardwinna's tail thumped as she cast her vote to stay where we were.

"Daddy needs to learn about the magic, too." Becca's remark was not a question. It was a statement. "He's a vampire, but he knows a lot of witches. It would be polite for him to understand them better."

Poor Matthew had been outvoted again.

"I think that's a grand idea," Aunt Gwyneth said.

"It's your decision," Matthew told me, still hoping I would choose another path.

I weighed familiarity and safety against curiosity and the unknown. I balanced Matthew's reluctance to uncover the secrets tucked into our children's lineage against my own horror at the thought that Becca and Pip might be swept up into the Congregation's desire for power and control. My fingers itched to begin doing alchemical experiments and learning curses—not to mention preparing some adequate wards to use when Meg challenged me at the Crossroads.

"Let it be the twins' decision," I said, reminding him of his earlier words.

"Very well," Matthew said, his expression one of grim resignation. "We'll stay at Ravenswood. For now."

There were whoops and hollers from Pip, Becca, and Granny Dorcas. Ardwinna barked along with their exuberant cries. Apollo took flight and soared between the rafters, coming to perch on one of the oak beams.

"Three came by land, and one by sea, and two were already present—blessed be!" Julie beamed at us from the entrance to the barn. She was wearing one of her wide-brimmed hats, knee-length white shorts, and a poppy-red shirt. "What's all this racket?"

"We're staying *all* summer," Becca said, dancing around Julie. "We're going to go to magic camp, and Mommy and Daddy are going to magic school—"

"Can we sail on your boat?" Like his father, Pip was dogged in pursuit of his objectives.

"Of course you can!" Julie conjured up two sparklers and gave them to the twins. "That means you'll be here for the Midsummer potluck."

"Potluck?" Matthew said, his face blanching.

"All the Proctors on the North Shore get together on Midsummer Eve to celebrate the summer solstice," Julie explained, conjuring up a couple of additional sparklers. She handed both of them to Matthew. "Here. Take two. It looks like you could use some brightening up."

"And it's not just a potluck for grown-ups," Julie continued, sticking more sparklers through the ventilation holes in her bucket hat. Thankfully, the sparks were made of witchlight, otherwise Julie's hair would have gone up in flames. "All of your cousins will be there, too. Everybody brings a signature dish, and sometimes all we get is dessert, but nobody minds. There are three-legged races to see who can fly the farthest, and egg-and-spoon games to test your prognostication skills, and cousin Rachel tells fortunes that will make your eyeballs fall out."

It sounded like a witchy version of the June Fete held at the children's school in New Haven. Except for the eyeball-popping predictions.

"Which reminds me," Julie said, handing Gwyneth another sparkler. "I thought we should gather at Ravenswood this year."

"Absolutely not!" Gwyneth exclaimed.

"It's been years since we celebrated Midsummer here," Julie said, her bottom lip pushed out in a pout.

"You children moved out and moved on," Gwyneth said, "tramping around Europe in the summer instead of staying at home. William has done a superb job hosting the annual picnic."

"I guess," Julie said. "But nobody likes his deviled eggs, and he can't light a clean witchfire so the barbecue always smokes. Besides, his backyard is too small for a proper egg-and-spoon contest, and we have to get in the pickup truck and drive for three miles just to dig for clams."

Becca and Pip listened to every word Julie spoke, dazzled by the prospect of the wonders in store. Julie had transformed a family reunion into a magical theme park, complete with rides and too much heavy food.

"Julie Proctor Eastey." Aunt Gwyneth was horrified. "What have you done?"

"Everything!" she said cheerfully. "It won't be any trouble at all. You won't have to lift a finger except to put on fairy wings and join the party."

Gwyneth did not find this reassuring, but it brought the twins to new heights of excitement.

"Can I wear wings?" Pip asked.

"Everybody wears them," Julie explained, as the children peppered her with additional questions. "Wait until you see Aunt Sally. She looks like a giant bumblebee, but she can still clear the tops of the trees when she flies."

"It's too late to change plans," Gwyneth protested weakly. "William's already bought the charcoal."

Matthew, for whom revenge was a dish best eaten cold, smiled with satisfaction as Gwyneth failed to persuade Julie to her point of view.

"Will's delivering it here tomorrow." Julie beamed at her aunt. "I told you. Everything's taken care of. Trust me, Gwynie. I know how to throw a party."

Chapter 14

After a few days of humid, variable weather, thick clouds rolled into Ipswich and the temperature plummeted once more. It was now part of our morning routine to gather in the barn after breakfast and make family plans for the day. The children drew logs from the woodpile and heaped them on the fire, bringing welcome warmth to the overcast day. Gwyneth presided over the teapot, while Matthew—who had made a second coffee siphon out of distillation equipment—made a fresh pot of his own favorite hot beverage. The happy buzz of family life filled the air, and Granny Dorcas puffed contentedly on her pipe in the rocking chair, stroking Ardwinna and then Apollo, who sat at her feet and gazed at her with soft eyes.

"I thought I'd get up on the roof and look at that leak," Matthew said, drawing a cup of coffee for Granny Dorcas. She couldn't drink the stuff, but adored the smell, which reminded her of long-ago evenings spent by the fire at Sparks' Ordinary, telling fortunes and fencing stolen goods.

"That would be fine." Gwyneth sighed with relief and eyed the dented kindling bucket placed in the corner to catch the drips. "I'm worried that if we have more rain the books might be damaged."

I was at the central worktable, shuffling the black bird oracle cards to see if they might reveal any insights into Gwyneth's teaching plans for the day.

"I don't think the oracle is awake yet," Gwyneth said with a yawn, bringing me some tea. "Patience, Diana."

Matthew deposited the mug of coffee at Dorcas's elbow, casting a wary glance in my direction. When I'd first shown him the cards, they flew at him and fluttered all over his face and body like butterflies drawn to a particularly sweet patch of buddleia. Since then, he'd kept a healthy distance from the deck when I had it in my hands.

Not so Becca, who had finished feeding the stove and was now hovering at my shoulder. The cards fascinated her.

"Can I try, Mommy?" Becca's fingers reached for the black bird oracle. The Sulfur card flew out of the deck and rapped her smartly across the knuckles.

"Granny Dorcas gave the cards to *me*, sweetie," I said looking across the room to make sure I was right to keep them away from my daughter.

She'll get her turn was Granny Dorcas's somewhat ominous reply.

"One day, someone will give you a deck of your own," I said, not wanting to bathe the cards in the allure associated with forbidden fruit. "Maybe it will be this one, maybe it will be one of the other decks in the barn."

"This summer?" Becca demanded.

"Rebecca," Matthew growled.

"When the time is right," I said firmly.

"Why don't you make a set of oracle cards for Tamsy to use?" Gwyneth suggested, steering our family ship out of troubled waters. "You can put your special pictures on one side, and write their meaning on the other." She set a pile of index cards on the table, along with a pot of colored pencils and crayons.

"Like what?" Becca said, clambering onto a nearby stool.

"Things that hold meaning," Gwyneth said. "Colors, books, food, songs. Anything you like. There's no right or wrong."

I wondered if all the Proctor decks had started this way, with a child drawing out their inner hopes and fears and refining them over a lifetime until they sang with power and insight. It was a good way to guide a young witch on how best to use her intuition. By freeing Becca to do whatever she fancied, Gwyneth had cleared any obstacles that might stand between my daughter and her witch's sixth sense.

The look on Matthew's face suggested that Gwyneth might have steered us out of troubled waters only to land us in the belly of the whale. My aunt had crossed one of Matthew's lines, and her plan for Becca seemed like coercion in his eyes.

"Would you like to color with Becca?" Gwyneth asked Pip, smoothly including her brother in the project to divert Matthew's attention.

"Nah," Pip said, his fingers tangled up with a ball of string. Gwyneth had been teaching the twins string games like Cat's Cradle, the Moth, and Jacob's Ladder. They were good for finger dexterity, which pleased Matthew. The games also taught the twins the basics of the Proctor method for building spells geometrically rather than relying solely on complicated knots. I, too, was learning this complex four-dimensional method as part of Gwyneth's curriculum covering protection spells and basic wards. It was unlike the weaving that Goody Alsop had taught me in London, but it helped that I had always seen spells in shapes and colors rather than words like most witches.

"Are you ready to learn the Witch's Broom?" Gwyneth asked, releasing Pip from the web of string. "Or would you like to practice on your spell-loom instead?"

"Spell-loom!" Pip said, running toward the wall where the family looms had pride of place. He took down his favorite. It was smaller than most of the looms, and simply carved with the initials MP.

Clever Gwyneth. The spell-looms had been carefully arranged so that those at a child's height would not tax their skills too much. As the children grew, they would have access to finer and more complicated looms.

Watching Becca and Pip with their great-great-aunt, I was struck by the physical similarities between Gwyneth and my father. They had the same crinkle around the eyes, the same patient expression, the same pursed smile that conveyed mischief as well as mirth. What might Dad have thought of his grandchildren? It was a question I'd asked myself many times over the years. Seeing the twins play with Gwyneth provided a kind of answer. Even though Dad would have disapproved of Gwyneth's subject matter, he would have been delighted by how their minds worked, and ready to guide them toward success with a light hand.

"This is hopeless." I kept shuffling the cards, but to no avail. "The black bird oracle isn't sleeping—it's gone on a cruise to the Bahamas."

Nobody gave my griping a moment's notice, or a drop of sympathy. Matthew tied on a leather belt with a pouch that held the tools he would need and climbed up into the rafters, scaling the bookcases and traveling across roof beams like an agile cat.

"Very nice," Gwyneth said, looking over Becca's shoulder at her drawing of a feather. "Did you see that on your walk?"

"No, it was in Penny's paddock this morning." Becca examined her drawing with a critical eye. "Only it wasn't black—it was greeny-bluey-blacky."

"Layer the colors," Gwyneth said, pulling out a green and a blue pencil and shading the feather. "See?"

Becca was amazed by the transformation and eager to try it herself. She was soon absorbed in her work.

"Everybody seems settled." My voice twanged with envy.

"You need something more active to do than brood over your cards," Gwyneth observed. "Come with me."

Happy to be excused from my chores, I tucked the black bird oracle into its bag. "Where are we going?"

"Mommy and I are going to the Old Place for the rest of today's lessons," Gwyneth told the twins. "Granny Dorcas will check on you while your father is up to his teeth in hammers and nails. She knows a great deal about oracle cards. I'm sure she'll share her knowledge with you if you ask nicely."

Granny Dorcas waggled her fingers, which set off a shower of sparks and tiny bubbles that popped when they burst.

"Bye, Matthew!" I called up to the rafters. I gave each child a kiss on the nose. "Have fun, you two. Learn things!"

At the Old Place, Gwyneth opened one of the doors in the tiny front hall to reveal a twisting flight of stairs. My aunt made slow progress up the uneven treads, pausing every few steps to catch her breath. She swore often, making her feelings on stairs, attics, the moon, the goddess, and the spirits of willful ancestors abundantly clear.

My eyes watered at her vehemence—not to mention the extreme detail—of her proposed remedies and retributions.

"Where are we going?" I asked again.

"To see to the ghosts," Gwyneth replied. "I'm jumping ahead in the lesson plan to the subject of living with the dead."

I wasn't supposed to study that until after I chose my path at the Crossroads. I clambered up the stairs after my aunt, tripping over my own feet in my excitement to learn Gwyneth's methods for keeping the Proctor ancestors in such good condition.

When we reached the top landing, Gwyneth removed a ring of keys from her pocket and pushed open the thin door into the attic. I was surprised that it was unlocked, then noticed the fuzzy ends of broken wards hanging from the lintel.

"Our dearly departed did that the night of the coven meeting," Gwyneth said. "No man-made lock will keep this bunch inside when a Proctor is in need."

My aunt cast an iridescent blue witchlight and sent it across the dark space. It hit an ancient tin sconce, the metal absorbing the magic and casting a bright glow throughout the rafters that revealed neat rows of trunks and boxes laid out like coffins in a graveyard.

"You'll find most ghosts pale in modern lighting," Gwyneth commented. "It dims their luminosity."

Many of the boxes, trunks, and coffers were tightly closed. Some had lifted lids, and personal items dripped out of them onto the scarred pine boards laid across the beams to make a precarious floor. I spotted bonnets, waistcoats, shawls, socks, the cardboard-backed *cartes de visite* of the nineteenth century, and ribbon-tied stacks of correspondence.

"It looks like homecoming weekend at Amherst," Gwyneth said, surveying the mess. "We'll have to clean this up before we let any more ghosts out. And make sure you get everything back in the right trunk. The old folk are possessive, and take note of every skillet and pillowcase before they can be put to rest."

I'd encountered a few household inventories in my travels through seventeenth-century archives, and I was familiar with the meticulous accounts that had been made at a time when raw materials and manufactured objects were precious and scarce. I pulled on a stocking draped over an old hook and held it up for identification.

"My mother, Damaris Proctor." Gwyneth pointed to a steamer trunk the size of a small child. It was covered with labels from ports of call throughout Europe and Africa. The corners were nicked and dented, and the leather surface worn through in most places, exposing the wood-and-metal structure beneath.

Inside, the trunk held crystal scent bottles and delicately embroidered handkerchiefs, along with a photograph album with a cracked spine and crumbling cover. A spectacular pair of satin-covered heels with worn soles proved Granny Damaris had tripped across many a dance floor. I folded the filmy silk stocking and slipped it into a heart-shaped bag embroidered with the name *DeeDee*. The old-fashioned epithet *Damaris* must have been too much for a stylish young woman of the 1920s.

Gwyneth made faster progress than I did, for it was not the first time she'd tidied up after her ancestors. My work was slowed by the attic's irresistible historical charms. I wanted to savor every item I touched, hear its story, and learn why the object was precious to its owner.

"And to think, we're going to have to do this again in less than two weeks," my aunt muttered under her breath, tossing a wooden toy into a trunk. "I hate potlucks. Who wants to eat nothing but desserts?"

I was not looking forward to the potluck any more than Gwyneth. Coven business meetings and ritual celebrations were bad enough. Potlucks were far worse, as they involved dozens of witches, enough food to satisfy a field battalion, and bruised egos once the event was over.

After Gwyneth and I returned the scattered personal bric-a-brac to their places, and the attic no longer looked as though a hurricane had blown through, we left the trunks open so that the ghosts would be drawn back to them by the power of their possessions. Gwyneth turned over an hourglass.

We waited for ten minutes while the sand trickled from one chamber to the other, but no ghosts returned.

"We'll have to use a stronger lure." Gwyneth went to a small cabinet set on bun-shaped feet. Unlike the attic itself, the cabinet was well protected with wards, hexes, sigils, and a stout iron lock. My aunt murmured the wards away and inserted a heavy key into the mechanism. Maybe Gwyneth would bring forward the unit on locks and keys, too. She drew the doors open and removed a small bottle with a ribbon tied around its neck. The ribbon bore a tag, inscribed with a spidery script like one of the bottles Alice found in Wonderland.

"*Nineteen October 1834*," Gwyneth read from the bottle's label. "*First frosts and final harvests.* That should fetch them."

The bottle reminded me of the tiny vials of perfume that my mother liked to keep on her dresser. Mom could never bear to part with them, even when the liquid was gone. Her empty bottles of Diorissimo were still on display in my parents' bedroom in Madison.

Gwyneth held the simple glass vessel up to the witchlight. It was securely stoppered, empty except for a single, crumbling rose hip. My curiosity must have shown.

"Whenever a handful of ghosts escape, there are bound to be problems getting them back into their trunks," Gwyneth explained, handing me the bottle.

I was surprised by its weight. The small vessel was far heavier than it should be, given its size.

"They like a good gossip, and there's a lot of weeping and wailing when it comes time to return," Gwyneth continued. "It's essential to have a plentiful stock of happy memories like this one. The elders find their lure irresistible."

"You *can* bottle happiness?" This was contrary to every bit of advice I'd ever received. I handed the precious bottle back to my aunt.

"No. Just the memory of it." Gwyneth's tone was tinged with regret.

My aunt twisted the cork in the neck of the bottle, cracking its wax seal and releasing a scent of fallen leaves and apple cider. I felt a crisp breeze on my skin, and the warm sun on my face. Children could be heard playing in the distance, their voices raised as they scampered across the meadow where piles of golden grass had been cut and gathered. A cow lowed, a bell sounded. A ship under full sail passed by The Nestling. I shielded my eyes to see it better, but my hand was not my own.

I was looking out at the world through different eyes, seeing what someone else had seen, a very long time ago.

Gwyneth put the cork back in the bottle and the scent of leaf mold and apples faded, taking the precious glimpse of the past with it. I was hungry for more, wanting to remain in that happy time forever.

I was not the only one. Greenish vapor trails appeared outside the fractured window glass, passing through the panes and resolving into small, angular rainbows that resembled those cast by prisms set out in the sun. The rainbows shone against the steep, pitched walls and along the pine boards. Some easily found their box and settled into it with a sigh. There, they brightened briefly, then went dark.

Gwyneth was ready with her wand as the wayward ghosts returned. She gently closed the lids and locked them, murmuring the spells that would keep them safely contained until Midsummer.

I watched my aunt work with interest, fascinated by the success of the happy memory bottle and intrigued by how it was created and used. The bottle had provided me with a brief timewalk into the past—one that didn't require a special outfit so you could blend in when and where you arrived.

"We won't get to the arts of memory this summer, I'm afraid," my aunt said, aware of my keen attention. "Those subjects are reserved for advanced initiates who are well beyond the Crossroads and nearing the Labyrinth." A few trunks still stood open, and she drew a weary hand across her brow.

"Who do those belong to?" I asked, lowering my voice in case there were still ghosts around who might hear.

"Naomi, Stephen, Julius Proctor, who was lost at sea." Gwyneth pointed to each box in turn. "Granny Dorcas, who is refusing to be re-homed at the moment, she's having such a fine time among the living. She'll need to replenish her energy soon. Maybe Julie and Put-Put will be able to cajole her inside with an open bottle of scotch and a cigarette. And that box belongs to Roger Toothaker, of course, who haunts the meetinghouse. He's only a relation by marriage and doesn't believe that he deserves a death sentence in the Old Place's attic."

I wanted to dive into each trunk and pull out every remnant of their lives. The dented camp trunk that had my father's initials on it and Naomi's purple suitcase were especially enticing.

"Perhaps I should . . . No." Gwyneth turned a question over in her mind. "It might be safer if . . ." My aunt trailed off again, then nodded. "We should let Tally out to help keep a lid on things as we get closer to Midsummer."

At long last, I was going to meet my paternal grandfather.

"I should have realized that Tally's presence would be necessary," she continued. "All those years in the Army taught him a thing or two about disciplining the troops. He'll keep the other ghosts from meddling with you at the Crossroads as well as ensure the potluck doesn't turn into Haverhill's haunted farm."

"I'm going to face Meg here—at Ravenswood?" It would be a considerable home-court advantage and I was surprised that the coven had agreed to it.

"Ann called late last night. It was Meg's suggestion," Gwyneth said, her mouth set in a grim line. "She's up to something— Oh hell, Meg's *always* up to something. Perhaps she thinks that the family ghosts won't be able to keep themselves from the Crossroads. Maybe she hopes the Proctors' ancestral bones will rise out of the earth and reject you."

It was a horrifying thought, given the number of bodies buried there.

"But Meg has no idea what powers are available to a Proctor in the Ravens' Wood," Gwyneth said. "This *maleficio* of hers is going to backfire. Meanwhile, we'll have Tally out and about to make sure nothing is brewing, spiritually speaking."

"You're sure Meg doesn't have Proctor blood in her veins?" I asked my aunt.

"Not a dewdrop." Gwyneth sat back on her heels. "Now that we know that her challenge will take place here and not at some other Crossroads,

I can take you to the exact spot where you'll meet Meg and look for your path. It will help to settle your nerves and give you a feel for the place. We can go there as soon as I get Tally out of his trunk."

Gwyneth carefully stepped across the boards to a row of footlockers tucked under the eaves. Some were stenciled with names, and I easily found the one belonging to Lieutenant T. Proctor, U.S. Army. The metal lid was dented and didn't close properly.

"Ike had to bash it shut last time," Gwyneth explained. "Once I unlock it, you'll have to pry the lid open. That boy wedged it tight."

Gwyneth went through her ring of keys and found the one that fit the lock. I worked the lid this way and that, putting all my might into loosening it. I even banged it up and down on the boards as though it were a giant pickle jar, hoping that would break the seal.

The lid opened with a pop and a whoosh of air that was pale green and nearly opaque. The strand of green grew longer and more transparent before it found a broken windowpane and dissipated through it and out into the air of Ravenswood.

"There goes Tally," Gwyneth said, wistful.

I was disappointed as well. I'd hoped that my grandfather would want to apparate before me, so that we could be introduced.

"Don't take it personally, Diana," my aunt said, gauging my reaction. "Tally was never one to linger. And he won't have gone far."

"Can I look inside?" I was still holding on to the rolled metal edges of the lid.

"I don't think your grandfather would mind," Gwyneth replied.

Gingerly, I lifted the lid higher. Folded inside was the white suit he'd worn to his wedding with Ruby. There was a brass Army buckle, too, and a wool garrison cap pinned with two bars and piped in black and gold cord. My aunt must have cast some formidable moth-repelling spells in the attic, for the cap was remarkably well preserved. Another flash of black and gold caught my eye.

I lifted a patch with neatly clipped threads still dangling from the edge. There were no division numbers, or other identifying marks, only a spade-shaped arrow that resembled the golden arrowhead that Philippe de Clermont had given me. It was always on a chain or cord around my neck, and I touched it regularly for comfort.

"What is this?" I asked.

"It's the badge for Tally's military unit," Gwyneth replied. "The OSS."

I knew Hitler relied on witches and their supernatural powers, but I'd never imagined the U.S. Army had done the same.

"Tally never spoke about his OSS days to me," Gwyneth said. "I know he was in Europe, unlike Putnam, who was stationed in the South Pacific. After the war ended, Tally was evasive about where he'd been deployed, and when."

I drew a small circlet of brass buttons from the trunk. They were tied together with a thin red ribbon, and rattled when I held them up to the witchlight. Once, they had ornamented the front of Grandpa Tally's uniform. Like his cap, they were in pristine condition. Reluctantly, I put the buttons back in his footlocker.

"I wonder what else he did during the war," I said, lowering the lid.

"Your grandfather was one of the finest men who ever lived," Gwyneth said, "utterly fearless and sound of heart. Whatever Tally did in the war was done with honor, you can be sure."

I nodded, thinking of Philippe. The two men sounded similar, and I felt certain that they would have been friends had they had the chance.

"Let's get some fresh air," Gwyneth suggested, soft-voiced with understanding. "I think it's time you saw the Crossroads for yourself."

We entered the Ravens' Wood through a narrow opening atop the rise near the witch's tree, rather than taking the familiar path from the Old Place. It felt like an entirely different place, with none of the deer paths and tree houses that served as landmarks in the lower wood. Here the wood was bathed in a perpetual twilight that cast strange shadows in all directions.

"This is where you'll enter the Ravens' Wood on the night you meet

Meg," Gwyneth explained. "Ann, Katrina, and I will be waiting for you here, and together we will go to the Crossroads."

"Where will Meg be?" I asked.

"Wherever she chooses," Gwyneth replied. "Some challengers meet their opponent outside the wood, in an effort to intimidate them, but I don't think that's Meg's style."

Nor did I. Meg would lurk in Shadow, then appear without warning.

The wood opened its thick underbrush to let us pass, then closed behind us.

"Ravenswood has become expert at hiding its secrets," Gwyneth explained. "It will only reveal what you are ready to see and comprehend."

"That's why the way to the river was so clear, and the path filled with tree houses," I said. The wood had only offered a curated glimpse of itself to Matthew and the children.

Mirages of graveyards and ghosts of fires long extinguished shimmered before me and disappeared. In the distance, I saw the ruins of a tower, the top crumbled away to reveal a room filled with women embroidering tapestries on spell-looms. They seemed real and tangible, but when I blinked, they were gone.

"This part of the wood belongs to Shadow," Gwyneth warned. "Nothing is as it seems, and you must learn to differentiate between truth and fantasy."

A witch sat inside a carriage made from a gigantic hollow egg, feet pressing against the pedals that kept its wheels turning.

"There goes one of the shades," Gwyneth said. "They're not ghosts, but manifestations of Ravenswood's magic and can be a help or a hindrance. I recommend you ignore them, until you become more familiar with their ways."

We crossed a glen and passed by an enchanted garden enclosed within a baneberry hedge. Though little sunlight penetrated this far into the depths of the Ravens' Wood, it was filled with blooms and the air was redolent with the intoxicating scents of flowers, fruits, and herbs that weren't normally in season at the same time.

"How?" It was the only word I could utter, my mind befuddled by the strong smell of rose, lilac, and carnation.

"It's my moon garden," Gwyneth replied. "It blooms according to lunar phases, not the progress of the sun. At the full moon, the garden reaches the peak of its growth cycle. After that, the flowers slowly wither and then set seeds under the crescent moon. The seeds lie dormant, gathering energy, until the moon waxes again."

On we walked, through another clearing and around a patch of red-and-white-speckled toadstools. We came upon curved stone walls covered in moss and lichen.

"This is all that remains of the Proctor family labyrinth," Gwyneth said, surveying the green mounds. "Before witches went to Isola della Stella, many communities maintained labyrinths. We trained our kin there, tested one another, and sent reports to Venice every now and then. Some were hidden in gardens, or marked out with tree trunks, or even scratched into the ground and swept clean later."

The Proctor labyrinth must have been impressive when it was first constructed. It still made a mark, even in its decrepit state.

Gwyneth led me past the labyrinth to the remains of a tree that had been stripped of its bark and polished to a high sheen, like the mast of a tall ship. Its circumference was easily twenty feet, and its flat top was large enough to stand on.

"What is this place?" I said, my weaver's cords animated beneath my skin.

"This is the Crossroads," Gwyneth said, her voice echoing in the hush. "Here is where you will meet Meg. Here you will find your path through Shadow."

"I don't see any paths," I said, looking at the dark ground.

"You have to find them," Gwyneth said. "It's difficult enough for a witch to do so without someone thwarting her at every turn."

"So Meg's challenge isn't typical?" My suspicion that Meg was targeting me, not Gwyneth, was confirmed. My aunt had simply been collateral damage.

"No, but they do happen," Gwyneth admitted. "Old grudges and feuds often bubble to the surface during these milestone rituals, and challengers step forward to distract their opponent so that they don't notice the paths the goddess prepares."

I thought I'd be playing defense in this challenge. It sounded as though the opposite were true.

"Meg's best chance of beating you is to wear you down so that you become frustrated and hopeless," Gwyneth continued. "Many witches turn away from the Crossroads after a few hours of fruitless searching. Most never return, though there are always opportunities for second and third chances."

"So being at the Crossroads is no guarantee I'll find a path forward into higher magic," I said slowly, beginning to understand how hard a task I'd set for myself.

"Not at all," Gwyneth said. "The goddess always has a trick up her sleeve that can't be foreseen."

"And if I find my Dark Path?" I asked. "What will Meg do then?"

"She will try to force you in another direction," Gwyneth said. "You wouldn't be the first witch to mistake Darkness for the Dark Path, and travel out of the Crossroads and into the territory of nightmares."

"Elsewhere," I said.

Gwyneth nodded.

A man sat under a tree, smoking a cigarette. He was long of limb and broad of shoulder, with golden hair touched with copper. I jumped, startled I hadn't noticed him.

"I'm going to leave you to explore on your own," Gwyneth said, squeezing my hand. "Stay as long as you like. Get familiar with the place. The ravens will see that you make it back to the Old Place."

"There's a man—" I said, pointing at the woods.

But there was no trace of him now.

"Take your time," Gwyneth said, releasing my hand and melting into the wood.

After my aunt vanished, I walked the clearing, wanting to make sure that no one was watching me. Satisfied that I was truly alone, I ran my hands along the smooth surface of the post. With no signs or markers pointing the way, it was easy to dismiss it as just an odd relic of a tree. I put my back to it and slid down until I sat at the base, resting against the stout trunk.

I inhaled, filling my lungs with the air of the wood. With each breath, I was changed. The wood altered my perception, so that I was more aware of the enchantment that was stored in every plant and tree. My ears tuned in to the flight of the birds and the sounds made by the small creatures who lived here. The weaver's cords in my left wrist tingled as they met the intricate web of power that extended across all of Ravenswood. My breath fell in sync with the soughing of the tree limbs and I felt a sense of calm like none I'd experienced before. I closed my eyes to savor it.

See. There's nothing to be afraid of.

My eyes flew open. The man I'd seen earlier was crouched before me, his forearms resting easily on his knees. He looked like Tally, but he was not so young as he had been in his wedding picture or even the formal shot of him in his officer's uniform. Bitter experience had etched the skin around his eyes, and a melancholy air surrounded him.

"Grandpa?" I held my breath, worried that he might be a shade of the wood and not a ghost at all.

Grandpa Tally nodded. His energy was bright after months spent in his footlocker, and he looked as solid and lively as I did.

"Thank you," I said softly, moved to tears. "Thank you for trying to save Philippe."

Shadow flickered around my grandfather, as Grandpa Tally smiled through his own unshed tears.

I had to try, Grandpa Tally said. *I kept trying, too, even though Madame de Clermont warned me to keep away.*

"It was unspeakably brave of you to go behind enemy lines, into Vichy France, and track down Ysabeau de Clermont when she was angry and hurting," I said. "Most witches wouldn't have dared."

It was the right thing to do, Tally said shyly, as though the decision had been a simple one. *I'd sworn an oath to speak out if I suspected that higher magic was being used for evil purposes. I couldn't break my word.*

"Gwyneth said you were fearless," I said.

.

Without fear, you can do the impossible, Tally replied. *That's what Shadow teaches us.*

"Ambiguity and uncertainty frighten most creatures," I said, thinking of Matthew.

Tally waited, knowing there was more to come.

"My husband was raised in a black-and-white world, where good and evil were clearly delineated. Shadow terrifies him," I continued.

But not you. Grandpa Tally was matter-of-fact. *Not your mother.*

"My mother feared losing my father," I said, bitter. "She turned her back on higher magic and kept me away from the Proctors rather than lose him. She put me in magical shackles and left me alone in Madison with no sense of who I was or what I might become."

Is that what you think, Diana Bishop? My mother stood behind Tally, hands on hips. She wore her favorite menswear: a secondhand brown tweed vest with a white shirt she nicked from my father and oversized trousers cinched at the waist with a belt.

Tally rose and drifted away, leaving me with my mother.

"You chose to turn your back on higher magic because Dad threatened to leave you if you didn't," I said, swallowing back tears. "How could you give up your power for him?"

I didn't give up my power for your father, my mother said. *I gave it up for you.*

I stared at her in disbelief. "Me?"

I wanted to be a mother—your mother—more than anything else in the world, Mom explained. *Nothing else mattered to me: not your father's wishes, or a seat at the Congregation table, or all the power in the world.*

"But—why?" I asked.

My mother's answering laugh was rich as honey and warm as firelight. Its comfort sank into my bones, relieving old wounds.

Because I dreamed of you at night and missed you by day, Diana, she said. *Before you were ever born, I knew I would do anything to hold you in my arms. I discovered that higher magic wasn't really my life's path—it was yours. And I wanted you to have it.*

"First I have to find it," I said, looking around the Crossroads.

You'll find it, my mother promised. *But only when you stop looking for it.*

T hat night, I lay in Matthew's arms, my legs twined through his, as I told him about my visit to the Crossroads and Meg's likely strategy.

"It may be for the best that Meg will be trying to deflect, rather than attack, me. I'm not good at defense," I confessed.

Matthew chuckled. "No, *ma lionne,* you are not. You have too much courage."

"Grandpa Tally was the same," I said, hoping that Matthew would tell me more about my grandfather, Ysabeau, and World War II.

"Hmm," Matthew said, his finger inscribing lazy circles around the scars on my back.

We both bore the traces of our past battles: mine with Satu Järvinen, Matthew's with hundreds of foes during centuries of conflict. They were a constant reminder that courage, like miracles, often left a mark.

"What are you thinking?" I propped myself up on his shoulder.

"That you need one of Baldwin's battle plans," Matthew replied. Baldwin was the family's master strategist and had been responsible for most de Clermont victories on and off the field.

"I'd rather have one of yours," I said, not wanting my brother-in-law to know about my upcoming ordeal.

"Mine wouldn't suit you," Matthew said. "I prefer to wait until my enemy reveals their weakness."

"Teach me how." I tried to tickle Matthew into agreement.

He barely moved.

"Pleeease." Maybe wheedling would work.

Matthew yawned.

I touched my teeth to his shoulder. A little nip usually got his attention.

Nothing.

"Damn you, Matthew, I'm just asking for some help!" I said, frustrated.

I found myself on my back, arms pinned to my sides, and Matthew on top of me.

"Being thwarted is your weakness," Matthew purred. "Impatience, too. You want what you want, when you want it. It's your Achilles' heel."

"Meg's entire purpose is to thwart me." I groaned. "I'm never going to find my way at the Crossroads."

"Would that be so terrible?" Matthew searched my face for clues.

"I want to succeed," I said, knowing it wasn't what he wanted to hear. "I'm afraid that if I don't, I'll hunger for what might have been."

Matthew listened, his face grave. "You've tasted forbidden fruit, eaten from the Tree of Good and Evil. You won't be satisfied without it."

"Not evil." I pushed against his chest with all my might. "Higher magic is not evil."

Matthew rolled so that I was on top, straddling his hips with my legs. My eyes sparked in warning, and the ends of my hair were aflame.

"What are you afraid of, Matthew?" I demanded.

"That if you do succeed, I won't like who you become." Matthew's fathomless eyes met mine.

I slid away, not wanting Matthew's truth, though I had demanded it of him—a truth hidden deep in Shadow, where it could damage all that we'd shared and built together.

How could I face Meg, now that I knew Matthew's fear? The arrowhead the goddess gave Philippe was warm on my skin, a reminder that she was not done with me, and my courage returned, carried on a wave of anger.

"You are a wolf, but I am a lion," I said, my voice fierce. "I will not be tamed. And whether you like me or not, a lion mates for life."

"So does a wolf," Matthew replied. "As for your battle at the Crossroads, you have no need of my advice. A lion survives on instinct and wits."

Wolves, like lions, were also apex predators.

"You don't want me to be your rival—your equal." I had heard what my husband had said. More importantly, I'd heard what he hadn't said.

"No." Matthew's eyes filled with sorrow. "I want you to be my superior—to refuse Darkness because I could not."

I lay beside him, staring up at the ceiling. Bridget Bishop once told me that there was no road forward that didn't include Matthew. I clung to her words, repeating them like a spell, relying on them like a prophecy.

"I love you, *mon coeur*," Matthew murmured. "I always will."

I reached through Darkness and found his hand.

My path forward may not be smooth, but it *would* have Matthew in it. I was not done with him yet.

Chapter 15

When I arrived at the witch's tree outside the Ravens' Wood, on the night of Meg's challenge, three witches awaited me as promised: Ann Downing, Katrina, and Aunt Gwyneth.

There was no sign of Meg Skelling.

The high priestess wore her black hooded cape of office to underscore the seriousness of tonight's proceedings. Ann was not the only witch to have dressed for the occasion. Mary Sidney had taught me the importance of being properly clothed—*armored* had been her term—when she prepared me to meet the queen of England in 1591. Then, I'd worn one of Mary's old gowns, carried a splendid ostrich-feather fan, and balanced a face-framing ruff on my shoulders. Tonight, I'd chosen a crisp white shirt, the cuffs pushed up in recognition of the warm weather, and a black linen skirt that swished around my ankles when I walked. For some reason, my habitual black leggings, though comfortable, didn't feel right and I went for a witchier vibe. I'd been sure to slide the fine wires of Ysabeau's pearl earrings through the holes in my ears. It would be comforting to have tokens of Matthew's formidable mother with me tonight. After I'd wrapped a bright woven belt around my waist and piled my hair atop my head in a loose knot, even Mary would have approved.

Matthew did, too. I'd feared our moonlit exchange would make him distant, splintering our partnership when I most needed his support. But honesty had brought new intimacy as our truths were led to Light, safe from the terrors of Darkness and Shadow.

"I'll be waiting under the chestnut tree when you're done," Matthew had promised me earlier before I left him at Orchard Farm. He'd kissed me, soft and sweet. I could still taste him on my tongue, taking some part of him with me into battle, too.

"Meg Skelling has challenged your fitness for the Dark Path of higher magic," Ann Downing said without preamble. "Do you accept it? There is no shame in turning away."

"I haven't changed my mind," I said, my chin rising above my turned-up collar. "It's the goddess's decision whether I pursue the path of higher magic—not Meg's."

"Very well. But there are no rules in a Crossroads challenge," Ann warned. "No magic is off-limits. Nor is there a set duration for the test. The contest continues until one of you yields."

Neither Meg nor I was the yielding type. We could be there for days.

"Goody Wu will watch over the challenge from here," Ann explained. "If she foresees there is danger to life or limb, she will call an immediate halt and give her judgment regarding next steps."

"Remember, Diana, that it takes most of us several attempts at the Crossroads to find our path, even without another witch trying to obscure it," Katrina said. "To try once and return to try again is not a mark of failure."

I nodded, eager to get on with it.

We walked to the Crossroads in silence. Once there, Ann delivered her final warning.

"No one knows what Meg's challenge will entail, or how treacherous the Dark Path may become," the high priestess said. "When two witches enter the Crossroads, the goddess is present. You will not only be meeting each other, matching wits and wands, but honoring her as well."

"Knowing this, are you ready to begin?" Aunt Gwyneth asked.

The stakes could not have been higher, and yet I found myself calm. I'd been through other tribunals before this, and survived other fraught moments with the goddess.

"I'm ready." My wand—a small stick of rowan with a pointed piece of agate mounted at the tip—vibrated in my skirt pocket. It was resting on

The Dark Path card from the black bird oracle, a lucky talisman for my encounter with Meg.

"This is where we leave you," Ann said, drawing the folds of her cape close. "If you require help, all you need do is call."

I would not be calling anyone. My expression must have told the three witches as much. Katrina's eyes glimmered with respect.

Aunt Gwyneth pressed her lips against my cheek in a final farewell.

"Catch you on the flip side," I said. It had been one of my father's favorite expressions, and I hoped it would reassure my aunt.

"Yes, you will," Gwyneth said with a smile, a tear threatening to fall from her eye. "Follow the footsteps of the goddess and she will keep you safe."

I watched until the three witches disappeared from view. Silence fell where the stake was driven into the heart of the Ravens' Wood. Any hope that a sign would appear that said DIANA'S PATH THIS WAY vanished. The polished trunk was just as it had been when I'd visited the place before: simple, straight, and unhelpful.

I scanned the ground, looking for any trace of a path. Here, too, I was disappointed. Gwyneth had told me that there was no way to predict what would happen at the Crossroads. She hadn't warned me that nothing at all might happen.

I stood, wondering what to do next.

After a few moments of silent indecision, I drew my wand and concentrated on the agate tip until it sparkled with an otherworldly blue-gold light. Hopefully the beacon would lure Meg out of hiding, just as Gwyneth's memory perfume had lured the ghosts back to the attic.

Here I am! my witchlight cried. *Come out, come out, wherever you are.*

Nothing.

The stake stood out against its wooded backdrop. I took a step toward it, then another, expecting a thunderclap or a falling tree or some other sign of divine agency. I lifted my wand high, hoping that it would illuminate my way in the murky wood.

All I succeeded in doing was casting long shadows.

Light is a resource, not a weapon, I reminded myself, lowering my wand so that Light, Darkness, and Shadow could return to their delicate balance.

My breath deepened, as it had when I'd spoken to Grandpa Tally, moving with the inhalations and exhalations of the Ravens' Wood and replenishing my power. Though a sense of enchantment settled into my bones, I didn't lower my guard.

Maybe I needed to utter one of the spells Gwyneth had had me weave to protect me from danger. It wasn't entirely satisfactory yet. When my aunt had told me to pick a text for my spell's gramarye, I'd chosen something from the complete poems of the witch of Amherst, and I wasn't sure they were fit for this purpose.

"*A Moment—We uncertain step / For newness of the night.*" My feet moved toward the stake at the center of the Crossroads and my eyes fluttered shut. "*Then—fit our Vision to the Dark— / And meet the Road— erect—*"

"Emily Dickinson? You're out of your depth, witch." Meg's condescending voice reverberated through the air, beating upon my ears from every direction so that I couldn't locate her.

The treetops above me whipped in a sudden wind and a black bird plummeted from the sky, falling toward the stake in the clearing like the raven had fallen to the pavement in New Haven. The creature was too large to be natural or even preternatural. Meg must have conjured it from some dark place.

"Stop!" I cried, knotting a netted ward to catch the bird before it impaled itself.

The bird tumbled in midair, revealing that this was no magical beast but Meg Skelling, using her black hooded cape like wings.

Meg landed lightly atop the wooden post. She bent her knees and wrapped the cloth around her so that she resembled a vulture. Her face was hidden in the depths of her hood, her features obscured by Shadow.

I directed my wand toward Meg, brightening my witchlight so that I could see her more clearly. The witchlight didn't improve matters, and I extinguished it.

"*I see thee better—in the Dark,*" I murmured, weaving a quick perspective spell to enhance my night vision and immediately clothing it in a half-remembered fragment of Dickinson's poetry.

My eyes adjusted further to the tenebrous environment of the Ravens' Wood, a play of dark on dark that flattened the trees into silhouettes and the undergrowth to a charcoal smudge.

"If you're looking for your destiny here, you're not going to find it." Meg was puffed up with confidence. "You're a Bishop, through and through. Go back to Madison."

A woman wearing a pale yellow shirt with a rounded white collar passed between Meg and me. Her hair was arranged in a loose knot, and a penny-farthing replaced her torso and legs. Gray wings sprouted out of the larger of the two wheels, and as it spun, the wings flapped up and down.

I was hallucinating. I closed my eyes to blot out the disturbing, surreal sight. When I opened them again, the woman was on the far side of the clearing, cycling around the perimeter in midair.

The bicycle-woman must be a shade of the wood. Perhaps she was trying to lead me onto the Dark Path. Though Gwyneth had advised me to stay away from the shades, I darted past the post at the Crossroads in pursuit of her.

"Oh, it's not going to be that easy." Meg directed her wand at my feet and the earth below me gave way.

I scrambled to remain upright but couldn't gain purchase in the crumbling soil. I grabbed for an exposed tree root to keep from being buried alive. I'd been thrown into an oubliette before and lived to tell the tale. Even if the ground beneath me was full of bones, I would somehow get out of Meg's hole, too.

The ancient tree swayed. A green face looked out from a hollow in its trunk with a serene expression. Here was another shade, this one wrapped in shrouds as though she had been laid to rest inside the tree.

A silver thread shot past my eyes, then a green one. I caught them, and rapidly tied a knot with six crossings.

"With knot of six, this spell I fix," I murmured, casting the knot into the air. Hopefully it would snag one of the oak's low branches and I would be able to pull myself free.

No sooner had I released the spell than a woman made of flame reached out of Shadow and clasped my raised hand. Her hair streamed upward, rising from the heat of her body in licks of brilliant red and gold. She held a glass alembic in her free hand, and a miniature mortar and pestle hung from a chain around her neck.

The acrid scent of burning feathers teased my nose. It grew stronger, as did the pressure of Darkness that surrounded the fiery creature.

Meg threw a silver athame in the shade's direction. "A green-and-silver knot? You think that will stop me? Pathetic."

Before the athame could cut my spell in two, the flaming shade stepped between the blade and the knot. The blade cleaved her in half and she turned an ashen gray, her hand disintegrating in mine. Darkness rushed into the void where her heart should have been, growing like a parasite.

Horrified, I put all my weight on a nearby tree's root and clambered out of the pit. I needed to redress the balance of power in the clearing, or I would never find my way out of the wood—never mind finding my path.

I cobbled together other fragments from Dickinson's poems that I'd read but failed to fully memorize.

"*Come to me, cling to me,*" I cried. "*Shadow, hear my plea. Go and tell the hourglass, Darkness is about to Pass.*"

I plucked at the threads of Light and Darkness that I could see in the gloaming and tied them into a chain using simple knots with only two crossings. I repeated the words of my spell, overlapping the strands until thick smoke creeped into the clearing. Shadow was rallying to my aid.

"So, you do have a touch of talent," Meg acknowledged, "enough to stop the Darkness. But do you have the courage to fend off the Light?"

Meg directed her wand to the night sky. The waning moon hung over us, surrounded by a watery silver penumbra. Meg twisted her wand like a distaff, winding a moonbeam around the tip. She cast it down from her perch, where it illuminated a patch of ground. Meg captured another, and another. Soon, Light would overwhelm Shadow and throw the wood into disorder once more.

Calling back the Darkness would restore its equilibrium, but I lacked the confidence to do so. I didn't have the expertise or the experience to win a protracted magical battle, and Meg had a greater arsenal of spells and counterspells at her disposal.

Think and stay alive, I told myself fiercely, repeating Philippe de Clermont's wise advice.

I searched among the shades gliding through the clearing, looking for potential allies. A shade reading a book approached. She pulled a small cart that carried a piece of distillation apparatus made from two alembics luted together. Fine multicolored threads emerged from small holes in the upper chamber of the stillatory and meandered into the world.

Perhaps the appearance of the thread twister was a sign that I should stitch up the shade who had gone from fire to ash. I searched the clearing and spotted her, walking widdershins through the trees.

"May I use some of your thread?" I asked the reading shade.

She tore her eyes away from her text and looked up. It was like looking into a mirror. The shade's face was my own.

Without reply, my simulacrum dropped her gaze back to the book, absorbed in the words. I pulled a white thread, then a gray from her alembic.

I dragged them over to the ashen shade who had once been so fiery and brilliant.

"May I mend you?" I showed her the threads.

Charcoal tears of gratitude streamed down her gray face.

I transformed my wand into a large needle and threaded the gray and white threads through the eye. I pierced the shade's ashen flesh, but the skin was delicate and crumbled into the pulsing Darkness within her ribs.

I would have to weave a patch instead. Swiftly, I drew the thread diagonally across the wound, creating the warp to hold the weft.

From her perch at the Crossroads, Meg swore, but I didn't have the time to focus on her next move. The shade's suffering was palpable.

A gust of poisonous green air tore through the trees, sending leaves flying. A moth beat its wings against my face. Another alighted on my shoulder. A third clung to my breast, its antennae moving. I batted the moths away, but whenever my fingers brushed against them, one moth became five. Soon I was shrouded in a cocoon of velvet wings, unable to mend the shade's riven body.

"*Owl Queen, teach me to see like thee!*" I drew once again on the succinct, evocative words of Emily Dickinson for inspiration. "*Alter Darkness and adjust my sight to midnight.*"

A wild shriek split the night and the moths fluttered away in alarm. Before me stood a woman with a mantle made from downy feathers. Her features were those of an owl, and she held a silver crescent moon in one hand and a net filled with moths in the other.

It was the Owl Queen from the black bird oracle. The shades here at the Crossroads were not arbitrary magical manifestations traveling between worlds. These spirits were specific to me, and the powers of higher magic that I possessed.

"Can you show me the way?" I asked the Owl Queen, elated at the prospect of finding my path to higher magic and foiling Meg's plans.

This is *the way,* the Owl Queen hooted. *Silence or secrets, wisdom or war. What is your destiny? What's your life for?*

Meg shrieked again in frustration. She was still atop the central post, still intent on keeping me from finding the way forward.

"You will never find your path here!" Meg held a ball of malevolent, green power in one hand and an inky orb in the other. She combined the two into a spitting sphere of Darkness and hurled it at me.

I watched in horror as the Owl Queen prepared to absorb Meg's malice, fearless in the face of the incoming threat. Her cloak thickened and fluttered in anticipation of the strike.

One shade had already been damaged by Meg's magic. I didn't want the Owl Queen to suffer the same fate.

"*Shadow, hold your breath!*" I cried.

Clouds obscured the crescent moon in the Owl Queen's outstretched hand, dimming its light and making Darkness dominant.

Another wraithlike shade appeared, pearlescent gray against the gloom. She looked like a refugee from a terrible war, her cheeks gaunt and her eyes wide and vacant as though she couldn't bear to close them in case her terrors found her. Her gray hair cascaded up into the night, the stiff strands resembling bare branches. This shade had a gaping wound at her core. Within the hollow space where ribs, heart, and lungs should have been I saw a forest that resembled the Ravens' Wood.

But it was the woven circlet around her body that drew my attention. Once, the shade's circlet had been a closed ring like the tenth knot, but it was in tatters now. The woman tried in vain to join the frayed ends and make the circle whole.

Help me, her lips mouthed, and she extended her arms so that the ends of the circlet brushed against my fingers.

At the touch of the frayed strands, my arms brightened with words and phrases inscribed in black, red, and gold. The shade's touch had awakened the Book of Life within me. I'd absorbed its contents from Ashmole 782 years ago in the Bodleian, but it hadn't manifested for some time.

I looked into the shade's haunted eyes and saw a dull glimmer of recognition.

"Naomi?"

The shade was the withered husk of my father's sister, hollowed out by Darkness and higher magic. But Naomi shouldn't have been a shade; she was dead, and should have been with the family's other ghosts, not trapped in this shadowland. Had a weaver cast the tenth knot around her? Was that why she'd chosen death—not because of some failure of her own but because another witch had set out to destroy her?

Naomi shivered, her eyes blackening as Darkness came nearer, drawn by her despair.

Help me, she cried silently, her mouth wide in an effort to break through whatever barrier kept her from speaking aloud. *I am Elsewhere.*

My thoughts froze. Becca had been *Elsewhere.*

Determined to save Naomi from everlasting in-betweenness, I wondered what would happen if I repaired the damaged circlet surrounding my father's twin. Would she be healed and freed? Or would she be destroyed and banished to an even darker reality?

I had only cast the tenth knot once, to destroy Knox and save Matthew's life, but I was prepared to do so again. Gently, I took the silver and black strands of the broken tenth knot and began the painstaking work of reweaving it, reciting the ritual Goody Alsop had taught me.

Naomi's shivering turned violent, her body writhing. She had suffered enough.

"With knot of one, the spell's begun," I said calmly, hoping my tone would relieve Naomi's agitation. "With knot of two, the spell be true. With knot of three, the spell be free. With knot of four, the power is stored."

I made knot after knot, one crossing, then two, then three, then four. My left hand gleamed with power, my black, silver, gold, and white weaver's cords shifting under the skin as I drew on higher magic. But another color had appeared on my index finger in a line of regal purple. It symbolized the goddess's justice. I was reassured by the sight of it, and knew I was doing the right thing. The hoop around Naomi drew close, and the Book of Life sparkled under my skin. The shade who looked like me, with her book and alembic, returned, drawing raven and silver threads out of her stillatory and twisting them together into a shining cord of Shadow. She handed the end to me.

"With knot of five, the spell will thrive," I said, weaving the shade's thread into my knot.

Naomi's head tipped back as a fresh wave of agony struck. I was chilled to the bone, aware of the imbalance in the wood as Darkness grew. All I could do to help my aunt, however, was continue with my weaving.

"With knot of six, this spell I fix," I said, making the six-crossed knot. "With knot of seven, the spell will waken. With knot of eight the spell will wait."

My fingers flew, and I continued to draw on the alchemist-shade's offering of strong, fresh thread to support my knots.

"With spell of nine, the spell is mine." This was the potent knot of endings and change, which Naomi sorely needed.

Naomi looked at me with gratitude as the racking pain left her body and its poison was absorbed by the wood. The energy around me shifted, too, tilting perilously toward utter Darkness.

A single knot remained. Would it bring relief to Naomi, or destruction?

"Are you sure?" I asked my father's sister.

Naomi nodded and closed her eyes with a sigh.

"With knot of ten, it begins again." I joined the two ends of the silver-and-black ring around Naomi's frail body, hoping that it would give her the blessing of closure and the ghostly rebirth that waited for her on the other side.

With a cry of joy, Naomi's shade disintegrated, falling to the ground in a cloud of silver and gray dust. A white raven rose from the ashes, cackling and calling to its kin. Owls came to bear witness to Naomi's transformation, perching on the branches and hooting with excitement. Two herons passed overhead, casting strange, bent shadows. A vulture sat, silent as a judge, observing the magic I'd made.

The ravens were the last to arrive.

They surrounded the white bird, their black wings caressing her with light touches. They tumbled and rolled in the air, welcoming Naomi's spirit home.

My eyes filled, and tears fell. Witchwater rose within me, and I released it so that it could wash away the residue of the dark magic I'd used to free my aunt from Elsewhere.

A path opened before me, extending to an oak tree, where the enormous gray owl I'd seen with my mother sat on a low branch. Her eyes glowed, twin orbs of yellow Light wrapped in feathered Shadow.

Feathers lined the path toward the magnificent bird. I stooped to pick them up, and with every new feather, the Book of Life shone brighter underneath my skin, until the line between its story and my own was indistinct and I felt the will of the goddess illuminating my way.

The owl blinked, the light of her eyes extinguished.

When she opened them again, I let them guide me down the Dark Path. I reached the oak and sank my nails into the bark, lowering my forehead in relief.

You chose your path. The goddess stepped from the tree's shadow. Her face was a web of wrinkles, and furrows marked her brow. The hands that held her curved bow were gnarled and knotted. *Your purpose is to use your full power—Light, Shadow, and Dark—in the service of others, just as you used them here. Some might have called on Darkness to subdue their enemy, or on Light to drive Shadow away. You have proven that you are suited to the Dark Path and its mysteries, daughter.*

I didn't know whether to weep with joy or despair at this new bargain with the goddess.

Do you have the courage to continue, sorceress, although there are thorns and brambles ahead? Or will you go back to the smooth, straight way of the mother whence you came?

This was my last chance to return to the life I'd known before. My fears fell away, and my choice was clear.

"I will continue," I said.

In return for your service on the Dark Path, I offer you the gift of my owl Cailleach, whose wisdom will help guide you on your way, the goddess said. *Will you take this gift, or will you refuse her as your mother did?*

"I accept." It was another obligation between me and the goddess.

The gray owl ducked her head in acknowledgment.

"Cailleach," I said, rolling the name around on my tongue, savoring its flavor of bitter knowledge and sweet mystery.

Cailleach took flight, scudding a few feet above the ground to follow a trail so faint only she could see it.

You must follow the Dark Path one step at a time, the goddess warned. *Do not rush, or you will lose your way.*

I cast my eyes toward the owl, and when I turned back toward the goddess, Meg stood in her place. I had been so consumed by the shades that I had forgotten about Meg and her challenge.

"I concede, Diana Bishop." Meg's strange eyes gleamed with an emotion I could not name. "You have found your path. So must it be."

A happy cry sounded through the wood at Meg's proclamation. Soon, the coven's three witches were at the Crossroads with Meg and me, offering thermoses of hot tea and blankets to ward off post-challenge chills.

I took a cup of steaming liquid from Gwyneth, grateful that the Book of Life was no longer visible on my skin and that my weaver's cords had faded into the tracery of veins at my wrist.

"As is our custom," Ann said, "the particulars of what happened here at the Crossroads must not be spoken of to any witch, even if they are an initiate or adept in the mysteries of higher magic. Do you agree to be bound by this rule?"

I carefully noted the conditions, especially the words *particulars, spoken,* and *witch.* I could share what had happened here with Matthew. One day, I could tell my Bright Born children, too.

"I do," I said, fully intending to exploit the loopholes in the coven law.

Meg agreed, and Ann drew my challenger away, leaving me with my two supporters.

"Congratulations, Diana." Katrina took my hand and squeezed it. "I am thrilled to have another oracle in our community."

"Thank you for all you've taught me," I said.

"We're just getting started," Katrina said with a laugh, looking at me over her spectacles. "I expect you at The Thirsty Goat on Monday morning. And don't forget your—"

"Cards," I said, finishing her sentence.

Katrina departed, and Gwyneth and I were alone in the clearing. She surveyed the Crossroads, took a sniff, and gave me a considered look before handing me a small journal.

"Your first book of shadows," Gwyneth said. "You've more than earned it, based on the magic unleashed here tonight."

I held the book in my hands, comforted by its weight.

"You've made it through an important rite of passage. Take a few moments to write everything down. You'll want those memories later."

I thought of the surreal shades who populated the wood. I heard Naomi's whispered thanks and saw the agony that had preceded it. I recalled Meg's spells, and how inevitable her victory had seemed. The taste of Cailleach's name lingered on my tongue, and the words of the goddess echoed in my ears.

"I can't believe Meg conceded." A cold finger of premonition drew down my spine and I shivered.

"Nor can I," Gwyneth confessed, a shadow falling across her features. "But tonight is for celebrating, not worrying. We'll talk tomorrow about Meg's surprising decision and make a plan for the rest of your summer lessons. Now we need to get you home. Matthew's been waiting for you."

When we left the wood, witchlights gleamed in every window of the Old Place, and smoke poured out of its chimneys. Orchard Farm was brightly lit as well, and the scent of cinnamon and chocolate filled the air.

Matthew paced back and forth under the witch's tree, his hands in his pockets and his hair wild. He was so preoccupied he didn't detect my arrival. I was given the rare opportunity to study his features and gait before he had rearranged them into something stoic and comforting for my sake.

I knew from the set of his shoulders and the expression of dread on his face that Matthew had been worried. Very worried.

"How long have you been out here?" I said softly, not wanting to startle him.

Matthew's head rose in relief. He took two long strides and gathered me to his breast.

"Forever," he murmured, burying his face in my hair.

Matthew held me tight before drawing away, my face cradled between his hands. His keen eyes searched every inch of me, looking for changes, wondering if I'd met with any harm.

"Still me," I said, pressing my lips into his palm.

Matthew pulled me into a deep kiss as though he needed to make sure, inside and out. His intensity was dizzying, but my need for reassurance matched his, and I put my heart and soul into our embrace.

"I found my path," I told him. "It has higher magic in it."

"I know. I can taste its Darkness." Matthew drew back the lock of hair that always found a way to tumble across my cheek.

I held out my hand. "Will you walk it with me, Matthew?"

"Yes, *ma lionne*—whether I like where it leads or not."

Tonight, however, our path was straight and short. We returned to the farmhouse, where Julie watched over our sleeping children.

"You did it." Julie flung her arms around me, relieved. She promised to come by tomorrow with cupcakes and champagne to celebrate.

We checked on the twins, our fingers intertwined. They were peaceful and deep in slumber. I tucked Cuthbert into Pip's arms and removed a pair of headphones from Becca's ears before we closed their doors and retreated to our room.

Without a word, Matthew reached for the buttons on my shirt and helped me get out of my magic-stained clothes. Smudges of Darkness marred the white cloth and a fine powder of Shadow clung to the folds of my skirt. Light had burned a hole through my shoe, and my toe poked through.

He glanced at the book of shadows I'd dropped on the bedroom floor.

But I didn't want to write down what I'd witnessed in the wood. Nor could I imagine retelling my story, not even to Matthew.

I drew Matthew toward the bed and lay upon it.

"Drink," I told him, arching my naked body so that my breast was close to his mouth, my heartvein dark and aching to reveal its secrets.

Matthew bit down, his teeth opening the wound that never quite healed that gave him access to all that I was, and all that I thought, and all that I experienced. He latched onto the vein, pulling my blood into his mouth.

At the first swallow, he shivered. I held him tight, wanting him to see as much of the Crossroads as he could while my memories of it were fresh and vital.

Matthew took another sip, then another. My head was spinning, and I lost count of how many times he drank. Shades passed before my eyes, on bicycles and in eggshell carriages. My lips moved, silently uttering the weaver's litany while I traced the knotted scars on Matthew's back.

My skin parted further, Light seeping out of my body and into Matthew's mouth.

I was Darkness. I was Light. I was an ocean of Shadow, waiting to be discovered.

Matthew drew away, amazed. He bit into his lip, and pressed a kiss onto my breast, his blood healing my flesh just as my magic had healed Naomi's wound.

"I understand," Matthew murmured between kisses. "Now I understand."

I turned toward him, curling myself tight as though he were a shell in which I could find refuge.

Matthew started to speak, but I was too depleted to listen. We had days—years—to talk about what had happened tonight, and what we must do tomorrow.

"Just hold me," I murmured. "Don't let me go."

"Never, *ma lionne,*" Matthew promised. "Never."

Chapter 16

It was Midsummer Eve, and waves of Proctors lapped up to Ravenswood starting at dawn, eager to celebrate my success at the Crossroads. They came by pickup truck and sailboat, crammed into SUVs filled with children and animals, in carpools and on motorcycles. One even came by horse, galloping down Great Neck and splashing through the marsh to reach Bennu's rock.

Since the Crossroads, Gwyneth and Julie had found a way to make sure the twins were comfortable among the many strangers who would soon arrive at Ravenswood. They put Pip and Becca in charge of handing out name tags. Proudly, the twins pinned their own to their shirts and waited by the witch's tree to introduce themselves to the family.

As for Matthew, meeting the Proctors was a next-level challenge. He'd gotten used to me casting cards as I drank my morning tea, and disappearing into the barn or the wood for my lessons with Gwyneth. We'd even begun the work of integrating higher magic into our daily lives. It all paled in comparison to meeting the tsunami of witches expected today.

The first to arrive were Julie and her husband, Richard, along with her sister, Zee—one of the two Susies who ran the magic camp. The nickname was how the family distinguished Z-Suzie from her cousin S-Susie—or Essie, as she was known. Becca and Pip swung into action, presenting Julie's sister with a Popsicle stick dipped in glitter with Z-E-E spelled out in uneven lettering.

By nine A.M., a steady influx of family filled the meadow where the Old Place stood. While Ike and Grace directed traffic, Gwyneth made sure the food was laid out in the long room that connected the kitchen to the keeping room. Tables covered with bright cloths were laden with pastries, fruit, and steaming plates of fresh eggs, sausage, and bacon, which were refilled as quickly as they were emptied. Ike's grown children, Tike and Courtney Mather, manned the fireplace—or enchanted it, to be more accurate. While their eyes remained glued to their phones, invisible hands lifted eggs, cracked them into a waiting bowl, whisked them into a foamy golden liquid, and then stirred them around in a huge cast-iron skillet. At another skillet, more spells ensured that the bacon was turned before it burned, and the sausage flipped the moment it was golden brown.

I watched their short-order magic, amazed at the way brother and sister had cast two interconnected spells to keep the hot breakfast items coming.

"I've always thought the Proctors should open a diner." Julie passed by, garlands of magical pocket watches around her neck, each one set to remind her of some organizational detail that would keep the party running smoothly. "But I've never worked out the accounting. How do you claim a spell as an employee?"

"You worry too much," Zee said, handing Julie an empty dish from the groaning buffet. Like Vivian, the head of the Madison coven, Zee was an accountant who had studied English literature. Like Gwyneth and the rest of the Proctor women—including Courtney Mather—Zee had graduated from Mount Holyoke.

Zee's daughter Tracy arrived with two gargantuan boxes of cupcakes and a small brood of children. They were around the same age as the twins, and slowed down long enough to devour blueberry muffins and drain cups of orange juice before they sped outside to play.

"I'm going to help Pip with the name tags," said a young boy with thick freckles and a name tag that read JAKE.

"So am I!" said his sister Abigail. She dashed out into the sunshine with a handful of strawberries and a banana.

The eldest of Tracy's children, Rose, stayed behind with Courtney and

Tike. Rose felt she was far too sophisticated to hang out with the other children—even though she couldn't be a day over ten.

More children arrived, and Julie corralled the boisterous lot at a table set up under the chestnut tree, where the materials for making paper boats, cinnamon brooms, and pinecone fairy-feeders had been laid out. Essie took charge and soon the children were absorbed in crafting these traditional Midsummer items.

I soon lost track of who was who and where they fit on the branches of the family tree. I squeezed babies and sympathized with young fathers about sleepless nights. I filled sippy cups for toddlers and provided mugs of tea and coffee to their frazzled parents. Still, the cars and vans kept arriving.

The only pause in the action came when Ike's mother, Lucy Nguyen, appeared with Put-Put. As the eldest living Proctor, Put-Put would be settled in one of the keeping room's chairs under the shade of the wisteria-covered porch. That was the plan, Julie said, but admitted that Put-Put suffered from selective deafness and would probably end up outside by the barbecue, where he could drink beer and watch the children.

Everyone clucked and fussed as Ike helped his grandfather out of the van and into his waiting chair. After settling in, Put-Put established himself as the head of the family by issuing a series of demands.

"Where's my coffee? I want a cinnamon donut, too. And don't forget the cream!" His sunken blue eyes surveyed the crowd. "Where's Stephen's girl?"

"Here I am." I bent to kiss him on the cheek, but Put-Put had other ideas. He grasped my chin with his gnarled hands and planted his lips on my third eye.

Usually, an unsolicited witch's kiss felt like a violation. With Put-Put it felt different, an inquiry into my state of mind so that he could be sure that all was as it should be after Proctor's Ledge and the Crossroads.

"You're Stephen's child, all right," Put-Put said after he pulled away. "But you've got the Bishop chin, just like your mother."

My face was still in Put-Put's hands. They were little more than skin and bones, but their strength remained.

"You were always one of us, Diana," he said with a touch of fierceness. "What happened at the Crossroads was for the coven, and their peace of mind. It was never for your kin. We knew the truth of it, no matter your path. You are a Proctor. Don't forget it."

"I won't," I said. Put-Put's complete acceptance, coupled with a Yankee's unvarnished truth, was a balm to my soul.

"Where is the rest of your pack?" Put-Put said, releasing me. "I like that husband of yours, even if he is a bit jumpy."

Matthew was at the grill, part of a circle of men watching Grace set the coals alight with a combination of witchfire and lighter fluid. Though the male members of the family outnumbered her three-to-one, and were offering unsolicited advice about how she could be doing a better job, Grace had no intention of letting any of them interfere. I pointed him out to Put-Put.

"Becca was with Julie, last time I saw her," I continued, unable to locate my daughter in the swelling crowd. "Goddess knows where Pip is."

"Here I am, Mom!" Pip clattered up to the porch with a baking tray filled with gooey pinecones, followed by a griffin and a swarm of flies and toddlers. Zee and Julie walked behind at a more sedate pace, each of them emitting a stream of opalescent bubbles from their mouths and noses that lingered over the parade of small Proctors.

We laughed at the sight of the two sisters, arm in arm, serving as animated bubble-makers to delight the children. Julie and Zee giggled, too, which increased the size of the bubbles and the speed at which they were released into the air.

"Off to feed the fairies!" Julie cried, waving at us. Her straw hat was decked with flowers and ribbons. "Who wants to join us?"

For all children, the line between magic and make-believe was fine and ever-shifting, but this was especially true of children born to witches. The newest generations of Proctors, enthralled by the prospect of seeing fairies in the wood, accepted each fresh expression of magic without a blink. Theirs was an enchanted world filled with the uncanny and the unexpected. What might my own life have been had I grown up embracing the family's magical traditions and the wild, playful power at their core?

"Everything all right, *mon coeur*?" Matthew murmured into my ear, tickling the flesh on my neck. He'd sensed my darkening emotions and come to see if I was okay.

"Better than fine," I said.

"Rebecca is in the midst of a gaggle of teenagers," Matthew said with a note of disapproval. "They're shuffling cards and telling fortunes."

"Leave the girl alone," Put-Put told Matthew. "Better out in the open with her cousins than off exploring the wood. Make yourself useful and find my coffee."

It was a rare occasion when Matthew took someone's advice, but today was a special day and he left Becca to her own devices while he fetched Put-Put's drink.

The Proctors' Midsummer potluck shifted into high gear now that Put-Put had arrived. Gwyneth sat under one of the chestnut trees, encircled by tween witches and wizards who were having a go at casting with spell-looms. The teenagers remained in small groups with their oracle decks and tarot cards, offering free readings to any adult who wandered by in search of a cold beer or iced tea. Tike left the cooking fire to whittle wands for the college students who were now of an age where they could begin using the magical staffs to focus their craft.

Hand in hand, Matthew and I wove our way through the crowd, exchanging a few words with the cousins I'd already met and stopping to have longer exchanges with others. I picked up a hot dog from the barbecue, where Ike and a score of other males exchanged yarns about football and baseball while Grace flipped burgers and slipped blistered sausages into buns.

"May I help?" Matthew asked, eager to assist my smoke-stained cousin. He was desperate for a job.

"Absolutely not," Grace said. "If I let you have a go, they'll all want a turn. Row over to The Nestling and get the clams. They should be ready."

After the last of the clams and lobsters were ferried over from The Nestling and the enormous bonfire lit, the atmosphere at Ravenswood went from playful to something more potent. Inch by inch the sun dipped below the western horizon and a slim witch's moon rose over the water.

As the shadows lengthened, I was aware that the longest day of the year was nearing its end. Light was giving way to Darkness in the eternal cycle of death and rebirth that carried all creatures into the future.

Weary parents tucked babies and toddlers into cots in the barn, propped up with dream pillows and firefly lanterns to comfort them if they woke in an unfamiliar place. The older children cajoled Aunt Gwyneth into a tour of the attic, but only after promising that they wouldn't scream and wake the babies—no matter what horrifying sights they might see.

I sat with Tracy, a bowl of magic marshmallows between us. I speared one with a stick and it immediately bubbled and browned.

"Fire-free toasted marshmallows. You could make a fortune with these, you know." I waited until the marshmallow was golden and popped it into my mouth.

"Hands off my marshmallows," Tracy said with a laugh, making another for herself with slightly singed edges. She sighed happily at the charred treat. "Just how I like them."

"So, what happens next?" I wondered. There was no sign of Julie, and Proctors drifted about the meadow, catching fireflies. Matthew, over Grace's strenuous objections, was dismantling the grills.

"I think we launch the boats," Tracy said, pointing to the flotilla of small paper craft the children had made. They waited at the edge of the marsh, each hull filled with flowers and berries.

"When does the real magic begin?" I asked in a low voice.

"It's all real magic," Tracy replied, making herself another marshmallow.

But there was more to Midsummer than these gentle enchantments. Darker sorceries were afoot, as well.

The excited cries of children alerted those gathered around the bonfire that Julie had returned, flanked by an escort of tweens and teens bearing torches that glowed with magical light. The individual personalities of the young Proctor witches shone through with rainbow flags and black neo-Goth outfits in a parade of solidarity and safety.

Ike rolled Put-Put to Bennu's rock, where he and Gwyneth could watch the children release their boats into the water. Some were old enough to conjure up a fluttering wisp of flame at the top of their Popsicle-stick masts. Most needed help to light the beacons, touching their sticks to those of their cousins who had succeeded in calling forth the flames.

"Bless these boats as they sail into Darkness," Gwyneth said, raising her hands and letting the power of the goddess work through her. "They carry our dreams and desires for the long nights ahead. May the goddess grant us love and luck in return."

The children waded into the wetlands of the marsh in search of the currents that would carry their offerings out to sea. The small boats scattered, their flaming masts shining. Matthew slid his arm around me as we watched Pip and Becca take part in their first Midsummer ritual.

Singly, in pairs, and in family knots, the Proctors returned to the warmth of the fire.

While the children gorged on magic marshmallows and chamomile tea spiked with lavender, the adults took charge of the entertainment. Instead of setting off fireworks bought from a roadside stand, Ike led a crew of pyrotechnical wizards and witches to conjure wheels of fire that rolled across the meadow. Their carefully crafted flames posed no danger to the vegetation or the animals, and instead of the shriek and boom that accompanied most human fireworks displays, these emitted the gentle sound of witches' bells.

Chamomile tea was not the only drink on offer. The steady flow of beer was augmented with pitchers of fermented honey, the magical elixir of antiquity. The more cautious Proctors were adulterating the strong mead with lemonade or adding it to beer to make the traditional brew bragget.

Someone called for music, and soon everyone was on their feet and dancing around the bonfire. Hands reached for Matthew and me, pulling us into the whirling circles of witches. The dancers broke into lines that moved in different directions, looping and twining until knots formed. The most daring took to the meadow, leaping over and through the flaming wheels like ballerinas.

The potluck's previous games and crafts had been fun, but these nocturnal activities showed the depths of the family's talent for higher magic. Darkness tickled children under the chin, and Shadow wove ribbons around their ankles. Elemental bonds of air, fire, earth, and water formed between one witch's hand and another in a voluntary association stronger than any coercive spellbinding could be. As the power around the fire mounted, a bell tolled in the distance, louder with each successive knell.

The crowd quieted, and the dancers stopped their spinning. From the marsh came a tall male figure clad in golden oak leaves so thick it was impossible to see who or what lay underneath. The children were amazed by the sudden apparition, and even the teens were impressed enough to look up from their phones and stop taking selfies.

"Who's that?" I whispered.

"The Oak King," Matthew replied, a slight shiver raising the flesh on his forearms. "Before electricity we all felt the turning of the year when the Light ebbed away. The Oak King was the guardian of Light, and the coming Darkness meant that he'd lost his battle with the Holly King. Winter would come again to plague us with hunger and sickness."

The Oak King didn't play a role in the Madison coven's Litha rituals, which were resolutely matriarchal and focused on the female powers of fertility.

"Who will be the Holly King?" Gwyneth cried.

"Your turn, Lisa!" Tracy said, pushing a cousin forward.

"Can't Put-Put fight him?" Tike piped up, trying to be helpful. "He's so old the Oak King is bound to beat him, and we'll have summer all year."

Put-Put wheezed and laughed, pleased with Tike's astute strategy.

"I'll do it!" Ike's mom, Lucy, volunteered to face the Oak King. "I'd like a reprieve from the snow and ice."

The Oak King circled the bonfire, his step deliberate, as the tension mounted. The teenagers pushed one of their number out into the open, but the boy scuttled back into the safety of the crowd. Others shook their heads and crossed their arms, daring the Oak King to pick them as his adversary.

The Oak King came to a stop and looked at me with open speculation. The family oohed and whispered. This was an unexpected development.

He extended an oak branch laden with golden acorns and leaves. The Oak King had made his choice.

"Me?" I'd already won one battle this summer. "Not this year."

"You can't refuse the Oak King," Grace said. "He's chosen you, and you must pit your Darkness against his Light."

What if I failed and the seasons were affected? Climate change was already a real threat. I didn't need to hasten the process.

"Shouldn't the Holly King be a man?" I said in a final, antifeminist effort to avoid the responsibility. The Mount Holyoke contingent—which was large—howled in outrage.

"Women can also be kings," Gwyneth said, with the calm certainty of someone who knew the burdens of leadership.

Resigned to my fate, I stepped toward the Oak King. When I came within reach of his gilded oak staff, the King touched me on the shoulder with its bright tip.

Magic spread from the point where skin and wood met. My body bloomed in response. Glossy holly leaves with sharp barbs erupted from my pores, decked with tiny white flowers and vivid berries. A coronet of holly branches twined around my head, and streamers of ivy wove through my hair. The circlet prickled, but not in an unpleasant way. In my right hand a white wand sprouted, carved from the pale wood of the holly tree.

I looked for Becca and Pip, wanting to see their reaction to my transformation. Had the sudden change frightened them?

The twins' gazes were filled with wonder and pride.

"That's my mom!" Pip said to Jake, whose eyes were round as saucers.

"Wow," Jake replied. "She's cool."

Even sprigged out in holly and ivy like the Ghost of Christmas Present, I was neither overwhelming nor unwelcome to my children— or my kin. My family's arms were wide enough to enfold me without pinching my magic out. As I looked around at the faces gathered around the bonfire—old and young, those who were now familiar to me and those I'd met for the first time today—all I saw was kindness and understanding.

"You're beautiful, *ma lionne*." Matthew braved the holly leaves to press a kiss on my cheek. "It's your job to win this fight. Show him no quarter."

To overcome my opponent, I would need to draw on Darkness. Matthew spotted the unspoken question in my eyes and nodded. Had it not been for the sharpness of the holly leaves, I would have hugged my husband tight. Instead, I turned toward the Oak King's golden splendor.

With a flourish of his oaken branch and a respectful bow, the Oak King invited me to match my wand to his. As the oak and the holly crossed, a low keening sounded across the meadow. The unearthly cry faded into an echo of something yet to come.

The Oak King drew his wand free, and the tip burst into stars that flew in every direction, their Light beating me back toward the depths of the Ravens' Wood.

I raised the holly wand to the sky in response, and called on the ebony moths that lived in Shadow. They came, drawn to the white tip of the wand, smothering the Oak King's stars. I pulled Shadow around me like a cloak as I advanced toward the Oak King.

He took a step back, and another. We made sunwise progress around the fire. The Oak King summoned more stars. They twinkled for a moment, but I called to the ravens, who swooped in and swallowed them with guttural cries.

Shadow lengthened into Darkness, its inky train blotting out the Light. I left a shimmer of powdered pearl behind me, a luminous promise of Light's return.

When we returned to the place where we'd begun, the bonfire's light was turning to embers and Darkness blotted out the stars. The Oak King lowered his bough into the fire, where it burst into spectacular multicolored flame. He bowed again, conceding to the Darkness, and melted into Shadow.

I was returned to my ordinary self, no longer clothed in sprouts and berries. Only the holly wand and the crown remained, along with a tingling aliveness that made me one with Ravenswood and its power.

"They've come!" someone whispered.

"Look! Look!" said someone else, her voice hushed with awe.

The Proctor ghosts had come out of the attic *en masse* to welcome Darkness's return and gathered in the Ravens' Wood. They spilled out from the trees and across the meadow. The night provided a tenebrous backdrop that revealed their every detail, from the sprigs of flowers on muslin dresses to the fine stitching on collars and cuffs. It was a marvelous spectacle, seen only one night of the year.

"Good job, Diana," Tracy said, patting me on the shoulder. "Sometimes the Holly King doesn't gather enough Darkness to bring them into focus like that."

Lucy pointed. "There's my Ike! And look, there's Gwyneth's sister Morgana!"

Morgana and Gwyneth stood, their hands raised and palms touching, in silent reunion. The former black bird oracle sent a glance my way, and dipped her head in thanks.

Sadly, there was no glimpse of Naomi.

A woman appeared at the edge of the Ravens' Wood, following in the footsteps of the ghosts. Her hair and limbs sparkled with eldritch light, and a sliver of crescent moon gleamed from her brow. Her cloak was midnight deep, and tiny winged creatures tumbled and flew around her feet. They got entangled in the folds of the cloak and freed themselves with the strong beat of gossamer wings.

"My God, is that—" Matthew began, eyes wide.

"The Queen of the Fairies?" I nodded. "Yes, I think so."

"The fairy-feeders worked!" Pip cried, giving his sister a high five.

Underneath all the otherworldly glow was Julie Eastey. Clothed in her power, and reveling in the glamour she cast, Julie was a sight to behold— one so breathtaking that it brought tears to the eyes of many.

Our Fairy Queen drew her wand and addressed her audience with the same words that generations of Proctors had used before her.

"*If we Shadows have offended,*" Julie began, her eyes bright with belladonna and magic, "*Think but this, and all is mended, / That you have but slumber'd here / While these visions did appear.*"

With a graceful twist of her wrist, Julie collected some of the surrounding Darkness and directed it into the heart of the bonfire, creating a molten black cauldron of bubbling fire. Gasps of astonishment sounded as Julie kept Darkness and Light in perfect balance. It was the performance of a lifetime, and even Matthew's London friends would have been forced to acknowledge the power Shakespeare's pen had given to this piece of Proctor spellcraft.

The bard's poetry took on additional potency with the family's alterations, which turned his words into pure magic.

"*And, as I am an honest witch,*" Julie continued, "*If we have released pitch, / Now to 'scape Midsummer's light, / We will, ere long, make it right. / Give me your hands, if we be friends, / And Shadow shall restore amends.*"

Cheers swelled as the rituals of Midsummer came to a spectacular close. We threw wooden torches into Julie's conjured cauldron, along with scrolls of paper containing spells, wishes, and dreams. Bits of magic popped and exploded like Catherine wheels and shooting stars, opening pathways through the night sky.

Amidst the cacophony of hollers and magic, I heard the low, sweet call of Darkness. My blood rose in response. I turned toward my husband, and pressed the length of my body against his. Our revels could continue in private.

For us, tonight's magic had just begun.

Chapter 17

It took days to recover from the Proctors' Midsummer celebration. Soon, Matthew and I had settled into our new normal at Orchard Farm, our bags no longer half-packed in readiness for a speedy exit. The suitcases went into the attic, and the laundry machine went into overdrive to keep up with the soggy clothes that accumulated with terrifying speed on the mudroom floor. Becca and Pip were ecstatic, running around Ipswich with their cousins and socializing with other magical families. Setting aside the plans we'd made for the summer—plans made long before we received the Congregation's letter, an embassy of ravens, and an invitation from Ravenswood—made the remaining months of our summer sparkle with renewed possibilities.

For Becca and Pip, these opportunities expanded by the hour as they learned how to dig for clams, supervised Matthew's renovation of the tree houses, and had lengthy conversations with Granny Dorcas about a wide range of topics, including headless horsemen and how to use handfuls of rosemary and sage to repel the green flies.

Julie dropped by Orchard Farm on the first day of July while we were still at breakfast. She brought with her fresh prospects for delight: magic camp registration forms and an invitation for the twins.

"Where is everybody?" Julie's voice floated through the screen door, along with the sound of canine feet scrabbling against the porch with excitement. "Some watchdog you are, Ardwinna. Here. Have a muffin. It's blueberry. Full of antioxidants."

Somewhere in the Eastey family tree there was a daemon—maybe two. I was sure of it.

"Come on in!" I called, gathering a fork and plate. Matthew was scrambling eggs this morning, and I was sure my cousin was going to want some.

Julie squelched into the kitchen, her knee-length shorts rolled up and her sneakers oozing with moisture and muck as though she'd waded here across the marsh. Despite her apparent route, she'd kept hold of a tiered cake plate, on which there was an assortment of muffins and cupcakes.

"I've brought the camp waivers for you to sign, as well as the registration forms," Julie said, using her mother's spell to conjure the papers out of thin air. "Here. They should be dry. Ooh, those look yummy. Are they for me? Is there ketchup?"

Matthew handed her a steaming plate with eggs, sausage, and fried mushrooms. Julie gave him a kiss on the cheek in return and settled down at the kitchen table with the twins and their entourages.

"Are you excited about camp?" Julie asked the twins. She and Gwyneth had applauded our decision to let the children attend the organized afternoons, where young witches were trained in proper magical etiquette and instilled with empathy for humans and other creatures.

Both nodded enthusiastically, unable to speak around the muffins they'd snagged from the cake stand.

"A daemon family from Rhode Island is sending their kids up here again, they had such a good time," Julie said, digging into her breakfast. "Becca and Pip will be the first campers with vampire blood. Isn't that exciting?"

Matthew took possession of the health-and-safety waivers. He was no doubt going to make sure that there were no suspicious rules that would indicate the camp management harbored anti-vampire sentiment.

"How would you like to go sailing?" Julie asked Becca and Pip. "The sun's out—for now—and the waters are calm."

The twins whooped with glee at the prospect of hours at sea with their beloved Julie.

"In a real boat?" Becca was game for anything that smacked of adventure.

"Is there another way to sail?" Julie asked, mopping up the last of her eggs with a bit of bread. "*Good Juju* is anchored out by The Nestling. She's too big to come closer to shore and I left the dinghy on board."

The dinghy was fittingly called *Bad Juju*.

"We'll have to wade out to her," Julie warned, "if you want to take her for a spin."

"Can we?" Pip said, jumping off his chair. "Can we, Mommy? Can we plee—"

"Philip Michael Addison." Matthew couldn't abide pleading, and the number of names he used indicated how far he thought the children had gone over the line. In this case, Matthew had stopped at three out of four, which meant Pip was on very thin ice.

Pip and Becca pressed their lips together to silence anything that their father might interpret as undue pressure. My mind was already made up, however. Fresh air and a new perspective would do them both good. And the peace and quiet that would descend over Ravenswood in their absence would bolster my sanity.

"Of course you can go sailing with Aunt Julie," I said, after exchanging a look with Matthew and receiving a reluctant nod of agreement.

"Will we see the ghost ship?" Pip had heard Julie's tale of the wrecked vessel caught on the rocks at the end of the neck, and the loss of all the lives aboard.

"It's the waxing moon! This is no time for spotting ghosts on deck," Julie exclaimed, dashing Pip's hopes. "They hide down below to avoid moonburn. You'll have to wait until the moon is dark again. That's when the captain raises the sails."

"Go get changed," I said, pointing upstairs. It was too early in the morning for talk of ghostly mariners and spectral ships. "You don't want Aunt Julie to miss the tide."

"Wait!" Julie reached into the back of her shorts to remove two damp T-shirts. "Wear these."

The shirts were hot pink and emblazoned with CREW in black letters across the back. On the front was the name of Julie's nautical pride and joy.

Pip and Becca clattered upstairs and soon returned to the kitchen, bursting like small explosives with further questions. Becca had Tamsy, who was dressed for a romp outdoors, with her skirts tucked up to show her ankles and a sturdy apron tied around her waist to keep her gown clean. Her feet were bare, and Becca had tied a wide-brimmed hat under her chin. Both children had their sneakers slung over their shoulders, the laces tied together.

"Good idea, Tamsy," Julie said, studying the twins to make sure they were outfitted properly for a day on the water. "We all need to protect ourselves from the sun—especially those of us with vampire blood. I've got sunscreen, and two baseball caps." Julie swung her own hat onto her head, tightening the cord so it wouldn't blow off in the breeze. She inspected Becca's shoelaces. "And we need to work on knots while we're out. If you tie up the *Good Juju*'s lines like that, we're sunk."

Julie conjured up her lightship basket, the preferred tote of Ipswich witches. From it, she pulled out two children's caps, one pink and one blue. Embroidered on each was the griffin emblem of the nearby Crane Estate.

"Look, Apollo!" Pip cried, waving his new hat at his familiar. "It's you!"

The griffin preened his feathers and thumped his tail in approval.

"We'll see you later, Diana," Julie said. She tucked a few of the cupcakes into her basket. "Thanks for breakfast, Matthew."

The twins ran straight for the marsh. Apollo used his wings to soar over the shallow water toward the bobbing masts of the sailboat anchored off The Nestling.

"I forgot his disguising spell," I worried, thinking of the tour boats that plied the nearby shore.

"Don't worry," Julie said. "The seagulls around here are unusually large. He'll blend right in."

Gwyneth came out of the Old Place to see the crew off, chuckling as Becca and Pip splashed their way into the marsh. Julie followed, her lightship basket balanced on her head to keep their cupcakes and ham sandwiches dry.

Matthew and I heaved sighs of relief and took Ardwinna out to the barn. She had elected not to go out on the *Good Juju,* preferring to sit by Granny Dorcas, where she would be petted and cosseted.

I gratefully accepted my third cup of tea from Matthew and settled at the worktable with the black bird oracle, running the cards through my fingers to receive today's guidance. One eye was on Gwyneth, however, who was working on a bespoke ritual oil designed to help me work safely with Shadow. She was bent over a small iron pot with three legs that resembled a cauldron. My aunt had begun with a powerful rose oil made last summer. To that she'd already added birch bark, wintergreen, spikenard, and an infusion of eyebright. These had been simmering over a low witchlight for the past twenty-four hours.

"What's that?" I asked, curious about what Gwyneth was adding to her concoction.

"Mugwort." Gwyneth used a dropper to add some more to her mixture. "We'll mix in the dragon's blood tomorrow, and then let it steep for three weeks."

Gwyneth set aside a large mason jar for the purpose. A bit of obsidian, a shard of clear quartz, lavender flowers, rose petals, and an old compact mirror rested on the bottom of the glass container, ready to add their magic to the mix.

I shuffled the black bird oracle a few more times, but my attention kept drifting toward the other end of the table, where Matthew sat, a stack of papers at his elbow. They were marked with grids and letters, like one of John Dee's magic squares.

"What are those?" I asked, picking up my tea and joining him. Now that I was closer, I could see that the letters were in strange, repeating strings like *EeCcDd* and *VvBbDd.*

"Mendelian Punnett squares," Matthew said. "I thought I'd track inherited traits among the Proctors. These help to map their appearance over generations, though they're not very good with multiple variables."

Matthew was using old-school genetics—the same techniques my ancestors would have relied on—to make sense of recurring patterns in the family's magic.

"Wouldn't we need genetic testing to really understand them?" This was the thorny issue that kept Matthew and Chris at loggerheads.

"Not necessarily," Matthew replied. "Diana mentioned you have a family tree, Gwyneth."

"I can't leave my pot," Gwyneth said testily, stirring the contents of her cauldron with a long-handled silver spoon. "Diana knows where it is. She can get it for you."

I dug around in a Victorian-era umbrella stand and soon produced the family tree. When I unfurled it on the table, anchoring its curving edges with my oracle deck and a mug filled with pencils and pens, Matthew's eyes widened in surprise. The silver boxes on the Proctor pedigree stood out from the names picked out in green, blue, or brown, and the fine black lines that connected them.

"The colors all mean something," I said, leaning my elbows on the table.

"Twins," Matthew said, immediately recognizing the significance of the silver boxes.

"A set in every other generation," I observed. "Regular as Swiss trains."

"Twins can run in families, but not like that. It's too neat," Matthew replied, driving his fingers through his hair to encourage his brain cells to work harder.

Matthew found Gwyneth's name, written in ink the color of strong tea. So was Grandpa Tally's, though their sister's name, Morgana, was written in blue.

"Does the brown ink indicate witches gifted with higher magic, while the blue ink highlights those with the power of prophecy?" I asked my aunt.

"Yes," she replied, wiping her hands on her apron. "Green ink signifies a knotter—a weaver. Goddess knows what we should have used for you, Diana. Something rainbow-colored, like the tails on those vile plastic unicorns?"

My name was written in black ink, as were the names of the twins, as though our magical identities had still been shrouded in Darkness when the tree was last amended.

"We'll have to mark Pip out in green, and Becca in blue," I said, ready to make my mark on the old scroll.

Matthew put out a hand to stop me, his irritation clear.

"We agreed not to make decisions for Rebecca and Philip," he said. "This is exactly why I don't want the children genetically tested, or their magical talents labeled by the Congregation."

"Matthew's right," Gwyneth said. "They thought I was an oracle, like Morgana. Then I hit puberty, and it was clear that I might be able to use the cards to see the future, but it was Morgana who had the real gifts. We will have to wait and see what the goddess has in store for the twins."

My aunt joined us at the table, and we studied the family tree together.

"The pattern explains why you are a chimera, too," Matthew said, looking up from the tree.

"Gwyneth and I thought so," I agreed. "The goddess had to break one of her universal laws."

"Thereby making you a doubly powerful witch, and preserving a place for both Rebecca and Philip," Matthew said.

"I'm impressed, Matthew," Gwyneth remarked. "I didn't think you'd be able to glean so much from the family tree."

"It's a start," he replied, hesitant, "but it only shows Diana's direct line of descent and the incidence of oracles, weavers, and adepts in higher magic. Look at Margaret Proctor. She gave birth to James Proctor in 1740, when she was thirty-seven. He might have been her last child, but I doubt James was her first."

Matthew was right. The family tree, extensive though it was, represented only a limited outline of the Proctor lineage.

"There's no possible way to include all the Proctors on a single tree. It would be as long as the Amtrak line from Boston to D.C., and as wide as the transcontinental railroad." Gwyneth moved toward the shelves. She returned with a leather-bound book. "There are more detailed family records here, in the Proctor grimoire."

Matthew opened the tome and was soon absorbed in his efforts to understand the family's lineage. I was envious that he was able to pore over the precious volume before me. Soon he was making his own genealogical chart, with all the siblings of my direct ancestors, on a long piece of butcher paper used for wrapping up dried herbs and flowers.

"I'll just go back to my cards," I murmured.

"Hmm," Matthew said, not looking up from his notes and grids, eager to find a way to map out the patterns of magic that emerged.

I was just settling down again when an earsplitting whistle cut through the air.

"Who can that be?" Gwyneth said, tetchy at another interruption.

"Were you expecting one of the Mather boys?" I asked as Gwyneth passed by, her silver spoon held in front of her like a wand.

Ardwinna cocked her head. Her ears perked up and she dashed for the open barn door, barking frantically.

"Yo! Where are you, squirt?" called a familiar voice.

It wasn't one of the Mathers.

"Oof." The sound was muffled by nearly a hundred pounds of ecstatic dog. "I missed you, too, Ardwinna."

"They're in the barn," said an unmistakable soprano. "Down, Ardwinna. I'm wearing new tights."

"It's Chris and Miriam," I said, shocked. "Matthew's colleagues from Yale."

"Who invited them?" Gwyneth was still out of sorts.

"I did." Matthew looked down at his watch. "I'm sorry, Gwyneth. They weren't supposed to arrive until after dinner. I was going to tell you at lunch."

"It seems that Ravenswood has accepted you as a member of the Proctor family, Matthew," Gwyneth said dryly. "I'm going to have to review my wards and adjust them accordingly."

My heart rose as Chris and Miriam stepped out of the sunshine and into the barn. I flew at Chris and flung my arms around him.

"Sorry we're early. Chris was afraid Matthew would change his mind," Miriam apologized. "You smell different, Diana."

"Nice to see you, too, Miriam." I gave Chris one last squeeze and released him. "Gwyneth, meet Chris Roberts and Miriam Shephard. This is my great-aunt Gwyneth Proctor."

"The witch who sent the oracle card." Miriam extended a hand. "Pleased to meet you. Do you have somewhere I could put these?" She lifted two Styrofoam cases marked BIOHAZARD.

Granny Dorcas woke from her nap and yelped in horror.

"Hi, I'm Chris." My friend walked toward her with a genial smile. "You must be Diana's grandmother."

I am her great-great-great-great-great— Granny Dorcas ran out of fingers. *Never mind. Who let a human into the barn?*

Chris stuck his hands into his pockets and shrugged. Granny Dorcas fixed her gaze on Miriam.

Another blood-letch, too. She chewed on her pipe in consternation. *Who's next? The Archbishop of Canterbury?*

"Is that—" Miriam asked, pointing.

Don't point at me, blood-letch! Granny Dorcas removed the pipe stem from her teeth and jabbed it toward Miriam. *It's very, very rude.*

"A ghost. Yes," Matthew said hurriedly, putting his bulk between Miriam and my grandmother. "Miriam meant no insult, Granny Dorcas. She was dazzled by the sight of you, and wonderstruck at seeing a ghost. Many vampires harbor a secret wish to meet the walking dead."

Hmph. Granny Dorcas stroked her elf lock, entranced by the idea that anyone would find her so desirable after so many years. A minuscule creature with the wings of a dragonfly fell from her hair, bent double with laughter, and rolled across the uneven floorboards.

"Here. This poor little guy broke free." Chris swooped up the fairy by the wings and offered it to Dorcas. "Wow. So you're a ghost. Cool. Have you met my great-aunt Hortense? Tall woman? Likes hats? Absolutely terrifying? Died about ten years ago?"

"Be careful!" Gwyneth warned. "Fairies—"

"Ow!"

The fairy had embedded his needlelike teeth in Chris's thumb. Chris tried to shake him off, but the winged sprite had no intention of letting go.

"Bite." I tickled the fairy between the wings until he released his hold. Granny Dorcas caught him and returned the tiny creature to her matted head of hair.

"So," Chris said, sucking on his thumb. "Where's my first victim?"

As usual, Chris was supremely unflapped by the presence of magic, ghosts, fairies, and other marvelous things. He was a scientist, and faced greater mysteries every day. Or so he claimed. I would wait and see what he thought of the shades in the wood with their mechanical limbs.

"What are you talking about?" Gwyneth demanded.

"Matthew said he needed help gathering DNA samples," Chris said.

I lowered myself onto a stool. Chris and Miriam's arrival had been a surprise; Matthew's apparent change of heart was nothing less than a miracle.

"We brought cheek swabs, equipment for blood draws, and a sequencer," Miriam said, looking around the barn. "But it's not going to fit in this shed. There's not enough space to prepare and isolate samples, and I doubt the electricity is up to the job."

"Shed?" Gwyneth's eyebrows rose. "I beg your pardon, Miriam, but this is my workshop and alchemical laboratory. There will be no *sequencer* in it, thank you very much."

"Slow down, Miriam," Matthew told his colleague.

"It's impossible to go any slower without shifting into reverse," Miriam retorted. "If I'd known all it would take to make you see the light about the twins' DNA was a family picnic, I would have arranged the biggest barbecue in Connecticut." She shuddered. "Revolting things."

"Why don't we sit?" I suggested. Brokering a truce between five research scholars and a ghost was not going to be easy. "I'll make tea and—"

"Whoa. Is that Diana's family tree?" Chris asked Matthew, transfixed by the scroll on the worktable.

"It's the Proctor family tree, yes," Gwyneth said, her tone as starched as one of Matthew's white shirts. "My sister drew it up, and we've been sure to keep it updated over the years."

"I've just started to expand upon it, adding people beyond Diana's direct ancestors." Matthew followed Chris to the table. "I plan on visiting members of the family to record their magical characteristics, and those of their parents and siblings. Some of them might agree to give a DNA sample, and then—"

"Jackpot," Chris said, gathering up the Punnett squares. "Jesus, Matthew. I haven't seen one of these since junior high."

"You can't just wander around Essex County with a tape recorder and a bucket of cheek swabs, interviewing Proctors!" Gwyneth told Matthew. "It's just not done!"

"Telepathy. Cartomancy. Bone dancing." Chris shuffled through Matthew's grids. "These are all your dad's people, Diana?"

I nodded.

"And some of them are still alive?"

I nodded again.

"Well, well." Chris exchanged a glance with Miriam. "Looks like Matthew found a few of Diana's missing links."

It's like Salem Town on market day in here, Granny Dorcas complained. *I can't think for all the chatter.*

Granny Dorcas was right. I banged the lid of Gwyneth's favorite seething pot against the stove. It crashed like a cymbal.

Once the room quieted, I spoke.

"Everybody. Sit. Down. Now. We shall start at the beginning," I said.

It required three full siphons of coffee, a pot of tea, and a shot of brandy for Gwyneth before Matthew managed to explain his new determination to understand the Proctor family's magic with nineteenth-century logic, twenty-first-century tools, and four hundred years of family archives.

Miriam and Chris, Matthew explained, would be back in New Haven analyzing DNA while he remained in Ipswich and correlated the results with the family lore.

"Who will assist you?" Miriam said. "You need someone to take notes, and manage the samples."

"I will," Gwyneth said. "I'm the only person who knows where Cousin Gladys lives, and you are definitely going to want to interview her."

"What about Diana?" Matthew frowned. "Your plate is already full, Gwyneth."

"Diana needs to do a bit more independent work. It will be fine," my aunt replied.

Will ye be able to tell if Thorndike Proctor's daughter was baseborn? Granny Dorcas asked, poking Matthew in the back to get his attention. *There were rumors, but never any proof.*

"I don't think we can determine that without the body or some of her mother's DNA, ma'am." Chris accorded Granny Dorcas the respect due to someone of her age and importance, even if she was dead.

Your science isn't worth much, if it's less knowledgeable than the Ipswich gossips. Still, if you need the body . . . Granny Dorcas mused.

Before Dorcas offered to unearth the unfortunate woman, I intervened.

"Let's talk about that another day," I said hastily, stopping Chris and Matthew from delivering an introductory lecture on genetics that would make sense to someone born in the seventeenth century. So far, Granny Dorcas was managing with lots of analogies to breeding heifers, but the comparison was wearing thin.

"It's getting late, and the twins will soon be home," I continued, glancing at my watch. "What, exactly, is your plan, Matthew?"

"To take every sample of DNA, and amass every bit of oral history, I can," Matthew said simply. "Then, I'm going to spend day and night trying to understand the Proctor lineage and its magic."

"What about Pip and Becca?" Chris asked. "When are we going to test them?"

"With all this new data, there is no need to analyze the children's DNA." Matthew's tone was clear and unequivocal.

Chris swore, Miriam stalked away so that she could vent her frustrations elsewhere, and Gwyneth looked surprised.

"Matthew's right," I said, taking his hand in mine. "We've got my genetic data. Matthew's and Sarah's, too. The information Matthew gathers this summer will make some of my genetic anomalies clearer, even if it doesn't solve every riddle."

Chris was listening.

"None of us can clearly see the future, no matter how hard we try, and DNA alone can't determine what the future holds for Becca and Pip," I continued. "But I truly believe that some combination of my history and your science can provide clues."

"That's a positively medieval attitude, Diana," Miriam said thoughtfully. "I like it."

Chris cocked his head. "You've changed, D."

"I came to Ravenswood and shed my old skin in favor of one that fits," I replied.

"I'm glad you realized that size extra-small doesn't suit you. It doesn't look good on most people, come to think of it," Chris said with a grin. "When you try to shrink yourself, or believe one size fits all, you aren't the only one who's uncomfortable. It makes the rest of us uneasy, too. Especially Becca and Pip."

"Wait until you see them, Chris." My eyes filled with happy tears. "They are so free here, able to be who and what they are."

"Sounds like everyone's got a lot to learn from the Proctors, and I don't just mean genetically," Chris said.

A clatter of oars and the cries of displaced herons alerted us that the twins were back from their boating excursion. The barn doors were still open and we had a clear view of the children's joy as they ran to be reunited with their godparents.

"Aunt Miriam!" Becca cried.

"Uncle Chris!" Pip said.

"There he is!" Chris said, adopting the hands-on-knees position of a veteran football player. "Give me what you've got, Pip."

Pip bowled into Chris, knocking his godfather backward onto the barn floor.

"Careful!" I warned. Chris may have been athletic, but he was still human.

Miriam and Becca's greeting was cooler, but no less sincere. "Hey," Miriam said, holding up her hand.

"Hey," Becca replied, slapping it and then twirling around twice.

"I'm sorry if I hurt you, Uncle Chris," Pip said.

"You didn't, squirt," Chris assured him, rubbing his elbow. "I just have a tender spot here. But what makes you strong?"

"Your tender spots," Pip replied.

This was a topic of frequent conversation between Chris and the twins—that vulnerability was a superpower, not a sign of weakness.

"Like this one?" Chris tickled Pip under the arms. Pip squirmed and giggled. "And this one?" Chris reached for the back of Pip's knees but my son's vampire blood kicked in, and he eluded Chris's attempts to catch him by running out of the barn. Chris leaped up, hot on his heels.

When Chris finally succeeded in catching Pip, he slung him over his shoulder like a sack of potatoes. He returned across the meadow with Pip flapping his arms and kicking his legs and Apollo imitating him.

Tike, who was carrying the oars for the *Bad Juju,* passed the pair of them with an indulgent grin. Julie was behind him with hats, life jackets, and of course her lightship basket.

"This is Chris!" Pip shouted. "Say hi, Tike. He's really cool. Like your dad."

"My goodness, another vampire!" Julie said, glancing at Miriam. "Do you want something to drink? Not blood, obviously, but we have wine and coffee."

"I'm good, thanks," Miriam said. "Do you need a hand with all that?"

"Please," Julie said, slinging the life jackets over Miriam's shoulders. "I'm Julie. You must be a friend of Matthew's."

"I'm Miriam. The one making an idiot of himself is Chris," Miriam said. "We work with Matthew at Yale."

"Oh, good," Julie said. "Maybe you can give him something to do. If he fixes one more thing on this farm, we're going to have to sell it. Gwyneth isn't used to all the machines working at the same time."

A familiar van pulled into the Old Place and trundled down the hill.

"Your father's here!" Julie called to Tike.

My cousin emerged from the van wearing a camouflage cap emblazoned with the letter H. Chris took one look at him and his jaw dropped.

"Mather?" Chris said, setting Pip down on his feet.

"Roberts?" Ike called. "Is that you?"

After a bloodcurdling howl and a rapid drumming of feet, the two men ran at each other, locking horns like two charging rhinoceroses before embracing.

"What was that?" I asked Miriam.

"Male-bonding ritual," she explained wearily. "I've seen a thousand versions of it. They're unmistakable."

Matthew's idea of male bonding consisted of drinking too much wine, debating philosophy, and playing games of chess and verbal one-upmanship, but perhaps he was unusual.

"My God, you haven't changed!" Ike said, swatting Chris with his cap. "Same scrappy seventeen-year-old I met at football camp at Harvard in the summer of '92. How do you know Diana?"

"Colleagues at Yale." Chris ran his hands over his head in his typical gesture of sheepishness. "You?"

"Cousins," Ike said, giving him another swat. "Wait until Put-Put finds out you're here."

"Your grandfather is still alive?" Chris looked at Ike in amazement. "He was ancient when I left Harvard."

"Goes to every home football game," Ike said proudly. "My mom's still with us, too."

"Good genes," Miriam said, thoughtful.

"This is Miriam," Chris said, putting his arm around her. Even draped in life jackets, her shoulders were narrow enough to fit easily inside his embrace. "I can't live without her."

Intrigued by this comment, Ike studied the vampire. Miriam gave him a wicked smile, and Ike laughed in return.

"Come on, Uncle Chris." Pip tugged at his hand. "I want you to see the tree house. And then I want to take Aunt Miriam into the woods. And then—"

"Whoa, tiger," Chris said. "Give me a minute to unpack and get Miriam a snack, okay?"

"Can I have a snack, too?" Becca asked, her stomach giving an audible gurgle.

"Do you mind if Chris and Miriam stay with us tonight, Aunt Gwyneth?" I asked, aware of the chaos associated with having two more houseguests around the place.

"Not at all," Gwyneth said thoughtfully, her eyes pinned on Matthew. "They're family, too."

Chapter 18

Chris and Miriam were getting ready to leave for New Haven the next morning, in the midst of the first day of magic camp chaos.

Matthew, who had been occupying the role of chef, bottle washer, and housekeeper, was under pressure from Miriam to focus solely on family research. The collection and analysis of the Proctor DNA was priority number one as far as she was concerned.

"I promised Gwyneth I'd fix her kitchen sink," Matthew protested.

"Julie told me the sink has been slow to drain since 1982. It's time to call a plumber," Miriam said severely. "I want the Proctor lineage updated on a regular basis. And please use the tag system I set up, rather than each witch's own characterization of their abilities. We need to keep the categories consistent."

As a historian, I took immediate exception.

"But it's important to preserve the traditional names," I protested. "Think of the Book of Life. You can't just update everything to modern nomenclature. You'll lose all the subtlety!"

"I'm with Diana." Chris glanced up from his cereal bowl. "Sorry, babe."

"Me, too." Matthew was weary from hours of negotiation with his lab manager. "We can categorize later. For now, let's just collect the information."

Miriam sighed.

"Apollo doesn't want to wear his dog costume to camp, Mommy. He's hiding in the closet and won't come out," Pip said, stomping with frustration.

I put down my cup of tea. "I'll see to Apollo while Daddy gets you breakfast."

"We gotta run, squirt. We're going to see Put-Put and Lucy before we head home," Chris said, digging once more into his marshmallow-studded breakfast.

"Hurry up, Mom!" Pip cried. "I want Uncle Chris to see them raise the camp flags!"

Despite Apollo's reluctance and several other small hiccups, we made it to the Eastey house just in time. As we drove in, we spotted the old flags and banners gathered from every barn in Ipswich rising above the treetops, their lofty height made possible by a barrage of levitation spells and some careful wind control on the part of the Susies. The secluded meadow behind the old house soon looked like Camelot, with call flags, ensigns, pennants, burgees, and jacks fluttering in the breeze to signal that magic camp was starting.

When the Range Rover came to a complete stop, Becca and Pip ran off with their milk pails filled with lunch and their rain slickers in case the heavens opened. They didn't cast a single look back at us.

"They didn't say goodbye," Chris said, glum. "Our babies are growing up."

Matthew and I stood with the other parents, worrying about how the day would go and whether there would be tears and upset tummies later. After we convinced each other that our children were in good hands, we said farewell to our friends and returned to Ravenswood.

Julie was waiting for us there.

"My big toe is howling, and all the dragonflies have left the meadow," Julie said, pushing a wheelbarrow laden with tools and a tub of fertilizer labeled SHOOTS FOR THE MOON toward the barn. "More rain's coming. If someone doesn't take charge, the wood is going to turn into a jungle."

"I have had one or two things on my mind, Julie." My aunt, unused to the hurly-burly of life with two six-year-olds, was showing signs of cumulative exhaustion. She had no business pruning shrubs. Before I could say so, Julie revealed her plan.

"That's why Diana and I will take care of everything," Julie said, straightening her hat. "It will be just like old times. Remember when Stephen, Naomi, and I went into the Ravens' Wood to look for toads? We wanted to kiss them and see if they would turn into princes and princesses."

Gwyneth hesitated, clearly torn, then shook her head. "No, Julie. Diana needs to stay here and work on her hexes."

I'd tried to hex a pail of water and had only succeeded in knocking it over.

"Diana will learn plenty about higher magic in the moon garden," Julie insisted. "I'll teach her how to pick a ripe baneberry without them spurting sap all over her, and where the pincushion moss hides. Diana needs fresh air and exercise, too."

My twenty-minute yoga routines in the front parlor weren't enough to satisfy my body's yearning for meditative movement, and my temper and stamina were suffering as a result.

"I've been looking for a secondhand Alden scull for Diana's birthday," Matthew said sheepishly.

I smiled at my husband, touched by his sensitivity.

"If Diana starts rowing, Matthew will want to fix up the old boathouse," Julie warned. "It will take six witches, a lot of lumber, and a vat of white vinegar to bring it back to life."

"Why don't we visit Gladys?" Matthew said, offering a lifeline to my aunt. "I'm sure she'll be more comfortable talking about her warts with you than with a stranger."

According to Gwyneth, Gladys Proctor shared the same bumpy skin affliction that had plagued all her female forebears. She could also levitate trucks and turn ordinary boats into hovercraft, but she was solely concerned with her dermatological distress.

Gwyneth agreed after eliciting promises that I wouldn't let the fire go out under her skullcap tincture or forget to stir the pot of chili cooking in the embers of the keeping room fireplace. She also scribbled out a list of plants and herbs she'd depleted at Midsummer and wanted to restock.

Gwyneth requested mistletoe, meadowsweet, and milkweed as well as bee balm, foxglove, vervain, and mugwort. My aunt had also asked for marigolds, roses, every rose hip left on the bushes (she had underlined this twice), rosemary, and sage. She scribbled *Rowan, Elder, Hazel* across the side margin. We'd be lucky to fulfill her order by sunset.

"Our work is cut out for us," Julie said as we approached the moon garden I'd seen on my way to the Crossroads. A seemingly solid wall of blackberry and baneberry surrounded Gwyneth's magical herb and flower patch. "What a mess. It's going to take us the rest of the morning just to hack through the baneberry."

Squeaks of protest erupted from the hedge and the white berries bobbed on their red stalks, a thousand disapproving eyeballs trained in our direction. The blackberry canes writhed in distress.

"You'll survive," Julie told the berries, her voice severe. "This is what happens if you let your witch's garden get the upper hand, Diana. Maintain a regular schedule, and you'll never have to argue with a hedge."

Julie passed me a set of trimmers with gleaming blades. I held them gingerly. Pops of alarm and bursting berries told me that the hedge wasn't pleased.

"Diana's going to give you a good trim, and I'll follow up with a styling," Julie said, clacking her secateurs reassuringly. "She'll be quick and merciful, I promise. One sharp cut, Diana, then another. No hesitant hacking around in the branches, or the sap will spray everywhere and the garden will look like a crime scene. Cut everything you see down by two feet. With conviction."

I closed and opened my hedge trimmers in what I hoped was a gesture of readiness.

"Charge!" Julie cried, secateurs held high.

I lopped off my first baneberry branch, and blood-red liquid dripped from the severed stalk. I made another cut, then another, until I lost count. After I was whipped on the thighs by a vicious thorned blackberry cane, Julie muttered soothing spells to keep the hedge compliant. Ninety minutes of hard work later, our efforts revealed the entrance to Gwyneth's secret garden. Julie lowered the intricate wards on the picket fence, and I swung open the gate so that we could pass into a place of carefully cultivated enchantment.

The garden expanded and contracted around me as I took my first few steps.

In, in, in, the leaves whispered as I absorbed the scents and smells.

Out, out, out, the boughs sighed as the rare essence of a witch's moonlight garden returned to me in the form of renewed magical energy.

Julie bent over to yank at a plant with a rosette of shiny leaves and a few faded violet flowers. It was growing at the base of one of the gateposts, and as the plant's thick roots came free of the earth, I saw that they resembled a human body.

Mandrake—the most famous specimen in any witch's garden.

Julie continued to pull, until the thick, twisted root turned into long, delicate fibers. At the end of the fibers was a baby carrot topped with a leafy sprout.

"Gwyneth's going to have a good crop this moon," Julie said, examining the roots.

"Of mandrake?" I asked.

"Mandrake and carrots both," Julie replied. "Gwyneth's moon garden draws energy from the sun that is absorbed by the vegetable patch in the meadow, and vice versa."

The garden had a rechargeable magic grow light. How typically Proctor to be witchy and practical in equal measure.

"Remember to gently sever the roots when you harvest vegetables at the farm," Julie warned. "It's one thing to draw a carrot into the Ravens' Wood, but another thing to pull a mandrake into sunlight. They make a terrible racket."

Julie giggled. "I remember when Naomi and Stephen used to compete to see who could make the most noise pulling enchanted plants out of the wood and into the meadow, but Tally put an end to their games. Let's get back to work. I'll gather the rowan, elder, and hazel. You start on the plants."

I took a grooved slab of foam from the wheelbarrow, the furrows created by the knees of all the other Proctors who'd labored here, and grabbed the second pair of secateurs.

Though I'd only been able to identify the most common magical plants when I arrived in Ipswich, I could now recognize dozens more by sight and scent. Gwyneth always had a botanical text and a book of shadows open on our shared worktable. Over the course of the day, she would offer me a mason jar of herbs to sniff, or a crock of salve to test on a bug bite or a patch of sunburn. It was another example of how the family wove higher magic into every day of their lives.

After Julie and I checked off all the items on my aunt's list, my cousin gathered supplies for her own magical needs. They were far darker than those Gwyneth required for her post-Midsummer concoctions. Julie moved among the beds with a fine pair of Japanese pruning scissors, collecting crocus and adder's-tongue, blackthorn and sea buckthorn, moonwort and enchanter's nightshade, and the long fronds of Solomon's seal. These were powerful substances, and Julie kept them separate from the more common herbs and flowers for safety's sake.

By the early afternoon, physical activity had worked its magic on my general outlook. My muscles had the heaviness that followed good exercise and the whirlwind in my mind had quieted. Julie was right; as long as I could garden, I didn't need a seaworthy Alden scull. And if Matthew picked up so much as a tape measure to fix this mysterious boathouse, Miriam would be back from Yale and out for blood.

We tucked into the lunch Julie had packed to sustain us. Juicy strawberries, deviled egg and cress sandwiches, and a paper bag filled with Tracy's delicate madeleines scented with orange and lemon were all perfect sources of fuel, and canteens of fresh, cold water rehydrated our bodies.

Our work revealed the structure of the garden, and Julie and I took the last madeleines with us as we strolled through its beds and pathways. There were thirteen separate sections divided by gravel paths. All were arranged around a central round bed covered in moss and low-growing herbs. There, a small apple tree decked with white blossoms and ripening fruit sent twisted limbs toward the sky.

I felt a prickle of someone watching us, and I looked around to see who it might be. Sitting in a witch hazel, her weight bowing a spindly branch covered in yellow blooms, was Cailleach.

The enormous gray owl was silent, her only movement the blinking of her brilliant golden eyes. The white crossroads between them stood out as a flash of brightness in the cool wood.

"Goddess and her train," Julie said, amazed. "That's no ordinary owl."

My cousin wasn't talking about the bird's size—which was immense— but the waves of power that streamed from her body, making the air around her sparkle and the breeze sing.

"That's Cailleach," I said. "We met at the Crossroads."

Julie, who knew the coven rules, tamped down her natural curiosity and didn't ask for more particulars.

"Ka-lyahc." Julie's pronunciation wasn't perfect, but the owl didn't protest. She only swiveled her head toward my cousin, and back again to me.

"I'm supposed to call on her if I need help," I told Julie, careful not to reveal too much.

"Ah. Cailleach is your higher magic guide," Julie said. "Everyone who finds their path at the Crossroads has one. They're not like Stephen's heron, Bennu, or your firedrake, Corra, or Apollo—a creature who comes unbidden to teach knotters their skills. You must summon your guide if you want her help."

"I didn't call her, and I don't need help now," I pointed out, "but there she is."

"Maybe you do and haven't noticed yet." Julie was more familiar with spiritual guides and guardians than I. "There's an Owl Queen and Owl Prince in the black bird oracle deck. Maybe Cailleach wants you to read the cards."

I had consulted the black bird oracle when I woke up, and there was not a hint of a distress call in its response—just a lot of alchemy, which seemed appropriate given how much time I was spending in Gwyneth's laboratory these days.

Cailleach pushed off her perch and flew low and fast across the garden.

She passed by in a whisper of magic and motion that left me dizzy and Julie starry-eyed, flashes of silver illuminating her brilliant aquamarine eyes.

The owl lowered her talons and grabbed the mandrake root, complete with trailing carrot, from the wheelbarrow. Cailleach circled and dropped her burden before me. Tangled in the roots was a stem with long, toothed leaves and a single lavender flower that gave off a sweet scent. Her work done, Cailleach soared off into the branches of a nearby oak.

Julie and I peered down at Cailleach's gift.

"Is everything all right at home?" Julie asked cautiously.

"Yes," I said.

"Hmm." Julie was doubtful. "Are you sure? Mandrake root and green dragon weed are used in the *ars veneris*."

"Love magic?" I laughed, thinking of Matthew and the post-Midsummer uptick in our lovemaking. "That's something I don't need, thankfully. A good hex, yes. A love spell? No."

"It was definitely a message for you." Julie considered the matter. "Maybe it's Cailleach herself who is significant. A gray owl signifies night. Trust. And balance, too, if I am remembering my owl lore correctly."

Stumped, I shook my head and shrugged.

"I'd think about it if I were you," Julie said. "You don't want an owl in the house, roosting on top of the Welsh dresser and hooting at you during breakfast."

"Has that happened before?" I asked, concerned.

"Oh, yes. Constance Proctor had a little owl named Minerva and when she didn't listen to her, the creature took up residence in her underwear drawer."

"Noted," I said, my knees weak at the prospect of Cailleach—who was not a *little owl* but stood over two feet tall—doing the same.

"Pick up your magic-mail, and let's get back to the barn," Julie said. "My right knee tells me Gwynie and Matthew are back, and you of all people know how angry teachers can be if you're late to class."

Later that afternoon, I checked the status of the angelica root, which needed to steep overnight to make one of Gwyneth's all-purpose antidotes. The mayapples simmered away over a magical fire on the distillation table, and I'd gathered the ingredients for a casting powder that promised to strengthen the boundaries of sacred circles. Redbrick dust, check. Solomon's seal, check. High John the Conqueror root, check. Vervain and yarrow were at the ready, too. All I'd need tomorrow was a tiny amount of the dried belladonna Gwyneth kept on a well-warded upper shelf so that curious fingers didn't ingest the deadly poison. Soon, I would be able to change out of my grubby work clothes and join the rest of the family for dinner.

I enjoyed the alchemical aspect of higher magic more than the intricate spellcraft required for effective hexes, wards, and charms. Even when I leaned heavily on the poems of Emily Dickinson for inspiration, my gramarye was not yet intuitive and didn't perfectly match my knots. To strengthen my spells, I would need to memorize more of the poet's work so that her words and images were so tightly woven into my thoughts they would come to mind unbidden. That process would take time.

But alchemical ideas and techniques were already part of my subconscious, and texts and images floated freely through my scholarly imagination. The time I'd spent in Mary Sidney's laboratory was proving invaluable whenever I read instructions on how to make a magical concoction, as I knew how to lute together glass vessels so they could withstand high temperatures, and select the most appropriate glass bubble or rough clay crucible to work alchemy's magic.

Mary Proctor's book of shadows waited for me on the laboratory bench. It was here that I'd found the recipe for *Tituba's Red Powder,* the making of which was my final task for the day. It had been handed down through the Hoares to the Proctors, and the legend that accompanied the formulary said that Tituba had perfected it using the knowledge of her own Indigenous people as well as the herbs and plants available to her in Barbados and New England. Due to the toxic nature of some of the substances in it, the recipe was accompanied by two full pages of warnings.

I lifted the book's front cover and flipped through it in search of the recipe. The book of shadows opened instead to an often-consulted recipe for *Releasing the Green Dragon.* The first ingredient was mandrake root, and its end result was a *veneficium*—a potion used for love magic.

I carried Mary's book over to the workbench, where I could study it more closely in the light from the high windows. Like most early modern recipes, it was part travelogue, part how-to, and part shopping list, all combined higgledy-piggledy.

For to stir the wild passions and unbridle your beloved's wild nature, first take your mandrake root and seethe it over a fire for five hours, I read. *Dry it in the sun, then slice a piece the thickness of a silver shilling and pour two glasses of wine over it. Let it steep in the moonlight along with four stalks of yarrow, two poppy seeds, and a pinch of dittany root. Strain it through your sieve. Pour your wine into two silver goblets.*

I turned the page.

Over the course of five hours, sip one goblet of wine from the blossoms of witches' bells. Cast the spent bells into your fire, and thereupon heat a wash made of vervain. Leave the other goblet of wine in a convenient place where your lover might find it, along with a single flower pluck'd from the green dragon weed that groweth in the Ravens' Wood.

I ran my finger down the rest of the text so that I could feel the underlying structure of Mary Proctor's spell. It was geometric, like most magic cast by the Proctors. In this case, the spell was built with two interlocking hemispheres.

When the moon is descending, enter the wood sky-clad and call the moths for a raiment. Leave a trail of green dragon blossom behind you, which sweet scent will entice your lover to follow his desires. Choose your bridal bed with care, and guard it with wolfsbane and poppy flowers. Do all of this on a Friday between Midsummer and the August Feast and you shall set the Green Dragon free and he shall lay with the Unicorn and they shall be as one.

I stared at the mandrake root and the spray of green dragon weed Cailleach had delivered to me. The cards in my pocket stirred, intrigued by Mary Proctor's arts of love. I thought of Matthew, playing with the ravens in the wood, and The Unicorn at the center of the complicated spread of cards I'd cast weeks ago. I heard my husband's weary voice at breakfast, and saw the fine lines that deepened around his eyes now that science and magic were intertwined at Ravenswood. Matthew was not the same man I had glimpsed that night, free and wild in the Darkness.

Perhaps Julie was right.

Perhaps Cailleach's message was a reminder that Matthew's daughter was not the only member of the family able to run with wolves.

On Friday evening, I kicked off my shoes at the limits of the Ravens' Wood. In my precious moments of private time in the barn, I'd studied Mary's love potion and researched its contents. I'd scoured alchemical texts for the many interpretations of the Green Dragon and the Unicorn. And I prepared myself to ensnare my husband in a web of magic that he would never forget—and might enjoy.

I set a silver goblet on a flat nearby stone and dropped a pink, tubular blossom into the liquid so that its honeyed apricot scent would perfume the wine. Around the goblet's stem I'd tied a tag on which I'd written *Drink me,* with an ensorcelled ink made of nightshade berries. I'd had no need to meddle with Lewis Carroll's gramarye. Since he'd committed the words to paper, every witch knew that this invitation would entice even the most resistant creatures to take a sip.

A few feet farther into the forest, I removed my top and bra. A few more feet, and I slid my shorts and underwear off, leaving me sky-clad. I caught a glimpse of myself in a puddle of water, astonished by my wild coppery hair and wide eyes. My pupils were wondershot under the subtle influence of Mary's elixir, which I had transcribed into my book of shadows as *Love Potion No. 9.* I'd drunk down my portion over the course of the late afternoon, dipping the foxglove flowers into the vessel and sipping down a few drops at a time. As the elixir entered my bloodstream, it brought a sense of freedom with it, washing away any inhibitions.

I made my way to Gwyneth's moon garden, scattering green dragon blossoms behind me while fireflies flocked to my side. Nocturnal creatures—moths, bats, and owls—circled my head as I became aligned with Shadow, allowing Darkness and Light to pass through me. The blessings and strength of the goddess filled my veins with liquid silver, and the golden arrow at my heart gave off a gentle glow.

The goddess approved of my actions here tonight. Would Matthew?

I lifted the latch on the gate, swaying as the powerful scents of the moon garden threatened to overwhelm my intoxicated body. Once steady, I entered and picked up a basket of poppy flowers that had been waiting for me since early this morning. I walked the inner circumference of the garden, dropping the scarlet poppy petals as I went.

"*Through bitter sweetness and delightful pain, I fall to the center and am drawn up toward the sky,*" I murmured. "*Desire spurs me on, while fear bridles me . . . What straight or devious path will give me peace, and free me?*"

The powerful words were not mine, nor were they Emily Dickinson's. They belonged to the sixteenth-century mystic Giordano Bruno, drawn from one of Matthew's favorite passages in *The Heroic Frenzies,* a poetic tribute to passion.

Matthew would have received my note by now, inviting him to meet me in the wood. I wondered if he was within earshot and could hear me utter his friend's words.

I took the path into the heart of the garden. White flowers were in full bloom under the dark sky: moonflower, white rose, lily, and jasmine. Gossamer ribbons of Darkness, Light, and Shadow streamed from my body. Threaded among them were the sparkling colors of my weaver's cords, those associated with higher magic and those that belonged to the craft. These proved irresistible to the moths, who lit on the strands with fluttering wings, clinging to their light. I called more of the velvet creatures, until they formed a cloak that fell from my shoulders and trailed behind me.

Matthew was close and getting closer. A ripple of anticipation swept over me.

Bruno's words had released the wild energy of the place, and with every step the moon garden became an ever-more-enchanted place, where ancient, epic forces were at play. An ashen owl wearing spectacles sat on the stump of a rowan, mesmerized by the light of a candle. The flash of a white tail streamed through the hawthorn, followed by a dull thud of hooves. A raven cried overhead, and I followed drops of blood to a nest filled with broken eggs tucked under a clipped boxwood. Toads hopped through the wolfsbane, and antlers gleamed through the spindly trunks of the staghorn sumac.

I'd chosen the soft ground under the boughs of the apple tree for our tryst. The tree was fruiting and blossoming at the same time, its gnarled branches as crooked as those on the Proctor family tree. A snake was curled around its trunk, sleeping with its head pillowed on its tail. When I stepped onto the fragrant patch of marjoram, chamomile, and moss, brilliant poppies sprouted around my feet.

"Magic is nothing more than desire made real," I whispered to the night sky.

I breathed in Darkness, and breathed out a beacon of amber light as Shadow settled in my bones. I climbed into the crook of the apple tree, letting my fluttering cloak cascade down. An apple was within easy reach. I twisted it from the bough and took a bite, the tart-sweet flavor flooding my mouth with danger and delight.

Another ripple of Darkness passed through the wood, alerting me that Matthew had found the goblet of wine. A throaty chuckle told me that he had read my second message.

My limbs were liquid with yearning. I hungered for Matthew's touch, for his wildness.

For his Darkness.

The soft air played on my flesh, foreshadowing Matthew's touch, sliding and slipping over my body with maddening lightness. My brain felt addled, my hearing and sight unusually acute as the elixir pounded through my veins.

I did not have to wait long before Matthew appeared, naked as I was under the moon. He had followed my trail of garments, the silver goblet pinched between his thumb and forefinger. His eyes swept over me, lingering on the places he knew and understood so well.

"And whom do I have the pleasure of addressing?" Matthew murmured. "Surely not the virgin huntress Diana. Alice? Eve? I believe your cousin has already claimed the role of Titania."

"What about Lilith?" I let my free foot drop toward the earth.

Matthew's eyes went to the shadowed valley between my thighs, then took a leisurely trip over my hips and breasts until they fell on my lips. The tension between us rose.

"Did you like my love potion?" A moth flew from my cloak and alighted on my nipple, maddeningly light compared to Matthew's firmer touch. "It was a special formula, designed just for you."

"You needn't have bothered with the magic." Matthew glanced down, his mouth twisting into a sardonic smile. "I was aroused from the moment I found the note on the kitchen counter telling me you wanted me to join you in the wood."

Matthew's responsive body had not escaped my attention. The ache in my breasts spread lower, and my fingers followed it.

"The potion you drank unleashes the wildness of the Green Dragon," I replied, my fingers playing in the sensitive folds between my thighs.

Matthew's nostrils flared slightly as he detected the scent of my desire.

"I've been sipping it all afternoon. With your metabolism, it shouldn't take you long to catch up." My eyes narrowed like a cat. "Do you trust me, Matthew?"

"Not entirely," Matthew replied, his breathing faster than usual.

"Good." I drew my fingers from hip to knee, leaving a damp trail on my thigh. "I don't entirely trust you, either."

Matthew growled. The wolf was wakening.

I slid down from the branch and landed, soft as an owl's feather, releasing scents of chamomile and marjoram into the air.

Matthew's fingers tightened on the goblet's stem.

"Becca isn't the only female in the family who likes to play with wolves. Or fire." I crept closer until the tips of my nipples brushed against his chest. I bit into the flesh over his heart, blowing gently on the red crescents left by my teeth. They sparked into moons of flame. The toothmarks would be quick to fade, but the dark traces of witchfire would remain for some time.

Matthew's pupils, already enlarged by the love potion, widened further.

"Or Darkness." I drew a thorny branch across my wrist and blood beaded along the fine lash. I carried it to my mouth, sucking my vital essence from the wound. "Do you want some?" I asked, drawing my wrist away from my mouth.

Matthew's lips tightened, but he didn't speak.

"You had your chance." I snapped my fingers and Cailleach swooped down on Matthew with a warning cry.

My husband, who was rarely taken by surprise, ducked to avoid a head-on collision with the owl. While Matthew was distracted, I loosened my cape of moths and lowered myself to the forest floor.

Then I ran.

It was something Matthew had warned me never to do. Never drink his blood. Never run from him. Never bait the wolf.

A growl filled the night. Cailleach hooted, and I dashed into a thick clump of hemlock, hoping the scent would mask my presence. I'd been doing more than researching plants and alchemical symbolism and picking poppies over the past several days. I'd done a deep dive into the hunting habits of wolves, using the work of one M. Clairmont. Sight and scent were a wolf's greatest assets; I suspected the same was true of vampires.

Matthew loped into sight. He stared into the thicket where I hid, holding my breath. His attention moved away, and he trotted off in the other direction.

Taking my cue from the ravens, I flew at my husband's naked back. His hearing would pick up my footfall so I skimmed the ground, hoping that magic would enable me to reach him before my scent did.

It worked. My teeth sank into his hip and he howled in fury. Matthew had explained in one of his articles that this was how wolves brought down their prey—by attacking its vulnerable flank.

"Diana," Matthew growled. "Don't—"

"—bite," I said softly.

Matthew lunged at me, and I shot heavenward, rising above the trees. I was beyond his reach, no matter how high he climbed or how far his long legs and strength might carry him.

"You'll grow tired before I will, *ma lionne,*" Matthew said in that throaty purr that was half warning and half invitation.

"I know," I replied, somersaulting in the air, copper hair tumbling over white buttocks. I was tantalizingly close. "I've learned a lot from one of the world's leading experts on wolves. They expend as little energy as possible in the chase, wearing down their prey."

Matthew swore.

"But I'm not weak, or sick," I said. "If you're going to catch me, my love, you'll have to do more than toy with me. Drop your civilized veneer, Matthew. It's like Apollo's disguising spell: uncomfortable and wearing thin."

"It's hard-worn—and hard-won." Matthew prowled back and forth. "So that's your game? You've put a spell on me that will force my Darkness into your Shadow?"

"You're under a spell of your own weaving, not mine." Tears fell from my eyes, and white lilies bloomed where they splashed to the ground. "Ysabeau's blood was all it took to put you to sleep, like a princess in a fairy tale."

My tears fell on Matthew's upturned face. He tilted his head back, catching a drop of moisture on his tongue. When his eyes met mine, they smoldered with dark intent.

"Sleeping Beauty was freed with a kiss," Matthew murmured. "Kiss me. If you dare."

If I wanted to prove that I was the lion to his wolf, I would need to accept the challenge.

I landed before him, feigning an attitude of indifference even though my desire was strong. The pulse at the base of his throat suggested that Matthew was caught up in the same divine madness.

Bruno was right. Passion was indeed the most heroic frenzy.

I pressed my lips against Matthew's chest, light as a butterfly. I walked around to his right shoulder and pressed my lips to the taut muscles there. I stood behind him, and Matthew's breath caught. I brushed my teeth and tongue across his spine.

"Do you trust me with your wildness, Matthew?" I stroked his back, lingering on the strong planes of his shoulders and sweeping down toward the small of his back where his trim hips rounded into a swell of flesh. I found the mark I'd left on him, and fluttered my right thumb across the red, sensitive skin.

Matthew's breath hitched, but he didn't move.

"Let me tell you a story." I conjured wolfsbane and belladonna into bloom. "Once upon a time there was a prince named Matthew."

It was a version of my mother's bedtime story, the one that had given me ribbons that I could follow to Matthew.

"He was tall and proud, straight and strong, darkly beautiful—a good man, with a soft heart," I continued. "But he was taught to hate his Darkness, and cast a spell so that he would never taste its sweetness again. The longer hate held him in its thrall, the hungrier the prince became. He needed the Darkness to sustain him. Without it, he was nothing but Shadow."

Seeds of wolfsbane and belladonna, green dragon weed and yarrow, floated through the garden. When they fell to the ground, the seeds blossomed into a carpet of dark indigo, maiden's blush, white, and yellow flowers.

"One day a witch found the prince, sleepwalking through life. He was a ghost of his true self." I drank in the sweet scent of the moon garden. "The witch had Darkness in her, too, and was learning to love it. The prince was still afraid.

"And so, the witch decided she would do everything in her power to release him." I faced Matthew. "But she would not do it by hiding from Darkness. She would be hard-worn and hard-won."

"Is this where your story ends?" Matthew said, advancing on me with lethal languor. "Here, in the *hortus conclusus*?"

I held my ground, and Matthew threaded his fingers through my hair.

"The maiden's bower." Matthew tugged me closer, his hand cupping the back of my neck. "The garden of earthly delights."

I relaxed into his fingers, letting him bear my weight. Matthew held me effortlessly, my body suspended in a bow from my toes to the crown of my head.

"The home of the legendary unicorn," Matthew continued softly, "held captive for the hunter's pleasure."

I opened my mouth to answer, but Matthew's kiss swallowed my words. When we parted he shook his head in warning.

"It's my turn to tell a story. Once upon a time there was a beautiful witch," Matthew said, nipping at my fingers to claim my attention. His lips moved down the curve of my neck, his teeth leaving a ribbon of pain against my flesh, soon gone. "She ruled over a magical land, filled with wonders."

He had my undivided attention now.

"Among the wonders of her kingdom was a creature who survived on blood and dreams." Matthew's hands cupped my buttocks now, massaging the flesh as he brought the curve of my body into contact with his.

"Soon the witch learned how to walk among the creature's fantasies, his nightmares—the secrets of his mind and heart—until she felt at home. The witch told the creature that she would never leave those dark places," Matthew continued. "She claimed them as her own, and planted the flag of her kingdom there."

Matthew's head lowered, slowly, slowly, until his lips and teeth found my breast. My body tingled with the love potion that coursed through our veins.

When his eyes met mine again, my breasts were flushed and rosy, and Matthew's lips were pink.

"But the creature could not be so easily conquered," Matthew said. "The beast in him was too strong. He howled with fury, and the witch cried with frustration."

"What happened next?" I said as Matthew dipped his head once more.

"You're the witch." He paused in his descent, his breath cool on my flesh. "You tell me what the future holds."

I kicked out, freeing myself. My hands were balled into fists, and I pummeled them against his heart.

"Goddamn your control. Why won't you let me in?" I screamed. "Why won't you let yourself out?"

Matthew absorbed every blow, the impact not registering as a bruise. His eyes were haunted with longing and hunger, along with a dark, terrible vulnerability.

It was then that I knew Matthew's true nature was not the wildness I'd seen in the wood, when he'd played with Becca and the ravens. He was this wounded creature, who needed so desperately to be loved that he couldn't bear the suffering that might accompany that joy. He could withstand the Darkness, and rejoice in the Light, but could not survive the liminal kingdom of uncertainty that lay in between.

"Fear and desire," I murmured. "Oh, Matthew. I am your greatest terror—and your deepest longings—made flesh. For I am Shadow, and neither your Darkness nor the world's Light has dominion over me."

"You want my Darkness?" Matthew grabbed my hands and held them between his. He raised my wrist to his mouth. "Then you shall have it, witch—when I choose to share it. Darkness is my realm, and you cannot command me there."

His sharp teeth lanced into my flesh and I gasped in pain. Matthew silenced the sound with a ferocious kiss that left me breathless, and I could taste my blood on his lips.

I sank my teeth into his shoulder in response, drawing Matthew's vitality into my mouth, tasting the cold fire of his vampire blood. It was syrupy and seductive, but it burned my throat and left an aftertaste so bitter it brought tears to my eyes.

I drew the tip of my tongue across my lips, savoring the strange, alluring flavor.

"I can taste the magic in your veins," I said, burrowing my head in his neck. "Can you taste it in mine?"

Matthew's answer was to carry me into the center of the garden. He laid me down under the apple tree and nestled himself inside me.

My muscles tightened, an effort to keep him there.

Matthew had other ideas and glided from my body.

There was a nibble on my cleft, a delicious swipe of his tongue. *God-*

dess help me, I thought, dizzy at the prospect of the pleasure in store from Matthew's soft lips and agile tongue.

My husband surprised me once more, lapping instead at the soft, satin skin that covered the hollow between my pubis and my thigh. He sank his teeth into me a second time, close to the femoral artery. I saw stars as he drank, trembling as he closed the wound with a bead of his own blood, my fingers gripping his head to stop the world from spinning out of control.

Matthew drew my fingers away and crossed my arms at the wrists. He lifted them above my head, pinning them to the ground with one hand. The fingers of the other delved into me. He kissed me, his fingers stroking me inside and his tongue teasing my mouth.

I tasted salt and iron, the unmistakable elixir of life. I cried out as ecstasy came within my reach.

My wolf was in no hurry, however, and his gentle strokes and soft kisses drove me to madness as I sought release.

When I couldn't endure the exquisite agony a moment longer, Matthew answered my plea, filling the space he'd made ready for him. My eyes widened as my passion released, the pleasure acute.

I held on to Matthew for dear life, not wanting the waves of my climax to end, praying they would continue forever. I cried my ecstasy into the night, as sharp and raucous as the ravens who haunted the wood.

Our dance was as timeless as the battle between the Oak King and the Holly King. Darkness bled into Shadow, Shadow lengthened into Darkness, until we were caught up in the Light of mutual passion. Sated, we lay entwined under the apple tree.

Matthew's fingers smoothed the skin on my collarbone, but he made no move to drink from the blue ribbon of my heart vein. Neither of us had held anything back this night, and there was no need for reassurance. Our bodies and minds were replete with the knowledge of what had happened in the Ravens' Wood.

"A parent's love for their child is so simple," Matthew said, "and wholly unconditional. You mistook its purity for freedom, *mon coeur.*"

I lifted my head from the notch of his shoulder, but the expression in his eyes stopped me from answering.

"What lies between us, vampire and witch, man and woman, is a love of terrifying complexity." Matthew's accent softened toward his native French. "We are both caught in its tangles and knots, sometimes the hunter, sometimes the hunted. And sometimes, we are so lost in love's magic that we neither know nor care whether we are predator or prey."

"Do wolves and owls ever play together like this, in the wild?" I asked, drowsy with satisfaction.

Matthew chuckled.

"No, my love," he said, brushing his lips against mine. "Wolves and owls have far too much respect for each other to do so."

Chapter 19

I should have foreseen that the happy bubble in which we floated through the end of June and into July was bound to burst. But the oracle cards, which I'd grown to rely on for daily guidance, did not warn me about the next visitor who would arrive at Ravenswood, or how her message would upend our lives.

Matthew had taken the twins to magic camp in the midst of a drenching summer downpour and was now back with Gwyneth and me in the barn.

"What on earth is wrong with the cards?" I said, trying to capture one of them that was flapping in midair. The rest of the deck was moving restlessly on the worktable, unable to settle into a legible pattern.

Gwyneth's wards clanged as a stranger tried to pass beyond the witch's tree. My heart skipped and I scrambled to gather the black bird oracle together and return it to its bag, away from curious eyes. Ardwinna's ears pricked, and she rose to her feet, growling.

"Good girl," Matthew told Ardwinna, stroking her head in reward before going to the door to see what had disturbed her peaceful sleep.

"No sane person is out and about in this weather." The damp was hard on Gwyneth's joints, and pain had darkened her mood. "By ash and bone, the winds have changed, and there's an ominous portent in the air. Maybe that's why the cards are misbehaving."

Matthew opened the barn door, revealing a car that was stalled out on the top of the rise. We were together at the threshold to witness a small woman get out of the vehicle, its headlights still on and the wiper blades swishing this way and that. She looked like Mary Poppins, with a carpetbag clutched in one hand and a black umbrella in the other. A bedraggled waxed cotton coat with faded plaid lining was slung over her shoulders to keep out the worst of the rain.

"Janet." Matthew was a blur, his feet digging into the slippery hillside so he could remain upright in the mud and the wind.

"It's Matthew's granddaughter. Something must be wrong." I slipped the oracle cards into my pocket before removing an umbrella from the old pickle barrel by the door. I dashed into the rain after Matthew.

"Are you all right, Janet?" Matthew took the bag and loosened her grip on the umbrella's bamboo handle. He held the serviceable black canopy over her, providing an elbow for support on the steep descent.

"Not really," she replied, her rolling Scots accent thick and strong.

When I'd first met Janet Gowdie, she'd been living under the guise of a beneficent old lady. Today, Janet wore a disguising spell to appear like a woman in her early forties, even though she was born in 1841. She was dressed in a crocheted patchwork cardigan and jeans, with a pair of orange rubber clogs that suggested she was of an artistic temperament, not afraid of strong color, and liked thrifting at the local secondhand markets. That there was a formidably powerful witch inside the Bohemian outfit, with enough vampire blood in her to live for another two centuries, was not immediately evident.

With Matthew and I accompanying her, Ravenswood recognized Janet as family and relaxed its wards so that the three of us could pick our way down the muddy incline.

"It's fine weather for ducks, but no good for other creatures." My aunt ushered Janet inside the barn. "I'm Gwyneth Proctor. You look like you need a cup of tea."

My aunt would not permit any further discussion until Janet was out of her sodden raincoat, into a pair of dry slippers, and ensconced in a rocking chair by the woodstove. Matthew hovered over his granddaughter's shoulder, and Gwyneth eased her aching bones into a well-cushioned Windsor chair.

"Bless you, Gwyneth," Janet said, taking a deep sip of the piping hot brew my aunt had provided. "Lapsang Souchong. Excellent choice. You don't happen to have a dram of whisky? The last three days have been hellish."

Matthew picked through the shelf of spirits in the alchemical laboratory. Gwyneth kept them handy for tinctures and to make the grounding spritzes she liberally applied to herself before family came to call. He poured a generous measure of a single malt from Islay into his granddaughter's mug. The resulting brew must have tasted like a peat fire, but Janet seemed pleased.

Matthew, having confirmed that Janet was not bleeding, broken, or otherwise harmed, broached the subject of what brought her to Ravenswood.

"What's happened?" Matthew asked gently.

"And how did you find us? Did Ysabeau tell you we were here?" I asked.

"I haven't spoken to Granny. There's been a clishmaclaver in Venice, and all hell's broken loose." Janet was a font of neglected treasures of Scots dialect. I had no idea what a clishmaclaver was, but Janet's sour expression indicated it boded ill.

"You know about the Congregation's message." I sighed with relief. "You needn't have come all this way to warn us, Janet. We already received it."

"Not that clishmaclaver," Janet said. "I'm talking about Meg Skelling."

"Meg?" I frowned.

"She challenged Diana's fitness for higher magic at the Crossroads," Gwyneth said.

"So she informed us." Janet drew a folded piece of paper from the pocket of her cardigan and smoothed it on her lap before donning her glasses and reading from its contents. "*Flashes of brilliant red and gold appeared all over Diana Bishop's white flesh, with terrible vibrancy and awe-inspiring power.* It would seem from Meg's letter that Diana and her book were a bit rory that night."

All of my line have a certain glaem about them. So what? Granny Dorcas apparated into the empty rocking chair beside Janet, her brow bristling and her elf lock trembling. Her sudden presence would have un-settled most creatures, but not Janet.

"There you are. I thought I smelled a wee ghostie." Janet clucked with sympathy. "The fae are keeping company with you, I see. How dreadful. You must be covered in bites."

Granny Dorcas scrutinized Janet head to toe.

And you're like the babes, 'twixt and 'tween. Granny Dorcas gave Janet a sniff. *More human than they are, though. Less powerful, too.*

"Right on both counts," Janet said mildly. "I'm Matthew's grand-daughter, though at three generations removed."

"This is Granny Dorcas," I said, making the introductions. I tried to calculate our relationship on my fingers. "Ten—no eleven generations—removed."

Gowdie, you say? Mumbling, Granny Dorcas went to the woodstove. She fished about in the flames with her bare hands, searching for an ember to light her pipe.

"The Congregation is aware that Diana has the Book of Life within her. Why is this an issue now?" Matthew asked.

Based on the knowing flicker in Gwyneth's eyes, she knew about the Book of Life, too. Gossip traveled quickly in witch communities, and news of my earlier discovery had apparently made its way from Venice to Ipswich.

"It's an issue because Margaret Skelling claims that Diana learned the secrets of bloodcraft from its pages," Janet said bluntly.

"The lost branch of higher magic?" Gwyneth frowned. "Diana knows nothing of that. No witch does."

"All appearances to the contrary." Janet's eyes sparkled with fury. "Let's see. What did Meg say? . . . *Flashes of brilliant red and gold* . . . No, I've read that bit. Ah, *illuminating the word BLOODCRAFT.* The wee besom put it in capitals, so we could find it easily amidst the rest of her screed."

Our secret was out. Until now, Matthew and I had kept quiet about the fact the Book of Life mentioned bloodcraft in connection with mixed-race children born to blood-rage vampires and weaving witches, though others had suspected as much—Gerbert D'Aurillac, Peter Knox, and Matthew's son Benjamin chief among them.

"And to think I let you into the Crossroads with this secret inside you!" Gwyneth cried. "No wonder Meg let you find your way in the wood. Your secrets were an open book to her!"

"And she was reading it closely," Janet said. "Though, to be fair, blood-craft would be impossible for any witch to miss. According to Meg, the word appeared in the middle of Diana's forehead, sealed with a witch-score."

Granny Dorcas was at my elbow. She drew her fingers through the space between my brows, first in one direction, then the other, passing over my witch's third eye. My skin tingled at her touch, and for a moment I was reminded of the white pattern of feathers on Cailleach's face.

The mark of the Crossroads, Dorcas said, her voice hollow, *left behind when a witch casts a* maleficio *and takes her sister's power.*

"But Meg didn't take my power," I said, confused. "Only Mom and Dad did, when they spellbound me. Not even Satu Järvinen succeeded in robbing me of it—though she certainly tried."

"Stephen didn't spellbind you, my dear." Gwyneth reached for my hand. "Your father didn't have the training or the skill to work such a complicated piece of higher magic. Only an adept like Rebecca would have the necessary knowledge."

"That can't be true," I said. "I spellbound Satu."

"Then she wasn't spellbound for long," Gwyneth pronounced.

"Do all the Congregation witches know higher magic?" A ball of lead formed in my stomach. Satu was a weaver, like me. Unless . . .

"They're all adepts," Gwyneth replied, "and all graduates of the Congregation's higher magic track. Only the most powerful witches are selected to play a role on the ruling council."

The lead ball in my belly grew. I buried my head in my hands and swore. My ignorance of higher magic had caused me to make a terrible mistake—one that could have damaging consequences for me and my family.

"Satu was a member of the Congregation when she left the witchscore on my forehead. She's a weaver, like me," I explained. "I have no idea what kind of *maleficio* she cast."

Gwyneth swore, too, and Granny Dorcas and Janet joined in. I couldn't bear to look at Matthew. What a mess we'd made.

A shrill scream and a barrage of whispers erupted from Granny Dorcas's tangled lock of hair. She sat bolt upright.

I remember you now, Mistress Gowdie! Smoke streamed out of Granny Dorcas's mouth and nose, and orange sparks escaped from her pipe. *'Twas you who visited us that night in the gaol. But you didn't take my memories on May Eve. Give Bridget's memories back to Diana, witch, or I'll hex you bald, blind, and blue.*

"It wasn't me you saw in Salem, Goody Hoare." Janet held up her hands in a gesture of appeasement. "You met my mam, Griselda Gowdie. I've come to find her memories of that night."

"Your mother's memories?" I was dumbfounded. "What about Meg and the Congregation?"

"Nothing is ever simple in this family." Janet pulled another folded paper from the other pocket of her cardigan and handed it to Matthew. The goddess knew what else she had stashed in there. "You both need to read this."

Matthew scanned the worn page. "It's a letter from Grissel Gowdie to her mother, sent from Salem on May Eve 1692 to Agnes Gray of Elgin."

May Eve. Walpurgisnacht. The night when people lit bonfires to burn witches—or their effigies. My blood thickened with fear at the memories of riding through the flames to flee Rudolf's court.

"Granny Janet was living in the caves of Covesea then," Janet explained. "My mam, Griselda, was born there. She didn't see the sun for the first five years of her life, only the reflected light from the water and the glow of the moon when Granny Janet let her run free at night. They spent the days weaving spells and telling old stories, and the wee hours hunting for treasures and food."

"She alludes to that in the letter," Matthew said. "*Blessed mother, I ar-*

rived in the colony of Massachusetts on the 13th day of April, as foretold by the winds' whispers on the day I was born and the tales Granny Isobel and Granny Janet wove around the fairy pool. You can rest now in the knowledge that the oath you swore has been fulfilled.

"*They have charged many of our kind and imprisoned them in a foul underground gaol in a town called Salem. There they await trial, along with many innocents who know nothing of our ways. One is a wee bairn not yet seven*"—Matthew's voice hitched on the child's age—"*who is shackled beyond the reach of her captive mother. Both are mad because of it, unable to give and receive comfort.*"

Mercy. Mercy. Granny Dorcas keened and swayed, tearing at her elf lock. *Mercy is gone.*

I soothed my grandmother's cries as best I could, but she was inconsolable. Matthew continued with Grissel's letter.

"*Our dam's yarnings are proven true daily, and at last I see a pattern in the goddess's weaving.*" Matthew's voice had the quiet solemnity of a prayer. "*It is just as the silvered one told Granny Isobel, who knotted the knowledge of it in the wind. The one who will be first to hang was brought to this place on the 18th of April. She is not surprised, nor her friends, nor even an unexpected summer traveler who has come here for some purpose of his own.*"

Matthew drew a deep breath before proceeding.

"*The silvered one did not reveal everything to Granny Isobel, however. I must leave what I have learned behind for fear that it will come into evil hands,*" Matthew read. "*Until then I give you the words from another oracle: 'For we know in part, and we prophesy in part.'*"

It was a passage from the Bible—a clever way to encode a message that would be acceptable to any Puritan official who might come by it. I suspected Grissel had done so again in her references to the *silvered one*— a traditional name for the goddess—and the mysterious *summer traveler.*

"*I do not know if the winds blow with or against my return, but I will seek to get this letter to you by whatever means I may,*" Matthew said, drawing to a close. "*Until then, keep time by the moon and the stars and remain close to the earth from which we all come and to which we will all return. Written from Salem on May Eve in the year 1692, by the hand of your devoted daughter, Griselda.*"

Matthew turned the letter over.

"*To Agnes Gray in Elgin via the captain of the* Golden Serpent, *Portsmouth.*" Matthew's mouth tightened. "I knew it."

I took the letter from Matthew. There was the address, just as Matthew said. In the upper right corner, where the stamp would have been on a modern letter, I saw a faint symbol.

"Jupiter," Matthew said. "My father's cipher."

"Did Philippe have eyes on the Salem panic?" I asked numbly. Like the *Golden Hind,* the *Golden Serpent* could only have belonged to one man. "Was the captain of Philippe's ship Grissel's summer traveler?"

"That's what I wondered—and why I'm looking for the memories Grissel left behind," Janet said. "The goddess only knows where she would have put them for safekeeping."

"Gwyneth and I used a memory bottle as a lure to catch the ghosts." I jumped to my feet. "Maybe Griselda's memories are stashed in one of the trunks in the attic."

"Have you reached the subject of mnemonics, Gwyneth?" Janet asked.

"The arts of memory?" I'd learned something about them in graduate school from a medievalist obsessed with Ramon Llull. And Janet was right: The subject hadn't been on Gwyneth's summer syllabus.

"The *craft* of memory." Gwyneth pushed her spectacles up to the bridge of her nose. "It's the branch of higher magic that preserves our history for future generations. Rebecca was a particularly skilled mnemonist before she stopped practicing higher magic. And no, Janet, our lessons haven't touched on that part of the curriculum."

Poor Bridget's secrets. Granny Dorcas wiped her eyes. *She shared them with the Gowdie witch, but they belong to you, Diana.*

"Only initiates and adepts are authorized to extract memories, as well as store, release, and maintain them," Janet added. "There's a great demand for the service these days—far greater than for love magic or protection spells."

"I've never heard of such a thing, and I don't think Sarah knows anything about mnemonics, either," I said.

"We all know about them," Janet replied, dismissing my claim. "Every family has one or two bottles knocking around in the back of a cupboard or tucked in a box with the Hummel figurines and souvenir teaspoons. The problem is that unless you look after them, the wax seals break, the memories escape, and people think their house is haunted. Sometimes the bottles get left behind for rubbish when a house is sold. It's a nightmare for new owners."

"If Grissel's memories of Bridget aren't here, then there's only one other place they can be," I said.

"The Bishop House," Matthew said, nodding in agreement.

"I've always wondered why the house insisted on going with them when they left Essex County after Bridget's hanging," I said. The rest of the house had been built around the old saltbox, which now served as Sarah's stillroom. "Maybe it's been holding on to Grissel's bottles for safekeeping," I said.

"I'm going to Madison to find out," Janet said with grim resolve.

"I'm coming with you," I replied.

"So am I." Gwyneth's expression was dark with satisfaction. "I think it's time Sarah Bishop and I buried the wand."

It was midafternoon the next day and a busy drone of insects, farm equipment, and lawn mowers provided a steady soundtrack as we turned off Route 20 and onto the lane that led to the Bishop House. I spotted it in the distance, its clapboard siding recently painted, the mailbox still atilt, and both the American flag and the progress flag fluttering in the wind. A COEXIST banner hung from the fence, too. Sarah must have run out of room for activist messages on her car.

The temperature reading on the bank's illuminated sign in Madison registered nearly ninety degrees, the heat clinging like honey. Ipswich's summer storms would have been welcome here in upstate New York. The only escape from the oppressive atmosphere would be in the movie theater in Oneida or the air-conditioned grocery store in Hamilton. The Bishop House would be purgatorial, even with every window in the house flung open.

All three of us were on edge, which had made small talk difficult on our journey west from Ipswich. Gwyneth found a classical music station, which should have soothed my raw nerves but didn't. Janet sat in the back seat and knitted, her needles clacking in time to the music, occasionally asking a question about the small towns we were passing through and the covens that were based there. I worried about my reunion with Sarah. She'd been texting me recently to see how we were getting on at the Old Lodge, and I hadn't replied. She may have started worrying that something was wrong.

"Not a decent ward anywhere," Gwyneth said disapprovingly as we proceeded up the drive. It wasn't pitted anymore—Matthew had seen to it that the surface was solid enough to support the weight of the Range Rover—but it was devoid of any type of protection, magical or human.

Wait until Gwyneth discovered that the front door didn't have a lock and the back door was on a latchstring.

"Sarah doesn't believe in wards," I replied, continuing with our slow progress. "She thinks they make humans uncomfortable and are bad for business."

Be Blessed, Sarah's organic foods and magical supplies shop, was similarly unprotected except for a bell on the back door that let out a gentle chime when someone opened it, and a sign in the front window that read GUARD CAT ON DUTY.

"Once we get inside, let me deal with my aunt," I said, turning toward Gwyneth. "She's my problem, not yours."

"Is she?" Gwyneth raised her brows. "Sarah has been a thorn in my side since before you were born. I should have settled things between us long ago."

"Ouch!" I cried as a sharp barb pricked into my flesh. "Gwyneth, could you reach into my pocket and take out the oracle cards? If they keep sticking their corners into me, they'll draw blood."

Gwyneth dipped into the cargo pocket on my favorite summer wear and pulled out the bag. It squirmed and wriggled like a colicky baby. She put the troublesome cards in the cupholder.

"Still fretful, I see," Gwyneth said with a sigh. "I know just how the black bird oracle feels."

I pulled up in front of the house and turned off the ignition. Janet was quick to spring out of the vehicle and help Gwyneth from the front passenger seat. I remained where I was and sent a text to Matthew to let him know we had arrived safely. Then, I gathered my resources. If we were lucky enough to find Grissel Gowdie's memory bottle, it was bound to be explosive.

I had settled my nerves and was ready to exit the car when my aunt burst out of the house wearing her favorite turquoise-and-gold kimono. Her hair was barely contained in a scarf, and she was wearing a pair of furry slippers that made her look like Bigfoot.

"Why aren't you dead yet, Gwyneth?" Sarah demanded.

All my resolutions to keep calm and carry on evaporated in a wave of outrage.

"You always were a touch feral, Sarah," Gwyneth observed calmly, looking down her nose at my aunt.

Sarah flung two cards at her. "Stop sending your damned birds. I've got plenty of tarot cards, thank you very much. Next time one of your ravens comes around here, I'm going to shoot it."

The black bird oracle, bag and all, propelled itself out of the cupholder and plastered itself against the window.

No wonder the cards had been so agitated and fretful. One of the family's ravens had absconded with two cards and carried them to Madison to prepare Sarah for our arrival.

"Janet. Hi," Sarah said, finally registering the presence of Matthew's grandchild. "You're welcome to come in, of course, but not her."

"*Och,* I think you'll find we're an inseparable trio, Sarah dear," Janet said, returning to the back seat to pull out her knitting bag.

"Trio?" Sarah said, peering through the car's tinted privacy glass.

"Hello, Sarah." I climbed out of the car. Things were off to a spectacularly bad start. I spotted The Bottle and The Owl Queen lying in the grime of the driveway. "Please don't throw my cards on the ground. They don't like it. Neither do I."

I held out my hand and the missing cards flew into my palm.

Sarah stared at me in astonishment. "Diana! You're supposed to be in England!"

"Gwyneth's not dead and I'm not at the Old Lodge," I replied crisply, slinging my bag over my shoulder. "As for the ravens, you weren't the only member of the family to receive a visit from them this summer. Becca did, too. My important messages came through the regular mail: one from the Congregation, and one from Gwyneth."

Sarah's eyes shifted to Janet then back to me.

"Because I have both a maternal and paternal history of higher magic, Sidonie informed me that they wouldn't wait until the twins turn seven to examine them," I said, recapturing my aunt's attention. "Janet came to warn me that the Congregation wants to know not only the twins' secrets but also the knowledge of bloodcraft that is written in the Book of Life. She wants her mother's memory bottle back, too."

"Memory bottle?" Sarah's voice was hushed. "How do you know about—"

"How do *I* know?" I demanded. "The same way that I know about the Proctors and the Dark Path. Gwyneth invited me to Ravenswood and I went. How could *you* keep me from my own family?"

"I made sure that Rebecca and Stephen's wishes were followed—that's all," Sarah replied, her voice rising.

"You sound so certain," Gwyneth said bitterly.

"I am!" Sarah snapped. "Stephen told me what they'd decided. He said—"

"I can imagine what Stephen said." Gwyneth's voice was steely. "But I find it hard to believe that Rebecca agreed with him. It's even harder for me to fathom why you were so quick to accept his word for it. You're clever, Sarah, like most Bishop women. You fell for Stephen's line completely."

"Stephen wanted *nothing* to do with you," Sarah insisted. "As for Diana, they both wanted her to be a Bishop."

"Well, she's a Proctor now," Gwyneth said. "Higher magic and all."

"Darker magic nearly killed Rebecca. It did kill Emily." Pain doubled the anger in my aunt's voice. "How many witches need to die before you people stop dabbling in forces beyond your control? If something happens to Diana or the children, I'm holding you responsible, Gwyneth!"

"I chose my own path, Sarah," I retorted. "It's my legacy, and my birthright."

"It is not." Sarah's face was the color of a rose hip.

"It is. Mom was one of the Congregation's talented adepts," I said. "But you already know that."

Sarah looked flustered. "The Bishops haven't approved of higher magic for a long time."

"Well, Mom got her talents from somebody!" I exclaimed. "She didn't summon them out of thin air one October morning. Who was it? Grandma? Or someone farther back in the family tree?"

A shadow flitted through Sarah's brown eyes. It was soon replaced by her usual stubborn glint. Silent, my aunt pursed her lips and crossed her arms.

"Typical." I entered the house, letting the screen door slam behind me.

"Every witch thinks they can practice higher magic without consequences," Sarah said, following me inside. "Emily and Rebecca learned the truth and turned their back on it."

"They did not." Of this, I was sure. I'd seen my mother scrying, and Emily had died trying to reach my mother's spirit for guidance. "Mom and Em knew you disapproved of the higher branch of the craft, so they hid it from you. Just like Mom hid it from Dad."

Janet and Gwyneth were still outside. "Why are you both standing there?" I called, exasperated.

"The house has taken the doorknob, Diana dear," Janet said apologetically.

"This place is very badly behaved," Gwyneth said, surveying the ceiling of the porch as though it were infested with wasp nests. "The Proctors would never put up with this kind of nonsense."

I let my aunt and Janet in and shouted into the heating vent. "Granny Bridget! Grandma! I want to talk to you!"

The keeping room doors sprang open. Two ghosts, startled from their sleep, looked at me bleary-eyed. Their transparent green outlines were startling after the substantial specters who haunted Ravenswood.

There's no need to shout, my grandmother, Joanna Bishop, said. *We're sitting right here.*

And have been since yesterday, Granny Bridget added. *When Dorcas's ravens came, I knew you would be here soon.*

Gwyneth spotted the ghosts. She turned on Sarah, angrier than I'd ever seen her.

"This is an outrage," Gwyneth said. "Those ghosts should be locked up. Look, Janet. They're utterly drained of spirit. I should report you to the Congregation for mistreating your elders, Sarah Bishop. Your neglect has reduced them to smudges!"

"You can't come into my house and order me around, Gwyneth," Sarah fumed, sparks flying from her curls in a rare display of temper. She clomped across the front hall, her Birkenstocks tapping out a drumroll of warning. "Get out! You aren't welcome here."

"There, there, Sarah," Janet said, trying to defuse the situation. "To be fair, Bridget and Joanna are in a ragged state."

The argument over the care and feeding of ghosts raged on, but I had eyes and ears only for my Bishop ancestors. Gwyneth was right—my grandmother and Bridget were so weak they wouldn't withstand much questioning. I had to choose my words carefully.

Were you canny at the Crossroads, daughter? Bridget wondered, venturing a question of her own.

"I'm not sure," I confessed, knowing better than to lie to such a witch. "You were right, though, about the secrets buried there."

There are more, Bridget said, toying with the laces on her bodice.

Don't worry, Bridget. Grandma was addressing my ancestor, but she was looking at me. *Diana has been walking the Dark Path since she was born. Rebecca and I spoke of it whenever we worked together in the stillroom.*

The stillroom was now Sarah's domain, and a place I associated with failure and loneliness. But the room had felt more welcoming to me after Matthew and I returned from our timewalk. It's where Sarah had revealed a cupboard that held my mother's enchanted clock radio that played nothing but Fleetwood Mac and a chunk of her dragon's blood resin. There was nothing else in it except—

Empty, dusty jars and bottles.

"Thank you, Grandma," I said. She'd anticipated my question and given me the clue to its answer before I could ask it.

I made a beeline for the back of the house.

"Where are you going?" Sarah said.

"I told you. We're here to look for something that belongs to Janet," I said. "Once I have it, we'll be on our way."

Sarah flapped after me, her kimono sleeves billowing.

I marched through the kitchen and stepped into the cool, dim depths of the old stillroom. Originally used as a summer kitchen, it still retained the wide hearth, the ovens, and the storage loft where flours and grains had been kept over the long, snowy winters. The cupboard that held Mom's radio and resin had been built into the stonework to the left of the old fireplace.

It was no longer there. I swore. The house was always rearranging things to suit its own arcane purposes.

In the corner, I spied a thin strand of amber tangled with a knot of blue. The warp and weft of time trapped things long forgotten in small spaces like this.

Hoping that the amber and blue threads might lead me to the cupboard's current location, I carefully inserted my index finger into the center of the knot. It tightened around my recollection of the old storage place, and around my finger, too.

An arc of blue spun across the room. I followed its path as it moved toward the stillroom fireplace. But it stopped before it reached the sooty brick. The end danced around the massive butcher block island and hit the doorframe.

The missing cupboard now blocked the passage to the kitchen.

I flung open its doors. My mother's scent—lily of the valley—escaped into the room, along with the now familiar aroma of petrichor and brimstone that I associated with higher magic.

The bottles were just as I remembered them: grimy jars with lids, some containing bits of dried roots and herbs, some large and some small. One bottle was encased in raffia and candle wax. Another had the distinctive shape of a bottle of Mateus. Behind them were older bottles with wax seals, and other glass and pottery containers. As for Mom's old clock radio, it was nowhere to be seen.

"What's in front of the door?" Sarah demanded. She tried to wedge her zaftig body through the slender gap.

"Step aside, Sarah. Let me give it a go." Janet used her vestigial traces of vampire strength to shimmy the edge of the cupboard so that Sarah and Gwyneth could pass through. The three witches joined me in front of the open cupboard.

"Look, Gwyneth. There are dozens of memory bottles here," I said in disbelief. "Who do they all belong to?"

With great care, I reached for one of the bottles. It was seemingly devoid of contents and had faceted sides like a condiment jar. There was a faded cocktail sauce label, and it was stoppered with a cork sealed tight with thick globs of dark wax. As soon as I had it in my hands, I knew it contained memories. It was heavy—far too heavy for its size, just like the bottled autumn happiness that we'd used to attract the ghosts.

I grabbed a cardboard box from the floor. It had held a case of Spanish wine—a gift from Fernando no doubt. It would be the perfect way for me to transport the memory bottles safely out of the Bishop House and back to Ravenswood, where we could examine them more closely. I used the cardboard dividers to hold the bottles securely, wedging several of them into each of the twelve compartments so that they wouldn't clink together and crack.

"You can't take those. They're not yours." Sarah grabbed for the same bottle I was lifting from the shelf. It had originally held mustard or maybe strawberry jam. Now it was empty, except for a few brown seeds.

"Mom left these memories for me—just like she left the radio." I closed my fingers around the jar and held tight, jerking my arm back to pull it out of Sarah's grasp.

The point of my elbow knocked painfully against the open door of the old cupboard, sending shock waves through my arm. Another bottle teetered precariously on the edge of the shelf.

Gwyneth rushed forward to catch it, but she was too late. It smashed against the floor. In our astonishment, Sarah and I let go of the other bottle. It, too, broke into a dozen pieces at our feet.

Glossy squares of cardboard rained down from the roof of the still-room, brightly colored and sparkling with magic. They were too large to be oracle cards.

But I had no time to determine what the flying objects were, or their significance. The memories that had been released from the bottles were overtaking me, only this time there was not one series of recollections but two, a chaotic blend of sounds, feelings, and impressions.

It was then that I learned that some of the memories were mine.

MEMORY BOTTLE, USE BY 1 JUNE 1982
I wasn't supposed to be in Mommy's room.

MEMORY BOTTLE, GUARANTEED FRESH UNTIL 24 APRIL 1982
"Wait until your father gets back," my mother
said, her hands on her hips. "You know he
doesn't like you to climb trees."

It smelled of Mom, like flowers and powder.
There was a glass dish on the bureau, with a soft puff in the top.
I took it out, and white dust fell on the glass. It was like snow.

"Why?" I was up in the crook of the apple tree.
"You'll have to ask him." Mommy sounded angry.
Tears fell, and soon I couldn't breathe through the
congestion.

There was a lot of snow today.
So much that I couldn't go to school.
Mommy went to school,
because she had boots and could get there on the sidewalks.
Daddy and I had to stay home,
because the buses weren't running and the T had shut down, too.

The ground was far, far below.
I had climbed farther and faster than
I should have, and now I couldn't find
my way down.
"Don't be mad, Mommy. I'm sorry."

I gave the powder puff another shake, sending flakes
onto the carpet and into the air.
It smelled like summer, but looked like snow.

I giggled.

"Summersnow," I whispered. "Bloom and blow."

The powder danced and whirled.

> "Not as sorry as you're going to be," Mommy
> said. "You're impossible, Diana. I left you
> alone for two minutes."
> It felt longer than that.
> Mommy went into the garden after lunch, and now
> it was snack time. My stomach was hollow
> and grumbly, and it was making the dizziness
> worse.

"Summersnow," I repeated, louder this time. "Summersnow."

Flakes of white whispered back to me in a language I couldn't
understand.

They created a cloud above my head.

"Bloom and blow. Bloom and blow," I sang into the cloud.

"Summersnow, summersnow, fast to come and fast to go."

> "Sorry," I said again, the tears falling.
> "Jump down," Mommy commanded. "Come on.
> Jump."
> "No!" It was too far. I would break something.

Wind whipped through the room, and the windows flew open.

I laughed, and the winter snow from outside sifted into the room,
blustering across the windowsill and forming a drift along the carpet.

It was clean and white and smelled like Aunt Sarah's garden in summer.

"Diana!" My father stood in the doorway, his eyes round.

> "I can't." I was sobbing now, my terror rising.
> "I can't."
> "You got yourself up there," Mommy said. "You
> need to get yourself down."
> "I can't!" I screamed.

"Hush. The neighbors will hear."

Mommy looked over the fence, but there was
    nobody outside.

"I won't always be here to fix things for you,
    Diana."

*"Look!" I said, picking up a handful of the snow and making a ball
from it.*

*As the snow warmed, it bloomed into white flowers that filled my cupped
palms.*

"I'll catch you," Mommy promised. "You won't
    get hurt."

"I'm scared."

My mother dashed her hand across her eyes.

    "Me, too. Now jump."

"No."

"I'm going to count to three." This was Mommy's
    final warning. "One. Two."

"Please don't make me," I pleaded between
    hiccups.

"Three." My mother held her arms up.

"Stop it this minute," Daddy said, his voice rough and angry.

Startled, I dropped the flowers.

They burst into stars when they hit the carpet, and . . .

I jumped. And fell up, up, up.

Chapter 20

A dark hole gaped in my chest, a wound shaped like a curtained window through which I could see an apple tree with a swing, white petals all around on the green grass.

I curled to protect my flayed torso, pulling the skin toward my sternum to make me less vulnerable. I cried out from pain and shock, even as I recognized that the window, the apple tree, the swing, and the petals that resembled a fine dusting of snow were all meant to be there.

I thought of the Crossroads, and the pale forest creatures with chasms instead of hearts, and limbs that only worked with mechanical assistance. Was I a shade now, trapped Elsewhere? I moved my arm to see what replaced my hand—a whisk? a pair of scissors?—and a wave of pain followed, along with persistent bites and pinches. Granny Dorcas's fairies must have hitched a ride to Elsewhere with me.

"Lie still." The voice was familiar, but it didn't belong with the apple tree. It belonged to another place, where the trees were taller, thicker, darker, and ravens and owls took flight.

"I'll fetch a broom."

This voice, with its distinctive burr of Scotland, was from yet another place, a room of ancient stone with a round table. Gallowglass? But no, this was a woman's voice, and I reached through my memories for the correct name.

"Janet?" I remained curled around the abyss in the center of my body. "Something terrible has happened."

Where was Matthew? He was my anchor, my healing balm, the one person who might be able to fix what was broken.

A warm hand settled on my shoulder. "You've got a bad case of memorylash, Diana. Give yourself a minute to recover."

In my mind's eye I saw a marsh with the sea beyond and the shadow of a heron falling over the long grass of a meadow.

"Aunt Gwyneth?" I whispered, relieved.

"Right here, Diana." A gnarled hand squeezed mine. "It feels worse than it is. You're lying on some broken glass, and Sarah is going to help you sit up."

Rough hands took my shoulders. The scent of henbane, mint, and cloves swept over me. *Sarah.* I'd know that scent, and the touch of her work-chapped hands, anywhere.

"Gently!" Aunt Gwyneth hissed.

I was still clutching at the edges of the skin on my chest when Sarah raised me to a seated position. I didn't want anyone to see my wound, and I kept one shoulder curved around it in defense.

"Thank the goddess," Janet said. "I didn't fancy letting Matthew know that his wife was lying in a pool of broken glass."

"The bottles." I grasped at the memory flitting through my addled mind, but my hands filled with broken glass instead.

"Are beyond repair, I'm afraid," Gwyneth said, prying open my fingers so that the shattered fragments fell to the floor, leaving my hands scraped and bleeding.

"How will we put my memories back?" I didn't want to lose these precious glimpses of my childhood. The thought of abandoning them in the stillroom, where I would only be able to visit them occasionally, was sickening. I began to scrabble in their remains, trying to gather up the pieces.

"Your memories are back inside you now," Gwyneth said gently, "where they belong."

I remembered the horrifying void in Naomi and shrank from my aunt's touch.

"I need stitches," I mumbled.

"You've got a few superficial cuts, that's all," Sarah said. "We'll clean them up and put my healing salve on them. You're going to need a new T-shirt, though."

I looked down, dreading what I would see. But my fingers were not gripping skin. They held folds of soft, cotton cloth. Confused, I pushed on my sternum, expecting my fingers to enter my chest cavity and touch the swing hanging from the apple tree. Instead, they met bone. There was no gaping hole in me as I'd thought.

"It can't be good for you to lie on the floor among all that glass dust," Janet clucked. "Can you stand?"

I nodded. Sarah grasped one hand and Janet the other, and they helped me rise. I stood on shaky legs. A piece of glass caught in my hair touched my cheek. I removed it carefully.

"I think we could all use some tea," Gwyneth said, taking charge. "Sarah, would you do the honors? Janet, could you sweep up the mess? Sarah must have a broom somewhere. As for you, Diana, you are going to stay where you are until you stop shaking. The only antidote for a sprained memory is time and rest. The headache usually goes away in a few days, but the wobbly legs and strange dreams can last for weeks."

Sarah, who had never had a meekly compliant day in her life, went to the kitchen without protest to gather supplies. Janet busied herself with a broom and a dustpan. I didn't want a shred of my missing memories to go out in the recycling, so Janet agreed to put all the shards and glass dust in a red-and-yellow coffee can. She gathered up the cardboard squares that I'd remembered raining down from the loft. These turned out to be some more of Mom and Dad's old record albums, which Janet stacked in a neat pile.

Sarah returned to the stillroom with a teapot and mugs. She switched on her coffee maker and plugged in the kettle. Sarah was a great believer in electricity. Gwyneth, who scorned innovation in favor of tradition, looked distressed at the thought of drinking anything made with the assistance of such a newfangled invention.

While Sarah busied herself at the stove, and Janet made another round with her broom, I studied the assortment of bottles and jars that remained on the cupboard shelves.

"Do you think those are all *my* memories?" I asked softly. The tender places around my heart, where the memories had flown, twinged in sympathy.

"Only the wee bottles and jars in the front," Janet said. "The rest of them are too old and dusty. The wax hasn't been renewed in ages. I wouldn't be surprised if no memories remain."

"Yours, however, were perfectly preserved, Diana. It's a testament to your mother's skill that she was able to capture those moments in such detail," Gwyneth said. "Morgana used to jump down and fall up like you did as a child. It must be an inherited trait, like blue eyes."

Janet's eyes were misty. "Such a sweet, wee spell you worked, using what you had at your fingertips. *Summersnow.*"

Sarah handed me a mug of tea. It was too weak for my taste, but she'd done her best. Janet joined Sarah in a cup of coffee, and Gwyneth decided on some cold water after seeing the tea bag's paper tag. We sipped our drinks in silence, and by the time I'd drained the steaming mug, I almost felt like myself again.

Janet took her mug to the cabinet and made a visual inventory of the shelves.

"Do you see Grissel's bottle?" I asked.

"None are labeled," Janet replied.

"I'm not surprised," Gwyneth said under her breath.

"Maybe their shape and size will help us find it." Braced with tea, I attempted to get to my feet so that I could help Janet look for her mother's memories. The room tilted this way and that as though I were on the *Good Juju.* I grabbed at the butcher block to steady myself.

"Given your current sense of balance, I think it's best you not handle anything breakable." Janet gathered the pile of albums. "Have a look at these instead."

"They must have belonged to Mom," I said, picking up the copy of Fleetwood Mac's *Rumours* that rested on top.

Sarah turned white. Thankfully, the enchanted clock radio was nowhere to be seen, so we would be spared an endless loop of Mom's favorite songs.

I riffled through the albums, which included every Fleetwood Mac record released between the *White Album* and *Mirage,* as well as a sampling of earlier recordings from before Stevie Nicks—my mother's idol— joined the group. There were a few other artists in the mix: Joni Mitchell, Creedence Clearwater Revival, Stevie Wonder, The Rolling Stones, Buffalo Springfield, and Simon and Garfunkel. I already had copies of a few of the albums, delivered by the house on a previous occasion.

"The greatest hits of the 1960s, '70s, and '80s," I said, repeating a tagline used by the Hartford radio station that the staff were always playing in the department office.

I flipped *Rumours* over. While the front of the jacket had the familiar image of Mick Fleetwood and Stevie Nicks engaged in a witchy ballet, the back had more casual black-and-white shots of the band horsing around during a photo shoot. I frowned as the cardboard wiggled.

"The record's missing," I said, peeking inside. I drew out the lyrics insert, which was covered with more candid shots of the band as well as the words to the well-known songs from their hit album.

Someone had underlined lines from the lyrics in different colors— black, red, blue, and green. The rest of the insert was covered in my mother's tiniest writing.

For releasing memory bottles
To enhance visions
For dreamwalking
To predict the future
To release the grip of the past
A protection spell for entering Shadow
To strengthen a witch in any Shadow work
To balance Darkness and Light
Love magic—proven by me, Rebecca Bishop
A spell to recite before gathering Graveyard Dust
A charm to make any magical work more resilient under
    curses and hexes
Before making an offering to the goddess

Years ago, the house presented a book of shadows to me that was filled with Mom's early spells and charms written out in round, childish letters. These were darker and far more sophisticated. She would have aced Gwyneth's syllabus.

"I think I found Mom's real book of shadows." My voice was faint. The Proctors relied on geometry and Jacobean literature, and I used the poems of Emily Dickinson, but it was Fleetwood Mac who inspired my mother's gramarye. There wasn't much to distinguish between William Shakespeare, Emily Dickinson, and Stevie Nicks. They were all bards, after all, with magic in their pens.

I showed Gwyneth the annotated lyrics. "She hid it in plain sight—in the words of her favorite songs. This is what she used to refresh old spells and keep them sharp."

Gwyneth gasped. "Rebecca used *music*?"

"Apparently," I replied, running my fingers across the underlining in "I Don't Want to Know." She'd written *A powerful method for uncovering old secrets* next to *Finally baby / The truth has come down now.*

"Mom borrowed from the songs and put the lyrics together in her own way," I said, noticing her careful excisions, changes, and additions. "And Stevie Nicks's lyrics were clearly her favorite."

"This day has been bad enough without bringing Stevie Nicks into it." Sarah tried to snatch the album insert from me, but my mother's magic was not going to go the way of my memories: reduced to shreds and lying all over the floor.

"Not this time, Sarah." I moved the album jacket and liner notes safely out of reach. "You were willing for me to have Mom's dragon blood resin and her first book of shadows. You shouldn't have a problem with me adding to them now."

Sarah lunged for the rest of the albums. Janet, with her vampire blood, beat Sarah to them.

"If these do constitute Rebecca's mature book of shadows, surely they belong to Diana," Janet said with a sweet smile on her face and a sharp blade in her voice. "Your niece's hexes might not be fit for purpose quite yet, Sarah, but mine are famously effective."

Janet handed me the albums. None had vinyl in them—just liner notes and pieces of paper covered with Mom's scribbles. Finding my mother's book of shadows in her album collection was a little like discovering the Book of Life inside Ashmole 782—surprising and a bit overwhelming.

During my first days at Ravenswood, Gwyneth had mentioned how useful it would be to have insight into my mother's magical thought process when I struggled with my gramarye. It would take time for me to come to terms with the trail of magical breadcrumbs my mother had left for me, but I was eager to begin.

"We'll take these back to Ipswich." I stacked the albums in a neat pile. "Let's find Grissel Gowdie's memories so we can go home."

"You are home." Sarah's eyes filled with tears. Two bright red spots burned on her cheeks, and her mouth was set in a firm, stubborn line. "And you're not taking anything out of this house—that includes your grandmother's memory bottle collection."

"You knew what these were when you showed me the cupboard the first time!" I cried. "All these years, you knew these bottles were here!"

"I should have thrown them away years ago!" Sarah grew more agitated, the color in her face deepening with guilt. "No one was allowed to touch them. That's why Mother enchanted that damned cabinet—so Rebecca and I wouldn't rummage through them when we were alone in the house."

"You can't just throw away family history," I shouted at Sarah. "It belongs to me, and to the twins."

"Too late!" Sarah crowed. "Mom destroyed some of them before she died, and the rest are probably empty by now."

A malodorous scent filled the air. My grandmother and Bridget Bishop slipped through the old cupboard and the kitchen to join us in the stillroom.

"Joanna Bishop would *never* destroy a memory bottle," Gwyneth said, pinching her nose shut to block out the scent of Sarah's lie. "She was far too great a witch."

"What are you afraid the memory bottles might reveal?" I demanded of Sarah.

"I'm not afraid of anything!" Sarah snapped. "Memory bottles can't be trusted. Leave the past dead and buried, where it belongs."

"The past isn't dead, and it's only buried by creatures who mistakenly believe it's no longer relevant," I retorted. "Past, present, future—they're all mixed up together."

Meg Skelling and the Ipswich coven had taught me that.

"I'm taking the memory bottles to Ravenswood, where they will have proper care so that Becca and Pip can know the Bishops who are gone," I said, my tone final.

"Over my dead body," Sarah replied through gritted teeth.

"Let's focus on my mam's bottle," Janet said, trying to de-escalate the tension in the room. She removed an amber bottle from the cupboard, handling it like a grenade with the pin pulled out, and placed it gently in the wine box. "Still, we might as well get the rest of them put safely away while we're at it."

"Here." Gwyneth handed Janet an orange tea towel with DRINK UP WITCHES printed on it in black, a Secret Sister gift Sarah received last Samhain. "Use that to pad the box."

"That towel is mine, Gwyneth!" Sarah exclaimed. "As for you, Diana, you're just as bad as Rebecca. You won't be happy until you've taken everything you want and I've got nothing but leftovers."

Sarah burst into tears.

This is what happens when you refuse to face Shadow, Bridget said sadly. *Sarah's sitting on a powder keg of secrets.*

She was so afraid of losing Diana after Rebecca died, she wouldn't let me tell Diana the truth, my grandmother said with a sigh, *even though it would have made things easier in the end.*

"What truth?" My witch's sixth sense told me that I was close to finding the root cause of all the half-truths and outright lies that Sarah had piled up over the years.

"If you tell Diana now, I will *never* forgive you, Mother," Sarah cried.

It's out of my hands, Sarah, my grandmother said sadly. *Rebecca's spells and bindings are too complicated for any of us to unwind. We just have to let her magic run its course.*

Rebecca saw the portents and read the signs, and knew what must be done. Bridget shook her head. *A great witch, gone too soon.*

"Perfect, precious, precocious, prophetic Rebecca!" A lifetime of resentment bubbled to Sarah's tongue. "I've always been second-best."

Darkness approached the house in a sudden storm, drawn to the windows of the Bishop House by Sarah's volatile energy.

"Higher magic got her in the end, though," Sarah said with a note of triumph. "Rebecca thought she was invincible. She was wrong."

"Sarah!" The depth of her venom took my breath away.

"Stephen warned me Rebecca could go the way of Naomi." Sarah's tears increased.

Sarah had known about Naomi, too. My own anger rose, and Darkness filled the stillroom.

"What's bred in the bone always outs in the flesh," Sarah hissed.

"If that's the case, why aren't you on the Dark Path, too?" I shouted back. "We share the same blood!"

"Wrong." Sarah's mouth twisted into a chilling expression as Darkness swept through her.

My phone rang.

Matthew. I answered the call.

"Has something happened?" I asked, my heart thumping with dread. "Are Pip and Becca hurt?"

"No, *mon coeur*," Matthew said, his voice low and calm. "I'm sorry to interrupt, but I've been going over your previous DNA results."

"And?" Surely this could wait.

"Are you somewhere you can talk privately?" Matthew sounded concerned.

"Hardly," I said, my glance traveling from my irate aunt, past the ghosts, and on to Gwyneth and Janet.

"Is Sarah there?" Matthew asked.

"Yes," I said.

"You'd better put me on speaker, then," Matthew said, his voice taut.

"Go ahead," I said, after pushing the button.

"As I was telling Diana, I reviewed her DNA findings. I wanted to compare them to Gwyneth's preliminary results and some of the other samples we collected. I also compared them to the tests we ran on Sarah years ago. I wanted to confirm we were identifying the maternal and paternal markers correctly."

Matthew hesitated.

"I'm sure this will come as a shock to you, Sarah," Matthew said carefully, "but you and Rebecca didn't share a father."

"It's no surprise to me," Sarah retorted. "Rebecca told me so when I was fourteen and she wanted to get back at me because I borrowed her book of herbal cures. She was the bastard of goddess knows who. Some soldier my sainted mother had a fling with during the war."

My mind reeled at the fact that I was not the granddaughter of Joe Green, the genial and beloved Madison chief of police.

Fear touched me with a cold hand. Had my grandmother had an affair with Tally Proctor, making me the product of an incestuous union?

His name was Thomas Lloyd, and it was not a fling, Sarah Estelle Bishop. My grandmother was brighter and more distinct than she had been before, anger fueling her spirit. *I met him when I was eighteen and we had seven glorious years together when we were reunited after the war.*

"You're a dark horse, Joanna," Gwyneth said, impressed.

"Goddess bless us," Janet murmured, eyeing me warily. She recognized the name Thomas Lloyd.

A sharp intake of breath on the other end of the phone told me that Matthew had, too. *Both* of my grandfathers had gone to Ysabeau in a fruitless attempt to save Philippe, who had himself been captured by the Nazis while attempting to liberate Ravensbrück.

I was holding on to the tag end of a weaving that was bigger than the Congregation's interest in me, or the twins, or even bloodcraft. The fuzziness in my head receded, and in its place was a crisp, white surface on which brilliantly colored pieces shimmered as they changed positions. I couldn't understand the pattern—yet. The cards reminded me that they were available for consultation, stirring in my pocket, but I patted them to indicate their revelations would have to wait for later.

I considered the options, but there was only one path to take.

"I think you had better call Baldwin," I told Matthew.

The intricacy of the weaving coming into focus terrified me—and the Bishops, the Proctors, and the de Clermonts were all tied up in it. It was vital we figured out how. Baldwin was the sire of the de Clermont clan. He needed to know what I'd discovered today.

My answer may have been unwelcome, but it was not unexpected.

"I'll call him now," Matthew assured me. "When are you coming back?"

"Tomorrow," I said, deciding to save the story of my own memory bottles and my mother's book of shadows until we were together.

The ensuing silence suggested that Matthew was disappointed.

"A lot has happened, and we all need a good night's sleep before we drive to Ravenswood," I explained.

And I had a few things I'd like to clear up with my grandmother. The Box from the black bird oracle deck swam before my eyes. My curiosity had brought chaos into our world, just as the card warned it might.

"Maybe going to Ravenswood was a bad idea after all," I said, lowering my voice.

"Everything we're facing—your higher magic, your grandfather's true identity, the twins' talents—was bound to come to the surface. Now it has," Matthew replied. "Nothing has changed, *mon coeur*. This has always been the truth, even if we weren't aware of it. Now we face it, together."

Tears sprang to my eyes. I dashed them away.

"I hope you still feel that way tomorrow," I said with a shaky laugh.

"I will." Matthew's voice was unwavering. "Can you take me off speaker?"

I did, sniffling into my sleeve. When Matthew spoke again, it was for my ears only.

"I've never liked or loved you more than I do in this moment, Diana." Matthew's voice rang with truth.

The shifting dynamic between us had threatened to bring the world crashing around our ears, and had drawn every skeleton out of the family closets, but still Matthew's love for me was inviolable.

After Matthew disconnected our call, ragged breaths filled the still-room. The Darkness outside the windows boiled and churned.

"I do hope you feel better, Sarah, after vomiting up these morsels of ancient history," Janet said bitterly. "I don't like to question a sister's trust-worthiness, but you've given me no choice. After your display of bile, I simply must have my mother's memories back."

Janet returned to the cupboard and systematically sorted through the contents. She examined each bottle in turn before placing them into the box at her feet, making prognostications about their contents based on their shape and age.

"Baby food. That belongs to Diana," Janet murmured. "Lydia Pinkham's Vegetable Compound to 'cure female weaknesses.' That predates Joanna's time, and the memory must have been bottled at the end of the nine-teenth century."

She reached into the back of the shelf for another bottle and froze.

"What?" Sarah said, suspicious. "What have you found?"

Janet drew a milky-green glass vial from the depths of the cupboard. It was small enough to fit into her palm, with a long, narrow neck and a bul-bous base so thin it looked as though a breeze could smash the vial to bits.

"That's an old bottle," Gwyneth remarked.

"I've never seen it before," Sarah said, frowning.

"It's from the seventeenth century," Janet said. "Granny Janet had a wee jewel box filled with them. They held Granny Isobel's memories and were her greatest treasure."

Janet cupped the bottle between her hands as though she were gauging the memories inside.

"This has the feel of Mam. It's heavy with fear and fury," Janet said. "She used a strong spell to close the bottle, one that has held through the years."

"Now what?" Sarah asked after a pause in the conversation, while we all considered our next step. "Aren't you going to open it? Isn't that why you came?"

"No," I said. "We aren't opening it here."

Too much had happened. Too many secrets still hung in the air. I hadn't yet fully recovered from seeing my own memories and feared I couldn't absorb anyone else's so soon—especially not if they featured my executed ancestor.

"We should open the bottle at Ravenswood, with Matthew present," Janet decided. "Mam was his kin, too, and her memories belong to him as well as to me."

"Is it safe to transport it?" Gwyneth asked. "I don't like the look of that cork, and there's hardly any wax left on the seal."

"Let me see." Janet crooned to the bottle in Gaelic. She nodded. "We can get it to Ravenswood, and open it, but we'll never get the memories back into the bottle. They may need to be rehomed. Is that something you can manage, Gwyneth? I've never been any good at it."

My great-aunt and Matthew's great-great-granddaughter were speaking a language that neither Sarah nor I knew. Bridget and Grandma seemed to share it, though, and both nodded their approval of this plan.

"Of course I can," Gwyneth said, adding, "though I might need the coven historian's help."

"Let's get the rest of the memory bottles packed in case the cupboard decides to hide itself again. Janet will watch over them in the keeping room," I said. "Gwyneth can use the guest room to rest, and I'll sleep in Mom and Dad's room."

"What about me?" Sarah demanded, her eyes red and cheeks swollen from crying.

"Honestly, Sarah?" I shook my head, weary. "I no longer know."

When I finally climbed the stairs to my parents' room, I left the memory bottles wedged between two needlepoint pillows on the keeping room's uncomfortable settee next to Janet's overflowing bag of needles and wool. Sarah was locked into her bedroom with a pack of cigarettes and a bottle of bourbon, smoking like a chimney and occasionally breaking into floods of tears. Gwyneth snored gently in the guest room, a picture of my mom and dad on their wedding day clutched to her heart.

I sat on the edge of the bed and trembled from head to foot, delayed shock and exhaustion hitting me in waves. Tears might relieve some of the emotional pressure I was under, but I found myself too bewildered to cry. All I could do was hug myself and rock back and forth on the edge of the mattress, hoping to comfort myself so I could face the choices that would have to be made in the coming days.

Though it was late, I was sorely in need of guidance. I reached into my pocket for the black bird oracle.

Who was my maternal grandfather? I wondered, moving the cards between my hands. *Who was this mysterious British officer, Thomas Lloyd?*

The oracle sprang to attention, releasing a flurry of cards onto the white eyelet bedspread.

The Unicorn. The Box. The Bottle. The Labyrinth. The Raven Prince. The Owl Queen. The Mirror. The Key. The Sun.

Concise meanings for the cards immediately came to mind, evidence that I'd been doing my homework.

Me. Chaos. Memory bottles. The Labyrinth. The Raven Prince—was that Thomas Lloyd? My mom. Prophecy. The answer to a dilemma. Enlightenment.

I collected the cards and posed another question. *How were the de Clermonts involved in my family's witchy business?*

The Unicorn. The Labyrinth. The Sun. The Raven Prince. The Key. The Bottle.

Me. The Labyrinth. Could The Sun be Philippe? Thomas Lloyd. The answer to a dilemma. A memory bottle.

I gathered the cards again, curious as to why the deck kept presenting me with the same cards though I was asking different questions. *What was I supposed to do next?*

The Unicorn. The Labyrinth. The Owl Queen. The Bottle.

Me. The Labyrinth. Mom. A memory bottle.

What bottle? I wondered. One of the hoard we'd found in the still-room cupboard? If so, which one?

Restless, I roamed around my parents' room. I picked up another picture of them as a young couple to search it for clues. It was sitting on the bureau, along with my grandmother's silver-backed brush and hand mirror.

I gazed into the mirror but found nothing there except my own reflection.

A bottle of Mom's favorite Diorissimo perfume was on a tray, along with the powder box that I'd seen in the memory bottle Mom had gathered.

If only she'd left the memories where they were, we might not be in this predicament now.

Maybe you wouldn't have met Matthew, my intuition whispered.

I sighed, newly aware that not all my memories had returned when my mother's spellbinding loosened. Some remained fresh, though, like my mother's delicate scent of lily of the valley touched with bergamot and lilac.

There was only a sticky trace of perfume in the elegant, amphora-shaped bottle, and a splash of eau de toilette in the black-and-white-gingham–trimmed bottle. But I knew that the scent, no matter how faint or faded it might be after all these years, would conjure up my mother's memory.

I pulled the stopper from the perfume bottle, expecting it to contain the strongest, truest impression of Diorissimo.

What I didn't expect were the memories that tumbled out of the bottle with it.

DIORISSIMO BOTTLE, CA. 1982

Rebecca was in the kitchen, clutching a disguising spell tightly
around her so that Peter wouldn't sense her nearby presence.

"She'll never amount to anything."

Rebecca could tell from his tone that Peter was angry.

"Coming here was a complete waste of time." Peter was hoping
for a reaction from Stephen, but her husband was too tightly controlled to give it to him.

Rebecca felt a pang of satisfaction. Peter didn't like being
thwarted.

"Ow."

Diana's voice was high-pitched and had a panicked edge that
sliced into Rebecca's skin, so she felt flayed alive.

"That hurts," Diana said with a whimper.

It took every ounce of self-control for Rebecca to stay where she
was. Her mind whirled with silenced spells, any one of which would
have laid Knox flat.

A child wasn't supposed to be terrorized like this when they were
tested for aptitude in higher magic.

Stephen knew that as well as she did, but he was feigning disin-
terest, allowing the wizard to bore into the sparkling rooms in her
daughter's mind and leave his special brand of Darkness behind.

Stephen had been right to bar her from the room. Had she been
there, Rebecca would have killed Peter Knox for his prurient interest in her child. It would have proved that Peter had been right
to suspect that all was not as it seemed in their family, and Diana
would be in even greater danger.

"I'm sorry you came all this way for nothing," Stephen said, his
voice low and even. "Let me see you out."

"I know you're hiding something, Proctor," Peter said. "I don't
believe that Rebecca was detained at work for a start. She would

have wanted to be here. I suppose you forbade her to witness her child's examination, just as you forbade her to pursue higher magic."

Stephen didn't reply. He never explained himself to anyone— not even his wife.

"Safe travels, Peter," Stephen said mildly. "I'll tell Rebecca you asked after her."

The front door closed quietly.

Rebecca's seething blood came to a boil.

"All right, pumpkin?" Steven asked Diana, trying to sound as though nothing was wrong, as though nothing had happened.

Unable to stand passively by for another moment, Rebecca burst from the kitchen and flew down the hall toward the front of the house and through the door that opened magically before her.

"Rebecca! No!" Stephen called after her.

But it was too late.

No one could stop her now.

She jumped down the porch stairs and onto the sidewalk of their sedate Cambridge neighborhood.

"Peter!" Rebecca's voice carried down the street. The heads of children and their parents, out for some exercise in the cool of the summer evening, turned.

Peter stopped. Even though it was Boston, and the night was warm, he was still wearing one of his pretentious tweed jackets. He turned and walked toward her, each step full of menace.

"I knew you were there, Rebecca," Peter said with a sneer. "Proctor's attempts to cover the truth are pathetic, and your protection skills are slipping. That's what happens when a witch isn't sufficiently challenged."

Rebecca couldn't say what she wanted to: that the greatest challenge a witch could ever face was to spellbind their own child as she had, replacing bonds of love with coercive restrictions—all in an effort to keep her safe from creatures like him.

"You sad, worthless man." Rebecca's voice was venomous, the words coming out in a hiss.

Peter chuckled. "Temper, Rebecca."

Rebecca blasted him with a concussive wave of Darkness, aiming it at the spot between his brows. She'd invented the third-eye-blind spell as part of her candidate portfolio before walking the Labyrinth, and it was a doozy. Knox wouldn't be able to cast a spell or work a charm for weeks, perhaps months. Her spell would render his magical sense of direction useless.

"Don't fuck around with my daughter," Rebecca said, pointing her finger at him.

But with her anger came her Darkness. Rebecca realized, too late, that she had given Peter exactly what he wanted.

He drank her Darkness into his lungs, savoring it as though it was manna.

Rebecca's stomach heaved with revulsion.

"I remember the scent of your dark power. I've missed it," Peter said. "Your memories don't retain it, you know—not with all its complexity and fire."

"What memories?" Rebecca asked, alarmed.

"The ones that the witches keep on Isola della Stella. Do you know what I do, late at night, when everyone else has left the island for their whores and their wine cellars and their parties?" Peter's eyes were filled with loathing—and lust.

Rebecca shook her head, suspecting—and dreading—his answer.

"I revisit the Labyrinth and trace the paths where we met before our combat in the memory palace. Do you remember what it felt like, when our magics clashed?" Peter drew another deep breath as though Darkness brought him nourishment. "I've never felt anything like it. Nor have you."

Rebecca swallowed down the bile that his words churned up.

"Stephen never brought out the best in you as I did, Rebecca.

Don't you ever long for that feeling of completeness, of purpose, of exhilaration as the Darkness and Light moved through you? Can this sad little life with your unpromising daughter and your talentless husband really satisfy you?" Peter demanded.

Rebecca didn't dare answer.

Peter's lips curved into a smile.

"But there's more," he continued softly, his face so close that she could smell the belladonna and monkshood on Peter's breath. He was high as a kite on one of his infernal elixirs. That made him dangerous, even though she had temporarily disarmed him.

"After I walk the Labyrinth and go over every step of our battle in the Theater of Darkness, and dissect how you beat me, I go up to the museum and take your memory bottles off the shelves and open them, one by one. I enjoy lingering in your mind, Rebecca."

The idea of him inside her, looking out at the world through her eyes, hearing her innermost wishes and fears, was repulsive. He was stalking her through her memories, amassing information to use as a weapon against her, against Stephen—against Diana.

"Your daughter resembles you in many ways," Peter continued, "but her mind lacks the brilliance and fire of a truly great witch like you. It's all rather dull in there, to be honest—just like her father."

Rebecca never should have listened to Stephen. She should have sent him and Diana away, and faced Peter Knox, witch to witch. Because of Stephen's stubborn insistence, this monster would carry this knowledge about Diana into her daughter's future—a future that did not have her mother in it.

"I plan on bottling my memories of the encounter with Diana when I return to Venice," Peter continued. "There was something— I couldn't put my finger on it, but I will figure it out one day. Until then, you can try to sleep at night knowing that you may lie beside your husband, but I am privy to your greatest secrets, your deepest fears, and your darkest desires. Not Stephen Proctor."

"You're sick, Peter. Not to mention a sore loser." Rebecca's voice dripped with contempt, but it was not enough to completely disguise how traumatized she was by his violation of her privacy. "The Congregation is going to hear from me about your abuse of your power and position."

"Not from you." Peter's voice was smug. "I know too much, Rebecca. Too much about you. Too much about the Proctors. Too much about him."

Knox glanced over Rebecca's shoulder. Stephen was standing on the porch holding Diana's hand.

"Are you coming back inside, Mommy?" Diana's voice was as piercing and demanding as only a seven-year-old's could be.

"Don't fuck around with me," Peter snarled, giving Rebecca a long look. "You won't beat me. Not this time. Not ever again."

Peter turned and resumed his progress down the street. Rebecca watched him go until he turned the corner and was out of sight.

"We already won." Stephen was now behind her, and Diana was with him.

Rebecca picked up her child, burying her face in Diana's silky hair. She always smelled like honeysuckle. Stephen said it was the herbal shampoo in the green bottle. Rebecca knew it was more than that.

She knew, too, that they hadn't prevailed over Peter Knox. He would be back. They had only achieved a hollow, temporary victory.

Rebecca feared that Diana would be the one who would have to pick up her mother's banner and continue to fight a war she had not started and might not ever win.

PART THREE

Chapter 21

The strange sight of Baldwin de Clermont, leader of a notorious vampire clan, sitting under a striped umbrella in the shade of the witch's tree, greeted us when we arrived the next morning at Ravenswood. A card table held his computer, and a long orange extension cord snaked between it and a tall green-and-white pillar candle decorated with a lightning bolt and a rabbit. It was well over ninety degrees, even in the shade, but the man still wore a suit. How wonderful to be a vampire now that the summer heat was here.

Matthew was playing catch with Becca and Pip in the marsh. He was quick to notice our return, followed shortly thereafter by the children and the animals. They clambered through the muck toward the meadow.

"Baldwin's here," Sarah said glumly.

I'd warned Matthew that Sarah was coming back to Ravenswood with us, and that the situation between us was tense. I couldn't leave her alone at the Bishop House after all that had happened.

I didn't tell him about discovering more of Mom's memory bottles on her bureau, contained within Dior perfume bottles. Sarah, Gwyneth, and Janet had no idea what I'd found last night, either.

"Let the fun begin," Janet said with false cheer. Having spent many years in Congregation meetings with my brother-in-law, she knew that *fun* and *Baldwin* seldom appeared in the same sentence.

"Julie's here, too," I said, eyeing the candle powering Baldwin's laptop.

"Why on earth is he sitting outside?" Gwyneth asked as we drove past.

I wanted to park as close to the house as I could for her sake; it had been a grueling few days.

"Hellooo!" Julie emerged from the back door of the Old Place with a bottle of red wine, some lemonade, and a pot of coffee. She had covered all the bases to soothe both mercurial vampires and Bright Born children.

What she hadn't done was make tea. Disappointed, I stopped the car and put it into park.

"The tea's steeping!" Julie announced as though she'd read my mind. "Hell's bells! It's Sarah Bishop. No wonder you all look exhausted. Come to the barn and have something to drink."

"Julie." Sarah gave her a cool nod. "I haven't thought about you for ages."

"Can't say the same," Julie replied, the honey in her tone belied by the anger that sparked in her eyes. "I think of you whenever I polish my hexes."

"Why didn't you let Matthew's brother in the house, Julie?" Gwyneth asked. "He can't be comfortable out there in the heat."

"I tried," Julie replied. "We all tried. Even Pip. But the wards won't budge. Baldwin says he doesn't mind, and that working outside reminds him of his days in the Roman army. He's been telling me about the Macedonian Wars."

Sarah was the first to climb out of the car, rushing to embrace the children. Ever the chivalrous knight, Matthew helped Gwyneth out before circling the rear of the vehicle to open Janet's door and then mine.

"I'm so glad to see you," I said as Matthew folded me into his arms. The longer he stayed at Ravenswood, the more he absorbed the ancient, homey scents of woodsmoke and salt. I tried to pull away, but my vampire held tight.

"Not yet," he murmured. "Not quite yet." When at last he released me, Matthew's eyes were bright with curiosity.

"Can you get the boxes out of the back and bring them into the barn?" I asked, my hand on his arm in a gesture of patience.

"Of course, *mon coeur.*" Matthew nodded.

"Don't forget the shoebox," I warned, thinking of the perfume bottles that were tucked inside.

"Please don't feel you have to rush to free Baldwin," Matthew said under his breath, lifting the box of bottles Janet had gathered from the stillroom cupboard as though it were light as down. "It's much better to let him bark orders into the phone and supervise his vast wealth out here."

Matthew was not the only creature who wasn't relishing the prospect of spending time with Philippe's eldest son.

"Is he staying long?" Sarah demanded.

"That's up to Gwyneth," I reminded her. "But Baldwin never remains in one place for more than a few days. I wouldn't worry."

"That's one way to avoid assassination, I guess," Sarah said dourly.

I climbed the hill and waited patiently for Baldwin to finish his call. As his blood-sworn sister, I owed him a proper greeting. The whole day would go more smoothly if I treated him with the respect due to the head of the extensive de Clermont family of which our Bishop-Clairmont scion was part. Besides, there was no point in interrupting Baldwin when he was making a deal or conducting a negotiation. He was doggedly determined and possessed of a laser focus—something that had benefited Matthew and me on more than one occasion. All too soon, his unwavering attention would be on us.

Baldwin glanced up as if noticing my presence for the first time.

"Your thirty minutes are up, Helmut," Baldwin said, studying his watch. "You've failed to persuade me this purchase is sufficiently promising to take on so much risk. The answer is no."

I heard sputtering on the other end of the line before Baldwin disconnected the call.

"Sister." Baldwin surveyed me from head to toe and back again, then approached and gave me a formal kiss, then another, one on each cheek. Ever the predator, it gave him an opportunity to gauge my heartbeat and scent. "Matthew said that you were a different witch, but I see no great change. You are, perhaps, a bit thin and under stress, but after Matthew's report I was prepared to find you at death's door."

Baldwin was like a bee trapped in a confined space; he had no choice but to sting.

"Thank you for coming, Baldwin," I said.

"Matthew mentioned that the family is implicated in a dispute you're having with the Congregation," Baldwin said, straightening his cuffs. "Naturally, I came at once."

"Shall we go inside and join the others?" I suggested, wilting in the humidity and eager to reconnect with the children, who had followed Julie, Sarah, Matthew—and the lemonade—into the barn. I turned toward the house, where Gwyneth stood. "That's my aunt Gwyneth Proctor. She's the owner of Ravenswood and graciously allowed you to be her guest here."

Be nice, I warned Baldwin with a stern look as we descended to the Old Place.

"I didn't want to interrupt your reunion with Diana—but I'm happy to officially welcome you," Gwyneth said, extending her hand. "I'm sorry about the wards. I adjusted them for Matthew and may have gone overboard."

"A pleasure," Baldwin said. "I believe one of your relations was on the Congregation with me—Taliesin Proctor."

"My older brother," Gwyneth said.

"Lieutenant Proctor was a brave soldier and a good man." Baldwin eschewed Gwyneth's proffered handshake for a more European greeting of two kisses. Having taken the measure of my great-aunt, Baldwin offered his elbow for her to lean on. "So was his friend—what was his name? The one who died in Prague sometime after the war."

"I think you mean Thomas Lloyd," Gwyneth said, her voice level and matter-of-fact.

Baldwin registered the change in my heartbeat and scent that had followed the mention of my grandfather. He looked at me quizzically.

"Let's limit our talk about my grandfathers and the war until I've caught up with the twins, and Julie has scooped them up for another adventure. They don't need to know what's happened—yet," I said. There was no point in prevaricating or believing that I could keep this information from Baldwin.

"Grandfathers?" Baldwin's ginger eyebrows rose.

I met his gaze without flinching. Baldwin saw the answers to some of his questions in my eyes.

"We have a lot to discuss," I said.

"Ah. I see." Baldwin bared his teeth in what some might have called a smile. I knew it for what it was: a promise that he would follow the trail of this new information until he possessed every morsel of it.

"Let's join the others," Gwyneth said, lifting the remaining wards on Ravenswood so that Baldwin could move freely around the property. "It may take time for the place to recognize you as its own, I'm afraid. You are a vampire, and the spirits of the place can be hasty to judge those they haven't yet accepted."

"Fascinating," Baldwin said, viewing the property with the speculative gaze of a real estate developer.

Matthew was propped in the doorway of the barn when we arrived. He straightened to let Gwyneth and Baldwin pass.

"Everything all right, *ma lionne*?" Matthew inquired lazily.

My bat-eared husband had heard every word of the exchange between Baldwin and me.

"Tea," I said firmly. "Before anything else, there must be tea."

When the pandemonium of our arrival subsided to manageable levels, the midday sun was streaming through the high windows of the barn, gilding the dust motes sifting through the rafters. After Pip and Becca debriefed Sarah on everything that had happened at Ravenswood in the past twenty-four hours, Julie whisked the twins off to town on the *Good Juju*. She used the pretense of needing to pick up clams and oysters for dinner, though I knew she dearly wanted to stay and hear our news.

Baldwin formally introduced himself to Granny Dorcas, not realizing she was a ghost until she disapparated before his eyes in protest at the increasing number of vampires who were disturbing her afterlife.

The boxes of memory bottles we'd retrieved from the Bishop House, along with an L. L. Bean shoebox and a cardboard box with my mother's book of shadows, were all waiting on the worktable. I pulled out a few of the containers for show-and-tell: short jars, tall jars, and a distinctively shaped flattened oval bottle that had once held my mother's favorite wine. Not only was this last example sealed with a cork, it was festooned with white, pink, and blue stalactites of wax that had dripped down the sides, evidence that the contents had been consumed over the course of a romantic evening sometime in the 1970s, when Mateus was the height of sophistication.

I didn't touch the shoebox, and Janet eyed it with curiosity. Gwyneth joined us with two test tubes and a roll of felt tied with woven strings. She indicated she was ready with a nod.

"This is your meeting, Diana," Baldwin said, looking down at his watch. "I have a phone call in an hour. Shall we begin?"

Matthew looked daggers at his brother, irked by his officious tone, but I didn't mind Baldwin's directness. After Madison, it was a relief to know exactly where I stood.

"Gwyneth and I took Janet to Madison to reclaim her mother Griselda's memories from 1692," I said, plunging straight into the heart of the matter. "She was in Salem and visited Bridget Bishop and some of the other accused witches in the gaol."

"Your reports are admirably concise, sister," Baldwin said, tenting his fingers. "Please continue."

"We brought it back to Ravenswood so we could open it safely," I said.

"I wanted Matthew to witness the memories as well." Janet removed a small bottle from its hiding place tucked into a ball of wool in her knitting bag.

"How extraordinary." Baldwin peered at the small bottle. "How many memories can a tiny vial like that contain?"

"There's only one memory in a bottle—unless something's gone horribly wrong," Janet said, carrying the relic around the table and depositing it on an impromptu book cradle I'd fashioned from two spell-looms propped between two grimoires. It would not have passed muster with Bodley's Librarian, but it would protect the precious object from clumsy fingers.

"Do you hold it up to the light to view the memory?" Baldwin asked, squinting at the bottle.

"Nothing so easy," Gwyneth said with regret. "Can you get me the smallest spider on my bench, Diana? The one that I use to hold phials of mercury. And a bottle of bladder wrack, please. Wet, not dry."

I knew exactly which piece of equipment she meant. It had been designed to hold a narrow bottle or small test tube. The bladder wrack was easy to find among the alphabetically arranged herbs and spices. Sarah, her curiosity caught, watched as Gwyneth withdrew a few damp sprigs of the seaweed that grew around the marsh. Gwyneth murmured a spell and the small green pouches swelled as though they were being inflated with a tiny pair of invisible bellows.

"Memories can only be viewed if they are released from the pressure of their confinement. We don't want any cracks to develop in the glass when we do so, however. There's quite a difference between volatile, pressurized memories escaping due to neglect or breakage and their release under controlled conditions." Gwyneth tucked a piece of bladder wrack around the bottle. "So long as I use plenty of this for a cushion, I think we can keep the neck from breaking."

"Let me hold that," Sarah said, using the tip of her pinkie to keep a strand of inflated seaweed in place. My aunt's enthusiasm for the study of magic was overcoming her previous fear and hostility toward the Proctors and their methods.

"Thank you, Sarah," Gwyneth said, accepting the offer of help and the olive branch that came with it.

"Where did you learn these skills, Gwyneth?" Baldwin asked. "They seem far more technical and precise than most magic."

"Higher magic is *techne,* Baldwin. A wonderfully nuanced Greek word, as you must know," Gwyneth replied. "It means art as well as craft, and skill as well as technique."

With great delicacy, Gwyneth added more bladder wrack to the aperture of the spider.

"As for the *techne* itself," Gwyneth continued, "I learned it from my mother, who learned it from her mother before her, all the way back into the mists of time where only memory can take us, before there were books and telephones and photographs."

Gwyneth slid the bladder wrack–wrapped neck of the bottle into the opening of the spider. She murmured another spell and the aperture gently closed around the cushion of air and seaweed while we held our collective breath.

"That's why it's best to learn higher magic from close relations," Gwyneth told Baldwin. "Every witch's talent for higher magic is as unique as a fingerprint, but it always reflects her lineage. That's why the oracles insisted I call Diana home. She needed to be among her Proctor kin to learn the *techne* of her people."

"I see." Baldwin understood Gwyneth's position—and her decision. The de Clermont family legacy meant everything to him.

"What comes next?" Sarah asked, eager to learn more. Because she wasn't an initiate in higher magic, neither Mom nor Grandma had explained the intricacies of memory bottles to her.

"Next, we need to create a memory chamber. There's no telling how dark the memories inside the bottle might be, so it's important to draw as much Light into the chamber as we can without breaking the integrity of the Shadow that holds the memories together." Gwyneth conjured a pearly bubble. It bobbed over the bottle, waiting for her next move.

"I'm about to enlarge the chamber. This is your last chance to leave the barn before I release the bottle's memories," Gwyneth warned. "Once you're under the memory's spell, you won't be free of it until Griselda's experiences are safely contained again."

"What are we likely to see?" Sarah looked uneasy. "A hanging?"

I shuddered at the thought.

"There's no way to know in advance," Gwyneth replied. "It's a bit like an experiment. Janet has a hypothesis, though."

"I think Mam's bottle contains memories she gathered in Salem *before* Bridget Bishop was hanged," Janet explained.

"Let's open it and see." Gwyneth blew gently on the bubble, which expanded until we were all contained within it. Surrounded with pearly light, we looked as preternaturally pale as vampires. The Light bleached

Sarah's thick red curls into a strange mauve, and even Matthew's black head looked more silvered.

My aunt walked us through the next steps of the complicated process, her teaching skills on full display.

"First, you want to be sure your chamber has enough room for the memory to breathe," Gwyneth continued. "Cast too small a sphere and the memory you experience will be short and abrupt, lacking flow and context. Make it too big, and the memory will be so diffuse and unfocused you'll struggle to know what's going on."

"And then you must factor in weight, age, pressure, and the number of viewers." Janet sighed. "It's all physics and I was never particularly good at maths. That's why I wanted Gwyneth to do the honors."

"Next, you want to carefully melt the wax seal on the bottle, using a shadowlight rather than a witchlight." Gwyneth conjured up a flickering, dove-gray spark. "A cool flame is essential. You don't want to burn the memory bottle's original fittings, and sometimes there are messages and other items stuffed into the neck."

I'd had many opportunities to watch Gwyneth at work this summer, and been impressed with her feel for higher magic, but her shadowlights were particularly beautiful. They were luminous without being hot, and bright without being filled with Light.

My aunt wrapped a blue-gray wisp of shadowlight around the wax closure that still clung to the cork. With a skill any sommelier would have envied, Gwyneth used the wisp of power to neatly separate the wax and cork from the glass. With a delicate touch, Gwyneth lifted the cork.

I braced myself for impact.

Nothing happened.

"Where's the memory?" Matthew whispered, looking around the room as though it might be hiding in the corner.

Gwyneth peered into the neck of the bottle.

"Ah. Janet's mother put a secondary closure in the bottle for safety," Gwyneth said. "It looks like a braided lock of hair tied with a bit of red string. A wise precaution."

"Mam was nothing if not thorough," Janet said.

"Some witches, like Meg, believe that hair-locks are a second line of defense to keep especially volatile and vulnerable memories from exploding when the wax seal is broken," Gwyneth said. "Others think they form tamperproof seals. If the hair had fallen from the neck of the bottle into the bulb, you would know someone had meddled with the contents."

"Like putting a thread, or a line of salt, across a threshold," Matthew said.

"Exactly," Gwyneth said. "If you could reach into that roll of tools and get my lorgnette and the extra-fine crochet hook, Matthew, I would be grateful."

Inside, in addition to the opera glasses and crochet hooks, were knitting needles, several pairs of tweezers, a long-handled mirror like a dentist might use, and a tiny scalpel.

"Those look like they belong to Sweeney Todd." Sarah shuddered. She would rather have been stung by hornets than have her teeth examined.

"Not quite so gruesome, Sarah, but an extraction *is* needed before we proceed," Gwyneth said, taking the implements from Matthew. "Is everyone ready?"

We looked at one another, dubious. The closer I got to witnessing moments from Salem's darkest days, the less sure I was that this was a good idea.

"Once I remove the hair-lock, the memories are going to come out," Gwyneth reminded us, the crochet hook poised over the opening. "They'll fill this memory chamber, then slowly sink under the weight of the past. I will direct them back into their bottle—or a test tube if the bottle is no longer viable—and reseal them."

"Proceed," Baldwin said with the crisp tone of a commanding officer.

Gwyneth gave me a silent nod, then cocked her head to indicate she was about to remove the hair-lock.

The next thing I knew I had tumbled into the body of Griselda Gowdie.

MEMORY BOTTLE OF GRISELDA GOWDIE, 30 APRIL 1692

LATE-SEVENTEENTH-CENTURY APOTHECARY VIAL OF ENGLISH MANUFACTURE

The stench emanating from the foul dungeon below the gaol was breathtaking. Grissel covered her nose and mouth, her sense of smell more acute than those of the prisoners or their human gaolers.

"Ye did come back." The man-at-arms whom the Salem officials posted at the entrance leered at her and wiped his mouth with the back of his filthy hand.

"I never break a promise," Grissel said, flipping her skirts to reveal her ankle and the earthenware bottle with the devil's face near the handle that was strapped to her calf.

"Give us a kiss and the ale, then," the man said, beckoning Grissel forward.

Grissel swallowed down her bile and did as he asked, settling like goose down on his knee and pecking him on the cheek before handing over his tipple and removing to a safe distance.

This, Grissel knew, was a small price to pay for a woman alone during a war. Others would be forced to surrender their bodies to survive, losing their souls to Darkness in the process. Grissel had been the plaything of English soldiers in Scotland, and Scottish soldiers in England, and Irish sailors on a boat somewhere off the Isle of Man, where she'd taken refuge in a storm.

In the war that had been raging for more than a century against the old ways and the creatures who still followed them, women were paying the ultimate price: their lives.

No matter the war, the devil often seemed to take the shape of a woman.

The potion Grissel put in the gaoler's ale pot would ensure that he would slumber as she took his keys and stole downstairs to offer what she could to the sisters and brothers held there. In daylight, she had taken food, drink, and blankets for the poor prisoners, as well as money for bribes, but they had denied her entry. She was not family, the minister said. Officials from Boston said it was too dangerous for a Christian woman like herself to be among the devil's kin.

But if the poor souls held in Salem, Ipswich, and Boston were Satan's minions, then Grissel was, too.

It didn't take long for her sleeping draught to work. Grissel made the potion using herbs she'd gathered deep in the woods where locals whispered that the witch Tituba had danced star-clad under the moon. They were potent and full of magic.

When the gaoler's snores drowned out all other sounds, Grissel lifted the keys from the man's belt. The daughter of one of the women held below had told her what key to look for and warned her that it stuck at the first turning.

Grissel locked the door behind her, aware that a casual passerby would notice the open door, even if they ignored the sleeping guard. She conjured a witchlight and crept down the stairs.

The half-light shone on the faces below: old and young, tired and gaunt with worry, bloodied and blue with cold. Though the April air was warming into May, here it was forever February, the only light and air coming from grilled openings close to the ceiling.

"I knew ye'd come back," said a woman in a tattered bodice. It had once been red, but was now a rusted brown from vomit, filth, and bloodstains.

The woman had been pricked by some man who had

repeatedly thrust a long brass pin into her body, into the private places of her sex, and the soft flesh of her nostrils, and the tender cavern of her mouth to locate the insensitive places where he believed the devil had suckled.

Grissel knew the signs, for she had been pricked at fourteen. She rubbed at the scars on her forearms where the pricker had thrust his brass bodkin, before he thrust between her legs and took her maidenhead.

"See, Dorcas," the woman told her friend, who was shackled to the wall. "My bones did not lie. The raven's daughter has come."

"Have you seen my Tabby?" Dorcas struggled to sit up. Her hair had been shorn, as had Bridget's, to ensure that there were no imps or fairies hiding within it. "Do you have my charm bag?"

"I do." Grissel pulled the small pouch from the pocket hidden in her skirts.

This had been Tabby's price when she'd asked the girl for help breaking into the gaol.

A man lay in the corner, his back to the wall and long legs stretched before him. His breeches were torn, and his wrists raw from the irons that bound him.

"You're as silent as a vulture tonight, John Proctor," Dorcas Hoare said. "Have you no words of thanks for our sister, who brought me my charm bag that I might ease our sufferings?"

"I brought food and blankets, too," Grissel said, looking around the chamber.

There was no sign of them. They had never reached the captives.

"She's not our sister, Goody Hoare." John Proctor's voice was more cultured than the country speech of Dorcas and Bridget. This was a man of education, and books. Grissel had good reason to dislike such a man.

"She has been among blood-letches," Master Proctor said. "I do not trust her."

"We have none other to trust, John," an older woman said. "I am Goody Nurse. What is your name, child?"

It had been many years since anyone had called Gris-sel *child*. Her mother, Janet, had never done so, preferring to live with her demons in the caves of Covesea rather than tending to her daughter.

"Griselda Gowdie," Grissel replied. "My mam is Janet Gowdie, the banshee of Auldearn, and my granny Isobel was pricked, hanged, and burned while she still lived, many years ago in Nairn."

Grissel nodded to John Proctor.

"And you are right, sir," she continued. "Granny Isobel had congress with a blood-letch, and my mother was the result."

Gasps of horror and whispers of dread filled the dank cell.

"'Tis unnatural," one woman muttered.

Bridget Bishop hummed and swayed, and a tiny slip of a girl joined in with an unearthly keening.

"Hush." The woman who comforted her from the shad-ows was visible only in a flash of dark eyes. "Hush, child."

"Mama's here, Dorothy," said a skeleton wearing blood-soaked skirts. "She doesn't understand, Tituba."

"None of us understand," John Proctor said, bitter. "Who can fathom it, neighbor turning on neighbor?"

"'Tis the Darkening time," Bridget crooned. "The Dark-ening time. From death new beginnings, from old spells, new rhymes. 'Tis the Darkening, Darkening, Darkening time."

It was a bloodsong, and Grissel's third eye opened wide in the presence of Bridget's prophecy. Her mam had told her of nights long gone by when women came together to sing bloodsongs to the goddess, so that she might help their families survive with new wind-knots and weaves. Grissell had never witnessed one of those gatherings, though.

Dorcas Hoare joined in Bridget's uncanny song, adding a new verse to the call-and-response.

"'Tis the flying time, the flying time," Dorcas sang softly.

"'Tis the Darkening time, the Darkening time," the other witches murmured.

"Bring us oracles, seers, and crones," Dorcas chanted. "What's carried in the blood will cut in the bone."

"'Tis the hanging time, the hanging time," Tituba sang, rocking little Dorothy. "The children in peril, their kinfolk in stone."

"The flying time," sang some.

"The Darkening time," sang others.

"The hanging time," John Proctor hummed. "When we'll meet our end."

"With vultures and herons, ravens and owls." Dorcas dared to raise her voice, hoping that the goddess would hear their cry. "Call forth your power, let your wolves howl."

Tituba thrummed her foot on the floor, and Rebecca Nurse joined in.

"Guide us through Darkness and on toward Light," John Proctor sang softly. "Protect us, Shadow, so we can do right."

Without warning or forethought, a verse of bloodsong bubbled up from her veins to her lips and Grissel added it to the others.

"What will befall us, what future is nigh?" Grissell asked the goddess. "Which of us lives, and which will die?"

The prisoners fell silent. They waited for a sign, a blessing, a whisper of the goddess's presence.

Death's head passed over the face of Bridget Bishop, who had started the song. It traveled over Dorothy's emaci-

ated mother, and Rebecca Nurse, and John Proctor, touching others in its path. Tituba, Dorcas Hoare, and the child
Dorothy were spared its grinning leer, though the child tried
to grab on to its jaw and howled when she failed.

"I will be the first, then. So must it be," Bridget said, her
voice a thin ribbon of acceptance.

"And what will become of us?" Dorcas demanded,
shaking her fist at Death. "After you've taken our kin and
kind, who will teach your maidens the ways of the ancestors? Which mothers will croon your bloodsong in the years
to come? Who will know to watch for signs in the flights of
birds when we are gone?"

"The goddess has spoken, Dorcas," Bridget said,
resigned to her fate. "So must it be."

"Haven't we lost enough—babes, husbands, farms?"
Dorcas cried. "Or is this the goddess's retribution for the evil
we wrought on those who were here before us, when we took
their babes, their husbands, and their sacred land? Why has
this horror befallen us?"

After a long silence, an answer came from the goddess
through the hollow voice of Bridget Bishop.

> *"With heron's bone and owl's wing,*
> *Through vulture's silence, the ravens sing."*

Tituba murmured a spell in a language Grissel had
never heard before, her hands weaving a blessing as Bridget
continued.

> *"Through absence and desire, blood and fear,*
> *A discovery of witches will carry them here.*
> *Four drops of blood on an altar stone,*
> *Foretold this moment before you were born.*

Three families joined in joy and in struggle,
Will each bear witness to the black bird oracle.
Two children, bright as Moon and Sun,
Will Darkness, Light, and Shadow make one."

"So must it be," Tituba murmured. "So must it be."

Boots clattered down the stairs.

"Dorcas Hoare! Make yourself known." The man's voice was gruff, and Scots, but not from the familiar lochs and mountains of Grissel's home. It was as wild as the moors and forbidding as the seaside cliffs.

Grissel melted into Shadow, hoping to avoid detection, fearing what this soldier from Scotland's Western Isles may have heard, or seen.

"Here." Tituba held up Dorothy Good. "She is here, sir. This is Dorcas. Take her from this foul place before she perishes."

The man held a lantern aloft, revealing the tawny hair of a lion and the shoulders of a bear. His face was grim and creased with sympathy.

"Would that I could, goodwife," he said softly. "I buried her sister Mercy this morning and have heard the bairn cry out ever since. 'Tis Dorcas Hoare that I am here for now."

"No. You are wrong. You have come for me," Bridget said, struggling to rise from the filthy ground. "You have come for Bridget Bishop. I am the first to die, not Goody Hoare."

The man's face whitened to the paleness of an owl.

"No one is to die tonight," the Scot said, regaining his composure. "Reverend Mather only wants to examine Mistress Hoare, nothing more."

"Nothing more?" Tituba muttered curses at the man of God, not caring who might hear.

Grissel knew the devastation that a pricker wrought in their "examinations," with their bodkins and pins. She stepped from the safety of Shadow, into the dangerous Light.

"Are you the pricker they've paid to torture these creatures?" she asked, her Highland burr strong and fierce. "Will you help him poke holes into a defenseless woman, you great brute?"

Eyes of ice and sea bore into her, so that Grissel could feel them touch her soul. This was no man. The Scot was a blood-letch.

"Do I know you, mistress?" he asked.

"Not unless the goddess moved your isle to Inverness." Grissel forked her fingers at him, to ward off his evil gaze. "Blood-letch."

Fear swept through the dungeon, sour and strong.

"Is this how we will die, then, Martha?" a man asked his wife. "Will it be the bite of the blood-letch, or the bite of the noose?"

"Da?" a young man asked John Proctor, his eyes wide. "Has he come for us?"

"I do not come for the life of anyone here. If it were up to me, you'd all be free," the Scot replied. He fixed his strange attention on Grissel. "But since it's not, you'd best give me those keys and away with you before the man upstairs dries off from his dunk in the trough. He'll be calling you a witch next if you're not careful."

"Maybe I am a witch." Grissel's chin rose in challenge. "What say you to that?"

"I say maybe you are, and maybe he has a weakness for drink." The Scot drew a gloved hand over his face. "I know which tale will save your life, lass."

"Here." Bridget reached into her bodice and pulled out a copper coin. "For Dorcas. For your pains. Spare her from the reverend's evil, I beg you."

"Keep your coin," the man said, his gruffness returning. "She'll come to no harm so long as I am with her, you have my word."

"May we know your name, sir, that we may remember you in our prayers?" Rebecca Nurse asked.

"William." He hesitated. "William Sorley."

Sorley. The legendary summer wanderer, who traveled the waters around Scotland. Her mam spoke of his return, and what it foretold: an end to the searching, an end to their hiding.

"Come," Sorley said, beckoning Grissel forward. "You hold the key."

Grissel's bones knew the truth of it, for Sorley had given her knowledge that opened many mysteries. She pressed the ring of metal into the Scot's hand, withdrawing her own quickly.

But she was not quick enough to avoid the cold touch of the blood-letch's fingers around her wrist, penetrating through his leather gloves.

"Take this, mistress," Sorley said, pressing a small silver disc into her hands. It was marked with a crossroads, the witch's sign of a choice to come. "It was my father's. He kept it always, for luck."

"And did Luck save him?" Grissel asked, closing her fingers around the coin, and pulling away from the stranger's grasp.

"No." Sorley's blue eyes darkened with pain. "But it might save you or yours, one day. For now, you must leave this place with all haste. Three days hence, a one-eyed man with a red beard and a gammy leg named Davy Han-cock will take you to a place called Philadelphia. They are Quaker there, and not like the creatures here. A boat will be waiting to give you passage home to Scotland."

Grissel had seen enough of the Massachusetts Bay

Colony, and done her duty to her granny Isobel and her mam. There was nothing else she could do for these poor souls of Salem, but bear future witness to their suffering.

"Remember what you have seen here, mistress," Sorley said, "but trust no one with the knowledge of it. Not even Hancock, though he is a blood-letch like me and will see you safe home."

"Why do you help us?" Grissel asked, for it was not the way of blood-letches to give assistance to witches in times of need.

"You are not the only creatures who watch for signs and portents," Sorley replied.

There was a crash and a groan above.

"Go. Now," Sorley instructed. "And do not forget what I told you. Three days. Be ready."

Grissel nodded. She would remember her meeting with this fellow Hancock.

Everything else she had learned in Salem Grissel would find a way to forget so that other witches might discover it, as the goddess had foretold.

"So must it be," Grissel murmured in farewell, before disappearing like a wraith into the night.

Chapter 22

When the memory faded, Griselda Gowdie's bottle was still intact in the spider, supported with a wreath of bladder wrack, neatly corked, and resealed with silver and gold wax. The tiny braid from the bottle's neck was the only thing that Gwyneth had not been able to return to the bottle. It was in one of the test tubes, sealed with a sturdy, modern closure.

"You did it, Gwyneth," Janet said, awestruck.

The rest of us remained silent. No matter how spacious Gwyneth's memory chamber, it was impossible to draw a full breath after what we'd witnessed. We had seen the events of those terrible days through Grissel's eyes and were forever changed by them.

Even so, we each had a singular reaction to Grissel's memories and what they revealed, for no two people perceived the same truths in preserved memories.

Reunited with a lost part of her mother, Janet was caught up in grief, and wept quietly.

Sarah had witnessed the rehabilitation of her ancestor Bridget Bishop. "See!" she said triumphantly. "Bridget wasn't as selfish as everyone makes her out to be!"

"Gallowglass?" Matthew gasped. "Here?"

I shared in his surprise that the summer traveler in Grissel's letter to Agnes Gray was his nephew. It was one of the few mysteries Grissel's memories solved, though it revealed even more complicated riddles.

It was the worn coin that had captured Baldwin's attention, shock etched on his face. "Hugh's coin?"

"I would never have sent it had I known." Already grieving for her mother, Janet was overcome again with the knowledge of the role she'd played in Philippe's capture and a blood-tear rolled down her face. I hadn't known that a third-generation Bright Born could shed such a vampire tear, and had always considered Janet more witch than vampire.

"No regret, Janet." Baldwin wiped the drop of blood from her cheek. "You used it exactly as Hugh would have wished."

Granny Dorcas, who was outside the pearly bubble, pressed her anguished face into the wall of the memory chamber so that the bumps of her nose and chin warped its smooth surface, wanting to be nearer her kin.

Whatever Gwyneth had seen and felt was tucked safely behind an expression that was schooled to give nothing away.

Bridget Bishop's prophecy was uppermost in my mind, for I knew in blood and bone it was the real reason Griselda Gowdie had left her memories in Salem. My lips moved as I repeated the words of her bloodsong and prophecy silently, trying to memorize them before they vanished.

"Quiet, everyone," Matthew commanded, noticing my intense concentration. He grabbed his laboratory notebook and thrust it in my direction, along with his favorite fountain pen.

"Write it down, *mon coeur*," Matthew murmured. "Now. Before you forget."

I did, first recording Bridget's words before turning to the rest of Grissel's memory. The pressure I put on the pen's nib was so heavy that I created a ghostly palimpsest on the underlying sheets, the ink blotting and splotching until it stained my fingers blue. I filled page after page, desperate to make sure that no detail was lost. I reached the end of the tale, then circled back to the beginning to see if I'd missed anything.

"Leave it as it is, Diana." Gwyneth's light touch brought me back to the here and now. "It's a rare piece of writing that doesn't benefit from an edit, but the description of a memory is one of them."

Reluctantly, I closed the notebook.

"It's time to leave Salem behind." Gwyneth used the tip of her wand to poke a hole in the memory chamber and it dissolved into gray particles that swirled in the air then disappeared into the nearest patch of Shadow.

The goddess and her hounds. Dorcas raised the hem of her skirt to dab at her eyes. *I'd forgotten how cold it was in that gaol. Put another log on the fire, young man.*

Baldwin did so, immediately.

Red stains, brighter than those I'd witnessed on Bridget Bishop's bodice in the gaol, bloomed through Granny Dorcas's sleeve. I drew the diaphanous linen and wool up toward her elbow, revealing red holes dotted along her forearms. She had not been saved from the pricker's bodkin, after all.

"Granny Dorcas! You're—bleeding," I said, the tips of my fingers red. Grissel's memories had opened the ghost's old wounds.

They haven't done that since Tabby had the twins, Granny Dorcas replied, pulling away from me. *They'll stop soon.*

Perhaps they might even heal, now that Granny Dorcas knew the memories of that dark night would never be forgotten by those who had borne witness to them.

Baldwin returned from the woodpile, not a hair or button out of place. "Are there other bottles like this one, Gwyneth?"

"Some. In the attic of the Old Place," Gwyneth replied, her words few.

"I brought all the bottles I found at the Bishop House to Ravenswood." I carefully avoided looking at Sarah. "There are more memory bottles in Venice, too."

There were expressions of disbelief around the table.

"What makes you think that?" Matthew asked.

I opened the shoebox and removed a seemingly empty bottle of Diorissimo.

"What I saw here. Mom kept some of her memories in her bedroom," I explained. "I accidentally opened this one last night, not realizing what it contained. There was no sealing wax or hair-lock to give its true purpose away, so I can't show you what it held. The memories are gone."

"Clever Rebecca," Gwyneth murmured, "coming up with a new memory bottle closure. She was such a talented mnemonist."

"What was in it?" Sarah asked.

"Mom's memories of the day when Peter Knox examined me," I replied, "and the altercation between them afterward."

I would never forget what I'd seen in the bottle. The tone of my voice alerted both Matthew and Baldwin that there was more to come. Matthew rested his hand on my shoulder in support.

"That bastard boasted that he viewed Mom's memories on Isola della Stella, over and over again. It made her sick to think of him inside her. There was something sadistic—even pornographic—about Knox's interest."

"The witches possess more memories than Rebecca's," Janet said softly.

"You shouldn't—" Gwyneth tried to stop her from saying anything further.

"I must," Janet said with firm refusal. "I'll lose my seat, and you'll be censured for failing to stop me, but after seeing Mam's memories, it hardly matters." Janet drew a deep breath.

"How many bottles do they have?" Baldwin asked.

"We lost count centuries ago," Janet replied. "Every time there was a war, a change of monarch, a religious controversy, or a famine, the Congregation sent someone out to gather whatever memories they could find that had survived what a witch's mortal body could not withstand. They returned them to Isola della Stella and put them into storage. Today, they're among the most treasured relics the witches possess."

"What did they intend to do with them?" Matthew wondered.

"I'm not sure anyone had a plan for them—at first. We had been persecuted for centuries. Whole villages were destroyed, and communities lost. Memories were all we had left, and we were determined to keep them," Janet replied. "Initially, the witches' efforts were focused solely on preservation. Now, the witches open them when they are seeking to appoint a new member to the Congregation. We did so recently, when we replaced Satu Järvinen with Tinima Toussaint."

Peter Knox had opened my mother's bottles repeatedly. Had he violated other witches' privacy as well?

"The memory palace at Isola della Stella contains a bottle for every witch who walked the Labyrinth and advanced to the rank of adept since the 1890s," Gwyneth explained. "Part of becoming an adept requires you leave your unique experiences behind so that they remain sacred—and secret."

"Whatever happens to a witch in the Labyrinth, there's one thing I know for sure," Janet remarked. "It lays bare her soul. I've seen the adepts emerge from their trials, blasted with power and eyes filled with a terrible wonder. It's only after their memories are taken away that they return to some semblance of normality."

"And the witches use the collection as a talent pool from which to draw only the best and brightest to sit in the Congregation chamber," Baldwin mused. "You have no recollection of what happened to you there?"

"None of us do," Janet said. "Sometimes, a shred of tattered memory rises to the surface of an adept's mind, but it's never enough to fully understand what the Labyrinth ceremony meant to us."

"My grandfathers, my grandmother, Mom, Dad's sister, Naomi." I ticked off the litany of names. "All of their experiences—whatever they were, whatever magic they stirred up—are on a shelf in Venice."

Matthew's lips parted in horror.

"There's a gap during World War I, when it was impossible for the Congregation to receive any new bottles," Gwyneth explained, hoping to lower Matthew's level of concern. "But after the Armistice, the witches renewed their commitment to developing the talents of the most gifted witches. It was seen as a way to prevent further damage to our culture and traditions."

"Why are the witches so interested in the memories from the Labyrinth?" Matthew finally asked, ominously quiet.

"To succeed in the Labyrinth and become an adept, a witch must face not only her deepest fears, as she does at the Crossroads, but her greatest desires, too," Gwyneth explained. "Dark, Shadow, or Light, what a witch experiences at the heart of the maze reveals her strengths and weaknesses, as well as the contours of her power."

"Her power." Matthew was thoughtful. Then his lips turned gray as the blood drained from his face. "They've been practicing eugenics. The witches are picking through the memory bottles looking not just for signs of talent but for specific, rare forms of magic."

Eugenics was bloodcraft by another name, one that masked the darkest side of scientific endeavor. Proponents of eugenics like Francis Galton believed that they could engineer a better human by banishing what they considered undesirable or uncivilized characteristics, including racial difference, sexual diversity, and disability.

"You say this emphasis on memory bottles started in the 1890s, and then revived in the 1920s?" Matthew asked Gwyneth.

She nodded.

"The timing is perfect," Matthew murmured.

"Wait, Matthew." Baldwin held up his hand. "Creatures have bred— and been bred—to improve their lineage since time immemorial, whether by marrying the daughters of tall men because height was an advantage in battle, or putting your neighbor's horse to stud with your mare because it was faster and better-looking than yours. It doesn't necessarily mean this was about achieving some ideal level of magical purity in a witch's blood."

"They're not vampires, Baldwin." Matthew's expression was grim. "The witches' goal wasn't greater purity—it was greater power."

Janet agreed. "The Congregation's witches were terribly concerned with our waning power in general, and the decline of higher magic in particular. It's not a huge leap from *higher magic* to *higher races.*"

Baldwin continued to look skeptical.

"Witches always preserve family records—grimoires, spellbooks, oracle cards—but Granny Alice thought we could do better," Gwyneth said. "When she was Congregation librarian, she put out a worldwide call for witches to gather their family memories, too, so they could be preserved in Venice for future generations."

"When was this?" Matthew opened his notebook and uncapped his pen.

"From 1875 to 1890," Gwyneth said, "during the first eugenics movement."

I never foresaw they would put my work to evil purposes! Granny Alice shouted as she sailed by on the library ladder.

"Were the witches hoping to learn something particular from these family memories, Gwyneth?" Matthew's hand raced across a page in his notebook as he recorded his thoughts.

"From what Granny Alice said—and mind you, I was a child and it was a long time ago—they were particularly interested in the rites. It's what led to the Rites Revision Covenant of 1919."

"What rites?" Baldwin frowned.

"The bell, book, and candle ceremony at age thirteen; choosing a path at the Crossroads before age twenty-one; walking the Labyrinth, for those witches who showed promise in higher magic," Gwyneth said. "It was Granny Alice who advocated for adding a new exam at age seven for children with a family history of higher magic, to see if there were early clues that it would later manifest."

"A test the Congregation's witches will administer to Rebecca and Philip in a few weeks." Matthew swore. "The witches may rely on the Labyrinth bottles to select their representatives, but testing children must be connected to a desire to groom that next generation of higher magic adepts."

"No one is grooming my children," I said, filled with rage at the prospect.

"What about Gallowglass?" Sarah asked. "Maybe he could help—if we could find him."

"What about Bridget's prophecy?" Gwyneth suggested. "If we focus on that, and decipher what it means, it might illuminate the path forward."

"What about the memory bottles on Isola della Stella?" Janet cried. "There's no telling what they might reveal!"

Baldwin held up his hand for silence. The clash of conversation died down.

"What will be done is up to Matthew," Baldwin said. "And Diana, of course. It's their responsibility to clean up this mess before the de Clermont family is publicly implicated in it."

When Baldwin had recognized Matthew's kin as a scion of the de Clermont clan, he had made it clear that any problems stemming from our branch of the family were ours to solve.

"Diana?" Matthew turned to me.

I considered the evidence of Peter Knox's malfeasance, and the mention of three families in Bridget Bishop's prophecy.

"We need to recover all of the family memory bottles from Isola della Stella," I said. "*Three families joined in joy and in struggle, / Will each bear witness to the black bird oracle.* The Bishops. The Proctors . . ."

"The de Clermonts." A spark of fury flamed in Baldwin's eyes.

"Fingers would naturally point in that direction," I admitted.

Baldwin's focus moved to another part of the prophecy.

"*Two children, bright as Moon and Sun, / Will Darkness, Light, and Shadow make one.*" Baldwin swore. "We must claim what's ours, for the sake of Rebecca and Philip."

I held up my hands, where weaver's cords snaked across my palms and wrists, creating a palimpsest with my veins and the words of the Book of Life. "We might not understand what the prophecy means, but it's clear the stakes couldn't be higher."

Matthew nodded, his eyes black.

"But—how will we reclaim them?" Janet said. "If I remove even one bottle from Celestina, the alarm bells will be heard in Milan."

"I'll go." This was not only my responsibility but something I felt compelled to do for my mother's sake.

"No, Diana. You'd have to pass through the Labyrinth to reach them," Gwyneth said. "On Isola della Stella, there are no second chances, and you don't have the knowledge or the skill to navigate its challenges right now. I should go."

My octogenarian great-aunt was not going to walk into the lion's den, either, not while I still had breath in my body. I was about to say so when Baldwin spoke.

"Matthew?"

My husband was astonished by Baldwin's deference. He soon regained his composure and flipped through his laboratory notebook. What the family tree and Mendelian Punnett squares had to do with memory bottles and stealing them from the Congregation, I couldn't imagine.

"Our priorities have shifted," he said, glancing through the pages. "First, we were concerned about the Congregation's examination of the twins, then about Diana's test at the Crossroads, as if they were isolated issues. But these are both rites of passage, as is the Labyrinth ceremony."

"*Four drops of blood on an altar stone,*" I murmured. "Do you think Bridget's prophecy may refer to another, connected ritual?"

"I think we need to find out," Matthew replied. "The bottles on Isola della Stella may represent our best chance of determining if—and, even more importantly, how—the pieces of this puzzle fit together."

Baldwin shot me a glance. In the de Clermont family, Matthew was known for his impulsive, often-bloody, responses to crises, not this methodical approach.

The black bird oracle hopped and buzzed in my pocket. I reached in and drew out the card that leaped into my fingers. *The Queen of Vultures*— the card of silence, and secrets. I put it down on the table so everyone could see.

"We need to call Ysabeau," I said.

"She's bound to remember something useful about this memory palace, perhaps some quirk of its construction that will help us storm the witches' stronghold." Baldwin cast an avaricious glance over the card as he spoke, no doubt wondering if he could use it to manipulate the international stock market.

Left to Baldwin, this dispute would rapidly escalate into something as ambitious and ill-fated as the siege of Damascus.

Matthew dialed her number, putting her on speaker.

"*Oui?*" Ysabeau's response was immediate. I suspected my mother-in-law had been waiting—perhaps for weeks—for this call.

"Hello, *Maman,*" Matthew said.

"Who are we destroying today?" Ysabeau demanded. "They must have threatened Rebecca and Philip, or Baldwin would be in Berlin. I would recognize his death march heartbeat anywhere."

Ten steps ahead, as usual.

"We're not at war, *Maman*. We're gathering intelligence, and wondered if you know anything about a memory palace the witches have in Venice. It would be part of the Celestina complex," Matthew replied, referring to the buildings that housed the Congregation on Isola della Stella.

"Does this have something to do with Lieutenant Proctor and Captain Lloyd?" Ysabeau's frank question stunned Matthew into silence.

The Queen of Vultures seemed to wink at me from the table, exuding satisfaction as she brooded over her pile of carrion. The likeness to Ysabeau was unmistakable. I decided to add to the heap.

"Matthew's been analyzing some new DNA evidence, and I've been at the Bishop House with my grandmother's ghost, and it seems *both* of my grandfathers visited you to discuss Philippe's situation." Hopefully these new morsels of information would be enough to stop the verbal jousting of which the de Clermonts were so fond. "We've learned that Janet's mother, Griselda, was in the Salem jail in 1692 to care for my ancestors. Gallowglass was there, too."

"Eric was in Salem in 1692?" Ysabeau asked, breezing past the revelation about Thomas Lloyd and Taliesin Proctor as though it were old news. "How extraordinary. I thought he was in Goa then, with Fernando. I shall have to make a note of it in my *aide-mémoire*."

Ysabeau's version of memory bottles took the form of slender volumes of appointments, cases filled with calling cards, and dance programs that still had their ribbons and tiny pencils attached so a woman could make note of to whom she'd promised the next waltz.

"We're concerned, *Maman,* because Griselda preserved her memories of Salem in a magical bottle." Matthew continued his vain attempt to bring his mother's wide-ranging recollections into focus.

"Just one?" Ysabeau made a dismissive sound. "*N'importe quoi.* I take it you have this bottle?"

"Yes, but Janet tells us there are more on Isola della Stella that contain Bishop and Proctor family memories," Matthew replied, pinching the bridge of his nose as though it would summon more patience.

"Ah," Ysabeau said. "Baldwin is afraid the Congregation will learn that the de Clermont family has been connected to Diana for longer than they suspected."

This, too, was old news to my mother-in-law.

"You don't sound surprised, Ysabeau." Baldwin's expression never changed, but his eyes glimmered with a dangerous combination of frustration and anger.

"It wasn't my tale to tell" was Ysabeau's prim reply. "Surely you do not need *my* help finding this cellar filled with old bottles, Baldwin. You and Matthew have spent far more time at Celestina drinking Philippe's wine than I have."

"The witches' memory palace, *Maman*," Matthew said, grinding the words out between his teeth. "Think. Please. Any scrap of information about how it was built, or when, could help us."

"Memory palace. Hmm. *Mais—non.* You cannot be referring to that vulgar folly the witches built in their water garden?" Ysabeau's tone conveyed an audible shudder. "It was so hastily constructed I thought it must have fallen into the lagoon by now. The witches wanted it to display their antiquities—old bones, a stuffed crocodile, their pyxes and amphoras— and trinkets they considered sacred relics, like Matthew's little vials of saints' blood. I do not know why they bothered, for few creatures were allowed to see them."

"Did *you* ever see them?" Matthew drove his fingers through his hair with frustration.

"Admission to their holy place was by invitation only." Ysabeau's response was a classic nonanswer. When had something like an invitation ever mattered to Ysabeau?

"Must you make this so difficult, *Maman*? I feel like I'm pulling teeth."

"I cannot imagine what you mean," Ysabeau said. "I am happy to tell you what you want to know, Matthew. As it happens, I went there several times with Roberto Rio, the daemon who drew up the plans. Construction was underway during the witches' Troubles, and the place was often unguarded. There were so few witches left, you see."

I winced, unable to meet the eyes of Sarah and Gwyneth. I was used to Ysabeau's dismissive remarks about witches, but her casual prejudice was nevertheless painful.

"As for these bottles, I never saw any there. I did look to see if they might have a few *flaçons de souvenirs oubliés* hidden away that would please Gerbert."

Leave it to vampires to come up with a more elegant name than *memory bottles*.

"He locked his collection in a casket—like the one he kept the head of Meridiana in." Ysabeau continued to drop breadcrumbs before us, this one relating to the powerful witch who had been an oracle of great repute. "Philippe possessed three *flaçons,* too, all very old. He considered them great treasures, but threw them into the Aegean in a fit of temper over something Gallowglass said."

If Gerbert and Philippe both showed an interest in memory bottles, then we were on the right track.

"I'm going to Venice," I said, my stool scraping the floor as I pushed back from the table.

"I'm going with you," Matthew said.

"I'll drive you to Boston," Sarah offered.

"No one is going anywhere." Baldwin scowled.

"What?" I was furious. "You saw the memories in Grissel's bottle! And heard what Peter Knox did with my mother's memories! We don't have time to waste."

"Diana's right," Janet agreed. "Sidonie and Tinima find a great deal to do in the Congregation archives these days. Rima told me they've been tracing early references to illicit vampire-witch unions, and noting down every strange power and odd occurrence that accompanied them."

I did not know the Haitian Tinima Toussaint—the newest member of the Congregation. She brought a fresh perspective to Congregation deliberations and highlighted the issues threatening Indigenous magical practices and its practitioners. The priestess's spell-casting skills were legendary, and her knowledge of African magic profound.

"It's only a matter of time before the two of them find something," Janet predicted. "Whether the clue lies in Crusader chronicles from Jerusalem, or in my granny Isobel's confessions about her love child with the devil, or in the accounts of the ghastly deaths of vampires in New Orleans—there is bound to be something that will pique their interest. Sidonie will ransack the memory palace if she thinks it will give her the whip hand over Diana and the de Clermonts."

"But she will not do so today," Baldwin said. "Nor tomorrow."

"Surely speed's an advantage. Why would we wait until they catch up to us?" I demanded.

Baldwin's hand met the table, palm flat, in a savage blow.

"Because you are my general, Diana, and I will not win this war by putting you on the front lines!" Baldwin exclaimed. It was a pointed reminder that Matthew and I may have formed our own scion but were still subject to the sire of the larger clan.

"General?" I said, numb. Ysabeau was the general of the de Clermont army—not me.

"I thought this was an intelligence-gathering operation, not a war," Sarah said.

"In this family, Sarah, they are often indistinguishable," Ysabeau said.

Matthew, who seldom took a side when Baldwin and I were embroiled in an argument, did so now.

"Baldwin is right, *ma lionne*," Matthew said. "We must tread carefully. Whatever the nature and duration of the connection between our three families, my father's fingerprints are all over it. Philippe loved intricate toys and complicated games that depended on strategy, memory, and risk. What could be more intricate and complicated than a family?"

"Agreed, brother. Philippe set something in motion—though the gods know when, why, or how—that has yet to play itself out," Baldwin said, "some mechanism to bring about a desired end that will remain mysterious until the final trumpet sounds."

"*Deus ex machina*," I murmured. God from a machine. It was as good a description of Philippe as I'd ever heard. I touched the golden arrow-head and felt the goddess's hand. *Four drops of blood on an altar stone . . .*

It was then I realized that Philippe couldn't have acted alone. He had to have had the goddess's help. I wondered if he'd had my mother's assistance as well.

"We have been caught in Philippe's spiderwebs before," Ysabeau said. "This is nothing new. *Plus ça change, plus c'est la même chose.*"

Ysabeau had put a new twist on one of her mate's favorite sayings: *endings, beginnings, change.*

"You need not worry, children." Ysabeau's voice dropped to a conspiratorial whisper. "I have a plan to retrieve the bottles."

Widespread alarm followed this announcement. Ysabeau sailed on.

"Diana must meet me tomorrow at Ca' Chiaramonte," Ysabeau commanded, "before sunset, when the gondola traffic will be at its peak."

In the eight years I had known her, Ysabeau had seldom traveled past Limousin. Venice may as well have been on the dark side of the moon. Our alarm turned to amazement.

"How—" Matthew began.

"Why—" Baldwin started.

But Ysabeau was not to be interrupted. "I trust you will be able to get her and Janet here in one of your infernal flying machines, Baldwin. It is the feast of Redentore and I received my annual invitation to return to Venice and commemorate the end of the terrible plague outbreak in 1576. I will attend services in the church we commissioned Signor Palladio to build so the city could mourn its dead."

"An invitation from whom?" Matthew demanded.

"From the doge," Ysabeau replied. "He was delighted that I accepted."

There hadn't been a doge in Venice since 1797.

"Domenico." Matthew shook his head. "This is a very bad idea, *Maman.* He will know you are up to something."

"That is my intention," Ysabeau said.

Baldwin was aghast. "I am not sending my sister into the chaos of a Venetian festival while you make a spectacle of yourself with Domenico

Michele! We must gather information—quietly—before we do anything that might cause speculation."

"Bah," Ysabeau said. "Philippe was never louder than when he was involved in something underhanded. If your father wanted to know an enemy's plans, he held a banquet and sent one of his daughters into their camp as bait. You should try to emulate your sire in this respect, Baldwin."

"I would need to notify the other vampire clans," Baldwin protested. "You cannot just show up and—"

"Marthe has informed Fernando of our arrival." Ysabeau would brook no opposition. "*Ça suffit.*"

"And Santoro?" Matthew asked. The family's Venetian majordomo resembled a mother hen and did not like chaos.

"Let it be a surprise," Ysabeau said.

"Your plan is what, Ysabeau, beyond adding to the city's fireworks?" If looks could kill, Matthew's phone would have been reduced to a mess of fried electronics and melted glass based on Baldwin's expression.

"I would never share something so important as my plans with you, Baldwin." Ysabeau purred like a cat curled before the fire. "Remember Jerusalem?"

Baldwin blanched.

"The memory palace has a tower, too, as I recall." Ysabeau let her words fall on Philippe's son like the glass shards of a broken memory bottle. "All you need to know is that I will be the *canard* this time, while Diana and Janet go to Isola della Stella and infiltrate Celestina."

"Duck?" I looked to Matthew for clarification.

"She means decoy," Matthew explained.

Ysabeau fell silent, waiting for Matthew and Baldwin to absorb her words and accept the steely determination behind them.

"It might work," Matthew said, clearly torn. "But the risk—"

"If the Congregation had Philippe's memories, or Hugh's, what would you do to get them back?" I asked Matthew.

"Anything." Matthew's response was whip-quick.

"Exactly. I need to do this, Matthew." My voice was soft, but sure.

"Excellent. I knew you would see the beauty of my plan, Diana. I will see you tomorrow—and Janet, too." Ysabeau chortled. "This is just like old times. The intrigue! The danger. How I've missed beating Philippe at his own games."

"Gwyneth will be furious if she finds out." I held tightly to Matthew's hand as we slipped past the witch's tree and into the Ravens' Wood.

"Is it wise to go without her?" In Matthew, worry and curiosity battled for the upper hand.

"Wise?" I shook my head. "But necessary."

I focused on letting my instincts lead and allowing my feet to follow. The black bird oracle was in my pocket, another precaution against disaster. The cards would tell me if I strayed too far into Darkness.

The moss-covered bumps and lumps that remained of the Proctor family labyrinth gleamed with an evergreen magic in the dark of the forest.

"We just need to find the entrance," I told Matthew. It would be difficult, given the labyrinth's ruinous state, but I wanted to avoid climbing over its crumbling walls if possible.

"I can feel its power," Matthew said, a note of awe in his voice.

Matthew walked the uneven circumference, looking at the rubble with a stonemason's practiced eye. He read the foundations, and the angle that the stones had fallen due to the pressures of weather and time.

"Here— No, the missing stones are just buried under an accumulation of leaves and pine needles," Matthew said when he spotted a break in the wall.

There were a few more false alarms before Matthew located the clean edges of the labyrinth's original entrance.

"This is the way in," he said, beckoning me forward. "And the way out, too."

"There's no exit?" I didn't like the thought of having to retrace my steps.

Matthew shook his head. "Not in a labyrinth. The object of walking it is to proceed inward and gain enlightenment before returning to the world the same way you came. It's a spiritual exercise, *mon coeur,* and one that I've undertaken many times."

"I'm glad you're coming with me, then." I would ask Matthew for further details about his inward journeys later. Time was passing, and with it this opportunity to better prepare myself for Venice.

"This labyrinth was built by witches. It might reject me," Matthew warned.

"Not if they're anything like me," I said, giving him a soft kiss for luck. "Let's do this, before we change our minds."

Matthew had reluctantly agreed that the best way to ensure success on Isola della Stella was to rehearse what might happen once I arrived. I wanted to make a practice run of the labyrinth here, in the Ravens' Wood. It would give me some sense of what the ritual space of the Labyrinth on Isola della Stella might demand of me if I was forced to go through it to find the memory bottles.

I squeezed Matthew's hand, and he grasped it tighter in return.

"I feel like we're about to timewalk," Matthew murmured, "and not in a good way."

We had stood just like this in the Bishop House, hand in hand, facing an uncertain future, before we had taken our fated leap into the past.

"I'm not the witch I was then," I said, hoping to comfort him.

"That's what I'm afraid of." Matthew looked down at me. "All right, *ma lionne.* Lead the way."

Our first few steps into the labyrinth were incident-free.

"This just feels like an ordinary walk in the woods," I whispered. "I don't feel anything magical at all."

Matthew's finger pressed to my lip in silent warning. "Philippe always told me the gods wait for a mere mortal to overestimate their power. It's only then that they pounce—a little like wolves hunting their prey."

I nodded, and kept my reaction to myself.

A few feet later, I felt the first prickle of something that was not of this world.

Three more feet, and the walls of the labyrinth seemed to be growing.

"Matthew, are they—" I began, my attention glued to the sprouting walls. They were still covered with lichen and moss, but no longer at knee and hip level.

"Erupting from the ground?" Matthew's sense of the change was far less organic and gentle than mine. He looked grim. "Yes."

Soon, we wouldn't be able to see the trees on the other side of the walls.

"Maybe I should call Cailleach," I said, uneasy.

"Your guide to higher magic?" Matthew touched the nearby wall, which was now even with his shoulder. "Won't that attract the goddess's attention?"

"I think we already have it. I wish we'd gone with our other option," I said, my anxiety increasing as the walls closed in, "and opened one of Mom's other memory bottles instead."

A glass perfume bottle, heavy with compressed memories, appeared in my free hand. I gasped.

Be careful what you wish for, the trees whispered.

I held it up before Matthew.

He swore. "You shouldn't have brought that with you, Diana."

"I didn't," I protested. "I was just thinking that it might have been better to have stayed home and opened Mom's bottles like you suggested, and . . ."

I trailed off. Gwyneth had mentioned something about the labyrinth, and a witch's deepest desires . . .

"I wish the moon was brighter," I said.

The clouds parted, revealing the silver orb.

"I wish my mother was here," I whispered.

Mom peeked around the next turn in the labyrinth.

"I wish to keep my children safe from harm!" I shouted to the sky.

An athame embedded itself at my feet, point down.

"I want to cast a proper hex," I cried.

A shimmering six-crossed knot floated through my mind's eye, and the gramarye that would secure it tickled my tongue.

After facing Meg at the Crossroads and meeting the shades, I had imagined the Labyrinth on Isola della Stella as a terrifying place of unimaginable horrors.

"I was wrong. A labyrinth is a place of dreams, not nightmares!" I turned to Matthew, elated with power and possibility. "Try it. Make a wish!"

Matthew hesitated. He shook his head.

"What about Lucas? Or Hugh? Don't you wish they were alive?"

Matthew paled. "Don't say such things, Diana."

But my words had already done their damage, for what choice did Matthew have but to hear what I said, take it to heart, and feel the longing in his soul?

Papa?

Matthew wheeled around. A slight boy stood behind us with hair cropped so short you could see his scalp. He was dressed in a stained linen shift and there were no shoes on his feet.

Matthieu?

Matthew's head turned. An ordinary-looking man with an extraordinary smile walked past my mother.

He laughed. *Salut, mon frère.*

"Hugh?" Matthew whispered.

The labyrinth's magic was more potent than I had suspected, able to conjure Matthew's deepest desires merely because he *thought* of them.

I didn't notice Darkness wrapping its hand around the athame's grip. Nor did I see Shadow loom behind Matthew's brother, ready to engulf him.

All I could see was my husband's ravaged expression as he came face to-face with those he had loved, and failed, and lost.

Granny Dorcas had warned me that Darkness was cunning. Gwyneth was adamant I was not yet ready for the perils of a labyrinth. They were both proven right.

"Cailleach!" I called to the moon. "Help me!"

But I had overestimated my own power in one of the goddess's most sacred spaces. Cailleach would not come to my aid.

I couldn't call on the Light, for it would only increase Darkness's hunger. All that I could do was draw Shadow around Matthew and me and leave the labyrinth as quickly as possible.

I whispered into the night, welcoming Shadow to meet me. I invited the moths to shroud us in their velvet wings. I pulled eldritch clouds over our heads in a shield, and summoned the spirits of my ancestors to rise up from the ground in an army of bones.

Matthew made an unearthly sound of pain as I dragged him past Lucas, forcing him to leave his son once more—and I was the cause of it.

Papa! Lucas screamed. *J'ai peur du noir!*

Matthew broke free from my grasp with a guttural cry, determined to save his son this time.

A wall of Shadow stopped him. From its depths emerged a man dressed in khaki and brown leather, tow-haired and freckled like Pip, with the lanky ease of an athlete.

"Grandpa." I had never been more relieved to see anyone in my life.

Steady, Matthew, Tally said, using the power he still possessed to keep Matthew from abandoning the Light and flying into Darkness.

My grandfather turned on me in fury. *You nearly lost him to Elsewhere, Diana. Vampires aren't welcome in any of the goddess's labyrinths—nor are you. Not yet.*

"I know," I said, tears streaming down my face. "I just wanted—"

"Don't," Matthew cried. "God help me. Please. Stop."

"I'm sorry, my love. I only wanted—" I protested.

Not another word, Diana, Tally said, his words low and threatening. His eyes shone through Shadow with the intensity of a spy slipping between worlds.

I fell silent, my breath coming in jagged gasps as the immediate danger to Matthew subsided.

This is how Naomi got into trouble, wanting to run before she could walk, believing that her goddess-given talents would always see her through, Tally said, supporting Matthew's weight. *Philippe believed in the enormity of his power, too. It was one of the reasons he didn't survive.*

Matthew's broad frame shook like a terrified child's at the mention of his father. He moaned.

The goddess may have given you the strength to get through any challenge—though if she did, you may well curse her for it in the end, Tally said. *But your husband? Your children? Think of them before you decide to do your own thing and to hell with the rules that were established to protect you.*

I nodded. Fresh tears welled up, but I sniffed them away. This was not the time for me to fall apart or give in to self-pity.

Get your husband back home, and get some rest, Tally said, as stern as he would have been to one of his subordinates during the war. *He'll recover. Vampires usually do.*

"I promise." This time, I'd follow his advice to the letter.

You'll need a clear head and heart in Venice. You can't afford a single snafu. My grandfather's tone suggested he had personal experience in this department. *Not with so many lives at stake.*

My grandfather draped Matthew's arm around my shoulders and I staggered under the weight he had so easily borne.

"Let's go home, my love," I said. "It's not far."

Matthew was wounded in heart and soul, rather than body, and vampire blood was useless for healing the injuries he'd sustained in the Proctor labyrinth. I would have to make amends for what had happened here—though only the goddess knew how I could ever do so.

What if the labyrinth's magic had changed how Matthew felt about me? What if he never forgave me? I wished I could—

Be careful what you wish for, Diana. Tally's voice whispered through the trees.

I turned my head and saw him in a fog of Shadow. He held back Darkness so that it would not keep us from the Light of home and family.

With a tilt of his head and a touch of fingers to his cap, Grandpa Tally melted into the gloom.

"During the war, we called your grandfather the Specter," Matthew said, his voice shaky. He, too, had seen Tally disappear. "Here one minute, gone the next."

"Oh, Matthew," I said, holding on to him tightly. "I never meant—"

"I know," Matthew said.

There was something in his tone that I'd never heard before. It frightened me more than Darkness itself.

Despair.

"I love you," I said, eager for his reassurance and expecting Matthew's usual reply.

"Let's go home," was his weary response.

Chapter 23

I was bobbing on Ca' Chiaramonte's landing with its silver-topped black-and-white poles, digging into my purse for the money to pay the *motoscafo* driver, when the palazzo's massive front doors cracked open and Santoro emerged, my brother-in-law Fernando behind him.

"Diana," Fernando said, his rich voice a balm to my jet-lagged and jangled nerves. "Janet. What a beautiful evening for your arrival."

"She is here! She is here!" Santoro's arms waved in the air.

Neither Janet nor I was the reason for the majordomo's agitation.

"No bed made with her favorite linens. No clothes pressed and waiting in the wardrobe. No flowers in the *piano nobile* as she likes." Santoro broke down in an unintelligible babble of Italian, Greek, and Arabic.

Vampires were famous for their composure—especially the vampires who served the de Clermont household. The cause of his distress emerged into the bright Venetian sunshine.

"My unexpected arrival may have been too much for poor Santoro," Ysabeau admitted, an épée in one hand. She paused to adjust her Dior sunglasses, providing the passing tourists with an opportunity to admire her quilted fencing vest embroidered with black bees and slim black trousers tucked into thigh-high boots.

Alain Le Merle, Philippe's former squire and still a venerated de Clermont retainer, slipped around her to help Santoro with our luggage.

"Janet," Ysabeau said, bestowing a kiss on each of her granddaughter's cheeks. "How was the flight?"

"Flawless and a bit cold. What you'd expect, really, flying on Baldwin's jet." Janet eyed Ysabeau's outfit and accessories. "You look well, Grand-mère. The French musketeer look suits you."

"If I look well, it is because of Venice's bittersweet beauty," Ysabeau said, dismissing the suggestion that clothes maketh the vampire.

"Permit me, *Serèna* Diana," Santoro said, taking the Bodleian tote bag from my grasp. "You and *Dònna* Gianetta must go inside now with *Ser* Fernando and *Dònna* Ysabeau. The tourists . . ."

"I believe Ysabeau's work is done," Fernando said, dimples flashing. "She's caught the eye of the curious, and set every vampire tongue wagging. Too bad we wasted Santoro's time running a message to Domenico. We could have just waited for the gossip to reach him."

Fernando's responsibilities on the Congregation had changed him. There were fewer ghosts flitting through his eyes, and he carried himself with a renewed sense of purpose.

"There is no better place to be noticed than Ca' Chiaramonte," Ysabeau said, brandishing her sword.

"And so news of Diana's arrival will be all over the Veneto by dawn," Fernando replied. He offered his arm to Janet. "A drink?"

"Whisky would be heavenly," Janet said, accepting his offer. "And do call me Gianetta from now on; I rather like it."

Ysabeau and I followed, leaving Santoro and Alain to argue over which suitcase would be next to enter the palazzo.

"You're very quiet," Ysabeau murmured, steering me around the prow of the de Clermont gondola, which was in the entrance hall and covered in piles of stained rags and tubs of polish. It would gleam and catch light like the waters of the lagoon by the time Santoro and Alain were finished with it.

"Bad night," I said, not wanting my mother-in-law to worry. Matthew had been subdued and distant when Ike picked us up to go to the airport, and the children had noticed. There were tears and pleas for me to stay. I was exhausted, anxious, and filled with guilt.

Marthe and Victoire, Ysabeau's trusted companions, waited for us at the bottom of the grand staircase, ready to lead us to the *piano nobile*.

I greeted them both, and they bestowed sharp glances on me. They, too, knew something was out of joint.

In the light-filled chamber overlooking the canal, with its sweeping views of the busy Venetian waterways and the grand houses that lined them, I traced the inscription chiseled into the decorative band under the mantel: *What nourishes me, destroys me.* It had been Matthew's motto long before it was Kit Marlowe's. Today it made me think of Naomi, and my mother, and the higher magic that even now rose in my veins. Would it destroy me, too?

"Do sit, Diana. Have some prosecco. Or tea, if you insist." Ysabeau held a silver goblet grand enough to have once graced the doge's table. "You will not bring your destiny closer by standing up to greet it."

Victoire disappeared to fetch a fresh bottle of wine and I rammed my hands into the pockets of my linen trousers to keep them from visibly shaking. The cards hopped to attention, shifting underneath the gauzy fabric.

Marthe and Ysabeau pitched forward, fascinated by the movement.

"The black bird oracle," I apologized. "It peeps when it wants my attention."

It was my attempt at a joke, and I smiled. No one else did.

"It has mine," Ysabeau murmured.

I drew out the silk bag and sat in the Savonarola chair by the fire. I hesitated before opening it, unsure how the cards would behave in a strange place surrounded by so many vampires. But the black bird oracle was as eager to see and be seen as Ysabeau. One tug on the silk cord and it took flight.

"Birds," Marthe said, wonderstruck at the sight of the flapping cards.

Marthe was right, as usual. How had I not seen the similarity before?

Ysabeau extended a regal, clenched fist as though she were on a hunt with Emperor Rudolf. Two cards settled on the back of her hand.

The Queen of Vultures. The Key.

Another card perched on Marthe's head. Breath. She chuckled at the card's tickle in her hair and another card came to rest on her knee. Earth.

A murmuration of cards surrounded Fernando. They dove toward his heart, then flew out to a slight distance, then dove again like humming-birds seeking nectar from a flower. Fernando gasped. Then he laughed.

I was used to Fernando's chuckles, his warm smiles, and his indulgent grins whenever Jack or the twins were around. His laughter was new to me, light and rich, full-throated and full-hearted, too.

The cards of the black bird oracle winged their way back to me, except for two that continued to buzz and hum around Fernando: The Phoenix and Spirit. When they'd taken their fill of Fernando's mirth and returned to my outstretched palm, I replaced the oracle cards in the bag for safe-keeping.

"Do they always do that?" Ysabeau wondered, flushed with excitement.

"Fly? Yes," I answered. "But not like they did just now. I think they were identifying you, so that I could recognize you if The Phoenix, or Earth, or The Queen of Vultures appeared—though to be honest, Ysabeau, I had you pegged as The Queen of Vultures all along."

"I am delighted," Ysabeau remarked, glowing at the dubious compliment. "Vultures feed on what others leave behind in the mistaken belief that it is of no value."

Marthe rose, responding to an unspoken cue from her mistress, and dumped a basket filled with paper onto the gleaming table set in the window recess where the light was strongest.

"Goddess above," Janet murmured. "Are those floor plans?"

"Some," Ysabeau replied, gliding toward the table. "I removed them from the rubbish on Isola della Stella. Most creatures do not appreciate the importance of such things, but I love a good map. There are always forgotten things to be found there, for those who wish to remember."

"Shouldn't they be in the Congregation archives?" Fernando said as we followed Ysabeau toward the light.

"Perhaps." Ysabeau waved a hand in the air, unconcerned with something so insignificant as legal custody.

Maps, diagrams, and charts unspooled over the table in all directions, finding the edges and draping down to the floor—a treasure trove of knowledge about the development of the Congregation's headquarters in Venice.

Victoire returned with a tray of glasses filled with golden, sparkling liquid. She distributed one to Janet and Fernando. I needed to remain clearheaded and refused.

"It seems you know where all the bodies are buried on Isola della Stella, Granny Ysabeau," Janet said, looking over the table in amazement.

"Corpses? They are in the plague cemetery by the old landing," Ysabeau said promptly, rummaging through the paper and vellum. She unrolled a 1483 floor plan that showed the changes that had been made to the island's monastery to transform it into Celestina, the Congregation's base of operations. I recognized notes in Matthew's hand, and Philippe's decisive scrawl. The central meeting chamber and cloisters were unmistakable, and other ranges of rooms were assigned to daemons, vampires, witches, and their personal servants. It was easy to forget that the vast, sparsely occupied buildings had once housed a multitude of witches, daemons, vampires, and even a few humans.

"Is this the Labyrinth?" I asked Janet, pointing to a small, meandering path surrounded by buildings outside the range marked *Casa delle Streghe*.

"No, that's just our wee maze," Janet said. "The Labyrinth is much larger. It was constructed later, too."

"The floor plan will be useful in case you need to make a quick escape from Celestina, but it will not help you find a way into the memory palace. For that we need another map." Ysabeau rummaged through her papers once more. "Here is the initial concept for Isola della Stella that Philippe laid out with Signor Lombardo before Matthew and his men broke ground."

The bird's-eye depiction showed orchards, gardens, a repair yard for boats, a place for small craft to unload cargo, and the aforementioned cemetery.

Adjacent to the Casa delle Streghe were courtyards and walled gardens that led down to the edge of the lagoon, one bearing the name *il Sentiero Oscuro*—the Dark Path—and another *Lo Stregozzo,* or The Witches' Processional. My third eye winked with curiosity about the history and purposes of these spaces.

I noticed something else. Floating in the shallow water of the lagoon off Isola della Stella was another tiny island. Venice's waterways were studded with these minute outcrops, some too small for even a single sheep to graze upon.

"*Il Memoriale delle Streghe,*" I said, reading from the marginal note. "The Witches' Memorial. Is that the memory palace?"

"That's Isola Piccolo." Janet pointed to a spot in the water between the drop of land and Isola della Stella. "The memory palace is here."

"It is now," Ysabeau said. "It was supposed to be on Isola Piccolo, and consists of only a three-story tower with a single room on each floor. Then Roberto Rio came to Venice, with his visions and strange philosophies, and the witches abandoned their first site and decided on something more ambitious."

Ysabeau pulled out a rendering of an elaborate structure studded with ornate architectural details.

"Roberto's plan was very ugly, but the witches liked it," Ysabeau commented, handing me the drawing. It was made with pencil, the delicate shading giving it depth and dimensionality. "Philippe made the witches enchant it so that none of us would have to see it."

Roberto Rio. I stared at the drawing, not believing my eyes.

"You mean Robert Fludd!" I exclaimed. "The English daemon devoted to the arts of memory."

"You have heard of him, Diana?" Ysabeau's delicate brows rose. "*Incroyable,* for he was an eminently forgettable creature. Philippe kept Roberto from ruining the meeting chamber with his bizarre frescoes, but only by encouraging the witches to employ him."

"*Incroyable,* indeed," I murmured, studying the façade of the witches' memory palace. Fludd had employed a raking view to give a sense of the layout of the witches' extension into the lagoon as well as how the elevation would look within the existing architecture of Celestina and against the backdrop of Venice. Fludd's memory palace on Isola della Stella resembled one he'd included in his massive encyclopedia with the equally monumental title of *Utriusque Cosmi historia,* or *The metaphysical, physical, and technical history of the two worlds, namely the greater and the lesser.* No wonder Philippe had required the use of a disguising spell before he permitted it to be built.

I'd known that Fludd traveled through Europe and into Italy at the turn of the seventeenth century, and long suspected he was a daemon, but never surmised that the journey was connected to the Congregation. Now that I did, Fludd made historical sense for the first time. The daemon was charismatic, pugnacious, and stubborn, with a creativity that verged on madness—a classic expression of daemon power. His contemporaries had not known what to make of him, and the intervening centuries had not always been kind to his intellectual reputation.

Ysabeau rummaged through the papers on the table once more.

"It was Roberto who proposed moving the witches' most valuable treasures here, to take some pressure off their overburdened storage," she continued. "He assured Philippe it would be straightforward to construct, only requiring posts driven into the mud to hold up a stone platform on which the building could rest."

My mother-in-law made it sound as though this were an easy proposition. On our tours of the palazzos that had been shored up by this method, including Ca' Chiaramonte, Matthew had convinced me it was fiendishly difficult, not to mention dangerous.

"The Labyrinth posed a far more difficult problem," Ysabeau said. "There was not enough room on Isola della Stella to plant one that would suit the scale of Roberto's *petite folie* while meeting the witches' peculiar needs."

Fernando coughed, tickled by the notion that Fludd's three-story monstrosity could be called *little,* even though *folly* was accurate.

"Before, the witches only wanted to reach the center of their Labyrinth and return to their chambers," Ysabeau explained with a moue of disappointment. "After they saw Roberto's designs, they wished to pass through the Labyrinth and enter the folly on the other side. This required not only an entrance, but a separate exit—which is not found in a labyrinth."

I closed my eyes against last night's memories of the Proctor labyrinth.

"You seem to know more about the witches than I do, Ysabeau," Janet said sharply.

Ysabeau ignored Janet's remark. "But this has not always been the case with labyrinths. Roberto and I conferred on how he might solve this impasse. *Et voilà!*"

My mother-in-law brandished a piece of paper. On it, in Ysabeau's unmistakable hand, was a note in Italian: *Here is the Babylonian maze.* Accompanying the note was a sketch of an intricate labyrinth with an entrance on one side, and an exit opposite.

"The Labyrinth isn't that intricate," Janet said after looking at the sketch.

"How could it be, when the paths are made of water?" Ysabeau replied. "Still, it was a start."

"Water?" I looked from Ysabeau to Janet, waiting for someone to explain.

"The Labyrinth on Isola della Stella, like the memory palace, was built in the lagoon," Janet said.

"How do you get through it?" I couldn't imagine a floating labyrinth, or a boat that could navigate its twists and turns.

"You row." Ysabeau gave me a brilliant smile.

"In a wee *mascareta* no bigger than an eggshell, not some whacking great Viking longboat," Janet added.

"But this does not matter." Ysabeau's smile widened. "You will not go through the Labyrinth, but around it."

"That's impossible, Granny," Janet protested. "The memory palace has unscalable walls and no windows. There's no way to get into it except through the front doors, and the only way to reach them is through the Labyrinth."

"Then why did they build this?" Ysabeau's delicate fingertip, with its exquisite French manicure, pointed to a place on the map where a small square was tucked against the side of the building.

We bent over the plan.

"Is that—a terrace?" Fernando squinted more closely at the tiny detail.

"It faces Venice. Maybe it's a platform to view city celebrations like Redentore?" Janet suggested.

"It is a landing for a boat. Not a *mascareta* but something larger," Ysabeau said, her expression triumphant. "See. There are four round posts on the corners."

They looked like dots to me.

"The witches could not move everything from their old tower to the new palace through the Labyrinth," Ysabeau replied. "It is one thing for a single witch to paddle a *mascareta,* but quite another to transport heavy objects and crates."

"Wouldn't we need to remove the disguising spell on the memory palace in order to locate the landing from the outside?" I asked. "Someone's bound to capture it in a selfie, and then Baldwin will have an even bigger crisis on his hands."

"After the fireworks start, there's utter darkness beyond Saint Mark's and Giudecca," Fernando said. "I doubt anything would appear in a photo at such a distance. To reach Isola della Stella before night falls, you would need to be beyond the festival traffic in Saint Mark's basin by late afternoon—"

"And past the pontoons by nine o'clock," Ysabeau added.

"It might work," Fernando said, cautious.

"But we'll still have to get onto the terrace, climb the stairs, and wander inside," Janet pointed out.

"No one in their right mind would build a mooring where there wasn't an easy way to unload cargo," I said, "not even Robert Fludd."

"*Exactement.* At last, you see." Ysabeau threw up her hands in relief. "Tomorrow morning, all eyes will be on Ca' Chiaramonte, which will be decorated with flowers from the rooftop to the landing, just as it was when Philippe was alive. We shall string garlands on the gondola, too, and I will visit friends along the Grand Canal. Later, I will meet Domenico's barge, and together we will process to the floating bridge for our *passeggiata* to Giudecca. You can make your getaway the day after, when I will lay flowers for poor *maestro* Titian and drink to the memory of *Dònna* Veronica. Perhaps I will be able to persuade Domenico to dry his tears long enough to read something from her verses."

With Ysabeau's cache of maps, Janet's firsthand knowledge of the Isola della Stella, and Fernando's Venetian connections, we soon had a plan for how to land on Isola della Stella and enter Celestina without detection. From there, we would commandeer a *mascareta* from the boatyard to take us around the outer walls of the Labyrinth to where we hoped the disused cargo dock was still in place.

"Honestly, it may no longer exist," Janet confessed. "I've certainly never noticed it. Then again, I wasn't looking for it."

"Fernando's right. Even if the landing is long gone, there must be some back or side way into Fludd's palace," I assured her.

"The only thing we haven't discussed is what to do about Domenico." Fernando poured a healthy glug of amarone into his glass. He had switched from fizz to something more fortifying. "He's as slippery as a fish and as two-faced as Janus."

"Leave Domenico to me. He may suspect my motives, and wonder about the reason for Diana's presence here, but he will not discover why we came to Venice until after we burgle the memory palace." Ysabeau's eyes gleamed with excitement.

Our supposed intelligence operation had turned into a heist.

W e picked up the delivery boat we would use in our criminal enterprise on the Santa Chiara Canal, at the far end of Dorsoduro by the train stations. Santoro piloted the craft through the traffic with the nimbleness of a salmon swimming upstream, darting in and out of the vessels taking passengers toward the festivities in Saint Mark's basin. We rounded the western end of Giudecca, skirting the southern shore until we passed by the domed, white marble church known as Il Redentore. The gondolas had not yet lined up to form the temporary floating bridge that would extend from the main island to Giudecca, though Ysabeau would be on her way there any moment.

We'd left Ysabeau in the salon on the *piano nobile,* draped in Dior from head to toe. There had been loose talk that she might please the locals in Dolce & Gabbana or some other Italian designer, but Ysabeau wanted to be visible against the sea of black and red favored by the Venetian elite. She had decided on an elegant beige crocheted dress for her afternoon boating. An ankle-length tulle confection with a satin underslip waited in a bag near her chair. The skirt was embroidered with emblems from the tarot—an homage to the black bird oracle, Victoire explained—and Ysabeau planned on donning the ensemble in the church before the fireworks began.

Santoro steered from Giudecca to the neighboring island of San Giorgio Maggiore, where another Palladian domed building—this one a Benedictine abbey—marked the boundary between the basin, the Grand Canal, and the larger Venetian lagoon. It was just four o'clock, but the traffic was already making Santoro's job impossible. We made slow progress as every conceivable style of boat from gondolas to *pupparini* entered the area to drop anchor for their evening picnics and the fireworks that would follow.

When we at last entered the farther reaches of the lagoon, I heaved a sigh of relief.

"I don't think we were spotted." Janet had been keeping a steady watch for members of the Congregation, while I scanned the waterways for a nudge, tingle, or icy touch that would indicate that a daemon, witch, or vampire was tracking our route.

"You should not worry so much, *Dònna* Gianetta," Santoro chided. "*Dònna* Ysabeau is a very fine distraction, and she has not been seen in Venice for some time. Every creature in the city will be transfixed by the miraculous vision of *La Serenissima* come home at last."

Whether the lack of traffic outside the city was caused by Ysabeau's magnetic presence, or the natural ebb and flow of a festive Friday evening, we soon reached Isola della Stella. Santoro shut off the motor and dropped anchor just outside the island's protective wards.

It would be hours before the sun set. Only then could we set our plan in motion.

"Now we wait," Janet said, tugging her hat lower over her eyes to shield them from the bright light playing on the water.

Chapter 24

It was nine o'clock before the twilight was deep enough to allow Santoro to restart the engine and slowly creep toward Isola della Stella. I'd taken this journey many times, and knew from experience that there was no sight of Fludd's memory palace or a floating Labyrinth from the lagoon. The witches must maintain robust concealment spells in addition to the other wards that protected the island from curious passersby and unwelcome visitors.

It was those complicated wards that would present our first real challenge. Janet and I hoped their magic would recognize Santoro as a regular visitor—even though he was driving a far less luxurious craft than was his habit—and release their hold for two visitors, one a former Congregation member who was also a de Clermont, and the other a current representative. We would not know for sure until we crossed into the shallower waters surrounding Isola della Stella.

The wards flexed and shifted as the prow of the delivery boat crossed one of the island's invisible channel markers. The wards were caught between a sense of familiarity and a suspicion that something was not quite right.

"Hold tight." Janet closed her eyes and murmured a spell in Gaelic. "Nobody panic. Any hint of panic will trigger the alarm."

Janet repeated her spell, and the wards whooshed open.

"We're in," Janet said, relieved.

"Nice work," I said, admiring her skill.

Santoro pulled into a covered bay marked with a hexafoil. It was not where I was used to arriving, for the de Clermonts used the vampire entrance nearby. He pulled the delivery boat level with the floating platform and I hopped onto its undulating surface.

I checked my watch. It was nearly nine-thirty and the fireworks would start soon.

"We must leave no later than four o'clock, *Serèna*," Santoro reminded me.

Venetian summer nights were short, and the skies to the east would be growing pale by then.

"Six hours is more than enough time," Janet said with a confidence I didn't share.

I helped Janet from the vessel, shivering in the cold air. If we were caught . . .

"Don't give in to fear, Diana," Janet warned. "Darkness is already interested in us. Stay in Shadow."

That meant embracing the uncertain outcome of our mission to Isola della Stella, rather than worrying about what might go wrong. I nodded and focused on our next challenge: getting me into the witches' precinct. I settled my Yale Crew cap more firmly on my head and zipped up the neck of my dark fleece pullover.

Janet conjured up a dim shadowlight. It was enough for me to see by but wouldn't draw attention if some member of the Congregation or its staff saw it. The island was full of haunts and shades, and Janet's glimmering bit of Shadow would be shrugged off without a second thought.

Janet walked with brisk purpose straight up to the door to Celestina. It had no handle, and no keyhole. The vampires employed a porter named Jacopo to check names against his roster of expected visitors, but the witches relied on magic. The portal would not open unless we were here on official Congregation business. Mere familiarity would not be sufficient to let Janet or me pass through this security checkpoint.

"Janet Gowdie and Diana Bishop, Yale University," Janet said crisply, putting her hand on the door's carved frame. "Here to visit the archives and consult the *Codex Incantamenti* to determine if Professor Bishop can understand its contents."

The door cracked open an inch and light spilled onto the landing from the torches on the other side.

"Put your hand on that moon just there," Janet said, nodding her head toward a carved crescent.

I did as she commanded. Electric tingles pulsed through my palm as the door's spells performed an entry scan that Miriam, whose laboratory security system was forever breaking down, would have envied.

The wards tugged and pulled, considering our request. Finally, they opened the door.

Welcome, sisters, a ghostly voice murmured. *The archives are expecting you.*

Before tonight, I had only been in the formal rooms where the witches held occasional receptions for Congregation members—never in this part of the Casa delle Streghe. The dark corridors Janet and I walked were covered with vivid wall paintings of mythical and magical subjects, and the carved beams were thickly inscribed with spells, curses, and sigils.

Shadow clung to Janet and me, fanning away from us as we proceeded deeper into the heart of the complex, avoiding the main thoroughfares in favor of old passageways once used by servants and rooms filled with moldering furniture and bric-a-brac.

"Mind your thoughts," Janet said, drawing a wand out of her knitting bag and swatting at a tendril of Darkness. "These bloody wards are better than an antidepressant in forcing you to adopt a positive outlook."

The doors of the witches' archives swished open to welcome us. Inside, the shelves bulged with curious objects and manuscripts, and apothecary cabinets stood where card catalogues would be in an ordinary library.

"We must at least open the *Codex Incantamenti*," Janet said, leading me inside. "If we don't, we'll rouse the wards' curiosity and that is the last thing we need. Thankfully, the thing is so enormous it's always out on a stand."

Janet directed me to a carved oak table that looked as though it had been specially built to accommodate the gigantic bound volume. The codex's heavy cover was studded with bosses, and I reached to touch them. Janet grabbed my hand.

"There will be no touching of books," Janet said. "Not after what happened with the Book of Life. Let me do it."

She lifted the cover, gave the codex a perfunctory riffle of the pages, and closed the volume with a bang.

"There. We've met the ward's conditions. How about a cup of tea?" Janet said, ushering me into an adjacent room.

The witches' common room looked like every Oxford University senior common room I'd ever been in, the walls steeped in tradition as well as the scents of tea, wine, old books, and tobacco.

Janet glanced at a Bakelite clock next to a kettle. "Fancy some fresh air instead?"

Janet was announcing every step of our journey through the witches' chambers.

"Hopefully the wards will get bored with all the innocuous chatter and go back to sleep," Janet murmured, taking me through a passageway that wound through the personal rooms that had been assigned to the three Congregation members. I spotted kitchens, laboratories, stillrooms, and storerooms, all of them jammed with personal items left by generations of witches. Once, there would have been staff to keep things tidy and neat, and some rooms still bore traces of their presence in narrow iron bed frames with lumpy mattresses, rickety clothing stands, plain ceramic washbowls and pitchers, and threadbare wool blankets.

"There go the bells," Janet said as the campanile chimed ten o' clock. A boom followed. "And there go the fireworks."

Janet let her wand drift through a marbling of Shadow and Darkness. A door straight out of a children's story appeared at the far end of the passage. It was arched, with simple iron fittings and a gap at the bottom large enough for a cat to slide through in pursuit of a mouse. Unlike the substantial slabs of wood and metal that guarded the Congregation meeting chamber, this ancient door looked as though it would fall off its hinges at the slightest pressure.

But things were not always what they seemed when magic was involved, as I knew from crafting Apollo's daily disguising spell. What appeared to be a rickety wooden door with cracks and gaps could be a superficial glamour placed over something far more impenetrable.

Janet touched the door and it opened easily, proving that some things were *exactly* as they seemed. A black cat streaked by us, hissing with indignation.

"One of Sidonie's moggies," Janet commented. "She'll be off to report to her mistress."

"Sidonie is *here*?" I said, my heart clenching into a knot.

"No, as that infernal cat will soon discover." Janet brushed aside the cobwebs of Darkness spun across the peak of the arch. "After you."

A flash of brilliant red, followed by green and gold, burst in the night sky. In the distance, I spotted the glimmer of water threaded between dark walls, and the gleam of a clock tower topped with a winged figure balanced on an hourglass and holding a scythe. The witches' memory palace may have been cloaked from outside view, but it was wholly visible from their precinct even though the rest of Celestina was spared the sight.

I studied Fludd's memory palace from its floating stone foundation to its tower finials with astonishment. I'd always thought of it as something imaginary. Seeing it constructed out of wood and stone was nearly as surreal as the shades of the Ravens' Wood.

"Unfuckingbelievable," I murmured, making use of one of Chris's favorite phrases.

"It really is an eyesore," Janet agreed. "Everything else at Celestina is Gothic and soothing, but that baroque monstrosity assaults the eyes like a coronet assaults the ears when it sounds reveille."

We took the route Ysabeau had traced on the map at Ca' Chiaramonte, and passed into the former monks' garden. The lush beds of herbs and flowers were well tended. The witches must still employ servants, for not even magic could maintain such an extensive garden with its carefully pruned grapevines and labels that indicated what was planted where.

Beyond the gardens was the orchard, as Ysabeau's map had promised. Most of the trees were in leaf, flower, and fruit, just like Gwyneth's garden in the Ravens' Wood. The trees were protected from the worst of the elements with a brick wall, creating a microclimate that would ripen their fruit more evenly.

Keenly aware of the time, Janet and I moved through another door in the wall and between trees along a dirt track that should lead to the *squero,* where the Congregation still employed master boatbuilders and specialist *squerarióli* to tend to their vessels. Once we reached the place where sawhorses and cradles awaited boats in need of repairs, the indistinct outlines of the Labyrinth's palings came into focus. I saw the arched bridge that spanned the short distance from the witches' formal gardens to the sloping bank where a witch would climb into a waiting *mascareta* to pilot her way through the Labyrinth's narrow, twisting waterways.

"There's a boat there," Janet said, pointing to the short, round *mascareta* that was lying upside down like an empty walnut shell. "Hopefully it's lagoon-worthy."

We carried it to the water and flipped it over.

"Do you want me to row?" I said, making sure that my baseball cap was securely in place and my ponytail pulled through the gap in the back as though I was about to enter a race.

"Have you ever rowed standing up, with one oar?" Janet blinked at me.

"Good point," I said, picking up the nearby oar and handing it to Matthew's granddaughter, who climbed aboard the vessel. Once Janet was settled inside, I pushed the *mascareta* into the water, jumping from the bank into the broad-bottomed craft as I did so.

It tipped under my weight, but Janet used her oar to keep level before pushing off the muddy bed.

"I'm getting too old for this kind of lark," Janet complained. "It's time for me to retire."

Circumnavigating the outer walls of the Labyrinth required that Janet leave the shoreline and enter the lagoon. Otherwise, we ran the risk of capsizing the boat due to its shallow draft or crashing into the palings, carried into them by strong currents and the stiff breeze that had risen as darkness fell.

That meant passing through the wards a second time. They shuddered in surprise, unused to boat traffic here. I held my breath, hoping the wards would relax of their own accord. Janet let out a stream of colorful Gaelic while she continued to steer the *mascareta* in a wide arc that headed back toward the memory palace.

It was only then that I realized the memory palace was no longer visible. It had disappeared behind the wards along with the Labyrinth. All we could see from our vantage point was the abandoned *squero* and the vine-encrusted wall of the witches' garden.

"How are you at dead reckoning?" I asked Janet, wondering how else we would find our way back to the palace without landmarks to guide us.

"I was born in Inverness," Janet said under her breath. "I'm used to poor visibility."

The wards were more than low-lying fog, however. They were a mirage of Shadow and reflected Light that would have disoriented even the most experienced sailor.

Janet was as good as her word, and steered unerringly toward a decapitated statue that was half-buried in the soft earth by the shoreline. We passed through the wards again. They were wide-awake now and tracking our strange movements with curiosity.

Puzzled but obedient, the wards parted and the memory palace shimmered before us once more.

"We're through." Janet heaved a sigh of relief.

I peered at the pale walls of Fludd's building, looking for Ysabeau's landing. "There!"

A listing, rickety dock was attached to a single rotting post. No one had landed on it for decades, and it was by no means clear we could safely do so now.

"That looks like a death trap," Janet commented, as the festival's final burst of fireworks filled the sky with light. Soon, it would be completely dark except for the lamps on the bows of the vessels taking home those few prudent souls who didn't wish to stay in Venice and drink themselves into a stupor.

I spied the outline of a bricked-up doorway where the dock remained tenuously affixed to its mooring. The cargo entrance was sealed. Had we come all this way for nothing?

Janet used her oar to snag a loose corner and pulled the *mascareta* into position between what remained of the dock and the foundations of the palace.

"What now?" I said, thinking of Gwyneth's Finnish TNT spell. Perhaps we could blow a hole in the wall. Hopefully, anyone within earshot would think it was just more fireworks.

Janet murmured a few words and poked the bricks with her wand, shredding the illusion cast over the door.

"Impressive," I murmured.

"*Och,* that glamour had seen better days," Janet said modestly, resting on the narrow bench that spanned the *mascareta*'s gunwhales. "You could see the latch right through the bricks."

The time had come for me to enter the memory palace. We had agreed at Ca' Chiaramonte that Janet could not enter for fear that its magic would recognize her and inquire after her purpose. She wouldn't be able to tell the truth, nor would she be able to lie.

"Remember, if the palace asks you a question, you must answer it as truthfully as you can," Janet warned. "Keep it short and to the point— that's how to stay on the right side of the remaining wards."

Sarah was an expert in half-truths, but I was not.

"The goddess only knows what Shadow and Darkness will throw at you inside, never mind the dazzles and glaems Light will produce to distract you," Janet continued. "When you find your memory bottles, don't wander or dawdle. If you do, you might be lost forever. The memory palace's magic is perilously mutable."

"Thank you, Janet." I opened my mouth to say something more, but Darkness was waiting to pounce, and Light snatched the words from my lips before I could utter them.

"There's no need," Janet said, the skin around her eyes creased with worry. "Listen to your instincts, Diana, and do not doubt them; they are how the goddess speaks to you."

I hopped out of the *mascareta* and onto the part of the landing that was still supported by the post. It sank a few inches, filling my sneakers with water, then bobbed up again. I reached for the iron latch on the door, but it had not been used for ages and the mechanism was stiff with salt and grime. I put my shoulder to the wood and pushed with all my might. Reluctantly, the door swung open, scraping against the floor on the other side.

Magic swept over me as I entered the memory palace, whooshing to greet me and passing through the open door. The force of it caused the door to bang shut, and I wondered if it could be opened from the inside.

But it was too late to worry about that now. I cast a flickering shadow-light so that I could get my bearings in the cavernous space. Holding it in my palm, I lifted it, hoping to see into the corners of the room. Darkness quickly absorbed its pale glimmer, but the illumination had lasted long enough for me to learn that I was standing in a wooden arcade with rectangular openings like unglazed windows. It reminded me of the stands at Hampton Court's tennis play, where spectators were able to view the action from a protected position.

I conjured another shadowlight and searched the panels until I found a simple catch. It snicked open, releasing a section of the enclosure so that I could pass onto the room's black marble floor. This was no tennis court. The lines and patterns in the marble were magical: a pentacle held in concentric rings, with an elemental circle at each point of the star.

My eyes adjusted to the absence of Light and I swept the room for further clues about its purpose. The ceiling was as dark as the four walls and the floor, and a silver crescent moon shone from it, casting the only light in the windowless space. A silvered frieze with the repeated legend THEATRUM TENEBRARUM wound around the room.

The Theater of Darkness.

This was where my mother faced Peter Knox in a magical duel, the conditions so gloomy that she wouldn't have seen the wand in front of her face.

Janet had warned me not to dawdle and I reluctantly left the *Theatrum Tenebrarum* behind me and found my way to a torch-filled hallway wide enough for four witches to walk abreast. A touch of witchfire would have illuminated them, but I couldn't risk detection.

In the hallway, Darkness was still present, but it was held in check by layers of magic and countermagic in a palimpsest inscribed and re-inscribed by hundreds of witches to keep the spells vital. But the loosening knots of the spells had not been re-tied with the shining threads a weaver like me used. These were woven out of Darkness, Shadow, and Light—the fabric of higher magic.

I passed by other rooms and sped down other corridors: a room lined with shelves, each laden with books; a dining room, with a table set for a banquet, and thirteen seats gathered around; a room like a theater, without players or audience.

I came upon the palace's kitchen, where a man in a dark jacket and knee britches sat by the fire, his back to me. He stirred a cauldron filled with something dark and fragrant. A black bird with a sharp ebony beak and a thickly feathered neck perched on his shoulder. The raven cocked its head to look at me.

The man felt my gaze and turned.

John Proctor. I recognized him from the carriage road and Grissel Gowdie's memory bottle. Why was he in the witches' memory palace?

There's nothing for you here, he said. *Hearth and cauldron will never be home for witches like us. You must climb higher to find what you seek.*

The raven rose from John's shoulder, leading me into another part of the palace. I followed the bird to a space where the light was pearlescent gray and shifting, rather than dark and thick. I searched high on the walls and wasn't surprised to see THEATRUM UMBRARUM—the Theater of Shadows—spelled out there.

A carved chair stood in the center of the room. A black bearskin—head and all—was thrown over the back and seat so that anyone who dared to sit in it would be held in the creature's legs. Next to it stood a bucket with a silver dipper and a chalice studded with jewels. Unlike the Theater of Darkness, the Theater of Shadows felt like a ritual space.

Curiosity saved the witch, croaked the raven circling above me. *You must aim high.* The black bird flew off in a flurry of dark wings.

I looked up, and saw another labyrinth suspended above me, this one made of air and Shadow rather than wood and water. Through some marvel of architecture and magic, the suspended labyrinth managed to be both diaphanous and solid, with the vaulted dome of the heavens visible above it.

Through the shifting clouds of the labyrinth I saw a glimmer, then a sparkle. I narrowed my eyes in an effort to see more clearly.

Glass. *Memory bottles.*

A spiral staircase rose behind the bearskin-covered chair. It was not until I put my foot on the first tread that I realized the stairs resembled a double helix, with two separate flights twining around a central axis.

As I climbed, the labyrinth grew more substantial. When I reached the top of the stairs, the landing was solid under my feet and I stood at the central point of the palace where the witches' memories were kept.

Signs pointed to *oriens, occidens, septentrio,* and *meridies*—the four cardinal directions. I stepped through the eastern arch and into a demented library of curved shelves and twisting aisles. Hundreds of bottles crowded the shelves, along with boxes of brittle call slips for indicating when a bottle had been removed, and a few odds and ends of unknown origin and purpose: a bird's skull, a crossbow with a wand for a bolt, a crumbling silk cap with a gold tassel. A thick layer of dust covered everything.

I scanned the labels on the nearest bottles. *Ema Howat. Ana Novak. Maja Krajnc.* These were Eastern European names, possibly from Venice's near neighbors Slovenia and Croatia. A few bottles suggested they belonged to witches closer to Venice, like the one labeled with the name *Zorzi Vascotto.*

Curiously, each label not only had a name but a six-digit code. *197402. 196813. 195101. 195904.* Could the first four digits be a date? If so, what did the last two numbers signify?

"Oh, Granny Alice," I murmured. She would be horrified by the jumble. If the numbers were dates, they should have been arranged in ascending or descending order. If they weren't dates, then the bottles should have been shelved alphabetically.

There was no time to bring order to the chaos, for I was in the wrong part of the memory palace. The bottles containing Proctor and Bishop memories would be in the *occidens* section reserved for witches who lived somewhere west of Venice.

I crossed the landing again. In the western part of the palace, the shelves extended as far as the eye could see in one direction, then twisted off into Shadow. There was no dust, and the slips that marked the places to reshelve bottles were fresh and crisp. I pulled one free. *Sidonie Von Borcke, 24 June 2017.* My nemesis had been here only a few weeks before, pawing through memories that didn't belong to her.

The bottles on the shelves closest to the entrance were labeled: *201701, 201705, 201713.* The next were marked *201603, 201607, 201608, 201611.*

My hunch was confirmed: The first four digits designated a year—probably the year the memories were collected from that particular class of potential adepts. The last two digits must be a secondary sorting system.

Matthew's mention of eugenics echoed in my thoughts, reminding me that the Congregation was not only interested in storing witches' memories but evaluating them, too.

"Rankings." My mouth twisted in distaste. After the witches removed the memories from the newly certified adepts, they were reviewed and assigned a rank according to their skills and power. Matthew's fears were justified.

These memories had been recently culled, so my mother's would not be among them. I tore myself away and went deeper into the library of bottles in search of hers.

I sped along the millennial shelves and reached the '90s. There were twice as many bottles here, but I had no time to wonder why. I ran down the next aisle, searching for the 1960s. I overshot the mark, and found myself among the memories of witches who had been here before World War II.

1932, 1933, 1934.

1935.

I breathed deeply, trying to quiet my racing heart.

Thomas Lloyd, 193601
Joanna Bishop, 193602
Taliesin Proctor, 193603
Nina Garnier, 193608
Janette Gardener, 193609
Viola Cantini, 193613

If the final two digits were a ranking system, then three of my grandparents had received top marks in their Labyrinth examinations.

I had no flowers to offer to their memories, as I had at Proctor's Ledge. Nor could I take the memories into my heart where they belonged. All I could do was reclaim them.

I pulled a rolled-up tote bag from where I'd stashed it in the waistband of my black leggings. One by one, I removed my grandparents' bottles, moving as quickly and surely as I could.

The aisle twisted to the left and I peeked around the corner. Another range of shelves extended into the distance. The past beckoned me to explore further, but I turned my back to it and set my sights forward.

This time, I used my instincts to find the other family bottles.

Gwyneth Proctor, 194802

I nestled Aunt Gwyneth's memories into the bag next to her brother's. The more family memories I reclaimed, the louder my power sang.

Janet Gowdie, 194903
Naomi Proctor, 195713

In the bottles went, the weight of the bag pulling on the straps.

I reached the 1960s, my fingers tingling.

Isaac Mather, 196503

I searched further, and found what I sought on the bottom shelf.

Rebecca Bishop, 196901

Mom had been top of her class, like her father before her.

I stooped to put my mother's memories into the bag and noticed another bottle beside it with her name and a date traditionally written out. It was *5 August 1976*—only eight days before I was born. I took that bottle, too, freeing a retrieval slip from the shelf. I grabbed it before it could pass through the clouds and fall into the room below.

There was a name, date, and description of the item taken—just like on a request slip at the Bodleian.

Bishop, Rebecca. Memory Bottle 3, 28 August 1983.

Fire and ice filled my veins. Some ghoul had taken my mother's memories on the day she had died.

"Peter Knox," I said, voicing my worst fear.

It was even more horrifying that someone else had custody of them now. I looked for the name of the witch who had my mother's memories, expecting to see Sidonie's initials.

Tinima Toussaint, 26 May 2017.

It was not Sidonie who had taken the bottle, but the Congregation's new recruit. She had done so on the day the ravens came to New Haven to give their message to Becca.

My eyes strayed to the shelves on the left, where I found other bottles that belonged to me and mine.

Emily Mather, 197405

Julie Eastey, 197606

Had some other witch been spying on Em, or Julie? Furious at the possibility, I put them in my bag, too.

The Bodleian tote couldn't hold any more items. The taste of unfinished business and unmet desire soured my tongue. It would remain there until I had reclaimed every shred of family from this place.

I was leaving the *occidens* section of the memory palace when one final bottle caught my eye.

Margaret Skelling, 200804

I hesitated. My intention had been to recover only what belonged to my kith and kin.

Take it, Darkness whispered. *It serves her right, after turning you and Gwyneth in to the Congregation.*

It doesn't belong to you, Light murmured. I made a Faustian bargain and slipped the bottle into my pocket.

"I'm sorry, Mom. I wish it had been yours," I said.

The floor underneath me went from solid to vapor and I fell—up, up, up.

I was flung into the inky sky. Instead of constellations, the Darkness was filled with a swirling galaxy of leaves, dragonflies, toads, and feathers. A ladder whirled around the center of the vortex, followed by a broom, a golden ring, even a doll's house, as though I had been transported to Kansas and would soon find myself in Oz.

I held the bag of memory bottles close, not wanting them to be sucked into this strange universe.

"Looking for this?" A tall, slender witch sat cross-legged in the middle of the dark galaxy, holding up a memory bottle. She was dressed in white, her head wrapped in a scarf. "I've been expecting you, Diana Bishop."

"That belongs to me." The air was thick with power and I struggled to swim through it.

"Not according to the label." Tinima's high cheekbones cast her fine features into Shadow until her face resembled Death's head. "You must be one of those witches who thinks all the magic in the world is theirs for the taking."

"And you must be Tinima." I hovered nearby, careful to keep my mind blank and not to wish or want for anything—not information, not this witch's sudden, painful demise, not even the return of my mother's remaining memories.

But I was not careful enough.

"This is not your first time exploring a labyrinth, I see." Tinima's eyes narrowed. "Someone's been walking where they hadn't ought. Only a true child of Shadow could have come so far, unchallenged. A little knowledge can be a dangerous thing, Diana."

"You knew I was coming to Isola della Stella," I said, "just as you knew when the ravens came to New Haven."

"The spirits have been restive," Tinima replied, "and the candle flames full of whispers."

I'd left the black bird oracle at Ca' Chiaramonte—thank the goddess. Hopefully Madame Toussaint was not yet aware that I, too, had a way of divining the future.

"Fireworks have never been my favorite poison," Tinima said, "so I remained on Isola della Stella to see you myself."

"Here I am," I said with a shrug that I'd learned from Ysabeau.

"Hmm." Tinima watched me closely, gauging my reactions. "Sidonie is obsessed with you, which tells me you have power. Janet barely mentions your name, which confirms you are a witch of great ability. She doesn't trust me and I don't trust her, you see, so we keep our secrets close."

Wise decision, I thought.

"And neither of them knows who—or what—they're dealing with when it comes to you," Tinima murmured, her eyes boring into me with a tingle that verged on painful, probing my strengths and making note of my weaknesses. "I'm glad I had the opportunity to judge you myself. You don't disappoint, Diana, even though you are in over your head."

I couldn't argue with that. But I was a quick study, and soon I would be swimming with the best of them.

"The bottle." I held out my hand.

Tinima laughed. "If you want it, you'll have to come closer."

I didn't want to be anywhere near Tinima Toussaint. I wished to be back on terra firma.

I blinked and found myself in the chair I'd seen earlier, the bearskin's head looking over my shoulder.

Tinima now watched me from the shadow of the staircase, her white lace dress blending into its stone traceries. Her expression had changed, and wariness darkened her features.

I rose to my feet. If Tinima was intent on a magical duel, I needed to be ready. More importantly, I needed to protect the memory bottles I'd taken from damage.

"If you're going to challenge me, let me put the bottles down first," I said. "Oh. I don't have a wand. It will have to be hand-to-wand combat, if that's okay."

The wariness vanished as Tinima's expression turned to outrage, her eyes smoldering. "How dare you suggest I would take advantage of a *novice.*"

The embers of Tinima's eyes burst into flame. With a strength that was not of this world, Tinima flung the bottle she was holding skyward.

"No!" I cried as my mother's precious memories joined the ring and the shells, the leaves and the ladder, the feathers and the dragonflies, swirling around the black hole in the strange galaxy at the center of the palace. The fiery bottle disappeared like a blazing star into Darkness, burning brightly before it was extinguished.

"How could you?" I cried, tears streaming.

"Go!" Tinima roared. "Take your bottles, and do not return here until Shadow calls you home."

I took a step back, then another, astonished that Tinima, like Meg, was letting me go.

The witch held up her hand in farewell, her eyes still burning bright.

"We will meet again, Diana Bishop," she promised. "Sooner than you think. We will settle the score then."

Chapter 25

The fallout from our intelligence operation–slash–heist was as serious as I'd feared it would be.

I was formally reprimanded for arriving at Isola della Stella without warning, and entering the witches' precinct without permission. The Congregation delivered a copy of the Witches Code of Conduct Regarding the Proper Manner to Approach the Members (a title worthy of Robert Fludd) to Ca' Chiaramonte after breakfast. The witches were at their most prolix in the document, which exceeded ten pages in length. As I had no desire to go back to Isola della Stella—or see Tinima—ever again, I threw the papers away.

Then, in an emergency meeting immediately after the festival of Redentore concluded, the Congregation's witches compelled Baldwin and Fernando to make assurances regarding my current whereabouts, and promises that I would make myself available for questioning if asked.

Finally, the witches summarily expelled Janet. She got the news on Sunday afternoon just before she left Venice. Janet confessed she was tired of the constant squabbling and the energy it took to stay one step ahead of Sidonie.

"It's a relief, really. Granny invited me to remain with her at Sept-Tours as long as I'd like," Janet told me when I accompanied her—along with Ysabeau, Marthe, Alain, Victoire, and an entire showroom of Louis Vuitton luggage—to Santa Lucia, where the party would board the Orient Express *en route* to Lyon.

"Janet and I shall do our best to stay out of trouble," Ysabeau told me when we said goodbye. "Unlike Baldwin and Fernando, we make no promises."

The disdain etched on Ysabeau's fine features indicated what she thought of those members of the de Clermont family who had acceded to the Congregation's demands.

Ysabeau was the only creature to emerge from the weekend in Venice not only unscathed but energized. The de Clermont matriarch had been the sensation of the 2017 Festa del Redentore, with one social media account rhapsodizing over the return of classic French elegance, likening Ysabeau's impact to that of Catherine Deneuve in 1967. As she crossed the station floor in a daring black Balmain suit, her arms filled with bouquets given to her by admirers, the moment was captured in photos that were quickly uploaded to the internet.

Later, I settled into my seat on Baldwin's jet with mixed emotions. I'd burned whatever precarious bridge to the Congregation I'd enjoyed as a member of the de Clermont family. The witches would not quickly forgive my raid on the memory palace, and they would never entirely forget it. Sidonie's animosity had deepened, along with her curiosity. Without Janet on the Congregation, Matthew and I had lost a crucial ally. As for Tinima Toussaint, I still did not know what to make of her decision to let me keep the stolen memories, or her seemingly impulsive decision to destroy my mother's bottle. I put a protective hand on the Bodleian tote, where each family bottle was now individually wrapped in a vintage Hermès scarf from Ysabeau's collection.

Matthew was waiting for me when I landed at the private airfield northwest of Boston. We embraced silently, relieved to be together again and awkward, too, after what had happened only a few days before in the Proctor labyrinth. At Ravenswood, I was delighted to find Sarah and Gwyneth had not strangled each other. Apollo and Ardwinna greeted me briefly and enthusiastically, then passed out under the chestnut tree from the heat and excitement. The twins were lightly tanned, healthy as horses, and eager to tell me everything that had transpired in their world over the past seventy-two hours. Once the reunions were over and the children were off to the river with Ike, I shared what happened in Venice with the rest of my curious family.

"I can't believe you managed to leave Isola della Stella with so many bottles!" Gwyneth said after seeing my heavily laden tote bag.

"I can't believe you didn't break any," Sarah said.

I asked Matthew to undertake the delicate job of unpacking the bag. He drew the bottles out of their wrappings, identifying each in turn until a bright assortment of Venetian glass bottles—some round, some tall, some plain, and others with elaborate colors and faceted stoppers— gleamed in the Ipswich summer sunshine.

"The witches must be in partnership with the glassblowers of Murano and Burano," Matthew said as he put the last of the memory bottles on the table.

"Which is mine?" Gwyneth asked in a shaky voice.

I looked for Gwyneth's gold-and-black bottle, as well as the green one that belonged to Tally. I placed them in front of my aunt in a reunion of siblings. Gwyneth touched them with reverence, her hands moving possessively over the bottles' rounded bases, her soothing strokes indicating that all was well now.

"It looks like the oldest bottles you found are from 1936," Matthew said, scanning the labels to make sure. "How far back does the memory archive go?"

"I didn't have time to find out," I explained. "Madame Toussaint discovered me looting the shelves and I had to leave as quickly as possible."

Matthew knew me well enough to suspect that this cool retelling was not the whole story. It would take me time to find the right words to describe what had happened, and to formulate the questions that remained.

I drew Matthew's attention away by drawing a rough floor plan of the palace, including the double-helix staircase that led to the floating library filled with memory bottles. I amused Sarah with tales of Ysabeau's antics in Venice, and showed her some of the pictures that had made it onto social media—none of which showed my mother-in-law's face in any detail. I told Gwyneth about my surprising encounter with Tinima Toussaint, the newest member of the Congregation.

While I spun my tales and sipped my tea, Matthew's eyes never left me. I was afraid to meet them, for I was unsure what I might see there. Love? Like? Neither? Both?

The clatter of footsteps and slap of wet life jackets outside the barn announced the children's return from their fishing trip.

"Look!" Pip ran in with a string of fish. "We caught dinner!"

Matthew and I dutifully admired the slippery trophies.

"What's in those?" Becca asked, dropping her fishing rod at the sight of what I'd brought home from Venice.

"People's experiences and memories from long ago," I said, drawing her into my arms so that she didn't knock any bottles over in her curiosity.

Ike entered the barn with the tackle. "Whoa. Are those all memory bottles?"

"They are," I said, making room for him next to me. "Thank you for taking the kids out today."

"No problem, coz. We had a great time," he replied.

"I have something for you," I whispered.

"A souvenir?" Ike looked pleased. "Did you get me a Juventus jersey?"

I laughed. No wonder he and Chris were such good friends. They were cut from the same piece of athletic cloth.

"I'm afraid I was on the wrong side of the boot." I located the tall, clear bottle with an amber double helix swirled through the glass. I twisted it so the label faced Ike. "This belongs to you and your mom."

Ike took the bottle as gently as though it were a tiny bird.

"These are Dad's memories?" Ike asked, wide-eyed.

I'd learned at the Midsummer potluck that Ike had never known his father except through photos and the tales that Lucy and the rest of the Proctor family told to keep the fallen soldier alive. I could only imagine what the memories might mean to a child who had never heard their father's voice, or felt their father's arms around them.

"Do you need a hug, Uncle Ike?" Pip was watching my cousin with vampiric intensity.

"I sure do, buddy." Ike gave Pip the kind of all-enfolding embrace that fathers give to their sons, the memory bottle still clutched in his fingers.

"I didn't know your father was an adept," Matthew said softly.

"We don't talk about it much," Ike said, releasing Pip. "Put-Put told me Dad had been examined on Isola della Stella in the summer of '65, but it was a wild time and Dad chose the Marines over the Congregation. 196503. Too many digits for a zip code, too few for a service number. What does it mean?"

"The year, followed by your dad's class rank," I explained. "The Congregation's invitation list was selective—no more than thirteen witches were invited to Isola della Stella to be tested."

"Third out of thirteen." Ike shook his head. "That's my dad. Always the overachiever. And neither he nor any of his classmates came back knowing what happened to them there?"

"Not unless they became members of the Congregation," I said. "With a seat comes access to the memory palace—and all the secrets there. You can recall anyone's memories you wish—enemies, friends, families . . ."

"No wonder ambitious witches compete to be selected," Gwyneth said. "Imagine wielding so much power over your fellow creatures."

"Who's looking out for the welfare of the other adepts, and the candidates who washed out of the program like Naomi?" Ike asked, his expression somber.

"No one," I said. "Their bottles were consigned to a shelf and forgotten unless one of the Congregation's witches thought they might be useful."

"Are there tiny people in the bottles?" Becca asked during the lull in the conversation that followed.

"No, moonbeam. Only memories," Matthew replied. "These are like the bottles *Maman* brought back from Granny Sarah's house. Remember how heavy they were?"

Becca and Pip nodded.

"They were warm," Pip added.

"And there were sparkles inside." Becca's tone turned schoolmarmish. "If we see an empty bottle that's heavy and warm and sparkly that's shut tight, we need to let Mommy or Aunt Gwyneth know."

I hadn't noticed a warm sparkle in the bottles, but I wasn't Bright Born and lacked my children's acute perception.

"That's right, Rebecca," Matthew said, bestowing a proud smile on his daughter.

"Who saved all of these from the recycling?" Pip asked, looking askance at all the bottles. "They must have a big house."

Matthew smothered a smile. The children, like many of their generation, were fervent eco-warriors who knew more about landfills and green energy than I had known about plastic and oil wells at their age.

"The Congregation." I wanted to be honest with the children, given their impending examination.

Pip scowled. The children were not fans of the Congregation. It had occupied far too much of my time, and now it deprived them of seeing Fernando as often as they would like.

"They put people's thoughts in jars like Marthe's pickles and then kept them?" Becca's nose wrinkled in distaste. "I wouldn't like that. And I wouldn't want Uncle Baldwin's memories kept in a jar, either. He tells the best stories, and they always start with 'I remember when.'"

"What are you going to do with them?" Ike asked me quietly.

"That's my question, too," Sarah said, surprised to be aligned with a member of the Proctor family. "Are you going to pull all the corks out? Or are you just going to stuff them in a different cupboard to be forgotten?"

"We're certainly not opening them now." As a historian, I was worried that releasing the memories might damage them in ways we couldn't anticipate. They were better off where they were.

Gwyneth looked relieved.

"Can we open them tomorrow?" Pip asked.

"Not today, and not tomorrow," I said firmly.

Not until I had an opportunity to talk to Matthew privately.

I waited for a few days before broaching the subject of Venice with Matthew. I'd expected him to be bursting with questions about what I'd seen and what Tinima had been like, but the distance that had widened between us since I took him to the Proctor labyrinth remained. My thoughts kept returning to that night in the wood and the hurt that I'd caused.

One day, when the run to camp went smoothly, the children were happy, the weather was fine, and Gwyneth had a meeting of the local garden club, I decided that it was time to mend fences with my husband. Not even Sarah remained at Ravenswood, as the guest speaker at Gwyneth's club was a visiting hedgewitch from Vermont who ran a seed-catalogue business and was addressing the topic "Seed Swaps: Preserving Historical Plants and Vegetables While Growing Stronger Communities"—a subject near and dear to her heart.

By late morning, only Matthew and I were left on the property. I was in the kitchen, making perfunctory notes on Gwyneth's latest alchemical project in my book of shadows. Matthew was in Tally's office, calling Grace to reserve some lobster for dinner. He'd already called Ike to review the best way to lay seaweed in a lobster pot and received his daily lab update from Miriam. Matthew couldn't avoid me forever. Sooner or later, he was going to have to return to the kitchen.

When he did, I pounced.

"I wonder if you'd like to witness one of Mom's memory bottles with me," I said, keeping my tone casual and my nose buried in my book of shadows.

Matthew's shoulders stiffened. He turned from the coffee siphon.

"Do you think it's wise to do that without Gwyneth being here?"

"It's not Mom's Congregation memories, but a bottle I found at the Bishop House. Gwyneth examined it and said it's in good shape and shouldn't be a problem," I assured him. Gwyneth's lessons had focused on how to care for and maintain memory bottles since I returned from Venice.

"Don't you want to wait for Sarah?" Matthew asked. "Rebecca was her sister. There could be a family memory in the bottle."

I slid the wax-covered Mateus bottle toward him. "I'm pretty sure this is from one of my parents' date nights."

Matthew opened his mouth.

"I doubt we'll be seeing anything X-rated," I said, deflecting his next argument. I bit back a sigh of frustration. "If you don't want to join me, just say no. I'll go to the barn and do it myself."

Matthew sat opposite me at the old kitchen table that had no doubt witnessed dozens of difficult conversations between husbands and wives.

"I don't want to be part of your attempts to work higher magic," Matthew said.

I wasn't *attempting* higher magic—I was mastering it, albeit haltingly and incrementally. I bit back my sharp response. Defensiveness wasn't going to improve matters between us.

"I understand," I said, and meant it. "It's your choice. I hope you can understand that I'm going to keep offering, though."

Matthew shrugged.

"Taking you to the labyrinth in the wood was wrong," I said. "I won't make a mistake like that again. I'm still learning and I'll make other mistakes—but not that one."

"You think going there alone would have made it all right?" Matthew's temper flared. "Christ, Diana. Neither of us had any business being there."

"I disagree."

Matthew threw his hands up in frustration and sat back in his chair.

"I learned important lessons in the labyrinth that night—lifesaving lessons," I told him, my own anger coming to a simmer. I was trying to hear Matthew's concerns. Was he listening to mine? "I underestimated how vulnerable you would be. I admit that. But after what I experienced in Venice, I would do it again—without you."

"Now that you have a toehold in higher magic, *your* vulnerability is no longer sufficient reason to turn away from something you don't understand?" Matthew leaned toward me. "This is the problem with higher magic, Diana. It gives you the false impression that you're godlike and invincible."

"I know my limitations better than you do," I replied. "My strengths and weaknesses, too. Every day I walk on the Dark Path, I discover more about myself—and it's changing me, Matthew."

Matthew took his own deep, shuddering breath. I was voicing his deepest fears, and they were difficult for him to hear.

"I do my best to share what I learn, so that you don't feel you're losing me," I continued. "But sometimes, words just aren't enough. Sometimes, I need you to experience it with me rather than *through* me as though I were already a memory bottle on a shelf."

The raw emotion in Matthew's eyes told me he was hearing me now.

"Mom and Dad's relationship is a mystery to me," I confessed. "I don't understand how they made it work without Mom being able to practice higher magic. I thought maybe looking in on one of their date nights might help. There must have been some reason Mom went to the trouble of saving this particular evening."

Matthew weighed the alternatives, and his face registered fear, longing, anger, even annoyance. I had no idea what his final decision would be—until he made it.

"All right, *mon coeur,*" Matthew said. "Where do you want to do it?"

"Here, in the kitchen," I said evenly, though inside I was jumping for joy that he had agreed.

"Is there enough room?" Matthew looked around the crowded space.

"Plenty," I said, conjuring a witchlight to cut through the wax seal. "You ready?"

Matthew was startled. "Now?"

I nodded. If I gave him time to reconsider, Matthew would come up with a million reasons not to be part of this.

I could give him only one reason he should.

"I love you, Matthew," I said. "Thank you for doing this. We're going to figure this out. I promise."

Before Matthew could warn me not to make a promise I might not be able to keep, I conjured the protective chamber that would keep my mother's memories from evaporating. The seal was already opened, and the edges of the stopper were above the lip of the bottle. I didn't need to tug it to dislodge the bit of cork. The force of my mother's memories sent it rocketing toward the ceiling. It returned to the table with a thud.

That was the last thing I noticed before the past met the present, and the unmistakable scent of my mother's Diorissimo filled the air.

REBECCA BISHOP MEMORY BOTTLE, DECEMBER 1975

Rebecca put the last of the witch balls on the Yule tree. They sparkled in the colored lights draped around the pine branches, brightening the room and shining through the falling snow to help guide Stephen home.

She put a hand on her abdomen and smothered a burp while surveying the room to make sure everything was perfect. The final exam Stephen was proctoring finished at five o'clock. He would be home any moment, having taken the T and then a bus. It was a long commute—far lengthier than her fifteen-minute walk—and on wintry days like this one, Rebecca liked to make date night extra special.

The fire was lit, and with a little magical help the chimney was drawing properly so there was no smoke. Soon enough it would be filled with the aroma of tobacco, though Rebecca was going to have to put her foot down about that. The bottle of Mateus was waiting, along with two glasses and a bowl of salted peanuts. Rebecca couldn't stomach the thought of their usual potato chips.

The sound of booted feet stamping on the front steps let Rebecca know that Stephen was home. Her heart lifted as it always did when they were reunited, even after only a brief time apart. It was ridiculous, of course, that the sight of a man could affect her so strongly. She had learned to school her features around her female colleagues and friends, all of whom were marching for women's rights. Rebecca was, too—only she was head over heels in love with the man she had married.

"Wow." Stephen stepped inside, closing the door to keep the snow from blowing through the house. "Somebody's been busy."

"Just in the holiday mood, that's all," Rebecca said, going to Stephen for a kiss. "How did the final go?"

Stephen sighed. "They're so strung out, it's hard to tell. Two of them have been existing on nothing but grapefruit, raisins, and coffee for the past five days. Needless to say, I'm not expecting much from their blue books."

Stephen divested himself of the worn brown-leather briefcase stuffed with the distinctive notebooks that were supposed to keep students from cheating on their exams, the scarf that Emily had knitted for him last Yule, and his dark wool coat. They all smelled of tobacco smoke, coffee, and peppermint. Stephen's students weren't the only ones existing on a subpar diet during this busy time of year.

"How was your day?" Stephen asked, giving her a second kiss. His frozen skin was coming up to room temperature, and the snow caught in his brown hair had already melted.

"Eventful." Rebecca took his hand and led him to the blanket she'd unfolded by the fire and their pre-dinner picnic. "It took me forever to find a tree that was the right size, and then I couldn't find the witch balls. I went to the hardware store to replace a few of the bulbs in the lights before the snow started."

Magic would have been quicker, of course, and the witchlight would never have burned out again, but Rebecca knew better than to enchant something that would be used every day for the next three weeks. Stephen would smell the magic, and he wouldn't approve. These days she saved her spells for private moments and important reasons.

"How do the bulbs burn out when the lights are unplugged and stored in the attic?" Stephen lowered himself to the floor with a groan. "God, it's cold out there."

Rebecca handed him a glass of wine, and took one for herself. They clinked them together.

"To us, and the years ahead," Stephen said.

"To us, and the memories we leave behind," Rebecca replied. This was their usual toast, but it had special meaning tonight.

Stephen propped himself against the nearby chair and opened his arm for a cuddle. A bubble of joy caught in Rebecca's throat as she settled into his arm.

"Mmm." Stephen sniffed her hair. "Did you make cranberry apple pie for dessert?"

"Yes." Rebecca laughed. "It was supposed to be a surprise."

"Hard to disguise that much brown sugar and orange zest," Stephen said, planting another kiss under her ear. "Did you get to see the doctor today, like you hoped?"

"Uh-huh." Rebecca's bubble of joy exploded into excitement. "I'm not allergic to potatoes. And I don't have stomach flu."

"Thank God," Stephen said, reaching for the peanuts.

"I'm pregnant."

Stephen was slack-jawed with shock. They'd been trying to conceive for years but hadn't had any luck. Rebecca had wanted a child for so long, and had given up so much for the promise of her—for the child growing inside her would be a girl, Rebecca knew.

"I hope you don't mind getting your Yule gift early," she said.

"Mind?" Stephen whooped with delight. "When are you due?"

"The middle of August." Rebecca laughed again, her excitement mixed with a touch of trepidation. "Not the best timing. I'll be the size of Mount Monadnock by the end of the semester and sitting in a bucket of ice cubes when the July heat hits."

"We'll get an air conditioner!" Stephen had resisted the purchase for years, as he considered the machines ugly and wasteful. Now there was a baby on the way, he felt differently. He rested his hands on Rebecca's abdomen, his expression awestruck. "We're having a baby."

"Yep." Rebecca put her hands over his. "One with

blue eyes and blond hair." Like the sex of her baby, Rebecca could already see the child she would become.

"I never want to forget tonight," Stephen said, after kissing her again. And again. "It's perfect—safe and warm by the fire, snowy and cold outside, and just the two of us—"

"Three of us," Rebecca corrected him.

"Three of us." Stephen stopped again, struggling to come to terms with the fact that they were now more than a couple. They were a family.

As for tonight's memories, Rebecca already had plans for them. She would put hers in the Mateus bottle (once Stephen had emptied it) and share them with their daughter one day, so that she would always know how much she was wanted and loved.

The thump of Stephen's heart under her cheek was steady and calming.

"They told me the baby's heart is already beating." Rebecca nestled closer, feeling wistful that she couldn't yet hear it.

The next nine months couldn't go by fast enough. After that, Rebecca wanted time to move so slowly that she didn't miss a moment as her daughter's life unspooled in a shimmering path like the yellow brick road in *The Wizard of Oz*. Rebecca would see her take her first steps, and cry over her first boo-boo, and take her to school, and watch her cross the stage to graduate from college.

Her daughter's imaginary path grew shadowed after that, and a dark silhouette of a man appeared, tall and broad-shouldered, obscuring the road ahead. But Shadow had never frightened her. Rebecca would find out why Darkness surrounded this man who waited in her daughter's future. She would make sure, too, that he was worthy of her.

"I'd like to call her Diana," Rebecca said, twisting a bit of Stephen's scratchy wool sweater in her fingers.

"I'm surprised you don't want to use a family name, like

Joanna," Stephen replied. "Besides, the baby could be a boy. What would you want to name him?"

The child would be female. Of this, Rebecca had no doubt. To appease Stephen, she said the first boy's name that came to mind.

"Gabriel. Gabe for short," Rebecca said.

Far ahead, on Diana's shining path, the man's head turned.

"An archangel? That's a strange name for a witch to give her son," Stephen said with another of his deep chuckles. "Have you been listening to too much Christmas radio?"

"It's a strong name," Rebecca replied.

Diana and her dark angel would need that strength. Rebecca's hand rested protectively on her belly. For now, all Diana needed was Rebecca.

For the first time in her life, Rebecca felt like she was enough.

"I love you, little one," Rebecca murmured. "Through all the years ahead, and all the memories I leave behind."

Chapter 26

Matthew dripped water across the bedroom floor as he left the shower in pursuit of his clothes, toweling off his hair and swiping at the moisture that clung to his skin. I made no secret of my enjoyment as I watched him get dressed.

"Hmm." I sighed happily as his muscles flexed and his torso twisted. "I like this new alarm clock way more than the one with the bells."

Matthew caught my eye and laughed. "Flatterer."

"All part of a wife's job," I said.

"What are your plans for the day?" Matthew asked, pulling a gray T-shirt over his dark head.

"I am not going to do *anything*," I said, wiggling my toes in anticipation. It had been a busy, stressful summer. Gwyneth was still putting me through my magical paces, and back-to-school messages were popping up on my computer screen with alarming banners of obligations to come. "Rest. Eat. Play with the children—if they ever come home again, that is."

Pip was at a stargazing sleepover. Becca spent the night with her cousin Abigail, who had a historical doll from the same series as Tamsy and an equally impressive array of period-appropriate accessories. The children were already experiencing nostalgia for their "Best Summer Ever" even though there were weeks of enjoyment still to come. Becca and Pip were determined to cram as many clams, cousins, and boating excursions as they could into what remained of their vacation.

I brushed aside the looming prospect of the twins' Congregation examination in September. I, too, wanted to enjoy the weeks between now and then as fully as possible.

"How about you?" I asked, propping myself up to get a better view of Matthew's backside.

"Miriam sent some new reports." One of Matthew's long legs went into his jeans, then the other. He pulled them up around his trim hips.

"And?" New information on the Proctor DNA was coming in regularly now that Matthew had sampled half of Essex County and interviewed everyone who would let a vampire into their house.

"And I haven't looked at them yet," Matthew teased. He climbed onto the bed and flopped onto his back so that I could cuddle into his shoulder. "Impatience really *is* a Proctor trait. I'm going to have to see if I can find the gene that controls it."

After a satisfying tussle and a full body search for the offending bit of DNA code, I was wide-awake and ready for breakfast. Matthew and I took our morning drinks onto the porch. I rocked and watched the play of sunshine on the water while Matthew sipped at his coffee and read the latest news from Yale on his computer.

"Combining DNA and family history is yielding results," Matthew said. "We knew that you had genetic markers for particular magical abilities when we tested your DNA in Oxford, but those identifications were based on general patterns. It was a bit like knowing that a specific line of genetic code is what makes your eyes blue. Now that we have the Proctor DNA to analyze, we're able to winnow down which of your ancestors might have passed that magical trait to you."

Knowing your grandmother also had blue eyes was nice. Knowing she was a genius with wizard bolts? That was priceless information.

"Any luck figuring out the identity of the first family timewalker?" I asked, happy that my tea was beginning to wash the cobwebs of sleep from my brain. Without it, I wasn't sure I'd be able to follow the arabesques Matthew's mind made when he was engaged with his research.

"Not yet," Matthew said, "but it's early days. There are a lot of Proctors who were prone to what's described in the records as 'wandering.' That might be an indication of timewalkers—members of the family known for disappearing for a few hours and then returning without explaining where they'd been."

"Granny Dorcas said John Proctor was a wanderer." I laughed. "I just thought that meant he liked to take walks."

Matthew grinned. I was delighted by his current happiness. Since we'd opened Mom's memory bottle, and he'd heard her speak his name, Matthew was enjoying being at Ravenswood as much as the children and me, from its bird-filled mornings to the quiet whisper of the water through the marsh at night.

"Gwyneth doesn't have the time-traveling gene," Matthew said. "It's possible Tally might have had it—but he's such a mysterious fellow it's hard to know whether his here-today-gone-tomorrow reputation was due to his career as a spy or his magical talents."

"And Morgana?"

"Gwyneth says not. She never had children, so I can't be sure," Matthew replied. "The stories I've heard about their mother, Damaris Proctor, suggest she was a timewalker, though. Your great-grandmother liked to give small but priceless Roman bronzes to her friends to mark special occasions."

"Don't tell Phoebe," I said, laughing. "We've got a beautiful, drama-free day ahead of us. Let's enjoy it."

I hadn't known then that I was tempting fate. Nor had the black bird oracle given me any reason to suspect what was to come. But the moment the mail truck showed up at the Old Place that afternoon, I was uneasy.

Gwyneth and Sarah were back from the garden club when it arrived. The coming of the mail was a highlight of Gwyneth's day, and there were always notes from faraway friends in it, as well as cheerful catalogues and print editions of various local papers. Gwyneth liked to have her afternoon tea while she went through her post. Today she took the mail from the box on the ridge, riffled through it, and froze.

I had braced myself to receive the summons from Venice requiring me to appear and explain what had happened on Isola della Stella during the feast of Redentore. Why did it have to be today, on this best of all summer days?

"The Congregation," I said, meeting her halfway.

"Not the Congregation," Gwyneth said, holding up a creamy envelope. "Just the witches."

I took the letter from Gwyneth and flipped it over, expecting to see the impression of Sidonie's familiar personal seal. Instead, I saw the witches' crescent moon pressed into green-and-black wax.

"Maybe Sidonie is afraid of losing face with the vampires and daemons if they learn how an inexperienced witch broke into their chambers," Gwyneth suggested.

"Inexperienced?" My eyebrows rose.

"When it comes to higher magic, you are still wet behind the ears, Diana Bishop," Gwyneth replied, putting me in my place. "Perhaps Tinima suggested they handle the matter internally instead. She has a reputation for being an excellent politician."

I cracked the wax seal and slid the witches' message from the envelope.

Dear Professor Bishop, the letter began. I read the rest of its message aloud.

"Following the charges made by Margaret Skelling, Ipswich Coven (f. 1634), formerly part of the Massachusetts Bay Colony Coven (f. 1629), we are scheduling a mandatory evaluation of your talents for higher magic, pursuant to the following guidelines (see enclosed)."

A copy of the Rules and Regulations Regarding Required Testing of All Children Born into Higher Magic Families or Exhibiting Higher Magic Tendencies—another verbose title that would have made Robert Fludd proud—was still stuck inside the envelope. I shook it out before continuing.

"We have launched an investigation into why your talent for higher magic, as displayed on the night of 14 July 2017 and witnessed by our member Tinima Toussaint, was not recognized prior to this summer, and we

look forward to learning how you concealed those talents while acting as the de Clermont representative to this governing body."

The answer was quite simple: It was all thanks to Peter Knox's obsession with my mother. I continued.

"To expedite matters, and make this process as efficient as possible, we will examine you and your children, Philip Bishop-Clairmont and Rebecca Bishop-Clairmont, over the course of a single day. We propose to come to New Haven on a date of your choosing that will not impinge on your teaching obligations, or the children's school calendars, ideally in the month of August. Please advise regarding your preferred time. We remain, yours sincerely, et cetera.

"I suppose I should have seen this coming," I said, "with or without the black bird oracle."

We returned to the barn to break the news to Sarah and Matthew.

"The Congregation is coming to New Haven sooner than expected," I said, holding up the summer's most recent special delivery. "They want to test my aptitude for higher magic, as well as the children's abilities."

"Ridiculous," Sarah said, pouring herself a fresh cup of coffee. She slammed the carafe back onto the warming stand. "What a waste of time. You broke into their damned headquarters and walked out with a bag of their memory bottles! Of course you have a talent for higher magic."

"It's just a formality, Sarah," I said, hoping to reassure her (and myself) that there was nothing to worry about. "And it's way better than facing a Congregation tribunal."

"I guess," Sarah replied, unconvinced.

"I only wish we didn't have to wait until we go back to New Haven," I grumbled, my mood souring further. "Now that Janet's been expelled from the Congregation, I suppose it will be Sidonie or Tinima who does the honors." I shuddered at the thought of either of the witches strolling around Memorial Quad.

"It would always have been Sidonie or Tinima," Gwyneth replied. "Witches aren't allowed to assess their own family members anymore. Too much grade inflation."

"If you don't want them in New Haven, tell them to come here," Sarah said, "to Ravenswood."

It was not her house—or mine—but the suggestion was intriguing. I looked to Matthew, wanting his reaction.

"Would that be allowed, Gwyneth?" Matthew wondered.

"We'd need the approval of the coven membership," Gwyneth replied, a note of caution in her voice.

"We aren't likely to get that," I said, "not with Meg Skelling agitating the atmosphere."

"I wonder," Gwyneth said, her voice thoughtful. "A date after Lammas might work. Julie should choose which one. She has a knack for picking auspicious wedding days."

In May, I wouldn't have thought it possible that I would be eager to bring the twins' examination date forward from September—but a lot had happened since then.

"Let's see what the cards say," Gwyneth said, rising to her feet with a determined light in her eyes. "I think it's time for a Proctor spelling bee."

"You've never been to a spelling bee!" Grace was astonished.

"Not since third grade, when I won the Madison Elementary School contest," I said, stacking cookies on a plate.

"Not that kind of spelling bee." Grace chuckled. "At a Proctor spelling bee, the family comes together to ask the oracles for guidance. Then we compare notes and figure out what spells we need to cast to manifest the best outcome."

"It's a sign the Proctors are at DEFCON One," Ike said, flashing one of his wide grins.

"Is all this really necessary?" I was going to pass the witches' test with flying colors, and there was no way to predict or prevent what the Congregation witch might do to assess the twins.

"Necessary? No. But the Proctors like to set themselves up for success," Ike replied.

"Besides, we haven't had a family spelling bee in ages," Julie said, rubbing her hands together with excitement. She did a quick head count. "We're eight, including Sarah."

"Me?" Sarah's eyes widened. "I'm not an oracle."

"Do you have any tarot cards with you?" Put-Put was holding a leather envelope, soft and supple.

Sarah nodded. "Always."

"Then you'll do," Put-Put said. "Where is Matthew, Gwynie? We need more coffee."

Matthew appeared with a fresh pot.

"There you are," Put-Put said. "You can be our ninth. The goddess prefers an uneven number at a spelling bee."

"I'm not an oracle, or even a witch, Putnam," Matthew protested.

"No, but you've begotten them," Put-Put said. "Get the man a deck of cards, Junior. Sit down and learn things, Matthew."

Matthew did what he was told as the rest of the gathering reached into pockets, purses, and fanny packs for their cards. Ike put an old deck of playing cards in front of Matthew that had been used for an oracle in the trenches of World War I and still smelled of explosives.

"Let's shuffle," Put-Put said. "Then we can let the oracles do their thing and have a sandwich."

We moved the cards through our fingers. Matthew's deft handling of them gave away one of his past lives as a gambler. The room soon fell silent except for the swoosh of the cards.

Put-Put was the first to release his cards on the table, where they formed the serpentine layout of the Dark Path.

Matthew was next, and put three cards face up before him in the past-present-future spread. He wasn't a witch but had been watching me handle the black bird oracle and had learned some of the basics. Sarah, seated next to him, laid out her tarot in a traditional Celtic cross arrangement.

The other oracles required more time to deliver their messages. When everyone's cards were finally on the table, two spreads appeared more than once: the Dark Path, and the complicated spiral of the Labyrinth.

As for my own cards, they had positioned themselves in an identical arrangement to Matthew's, shedding light on past, present, and future.

I looked at the images before me. *The Skeleton. Salt. A Flight of Herons.* Change. Strong boundaries. Cleverness and patience.

The Proctors surveyed the table, looking for synchronicities and patterns. Cards shot into the air as options were considered and discarded, rearranging themselves to illuminate new possibilities.

In the end, the plan we concocted had the virtue of being utterly transparent, and so simple a child could execute it.

All I was required to do was lay my cards on the table before the Ipswich coven, along with a single memory bottle.

A nn, Meg, and Katrina arrived at Ravenswood later that afternoon to hear our request for a change of venue. Gwyneth and I met the coven representatives in the Old Place, and we took seats under the wisteria's leafy canopy. It was well past flowering, but it provided welcome shade on this warm day. Gwyneth had Katrina's tea ready, properly made according to her liking, as well as a rotund Brown Betty pot filled with her own favorite oolong.

"Thank you for coming on such short notice," I said, once everyone had a cup or mug in hand. "I need your help."

Ann looked surprised; Meg, suspicious.

"That's what a coven is for." Katrina's lenses were tinted pale yellow today. "What's on your mind, Diana?"

"The Congregation witches want to examine me to determine if I have a talent for higher magic," I replied. "They want to test the twins at the same time. They'll be seven this autumn."

"The higher magic aptitude test is given to children, not adults." Ann frowned. "Besides, they already know you chose the Dark Path at the Crossroads."

"It seems the Congregation wants to go by the spellbook when it comes to Diana," Gwyneth said.

"I don't blame them," Meg muttered.

"Nor do I."

My prompt acquiescence startled her.

"There have been so many procedural irregularities—not to mention my former status as a vampire representative on the Congregation—that they want to dot every *i* and cross every *t*," I said.

Gwyneth handed the Congregation's letter to Ann, who read it swiftly.

"Meg!" Ann was shocked at the letter's reference to one of her witches. "You broke your vow of confidentiality and shared particulars of the Crossroads with other witches!"

"She did what she thought was best, Ann," I said, wanting to avoid any further mention of bloodcraft. "Given that the witches refer to the coven in their message, I wondered if you would be willing to request a change of venue and date, so that the twins and I could be examined here, at Ravenswood."

Ann looked to Katrina. "What do you think?"

Katrina scattered a handful of bones on the table. She studied their arrangement. "There's more to this request than a missing signature on a form."

"There always is with my family." I sighed. There was no good way to tell the witches what had happened on Isola della Stella, so I simply blurted out the truth. "I burgled Celestina and took items from the witches' memory palace."

"You did *what*?" Ann cried.

"Memory bottles?" Katrina asked, intrigued.

"Yes, all of them filled with the recollections of potential adepts when they were examined on Isola della Stella," I said. "I don't think the Congregation has a right to keep them."

I picked up the bubble of blown glass with Meg's name and number on it. "These are yours."

Meg's normally narrowed eyes widened.

"I saw it on the shelf as I was leaving," I explained. "I'd already taken as many bottles as I could that belonged to my own family. I hope you don't mind that I took yours as well."

"You opened it?" Meg said, wary of my gift.

I shook my head. "I thought about it. But they belong to you, just as my memories of the Crossroads belong to me."

Meg's cheeks turned red. Her fingers reached for the bottle, brushing against mine.

"How many bottles do the witches keep on Isola della Stella?" Ann asked.

"Hundreds," I said. "Thousands? I don't know for sure. Only the chosen few witches who sit at the Congregation table ever have a chance to see them. I think that's wrong, too."

"I agree with you," Ann said, her voice rough. "Meg? Katrina?"

"Agreed," Katrina said promptly.

It took Meg a little longer to decide. Finally, she nodded.

Ann looked relieved. "Let me run it by Hitty first, but if she gives me the go-ahead I'd like to put it to the membership soon."

"How soon?" Gwyneth asked.

"So long as Hitty doesn't rule it out, I suspect she'll let me conduct a vote via the phone tree. Once they've heard the specifics of the situation, I have no doubt that the membership will decide that it's in our collective interest for the examination to take place here in Ipswich, where Diana's home coven can be available for support if necessary."

"Home coven?" I repeated blankly. "I'm a visitor."

"Are you?" Gwyneth asked.

This was another decision that I needed to make myself, without asking Matthew to weigh in on the matter.

"No," I said softly. "I'm not a visitor. But I'm not a member of the Ipswich coven, either."

"You will be if you want me to write this letter to the Congregation," Ann said sharply.

Chapter 27

Julie selected August 13 as the best day for the examination. It was later than I'd hoped—and my birthday.

"I still don't think I should have to take a test on my birthday," I said, opening the card she'd given me to mark the occasion. It was Naomi's birthday, too, and I couldn't help but think of her experience on the Dark Path.

"What could be better?" Julie replied, pleased with this obvious sign from the goddess. "Everybody needs a cake and sparklers after they finish their MAT."

The Magical Aptitude Test, I learned, was a far more exciting milestone for witch children than a visit from the tooth fairy. Not everyone shared this view, however. Matthew had been a bear all morning, growling at every perceived slight or hint of rudeness.

"My toe aches and I dreamed of a vulture last night," Sarah said, clomping into the kitchen in search of coffee. "It circled over Ravenswood, hissing. I think it's a bad omen."

I had already consulted the black bird oracle this morning and held up the Quintessence card so Sarah could see it.

"The fifth element. Not a vulture in sight."

Pip was toying with his oatmeal spoon, just as unhappy as Sarah with our plans for the day.

"It's not fair. Why do I have to take a test? Why can't we be like other kids? Why do you two have to be such *professors*?"

"It won't take much time," I assured him, even though I had no idea how long the twins' ordeal would be. My mother's memories of my examination pressed on my heart, and my anxiety rose.

"Tamsy said the same thing, Pip," Becca told her brother, doling out some of her blueberries for the doll.

"How does *she* know?" Pip demanded, glowering at his sister's companion.

"Tamsy does her cards every morning, just like Mommy," Becca said. "Today the card was a puffy cloud in a blue sky with a big yellow sun. You know how sunny days are always better, and they go by more quickly than when it rains?"

"Ohh." Pip looked impressed. "Is 'Nando coming?"

"No," I said with a laugh. "A witch is coming, but I don't know who. It's a surprise."

Without the prospect of their uncle 'Nando showing up, the children scampered off to the barn to play with Granny Dorcas and the spell-looms. I went back to my own worries over whether Tinima or Sidonie would be proctoring the exam.

Matthew brought me a pot of tea and my oatmeal. He searched my face for clues about how I was doing. I laid my palm against his cheek.

"I just want this over with," I said.

"Soon, *mon coeur*," Matthew replied.

There was one last thing I wanted to do before the witches' representative arrived. I asked Gwyneth if she would join me in the Ravens' Wood.

My aunt agreed without question. Sarah would have peppered me for more details, but Gwyneth was content to put her arm around my elbow and let me help her into the wood's green coolness.

We reached the Crossroads. It seemed a lifetime since Meg had issued her challenge.

"Can you teach me how to cast a circle to summon a spirit?" I asked Gwyneth.

"Yes," Gwyneth replied. "That doesn't mean I'm going to. What are you up to, Diana?"

I pulled a memory bottle out of my pocket.

"I want to give these back to Naomi. I know I'm not supposed to tell you what happened at the Crossroads in any detail, but I met her shade here, when I faced Meg, and she had a hole in the center of her chest." I pressed my hand against my sternum, where my aunt's wound had been.

"I intended to patch it," I continued, "but Naomi wanted an end to her suffering. I wove the tenth knot—the knot of creation and destruction—and released her from Elsewhere. I'd hoped she would return as a ghost, but I didn't see her at Midsummer."

Naomi materialized from the trees, apparating from the dark hollow in an old oak without any help from me or Gwyneth. She was no longer the eerie wraith she had been as a shade, but she was not as clearly delineated as most Proctor ghosts. Naomi's hands were crossed protectively over a dark depression near her heart that was not fully healed.

"Naomi?" Gwyneth whispered.

Hi, Aunt Gwyneth. Naomi waved. *Long time, no see.*

For a moment Gwyneth's joy was strong enough to push back the Darkness that still lingered around her niece.

"I brought your memories from Venice," I told my father's sister. "Where should I put them?"

Where they belong, Naomi replied, opening her hands so that we could see the place behind her ribs that was still waiting to be filled.

With Gwyneth's help, I released Naomi's memories. For a moment, Darkness threatened to engulf the fragile ghost and we lost sight of her. Shadow tipped the balance in the end, and Naomi emerged more substantial than ever.

Thank you for making me whole, Naomi said, her voice breaking on the last word. *I'd lost hope, and couldn't imagine a witch who could work such magic.*

It would take months—perhaps years—for Naomi to fully integrate with her memories. They were visible beneath her skin, swirling and shimmering just like the words of the Book of Life moved within me.

"We should go," I told Gwyneth, mindful of the time.

Be sure to come back, Naomi said, wistful at our departure.

Gwyneth and I emerged from the wood with lighter hearts. Then I saw who was waiting for me on the bench underneath the witch's tree, and Light turned to Darkness.

"Hello, Diana."

"Satu." I stifled my instinct to scream in warning, knowing that Matthew would hear me no matter how quietly I spoke. "Why are you here?"

"I'm here for you, of course." Satu stood, her platinum pixie and pale skin gleaming in the summer sun. "And your children."

Gwyneth had been right. Satu was no longer spellbound. My attempt had been impassioned, but lacked the skill that would have kept the bindings on her magic in place. And my efforts to curb her powers had backfired spectacularly. It felt like they had increased, the air between us electric.

Matthew burst out of the farmhouse, his eyes pinned to the ridge.

"Could you find the children?" I asked Gwyneth, though I was really speaking to Matthew. "I think they're in the barn with Sarah and Granny Dorcas."

"If so, they have no need of me at present," Gwyneth said, her eyes steely. "Miss Järvinen. How unexpected."

"Really, Miss Proctor?" Satu replied. "Has the gift of prophecy been taken from you? I'm surprised, knowing the strong tradition of oracles in your family. Diana has always had a touch of the oracle about her. I knew it the first time we met."

A slight twist of Gwyneth's fourth finger suggested that she had triggered some alarm. Hopefully it would alert the coven that something was wrong at Ravenswood.

"Our high priestess isn't due for another hour," Gwyneth said.

"My flight was early," Satu said with a mocking smile. "Tailwinds over the Atlantic."

Matthew had joined us, which meant the children were indeed safely in the barn.

"I told you it wouldn't be Sidonie." I glanced over my shoulder, wanting to make eye contact with Matthew. "You owe me five dollars."

"Poor Sidonie has been under so much pressure since Janet's abrupt departure and the unexpected vacancy on the Congregation," Satu said, her voice silky. "My name was at the top of the list of replacements, and I was happy to be of service."

I should have looked for Satu's bottle when I was in Venice. But it had never occurred to me that she might still pose a threat, not even after Gwyneth's warning.

Matthew placed his hand on the small of my back, close to where Satu had branded me with his family seal as a reminder that I was tainted by my association with vampires. The scars were a lasting symbol of Satu's cold-bloodedness. My courage, which had been wavering, revived.

"I've already notified the Congregation that your appearance here is unacceptable, after your violence toward Diana," Matthew said. "They'll have to send someone else to examine her and the children."

Satu's laugh was as brilliant and brittle as Griselda Gowdie's memory bottle.

"This is an internal matter, Matthew. The other members of the Congregation have no jurisdiction over the affairs of witches." Satu's smug expression left little doubt that Tinima and Sidonie were aware of what Satu had done to me in the past, and had sent her here anyway.

"It's okay," I said, putting my hand on his arm. "She can't do anything to me or the children."

"That's right, Diana. Ravenswood protects its own." Gwyneth fixed a basilisk stare on her visitor. "You're on Proctor land, Satu. There are forces here that are beyond even the reach of higher magic."

"I'll be careful," Satu replied with a twisted smile.

A howling wind of protest swirled past my shoulders and nearly flattened Satu.

"Be more careful," Gwyneth said. "That's the last warning you'll get."

"No harm will befall Diana or the children. Today." Satu paused long enough to give her words a malicious shimmer. "Today is all about ticking the boxes so that there are no questions later. Shall we get started?"

"Follow me," Gwyneth said, directing Satu toward the Old Place.

I took Matthew's hand and pulled him in the direction of the barn, away from Satu's veiled threats, and toward our children.

"How did your oracle not foresee *this*?" Matthew snarled in fury.

"We'll deal with the intelligence failures later," I said, taking his face in my hands. "Right now, I want the children with us and their examination in the rearview mirror."

Matthew drew a shuddering breath, gathering his composure. His eyes were stormy but not yet fully black. Matthew was in control of his blood rage—for now. He nodded.

When we entered the barn, Sarah was ready to fight—not with magic but with Granny Dorcas's favorite fire poker. She dropped it with a clatter.

"It's time for your test," Sarah told the twins brightly. "Who wants to hold my hand? I hate tests. I was terrible at them."

"Me, too," Pip moaned.

"I like tests," Becca said, slipping her hand into mine. Something warm and sharp bit into my flesh.

"You're wearing your ring," I said, looking down at her fingers.

"Tamsy told me I have to wear it from now on," Becca explained. "She told me it belonged to a great witch and that I would be a great witch one day, too."

Thank you, Tamsin Proctor, I said silently. For the first time since my ancestor's spirit took possession of my daughter's toy, I was grateful. Tituba's ring retained some of her power, and Emily's ancestor would be with Becca when she faced Satu.

In the end, we all held hands as we crossed the green expanse of grass and flower beds between Orchard Farm and the Old Place.

When we reached Gwyneth's house, Sarah let go of Pip's hand. "There you go, squirt. Your mom will take you and your sister inside. There isn't room for your dad and me in Gwyneth's poky front parlor. We'll wait for you out here."

Matthew was surprised. "I'm going—"

"No, you're not," Sarah said firmly. "Everybody needs to focus, right? We don't want to distract anybody."

I thanked the goddess for Sarah's unusual restraint. Rather than adding to the tension, she found a way to remind Matthew he had an important role to play in today's proceedings.

Reluctantly, Matthew nodded.

"Who wants to go first?" I asked the twins.

"ME!" Pip and Becca shot their hands in the air and shouted in unison.

"Ladies first," Pip said with a little bow to his sister.

"No, Pip." Becca took her brother's hand. "We'll do it together."

I took Pip's other hand and cast one final look at Matthew.

Matthew traced a cross in the air between us.

"*Angele Dei, qui custos es mei,*" he murmured. "*Me tibi commissum pietate superna; Hodie illumina, custodi, rege, et guberna.*"

Pip and Becca both recognized this ancient prayer to one's guardian angel immediately, as did I. Matthew had taught it to the twins as soon as they could speak, and both children repeated it whenever they felt uncertain or distressed.

"Amen," Pip said in response.

"Catch you on the flip side, Daddy," Becca said, adding my father's favorite farewell to the litany.

Satu and Gwyneth sat in silence in the keeping room. The rest of the witches present had plenty to say, however.

That despicable hag has no business being here! Granny Dorcas said, shaking a frying pan. *Pallid creature. And her skills are shockingly crude.*

Better we smoke her out, Granny Dorcas, than mount a frontal attack with kitchen equipment. Grandpa Tally was propped against the fireplace, his eyes glued to Satu with deadly intent.

This witch from the north is not a great lover of books, Granny Alice said with a sniff. *No wonder her knots lack structure. There's barely enough gramarye to hold them together. She needs to acquaint herself with more disciplined prose.*

Naomi was here, too.

Darkness always recognizes its own kind, she said, her hair sparking. *I felt her presence at once.*

"Who is she?" Becca whispered, hanging on to my hand as we entered the keeping room.

"I am Satu Järvinen. I've come to do some spells with you." Satu smiled in a vain attempt to look less terrifying.

"Not you." Becca frowned. "That lady there, with the sparkly bottle where her heart should be."

"That's your aunt Naomi," I said. "Grandpa Stephen's twin sister."

"Grandpa was a twin? Coo-el," Pip said, his anxiety surrounding tests temporarily alleviated. It soon returned. "What kind of spells?"

"All kinds," Satu said.

Hopefully these would not include timewalking, flying, or any other use of magic that might cause Pip to disappear and not be seen or heard from again.

"My spells don't always work the way they're supposed to," Pip confessed, glum about his future prospects.

"How marvelous for you. Let's see if we can figure out why." Satu pointed to a vase holding the last of the summer roses. The blooms were past their prime, and mottled with brown spots. "See if you can make one of those wilted flowers come back to life, Philip."

Pip screwed up his face in concentration. A quiet glow appeared around him, as it usually did when he was focused on casting a spell. He murmured a few words.

The flowers disappeared.

"Where did they go?" Becca wondered, searching for the vase.

Pip shrugged, his cheeks pink with embarassment.

"I think they're in the meadow." I pointed through the window to where single roses were sprouting out of the grass like dandelions. Pip had not only restored the flowers to life, but to the ground as well.

"Clever boy." Satu made a note in her leather-bound journal. "You've got a lot of earth magic in you, Philip. It's so warm today. Can you make a gentle breeze to cool us down?"

"Gentle," I emphasized, thinking of the state of the clapboards.

More confident now, Pip muttered something unintelligible and waved his hand in the air.

A whoosh of wind blew down the keeping room chimney, along with a soot-covered Apollo. He stood on unsteady lion's paws and spat out a mouthful of ashes.

The sight of a blackened griffin didn't faze Satu.

"Looks like your chimney needs a good cleaning, Miss Proctor," Satu said. "Air, too, I see. How about we try—"

"Not fire," I said firmly. "The house is a national treasure."

Satu frowned at my interruption. "Yes, fire. Can you light the candle on the mantel, Philip?"

"Sure!" Pip said, tripping over his familiar to reach the fireplace. He puffed on the nearest candle wick.

The ornamental birch logs in the grate burst into roaring flame.

"Oops," Pip said, giving Gwyneth a lopsided grin. "Sorry, Aunt Gwyneth."

"You kept the fire in the fireplace this time," my aunt said, beaming at him. "Well done, Pip."

"And fire." Satu made another note.

"Like Mommy," Pip replied. "She can shoot a fire arrow."

"Yes, I know," Satu murmured. "Can you empty the water from the glass on the table without touching it?"

I closed my eyes and prayed that Pip would not cause a tsunami that would require coastal evacuations.

Pip stood in front of the table and concentrated on the glass of water. It lifted from the table's surface, wobbled a bit in the air, then tipped its contents over the African violet sitting on a doily. The glass landed on the table with a thud.

Becca clapped. "You did it, Pip!"

I opened my arms to give my son a hug.

"You were magnificent," I told him, smoothing the piece of blond hair that had fallen into his eyes.

"There's just one more test, Philip," Satu said. "Come stand in front of me."

Pip did so, although he kept a prudent distance between himself and this strange witch.

"I want you to close your eyes," Satu said. "What's the first thing you see?"

"A gray cat." Pip had been asking for a cat all summer, and intended to call it Spike after Chris's favorite character in *Buffy the Vampire Slayer.*

"Can you invite the cat to join you, Pip?" Satu asked, eyes gleaming with curiosity.

"Is this really necessary, Satu?" I pointed to Apollo. "You've seen his familiar."

"Don't interfere again, or I'll have to ask you to leave," Satu warned. She would do it, too.

Pip concentrated, screwing his eyes shut. He cracked one open. "Is Spike here?"

"Not yet," Satu said. "Ask him nicely."

Pip pressed his lips together and lowered his eyelids.

Nothing.

Pip stomped his foot impatiently, and the floorboards shook at the impact. "Come here this minute, Spike!"

"Spike must not be available," Satu said. "Thank you for trying, Philip."

Pip's face fell in disappointment. He opened his eyes and turned to me. "Did I do something wrong?"

"Not at all," I said.

"You are a very talented witch, Philip." Satu made a few more notes in her book. My fingers itched to snatch it from her, so that I could see what they said.

He smiled and turned to his sister. "Your turn, Becca."

"That's it?" I was blank with astonishment. Where was the pain? The threats? The sense of violation? Satu's examination was nothing like what

I remembered from my encounter with Peter Knox, or my mother's memories, either. Mom had been angry at Dad for allowing Peter to proceed with his unorthodox methods, but I hadn't understood how different my experience had been.

"What were you expecting?" Satu asked, genuinely curious.

I smothered my fractured memories of Knox's visit to Cambridge, not wanting Satu or the children to see my distress.

Becca shot me a nervous look, which suggested she had, as usual, picked up on my emotional turmoil.

"You'll be fine," I said, plastering a wide smile on my face.

"It's not hard, Becca," Pip said, taking his sister by the hand. "*Courage.*"

With her brother's support, Becca walked the few steps that stretched between her and Satu. Granny Dorcas walked beside her, chewing on her pipe.

"I'd like you to—" Satu began.

"Make a wilted flower bloom," Becca said, ready to make magic.

"No," Satu said sharply. "You must listen carefully to my instructions, Rebecca. I want you to fill that empty glass on the table."

Rebecca's chin lifted. "Water, milk, or lemonade?"

Gwyneth choked down a laugh.

Take that, you pudding-headed hoyden! Granny Dorcas brandished her frying pan.

"Witch's choice," Satu replied, her tone vinegar.

Becca pointed her ringed finger at the glass, and it filled slowly with lemonade from top to bottom, rather than from bottom to top. It was neatly done, tightly controlled, and very naughty.

An expression of astonishment slipped over Satu's features, and quickly left.

"Very good, Rebecca." Satu pointed to the candles. "Can you light them?"

Becca walked to the fireplace and blew gently on one wick. It burst into golden flame. She looked over her shoulder at Satu, cunning as a cat, before twirling around and setting every wick in the room alight.

"Settle down, poppet," I warned. Rebecca was too young to have enemies—especially one like Satu.

"How about the rose in this picture?" Satu pointed to the pink blossom held in the fingers of my ancestor. "Can you make it wilt and shrivel up? It's just like making it bloom, but backward."

I opened my mouth to protest. Making things die was not a talent I wanted my children to have.

"Okay." Becca pointed her index finger and walked toward the painting.

Nothing.

"That's all right," Satu said briskly, ready to move on. "You've got plenty of fire and water in you, Rebecca."

But Becca was a competitive child. Her brother was outscoring her in magic. She scowled with displeasure.

"Please draw a breeze in from the garden," Satu said, setting Becca a new task.

Becca tried, waving her arms around like a windmill, but the air in the room didn't stir. We had always known that Becca's magic was not as diverse as Pip's, even before Apollo showed up and let us know our son was going to be a weaver.

Becca stomped off and sank into a chair by the door, her lips jutting into a pout.

"You still have one more test," Satu said, calling her back.

Becca returned with ill-disguised reluctance.

"Her teen years are going to be a nightmare," Gwyneth murmured.

"This test is stupid," Becca grumbled.

"Close your eyes, Becca." Satu's voice was hypnotic. "Keep them closed. Tell me what you see."

"A raven," Becca said promptly, "but not the one who died on the pavement."

Gwyneth and I exchanged worried glances.

"Can you invite the raven to join you here?" Satu pressed.

"His name is Fiachra," Becca said.

My grandfather straightened.

"I'd like to meet Fiachra," Satu said.

"Me, too." Gwyneth stood on trembling legs.

A black bird with silver eyes and a silver ruff swooped past the window, beating its wings at the glass. It dropped to the windowsill. The window was cracked open, but not wide enough to let the raven in.

"Can I open the window?" Becca asked Gwyneth.

"Of course," Gwyneth said, her voice trembling.

Becca flung open the window so that Fiachra could hop through it. Outside, Matthew and Sarah were peering at the unusual bird.

"You sure you have room for a raven in New Haven, as well as a deer-hound and a griffin?" Sarah asked my husband.

Becca waved. "Hi, Aunt Sarah! Look, Daddy. This is Fiachra. He's the bird who came to New Haven and talked to me after his friend died."

There had been no silver feathers on the raven I'd seen in New Haven. It was as though the bird had been given a collar of office, a mark of the goddess like the cross between Cailleach's eyes.

"Fiachra?" Gwyneth whispered. "Is that you?"

Fiachra turned his brilliant silver eyes toward my aunt. He ducked his head and cawed with recognition. Fiachra hopped a few steps and then took flight, landing on Gwyneth's outstretched hand.

"It's good to see you, old friend." Gwyneth's eyes filled with tears. "How wonderful that you came when Becca called."

Fiachra clucked and warbled, bobbing his head in Grandpa Tally's direction.

"He did?" Gwyneth smiled at her brother.

Fiachra spread his wings and returned to Rebecca and Pip, watched closely by a curious Apollo.

"Apollo doesn't mind if you fly, too," Becca assured Fiachra. "Mommy flies sometimes. You can still be friends."

Fiachra uttered a strange chirp. He paced up and down the windowsill, undecided. Finally, the raven flew into the room and landed on top of Apollo's head. He pecked at a bit of soot that was trapped in the feathers between the griffin's eyes.

See, Granny Dorcas. The Proctor legacy is safe with Rebecca, Grandpa Tally said, a twinkle in his eye.

Hmph, Granny Dorcas replied. *That imp is bent on mischief. Best not to cosset her, or Darkness might follow.*

Darkness wouldn't stand a chance against Becca.

Satu returned her pen to the elastic loop on her notebook. "I think that's enough for my report. Once I've filed it, you will receive a copy."

"Aren't you going to test Diana, too?" Gwyneth asked.

"I know what kind of witch she is," Satu said, slipping her notebook in her bag. "She is strange and Dark. Like me."

A sense of impending danger prickled along my hairline. Satu was up to something.

"Tinima already wrote a lengthy report about Diana's abilities," Satu said. "It was a last-minute filing, and it was too late to notify you of our change of plans. I'm sorry if we caused unnecessary concern."

I wrapped my hands into tight fists to prevent myself from trying out one of my newly polished hexes.

"But we'll see you next summer, Diana. In Venice." Satu drew another Congregation missive from her bag. "Here's the official notification that you've been selected to join the potential adepts in the class of 2018, as well as instructions on how to certify the skills you need to acquire before arriving in June. I'm sure that your aunt or the Ipswich coven will be able to attest to them using the enclosed form."

"What?" I hadn't foreseen this, either.

"You didn't think we'd let you walk some other labyrinth, now that you've seen the one on Isola della Stella?" Satu's voice dripped with scorn.

Matthew had had enough. He came into the room and stood next to Grandpa Tally in the same vigilant pose: arms crossed, limbs still, and his eyes everywhere.

"Congratulations, Diana. It's a great honor to be invited to Celestina for your next examination," Satu continued. "Thank you for your hospitality, Miss Proctor."

Satu headed for the door. I slammed it shut before she could leave, trapping her inside the Old Place.

"That's Professor Proctor," I said, seething. "I'll show you out, Satu. This way."

"As you wish," Satu said, inclining her head.

I led her through the kitchen, across the uneven granite stones, and into the sunshine.

"Go." I pointed up the hill. "And don't come back to Ravenswood, or within a hundred miles of my children again. Understood?"

"You don't order me around, Diana," Satu said softly. "I order you around. Remember?"

"Oh, I remember," I said. "But those days are over."

I felt the press of ancestors and family gathered at my back, and the power of Ravenswood under my feet.

Satu smiled. "We'll see."

She climbed the hill without hurry, gradually making her way to the witch's tree, where I'd first seen her.

Infuriated, I followed.

"Stay with Pip and Becca," I told Matthew, who had joined me outside.

I heard the sound of a car engine and flew over the top of the hill. I stopped the car with a drift of stones conjured out of the carriage road's loose gravel.

"This isn't over, Satu," I said, landing on the hood of the Volvo.

Satu turned off the ignition and climbed out of the car.

"Oh, I've only started," she replied.

"I'm not the same witch," I warned. "You won't defeat me as easily as you once did."

Satu turned her palms to face me. They were bright with weaver's cords, the colors extending to the tips of her fingers.

I gasped. Satu had found another weaver—one able to train her in the art of making new spells. I'd suspected she was a weaver. Here was proof.

"I'm not the same witch, either," Satu said. "And you're not as special as you thought. There are others like us."

Maybe, but I doubted they had Goody Alsop's expertise. And Satu may not have the ability to weave the tenth knot as I did.

"As for higher magic, you can't hold a candle to your daughter," Satu continued. "Rebecca will eclipse you in no time. The witches will have big plans for her once they see my report."

The temperature dropped suddenly, and I shivered. I'd feared this might be the case, ever since Rebecca had danced with the ravens in the wood.

"You'll know soon enough what lies in store for your daughter," Satu said, her eyes gleaming with evil intent. "But what will the witches do when they find out about Philip, I wonder? What will they make of his unique inheritance?"

The earth shifted below my feet, just like the floorboards in the keeping room had when Pip stomped his foot.

Satu smiled, malevolent. She pulled on a yellow thread, then a green, flattening the rocky dune and clearing her way forward.

"Until next year," Satu said as she climbed into the car.

I watched her car as it traveled down the carriage road, away from Ravenswood and the children.

Darkness gnawed like a poison in my stomach, feeding on the fear prompted by Satu's words.

I beat it back with the Light of truth. I was a trained weaver who could tie the tenth knot. I was an initiate in higher magic. I was the mother of gifted twins, and the wife of an extraordinary man. I was more than the sum of my Bishop and Proctor ancestors. I was more than a match for Satu.

Helter skelter, hang sorrow, care'll kill a cat, up-tails all, and a louse for the hangman. Mary Proctor's ghost forked her fingers in the direction Satu had departed. She spat on the carriageway for good measure. *Take that, you bald-pated lummox.*

We stood together in silence as the dust churned up by the car's wheels settled.

They've been looking for you, Mary said, holding the bag containing the black bird oracle. It was bouncing up and down with agitation. I hadn't wanted them with me when I took the witches' examination in case they roused the witch's curiosity, and had left them safely at the farm.

"Thanks," I said, taking the cards from the ghost.

When my fingers touched the bag, the weaver's cords on my left hand flashed with the colors of higher, darker magic. A single card wormed its way out of the protective enclosure and fell to the ground, face up.

Blood.

"Four drops of blood on an altar stone, / Foretold this moment before you were born. / Three families joined in joy and in struggle, / Will each bear witness to the black bird oracle. / Two children, bright as Moon and Sun," I said, the power of Ravenswood flowing through my veins and imbuing Bridget Bishop's words with the power of all the witches who came before me. "*Will Darkness, Light, and Shadow make one.*"

Nothing—and no one—would stop Pip and Becca from choosing their own paths forward. I would make sure of that.

I traced my own sacred symbol in the air to seal my oath. It was not Matthew's cross but the simple circlet of the tenth knot, the ouroboros, a beginning with no ending, the powerful sign of creation and destruction.

It shimmered before me, black and silver like Fiachra's feathers.

"So must it be," I said, as the wind carried the tenth knot Elsewhere. "So must it be."

Acknowledgments

I am deeply grateful to all of the people who helped me through the endings, beginnings, and changes of the past few years: my wife, Karen, first and foremost; my family of Harknesses, Halttunens, Kagans, Hurleys, Pagnottas, and Martins; my friends; the Circle of Light who cheered me on and gave me a soft place to land amidst life's uncertainties (you know who you are!); my physicians and nurses and all those who cared for my body and soul.

To my writerly friends Brigid Coady, Liz Fenwick, and Tonya Hurley, I give endless thanks for supporting me as I slowly came back to life through the words on the page.

My spectacular teams at Park & Fine Literary Management, Emerge Business Management Los Angeles, and Ballantine have walked me through the challenges and opportunities associated with a new path into the future. I am so grateful for all of their support.

Not a day goes by in which I don't rely on the steadfast presence of Annie, Bridget, Cat, Clarisa, Jill, and Sascha. As they know, it takes a village, lots of snacks, and even more yoga to birth a book.

Two extraordinary women, Grace Nicklas Warne and Tracy Hurley Martin, lost their lives to cancer and did not live to see this book published. I miss them each day and trust they don't mind being a permanent part of my magical world.

About the Author

DEBORAH HARKNESS is the No. 1 *New York Times* bestselling author of *A Discovery of Witches, Shadow of Night, The Book of Life, Time's Convert,* and *The World of All Souls.* A history professor at the University of Southern California, Harkness has received Fulbright, Guggenheim, and National Humanities Center fellowships. She lives in Los Angeles.

deborahharkness.com
Facebook.com/AuthorDeborahHarkness
Instagram: @debharkness
X: @DebHarkness

About the Type

This book was set in Garamond, a typeface originally designed by the Parisian type cutter Claude Garamond (c. 1500–61). This version of Garamond was modeled on a 1592 specimen sheet from the Egenolff-Berner foundry, which was produced from types assumed to have been brought to Frankfurt by the punch cutter Jacques Sabon (c. 1520–80).

Claude Garamond's distinguished romans and italics first appeared in *Opera Ciceronis* in 1543–44. The Garamond types are clear, open, and elegant.